The rubber raft, with four men all dressed in black, their faces corked, materialized from the darkness, and Schey helped pull the boat up on the beach. All four of the men jumped ashore.

"*Heil Hitler*," one of the men said, raising his right arm in salute.

Schey returned it, a sudden surge of pride coming over him. It had been a long time since he had been among friends and had been able to use that greeting. Schey pulled the tightly wrapped package from his pocket. "This is very important, Lieutenant."

"You don't have to tell me, sir. We came all the way across the Atlantic to pick it up."

The three crewmen had wandered up the beach. When they returned home, they'd be able to brag to their friends that they had actually invaded the U.S. Suddenly, Schey saw the crewmen racing back, waving their hands frantically.

"There's someone up there," one of the crewmen gasped.

"Probably the coastal watcher," Schey said. "Get the hell out of here; I'll take care of this."

Look for this other TOR book by David Hagberg

HEARTLAND

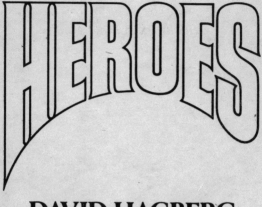

HEROES

DAVID HAGBERG

TOR

A TOM DOHERTY ASSOCIATES BOOK

THIS BOOK IS FOR LAURIE

HEROES

First printing: January 1985

A TOR Book

Published by Tom Doherty Associates,
8-10 West 36 Street,
New York, N.Y. 10018

ISBN: 0-812-50409-7
CAN. ED.: 0-812-50410-0

Printed in the United States of America

ACKNOWLEDGMENTS

This is a work of fiction, based in part on fact. I must give thanks to the historians for their work: to Heinz Höhne for his perceptive book, *Canaris*, Doubleday; to Joseph E. Persico for *Piercing the Reich*, Viking; to David Kahn for *Hitler's Spies*, Macmillan; to Lynn Montross for *War Through the Ages*, Third Edition, Harper & Row; and no novel encompassing any portion of the war in Germany would be possible without reference to William L. Shirer's *Rise and Fall of the Third Reich*, Simon and Schuster.

—David Hagberg
July, 1984

I pledge allegiance to the flag
of the United States of America,
and to the republic for which it stands,
one nation, indivisible, with liberty
and justice for all.

> —The United States
> Pledge of Allegiance
> (1944)

I swear to Thee, Adolph Hitler,
As Führer and Chancellor of the
German Reich,
Loyalty and bravery.
I vow to Thee and to the superiors
Whom Thou shalt appoint
Obedience unto death,
So help me God.

> —Nazi SS Oath
> to the Führer

—Look, we had our heroes in Nam, too; so don't ride off on your high horse. There was the kid from South Dakota—Terry, I think his name was—who later went to work for the Associated Press in Sioux Falls.

—Hell, he held back or something—to take a piss, I guess—when out of the corner of his eye he saw the little slope coming out of the hill.

—Terry spun around, scared shitless, pulled out his .45 and blew the mother away. Let me tell you, when his pals all ran back to find out what the hell was happening, they found Terry puking his guts out. He was just a green kid, but he did his job. Saved the entire platoon.

The story was familiar to the older man, who at forty wasn't really much older, actually, and he raised his beer in salute and took a deep drink. He was remembering, just like the kid was. Only he was going back further, when he was really just a snot-nosed kid from Wisconsin. Frightened. Unsure of himself, the way all kids are. But back then people were certainly not as naive as the young buck seated across from him seemed to think everyone was. Hell, there were Benny Goodman, Ike (forget about Truman for the time being), the New York Times, and Edward R. Murrow. What'd they have nowadays: Dan Rather, Miller Lite, and Star Wars?

The younger man brushed his long hair back. He didn't look so good. Probably the dope he was smoking.

—Major Fisher. Now there was a bonafide hero. Even got the Medal for what he did up in the Ashau Valley. Fuckin' A. Four thousand VC against four hundred fifty Special Forces. They were steamrolling us, when Fisher and his Air Force pals came to the rescue in their A1E's. Meyers went down and Fisher just went in after him. Screw the VC and their machine guns and

7

mortars; screw the whole bunch of them. Fisher was goin' after his buddy. He pulled it off.

The bar was a sleazy joint, and they had to shout to hear each other over the noise of the jukebox. Normally, the older man wouldn't have bothered, but at this juncture in his life, for some reason even he could not define, it was important for him to make the younger man understand. *—How about the Viet Cong themselves?*

—Those motherfuckers? What about 'em?

—How about their heroes?

The younger man looked across the table at the other, incredulously, as if he had just committed a sacrilege. *—Man . . . oh, Jesus . . . man, you just don't know what the fuck you're talking about.*

—Heroes.

—Fuckin' A—heroes, not slopes! The little bastards didn't know what the fuck they was doing half the time. They had their sack of rice, some dried fish, and a little wine, and they was set. Shit.

The older man was thinking back again to the stories he had been told, and the younger one reached across the table and punched his arm.

—Come on now, don't go space-city on me. I didn't mean nothing. I just like hearing about the old days, that's all, and you know what you're talking about most of the time. Makes me think of the way Nam could have been.

Heroes, the older man thought to himself. The kid had absolutely no conception of what it was all about. Oh, he had been doing a lot of talking about heroes—genuine heroes, all right—but he was just like a bird, like a parrot or something, just mouthing words that meant nothing.

Christ, but it made the older man mad. Yet he didn't want to antagonize the kid. Maybe start a fight or something. He wanted the kid to understand. That's all. Just understand.

But then he had to laugh. The kid at least had Vietnam. He had actually fought over there. Pleiku or someplace that sounded like that. But the older man had missed it all: He had not been born until 1943. He had been too young for Korea, and somehow he had missed Vietnam. The kid had his war fresh in his mind. The older man had only the stories from his father and, of course, his collection.

—*You started out by telling me about some heroes from the big war.*

The older man looked up. Would the kid understand? Could he?

PART ONE
SPIES
January–February 1944

1

The weather was very bad, even for this time of the year, and Dieter Schey, alias Robert Mordley, was more than a little concerned about the rendezvous. The wind blew snow from the northeast, and he had to bend forward against it as he trudged along the beach at the head of Frenchman's Bay, south of Bangor.

He hadn't heard a thing from his control at Hamburg for three and a half weeks now. Twenty-seven days of wondering what the hell would happen if the sub could not get here. If the FBI closed in. If he could not get away from Oak Ridge long enough to make the drop.

They were asking a lot.

Schey was a ruggedly good-looking man, who at thirty-three could pass, and often had, for ten years younger or ten years older, depending upon the clothing he wore, the way he parted his hair, the expression on his face, and how he held himself. He was blond, and fair of skin, his eyes a deep blue that, he was told, turned almost steel-gray when he was angry. This evening, however, he didn't give a damn what image he projected. Not out here. Not in this bloody storm.

His last communications with Hamburg had been on the fifth and sixth of December, when he'd reported that he had important films to send out. The reply came back the next evening:

> U293 TO GRID 158-277 2.1.44
> 2300 UNTIL 0400 REGARDS

That had been it. A simple rendezvous order giving the time, the date, and the grid reference, which was here, on the Maine coast.

Three times since then he had driven out of town, back up into the Cumberland Mountains of Tennessee, had set up the portable transmitter, and had sent out messages. But Hamburg had not replied. It was as if they no longer existed.

"Most of the time you will be very much alone, very much on your own resources," his instructors at A-Schule West, in Park Zorgvliet, had drilled into his head. "Never rely on your cover-identity friends. They'll betray you the moment they suspect who you really are. Even your wife, if you follow our advice and take one, must be guarded against. Vigilance is the price of freedom."

He stopped again to peer into the darkness out to sea, but in this weather he could not even make out the lights of Bar Harbor, four miles to the south on Mount Desert Island, nor the Naval Reserve Station across the way at Winter Harbor. But the U293 and her officers and men would have to make it undetected between the two. So it was just as well the weather was bad.

Three miles back, Catherine and the baby were sleeping. They had had a tiring three days getting here by train and then by bus. Catherine had not even moved when he had carefully climbed out of bed, got dressed, and left the cabin.

He touched his pocket. The film was there. A thousand miles to the southwest his job as a machinist at the Oak Ridge Manhattan District project was waiting for him.

"Damned funny time to take a vacation, if you ask me," Tom Riley, his foreman, had said. It was the only difficult moment. If too much of a fuss was made, someone would be coming around to take a closer look at him.

"I have nowhere to go in the summer that I like any better than here," Schey said. His English was so Oxford-perfect that he had to work constantly to inject a nasal twang into it, an accent that most people suspected was Connecticut Yankee.

"Where're you going, anyway? Don't you know there's a war on?" Riley had complained. He was from Biloxi, Mississippi. Everyone working on the huge project was from somewhere else. It was what had attracted German intelligence to Oak Ridge in the first place.

Schey shrugged. "Maine. I just want to get away with my wife and kid. Haven't had a vacation in eighteen months."

"You know people up there?"

"No. Just heard it was a nice place. Got cabins for rent. Cheap this time of year. It'll be just me and the family."

They were in the main machine shop to the southwest of the

gigantic gas diffusion building with its miles of piping. There was a lot of noise. Riley looked around at the work going on. Everyone seemed to be racing at a feverish pace. He resented being pulled away like this.

"What the hell am I supposed to do without you?"

Schey laughed with just the right inflection. If worse came to worst, he'd have to quit. It would cause a lot of suspicion, but he was going to have to make the rendezvous. No matter what. It was vital that the photographs and drawings get out. The Americans were not too far now from their new bomb.

"If it wasn't for the board, I'd hit you up for a raise after a remark like that."

Again Riley shook his head.

"Well? Do I get my ten days or do I have to arm wrestle you for it?"

"Go on," the burly foreman had said finally. "Get the hell out of here before I find my overtime board and sign you on."

He came to the frozen creek that crossed under the highway a few hundred yards upstream, then looked at his watch. It was a couple of minutes after eleven. He looked out into the bay, and an almost overpowering feeling came to him that the submarine was there. He strained to listen, but he couldn't hear a thing except for the wind in the trees and rocks behind him and the waves washing up on the beach at his feet. But the boat was out there. He could almost smell the diesel fuel.

He pulled a large flashlight out of one of the pockets in his dark pea coat, pointed it directly south, and sent four flashes. He waited thirty seconds, then sent four more flashes, and followed them one minute later with a final four.

The answering sequence came almost immediately. Perhaps no more than a couple of hundred yards offshore. It was possible they had come that close. The water was very deep here. He had heard the local fisherman talking about it this afternoon, when he had gone into the country store for some food.

From the charts he had seen back at the cabin (he supposed they had been left there by the previous tenant, a fisherman), the sub would probably have come up the east side of the bay, well away from Bar Harbor itself, before angling back to the west to Peck's Point.

There was a very brief flash of red light, as if someone had opened the wrong hatch or something, and then, over the wind,

Schey was certain he could hear the sounds of oars dipping in the water, and someone grunted.

He looked both ways along the beach. There were coastal watchers here. Or at least along a lot of coastline there were old men with nothing better to do than snoop around at night. He wasn't really afraid of them; he just didn't want the nuisance.

The sounds of someone rowing a boat came much clearer now, and Schey flashed his light a couple of times for them to home in on as he waited impatiently. Every minute he was here like this, he risked exposure. There was too much work yet to be done for him to have to run. There was another reason he did not want his life turned upside down at this moment, but he pushed that thought to the back of his head.

He had not had enough time to find out for sure if beach patrols were maintained on a *regular* basis in these parts. A mistake on his part, he thought with recrimination, but it was too late now to do anything about it.

The rubber raft, with four men all dressed in black, their faces corked, materialized from the darkness, and Schey helped pull the boat up on the beach. All four of the men jumped ashore. They had huge grins on their faces.

"Die Vereinigten Staaten. Wir sind hier!"

"Welkommen," Schey replied.

"Heil Hitler," one of the men said, raising his right arm in salute.

Schey returned it, a sudden surge of pride coming over him. It had been a long time since he had been among friends and had been able to use that greeting. Power. The destiny of Germany. Brotherhood. Authority. It bespoke a rich patina of all those feelings and more for him.

"Hamburg sent us. You must be Captain Schey," the naval officer said. He was young, probably twenty-five, and wore a short, well-trimmed beard.

Schey nodded. "U293?"

"Right. Lieutenant Kurt Voster, communications and security officer. You have something for me, sir?"

Schey pulled the tightly wrapped package from his pocket. "This is very important, Lieutenant."

"You don't have to tell me, sir," Voster said, taking the package and pocketing it. "We came all the way across the

Atlantic to pick it up. Do you realize what that means these days?"

"Sorry," Schey said, and he meant it. "How are things at home?" He did not trust the news he was getting here from the radio and the newspapers. There was too much propaganda.

"Not good, let me tell you."

The three crewmen had wandered up the beach. When they returned home, they'd be able to brag to their friends that they had actually invaded the U.S.

"They talk about bombing. Is it true?"

"Unfortunately," Voster said. "The bastard Americans come over by day, and then at night the British come. We have the Norden bombsight—or at least that's the rumor going around—but that doesn't do us any good."

Schey was sick at heart. "Berlin, too?"

Voster nodded. "Dresden. Köln. Munich. No place is safe." He looked over toward the diminishing figures of his men. "There's a gag going around. I heard it when I was home on leave for Christmas."

It hurt hearing this, but Schey said nothing, letting the man go on.

"They're asking what's the shortest joke. When you say you don't know, they answer: 'We're winning the war.' "

"That bad?"

"I'm afraid so, sir. What about you here? How much longer will you be able to hold out?"

"That depends upon the photographs and drawings. It's up to the Admiral."

An odd expression came over Voster's face. "Perhaps not," he said enigmatically.

Schey was about to ask him what he meant by that, when the crewmen raced back, waving their arms frantically, but making absolutely no noise.

Voster spun around and pulled out his pistol. Schey held him back.

"No!" he whispered urgently.

"There's someone up there," one of the crewmen gasped, out of breath.

The other two were pushing the rubber raft off the beach.

"Probably the coastal watcher," Schey said. "Get the hell out of here; I'll take care of this." He looked into Voster's eyes.

"The photographs and the drawings are important, Lieutenant! Very important! *Verstehen Sie?*"

"*Ja, und Gott Sie dank,*" Voster said. He jumped in the raft with the others, and as Schey hurried back up the beach, they disappeared into the darkness.

Almost immediately he could hear someone above in the rocks, on the west side of the creek. He froze in his tracks as a powerful beam of light flashed on the beach behind him. When it swung out to sea, he raced across to a long, low outcropping of rock.

"Here, what's this?" someone shouted from just a few yards off the beach.

The beam of the light shone on the skidmarks from the raft and the footprints in the sand. The light flashed out to sea again.

"Holy Mother of God!" the man shouted. "The Nazis!"

Schey climbed up from the beach on the other side of the rock outcropping and quickly scrambled above where the man had been standing. But he was gone. Schey held his breath, listening, and he could hear someone farther up on the rocks, back toward the highway.

If the man got to a telephone, the U-boat wouldn't have a chance. At first light the Navy's spotter planes would be up, and every boat in the area would converge at the mouth of the bay.

Schey headed up toward the road, dropping all attempts at stealth, his powerful legs like hydraulic rams propelling him upwards, and recklessly he leaped from one rock to the next, mindless now of the cold and the blowing snow.

The coastal spotter, frightened that he had actually spotted the enemy, here in Maine, was puffing like an old steam engine by the time he made it to the side of the road, so he had no idea that anyone was behind him, until something leaped out of the darkness on his back, and he thought it was some sort of wild animal.

Schey jammed his knee in the man's back, then sharply pulled his head back, breaking his neck.

It was over in a split second, although the man's legs jerked spasmodically for several minutes afterwards.

Schey didn't like this at all. He looked down into the man's open eyes. He'd been nothing more than a coastal watcher. An amateur. Almost certainly a family man, too old for active service, so he had chosen this. Just doing his bit for the war effort.

"Verdammt," Schey swore out loud, his stomach churning. But it was war—total war. The Führer had ordered it.

Just down the highway was the spotter's old, beat-up pickup truck. Without having to think it out, Schey carried the man's body over to a spot a few yards behind the rear of the truck and laid it half in and half out of the ditch. He lined the head and neck up with the inside rear wheel.

The man looked to be in his early to middle fifties, and Schey wondered what men like him would do after the war . . . whichever way it went. Would they fit in? He sincerely hoped so. There had been enough suffering now; more was not needed.

Back at the front of the truck, he released the parking brake, put the gear shift in neutral, and gave the truck a shove. It started back slowly at first, but then, as it angled over to the ditch, it picked up speed, the rear wheel bumping up over the dead man's face and neck with a sickening crunch.

Schey hurried off the side of the road and scrambled down the rocks toward the beach even before the truck had come to a halt in the ditch.

They'd find the man in the morning, run over by his own truck. A freak accident.

Catherine's body was warm and soft beneath her flannel nightgown when Schey climbed into the small bed in the front bedroom. She moaned softly, and automatically turned to him.

"Hmmm?" she said, starting to wake up.

Schey's stomach was still churning. He kept seeing the dead man's eyes looking up at him. "Go back to sleep, Katy," he whispered.

But she was awake. There was a small amount of flickering light in the room from the isinglass window in the oil burner in the living room, just enough for him to see her face. She was smiling.

"Did you go outside?" she asked. "You're cold."

"I went out for a smoke."

"Are you worried about your job?" She was always concerned about him. She was certain that she loved him more than he did her, and it frightened her at times.

"A little bit," he said softly.

She kissed his nose and his cheeks. "Maybe we should go back. Our little house in Oak Ridge is nice."

Schey smiled. Their little house was, besides the baby Robert, Junior, her source of intense pride. Damned few of the other women she knew had houses. But they had come to Oak Ridge much too late, after houses had become all but impossible to find.

"We'll think about it in the morning," Schey said, and he drew her closer, pulling her nightgown up so that he could feel her legs and stomach and breasts against his body.

Neither of them heard the baby coughing in the other room.

2

It was snowing in northern Germany, too, as Lieutenant Robert David Deland, alias Edmund Dorfman, stepped out of the mathematics center at Versuchs-Kommando Nord and hesitated a moment to pull up his coat collar.

For the first time since the OSS had sent him to Germany, he was seriously considering running. It was getting to be too much for him. Major Preuser had been at him again this afternoon, and this time it was serious.

Deland had been hired nearly nine incredible months ago, for his expertise in trajectory mathematics. A background out of Göttingen had been prepared for him, and so far it had stood up. But now he wasn't so sure.

Preuser had been on him about his snooping around. He had tried to explain to the major, who was chief of security for the M-Section at Test-Command North, that in order to come up with acceptable trajectory mathematics, systems that would work, he needed to know specifics about the mammoth rocket—the V2, they called the earlier models. That's when the trouble began; Preuser had accused him of being a spy, rhetorically of course, but it was creating too much attention.

The frigid wind whipped across the island of Usedom from the Baltic, and Deland had to turn his face away from it as he hurried toward the S-Bahn terminal before the rush started.

He looked more like a farm boy than a mathematician. At just under six feet, he was big-boned and dark-haired with a ruddy outdoors complexion. In actuality, he had attended the University of Heidelberg, then Göttingen, where he had studied mathematics from '32 to '36. There were times when he'd admit to himself that those were the very best years of his life. The camaraderie. The student pubs. The hard work with Dr. Alois Reichert. God, it had been grand. But now he mostly hated

Germans and what they stood for. He had heard of Auschwitz. He could not believe it, and yet he knew it was true.

There was a lot of activity in the compound this afternoon, despite the nasty weather. Deland supposed they would be firing another V2 sometime tomorrow. Before long there'd be others, though: V3's, V4's. He had been doing a lot of work lately on intercontinental trajectories: Ireland to the U.S. east coast. Farfetched, Dulles had called it; nevertheless, it was frightening, because if the Germans could hold out for another couple of years, they'd have the V9 or even the V10, with enough power to span the Atlantic.

He noticed all that and more, including the truck coming from the liquid oxygen plant toward the *Preufstande* where the rockets were fired.

Also, there had been a lot of big wigs coming on base all day, including an SS General who had been in the mess hall at the VIP table with Von Braun himself.

Something definitely big was set for tomorrow if the weather and the Allies cooperated.

The little five-car electric train rattled under the canopy across the main road; Deland rushed across to it and took a seat in the last car. There were only a couple of dozen people, some of them officers, but most of them civilian engineers and technicians. No one Deland knew, which was just as well. He wanted to keep to his own thoughts long enough to calm down.

It was just after four in the afternoon. The main rush wouldn't begin for another hour, when most of the four thousand employees here at Peenemunde would head home to Koserow farther down the island or to Swinemünde and Wolgast on the mainland.

The S-Bahn rattled out of the terminal, picking up speed as they crossed the base to Werk Süd, where they stopped for another dozen passengers, then headed down to the main highway for the first checkpoint this side of Zinnowitz.

The others on the train were in a good mood this afternoon. Laughing and joking. "They may be bombing Berlin, but they haven't been at this little nest lately," was the consensus.

"Besides, it's Wednesday, already the halfway point. Can Sunday be far behind?"

Except for the big concrete buildings like Werk Süd, the base looked more like a small town than a rocket research and testing facility. Most of the buildings were neat two-story structures nestled in and amongst thick stands of pine. In fact, he had been told, Peenemunde had once been a very fashionable resort area. He believed it. In the summer the place was lovely.

They came down the long, open southern stretch, the sea to their left, and Deland's stomach tightened as it did each time he got to this point.

A large sign moved slowly past them, and he did not have to look up to read it. The words were burned indelibly into his mind. He even dreamed about them.

WHAT YOU SEE
WHAT YOU HEAR
WHEN YOU LEAVE
LEAVE IT HERE

Just beyond the sign the S-Bahn made a wide loop, coming around to the main gate and to the transfer point for the regular train and for the parking area where Deland kept his bicycle. Barbed wire and tall fences surrounded the entire area. A dozen SS guards were waiting as the S-Bahn came to a halt at the platform, while other SS guards patrolled outside the fences with their German shepherds.

It was nothing more than routine, Deland told himself, as he told himself every day at this time. He was taking nothing out with him, nothing other than what he had catalogued in his mind. He had no need to take anything with him; he had total recall—a photographic memory.

His instructors in Virginia had been delighted with him, and Wild Bill Donovan himself had come out to the school one afternoon to meet with the whiz kid, as he was then called.

Six lines were formed, each passing through a turnstile manned by a pair of guards who checked papers, retrieved passes, and searched parcels, lunch boxes, and even pockets.

"If they were really sharp, they'd understand that none of us is interested in rocket parts; all we want is bread," someone behind Deland quipped.

Someone else laughed. "A little meat wouldn't be so bad either."

"Meat . . . what's that?" the first one shot back.

It was Deland's turn. He handed over the badge which he wore clipped to his lapel, his identity card, his work permit, and his military classification card, which exempted him from service as long as he worked on a priority project such as Peenemunde.

One guard looked at his papers while the other quickly and efficiently frisked him. He carried nothing but his wallet, a package of cigarettes, a lighter, and fifty or sixty marks—yesterday, the first, had been payday. The bicycle lock key he kept on a string around his neck. The guards never searched there.

He was allowed through the turnstile; his papers were returned to him, all but the security badge which would be kept here at the gate, and he hurried across the entry area to where he had parked his bicycle.

It would be a long, cold ride into Wolgast, 10.5 kilometers to be exact, but he never really minded the ride. He got to see more of the comings and goings from Peenemunde (many of the VIP's visiting the station came on the ferry from Wolgast), and it gave him the time to settle his nerves, which by the end of the workday were usually frayed. Today he was really jumpy, and it took him several minutes to thaw out his lock so that the key would work.

"Dorfman," someone called from behind, and Deland nearly jumped out of his skin.

"Wollen Sie mit mir gehen?"

Deland had tried to be a loner, but with Rudy Schlechter, a mathematician in fuel management systems, it was nearly impossible. The man had an infectious grin and manner. Even when his superiors were chastising him for one thing or another (he was also a practical joker), they'd be doing it with a grin.

He was a tall man, somewhat on the thin side, with graying temples that would have made him look distinguished except for the fact he always seemed to be dressed in crumpled suits, his tie dirty and his shirt stained. He stood by the open door of his Volkswagen—one of the new Hitler cars—grinning. How he managed to get the car in the first place was a mystery, matched only by the mystery of how he managed to get gasoline ration coupons.

"Come on, Dorfman, we'll tie your bicycle on the roof. You can ride up there on it, if you wish."

Deland laughed, forcing himself to sound natural. He walked his bike across the roadway. "I suppose you have some wine and cheese in there. Perhaps a fat sausage."

"And dancing girls. Don't forget the dancing girls," Schlechter laughed, helping Deland raise his bicycle onto the roof of the tiny car. He got some twine out of the trunk, and they tied the bicycle frame to the front and rear bumpers.

Ordinarily, Deland would have refused such an offer, but he had been very carefully cultivating the other man. Schlechter had an enormous intelligence potential. As the fuel flows, so does the rocket. In another time, Deland thought, he and Schlechter could have been friends. It was saddening.

"It will be among your more difficult problems over there," one of his instructors had told him. "There will be no safe haven. Unlike here at home, where you can make friends freely, without worry, in Nazi Germany you will be watched twenty-four hours a day. Never forget it. Your life may depend upon your remembering it."

They pulled away from the parking lot and headed west on the main island highway that led to the ferry to Wolgast. A half-dozen heavy Army trucks passed them on their way to the station. Schlechter glanced in the rearview mirror after them.

"We're supposed to have a storm tonight. I don't think they'll be able to fire the rocket tomorrow."

Deland looked sharply at the man. Was it some sort of a test, or was the man being a fool? "I don't think we should talk about that sort of thing, Rudy," he said.

Schlechter glanced at him and laughed. "You're right, of course. They'd probably hang me by the thumbs."

Careful, Deland told himself. "Are you fellows having problems over in C-Hut?"

This time Schlechter laughed out loud. "Problems! It's not the word for the mess we're in. No one knows what's going on. Von Braun himself was in today, ranting and raving about what incompetent fools we were." He chuckled. "When he left, he forgot his hat and gloves."

"They have us working on the Irish thing."

"What's that?" Schlechter asked casually. Too casually.

"Oh, you know, trajectories for the V9 and V10."

"I don't know what you're talking about."

"Forget it," Deland mumbled, his stomach churning. He wished he had ridden his bicycle.

"No, I'm serious. I don't know what you're talking about, but I have my own questions."

Deland said nothing.

"They took us off the alcohol problem, and we're supposed to be designing pumps for corrosive liquids. But they never tell us exactly what sort of liquids we'd be working with. Have you any idea what the hell they mean?"

"They are working on new fuels; I did hear that. Supposedly much more powerful than alcohol. But they'd still need liquid oxygen. I can't see any way around that."

"There're ways," Schlechter said. "But we've not been asked to do away with the Lox pumps, just to design a pump to move corrosive liquids at very high speeds." Schlechter shook his head. "It's crazy, you know, Dorfman, but we're probably losing the war, so none of this will matter much in the end."

"Don't talk that way, Rudy," Deland said sharply.

"Sorry." Schlechter shook his head again.

They passed through the tiny village of Bannemin, then a few kilometers later crossed the Peene River into Wolgast, the wind kicking up whitecaps on the water.

Before the war, Wolgast had been a commercial fishing center of about ten thousand people. But the work at Peenemunde had swollen its population by nearly half. Deland lived in a rooming house on the far north side of the city, and he was about to direct Schlechter that way when the man pulled up and parked in the square downtown.

"What's this?" Deland asked.

"Just hold on there, Dorfman; I've got a little surprise for you."

"I really . . ."

Schlechter turned off the ignition, opened the door, and jumped out of the car. "You can stay here and freeze in the car, if you'd like, but I really need a big favor from you. It won't take much of your time. But it'll be worth it. You'll see."

Deland laughed after a moment, his earlier dark mood deepening. His gut was killing him and his heart was hammering, but there was no way of refusing this man without arousing suspicion. He had only known Schlechter for a few months, since the man had transferred in from the research station at Bleicherode. Before that, he said, he had been at Kummersdorf West, near Berlin. Until today, Deland had liked the man, so far as a Nazi could be liked. But he was getting a bad feeling about him now. Something was not quite right.

He got out of the car, nevertheless, a grin on his face. He was either going to stay and do the job he had been sent to do, or he was going to turn tail and get the hell out. He wasn't going to sit on the fence any longer.

"My supper is waiting for me," he said weakly.

"I'll buy you supper. And a beer, too," Schlechter said. He started across the square, and Deland hurried to catch up.

"What's going on, Rudy? Why the mystery?"

"Just wait and see, my boy. Just wait and see."

They had to wait for an Army jeep to pass; then they crossed the cobbled street and entered the Hansa Haus. It was early, yet the *Bierstube* was already crowded and noisy. A pall of smoke hung just below the wood-beamed ceiling, curled around the wild boar and deer heads on the walls, and completely wreathed the heads of the old men at the long *Stammtisch*. Deland had never been in this place, although he had heard it was popular with the young office workers of Wolgast. Many of the routine administrative functions for the research station were carried on here in town.

Schlechter seemed to be well known in the place; they stopped a half a dozen times to shake hands and say hello. But finally they reached a small table around the corner from the long mahogany bar. Two women were seated there. One of them was older, with a thin, angular face and a self-assured expression, while the other was much younger, much prettier, with long blonde hair up in a bun, a tiny round face, and lovely hands folded in front of her on the table. The swell of her bosom rose and fell beneath her white blouse. She seemed nervous. They both had been drinking wine.

Schlechter kissed the older woman on the cheek and smiled at the other. "You're looking lovely this evening, Katrina," he said to her. "I've brought someone to meet you."

The girl nearly jumped out of her skin, and Deland realized with a sinking feeling exactly what it was Schlechter had in mind. A couple of weeks ago they had talked over lunch at the mess hall on station about Deland's love life, which was zero. Schlechter had pried. This was the result.

"This is Edmund Dorfman, who works out at the station with me. He is not nearly as serious as he seems at this moment, but I think the poor boy is frightened." He laughed; the older woman tittered. "Dorfman, I'd like you to meet Katrina Mueller. She works in KwE/3 in town."

"Herr Dorfman," she said politely. She had a gently enchanting voice.

Deland nodded, flustered.

"This is Maria Quelle," Schlechter said, introducing the other woman. "We've been friends since Berlin."

The woman smiled. "We go back too far," she said. "I'm pleased to meet you, Herr Dorfman. Rudy has told me so much about you."

Schlechter shoved Deland down next to Katrina, and Maria got to her feet and collected her handbag.

"Sorry we have to run like this, Katy, but I'll see you in the morning," Maria said.

"You'll like the sauerbraten here," Schlechter said, and before Deland could do a thing, or even remember about his bicycle, Rudy and Maria had turned and were threading their way toward the front door. They stopped to talk with the big, burly woman behind the bar, and then they were gone.

Deland turned back and Katrina jumped again. She had been studying his profile.

He smiled. "I'm sorry."

"About what, Herr Dorfman?" she asked timidly.

"Please," he said. "My name is Edmund."

She hesitated a moment, but he smiled. "Edmund," she finally said.

"I didn't realize that Rudy was going to pull something like this."

"Neither did I suspect it of Maria," she said. She reached for her purse and started to get up.

"Where are you going?"

She looked down into his eyes. "Home," she said matter-of-factly.

Deland's heart was pounding. He felt like a complete fool. "Please don't. We're here together now. Have supper with me?"

Again she hesitated.

"Please?"

She smiled. It was warm. "They *did* go through a lot of trouble," she said, sitting down.

The barmaid brought him a beer and Katrina another glass of wine. They both ordered the sauerbraten.

"I'm not sure I know what KwE/3 is," Deland said when they were alone again.

"*Kriegswerke Erwerbungen*. It is the war plant acquisitions office. I'm in section three. Nothing very important, I'm afraid."

"You're being modest."

She laughed; the sound was like music, and it went right through him. He shivered. "No," she said. "We purchase soap and towels and bed sheets, those sorts of things." She lowered her eyes. "And you?"

"I'm a mathematician."

Her eyes widened. "You must be brilliant, then, like Maria's Rudy."

3

Admiral Wilhelm Canaris, chief of Amt/Ausland Abwehr, hesitated a moment on the top step of his private railway car before stepping down to trackside, as an extraordinary thought crossed his mind. There was no one—not one single person here in Germany—whom he could completely trust.

He and his wife Erika had never been close. Which in a way was good; when it all ended, his taint would not reflect on her.

His adjutant, Lieutenant Colonel Jenke, was a fool. He was a reasonably capable administrator, but he had no vision, no creativity, and he certainly was not one to be relied on.

Hansen in Abteilung I, who had taken over from old Piekenbrock, was a raging Nazi, as were Loringhoven and Jacobsen.

There was no one. It gave him an odd feeling at the moment to realize it, almost a sense of freedom.

They had stopped outside Hamburg, near the tiny suburb of Reinbek, but even this far out the destruction from the Allied bombing raids was awesome. The air smelled of plaster dust and burned wood.

Several large staff cars were parked on the road behind the burned-out shell of a station. Two officers and a half-dozen men were waiting as Canaris stepped down.

They all saluted.

"So good of you to meet me here with a car," Canaris said. His voice was very soft, and he spoke with a slight lisp. He was a small man, five feet three, slight of stature, with white hair, bushy eyebrows, and an air of fatigue about him, as if he had not been getting enough sleep. His uniform was on the shabby side. The Iron Cross on his tunic was just visible beneath his unbuttoned overcoat.

"Major Loetz, sir," the senior Hamburg officer introduced

himself. He was the new man up here, and Canaris strongly suspected he was reporting to Department VI of the RSHA.

They shook hands.

"We only just found out you were coming, Herr Admiral."

"The tracks still have not been repaired through the city?"

"No, sir," Loetz said. He turned and introduced the other officer. "Captain Hans Meitner."

Canaris looked at him. "Chief of Communications Branch?" They knew each other, but Loetz wasn't aware of it.

"Yes, sir," the captain, a thick-waisted older man, said. He was from the old school. Canaris liked him.

"Nothing further from our friend in Oak Ridge?"

"No, sir."

"Or from Lieutenant Voster?"

"No, sir. But if the boat has gotten away, and everything was as it should be, we were not due to hear from them until today in any event."

"What's this?" Loetz asked impatiently.

They could not hide anything from the man, so between them, Canaris and Meitner had decided to handle the affair as a routine matter. Dangerous, but it was the only way.

"It's nothing," Canaris said. "Let's go out to the communications center." He marched across the tracks and climbed into one of the staff cars. Loetz and Meitner got in with him, while the soldiers piled into the other vehicles, and they headed away from the station.

Dear God, he was tired. Sick to death of the senseless destruction. It was horrible in Berlin, but this was even worse. He felt a constriction in his chest as they passed block after block of knocked-down buildings, burned-out hulks of homes, piles of rubble that had once been thriving factories.

"I hadn't realized the destruction was so complete," he said half to himself. Reading the daily reports was one thing; seeing the damage first hand was something else.

"It will be a happy day when New York and Washington are reduced to this," Loetz said.

Canaris looked sharply at him. "Good God, man, isn't this enough?"

Loetz bridled. "I only meant, sir . . . that is, we can't leave this unrevenged."

"Can't revenge take another form?"

"I . . . don't know what to say, sir," Loetz stammered, embarrassed. Captain Meitner was looking the other way, out the window.

"Do you actually think we're going to win this war, Herr Major?" Canaris said. He knew that he was going too far, but he could not help himself. He was worried, at the moment, about Dieter Schey. Deeply worried about the information he was sending over. If Schey's early transmissions had not been exaggerated and if their other intelligence units had been on the button, then the Americans would very soon have the new bomb. Germany might have it, too. Oster and Dohnanyi had both agreed that such a possibility would be totally unthinkable. It would have to be blocked at all costs.

"I'd pull the trigger on Hitler myself before I allowed such a monster weapon into the Luftwaffe's hands," Oster had cried.

Canaris ran a hand across his eyes. "I'm sorry, Major Loetz. I'm just very tired."

"I understand, Herr Admiral," Loetz said coldly.

They passed the ruined outskirts of Hamburg to the north, toward Ahrensberg, where the highway turned down a narrow country lane that ended a few kilometers later at *the house*, as it was called, that housed the Abwehr's Hamburg radio station. The two-story stucco house, with an odd-looking turret at the rear, was one of the few things in Hamburg that Schellenberg and the RSHA had not yet taken over. They had snatched many of the intelligence-gathering functions from the Abwehr, and even the cream of the Brandenburg Division, but for the moment at least, the Abwehr's link with her agents around the world was still secure despite Loetz.

Inside, they went immediately upstairs to the radio rooms themselves, which occupied the entire second floor. Tiny tables equipped with radios and notepads were stuck everywhere, even in back closets. Power cables had been strung beneath the floorboards, but the connections to the antennae, which bristled in the trees outside, came through cable runs across the ceiling.

There was a lot of activity this afternoon. Messages came and went from the radio operators, via copy boys, to the message center behind a large window in one of the back bedrooms. From there, after decoding, the plain German texts were sent downstairs, where they were typed on message forms and sent to the addressees by various means, depending upon the urgency of the message.

A young lieutenant in the message center jumped up from his desk when he saw Canaris and the others coming up the stairs.

He rushed across the room to them and saluted. He was excited. "It came, Herr Kapitän. We have word from U293." He held out a yellow message form to Meitner, who passed it on to Canaris. It had not yet been sent downstairs for typing, but it had been decoded.

> PACKAGE SECURED HAVE CLEARED
> 158-277 ETA 001-358 30.1.44
> REGARDS VOSTER

Double-o one, was Portugal; 358, somewhere along its coast. It would take nearly a month for the submarine to make the crossing, if all went well, and another couple of days for the Lisbon messenger to meet Voster, pick up the film canisters Schey had radioed he was sending over, and then make it across the border into Spain.

Four weeks. Canaris hoped he could hold out that long. It was going to be difficult.

Loetz wasn't the least bit interested in the message, assuming it was nothing more than routine traffic. Canaris often meddled in the day-to-day routine of his outstations. This was no different.

"You needn't make copies," Canaris said softly.

The young lieutenant was startled. "Sir?" he said. But Meitner nodded, and the lieutenant saluted and went back to his desk.

"We'll have to log it, Herr Admiral," Meitner said, taking him aside. Loetz had gone across the room to check on something.

"As a routine transmission from one of our coast watchers," Canaris said.

Meitner managed a slight smile. "Of course, sir; it was nothing more."

Loetz came back. He was rubbing his hands together. "And now, Herr Admiral, we are ready for your inspection."

Canaris had pocketed the message, and he reached out and patted Loetz on the shoulder. "That is not why I came up here today."

"Herr Admiral?" the major said. He was suspicious.

Canaris looked around at the radio operators and the equipment. The house was warm. It smelled of electrical apparatus and human bodies. It would be much worse for them in the bunkers at Zossen, outside Berlin. But it couldn't be helped if the SD was to be thrown off.

"The bulk of operations here are to be immediately suspended."

It was a bombshell. Even Captain Meitner, who for the past seven months had acted as Canaris' eyes and ears for the entire Hamburg station, was stunned.

"The A and B circuits, of course, will be moved first. Specific written orders have been cut. They'll be here very soon."

"Are we to join you at Maybach II, sir?" Meitner asked.

"Yes. The technical staff has already begun attending to your electrical needs. But Captain Unterman will be liaison. He'll handle the details." Canaris looked down the corridor past the message center to the radio operator positions in one of the front bedrooms. Three of the operators, their earphones shoved down around their necks, were looking this way. When Canaris caught their eye, they turned back to their radios.

"This comes as a great surprise to me, Herr Admiral." Loetz was clearly unhappy. In Berlin he would not have as much autonomy as he enjoyed here.

"You mean Brigadier Schellenberg has not informed you?" Canaris snapped sarcastically.

"No, Herr Admiral . . . I mean . . ." Loetz blustered.

"Then you may so inform Department VI, if you wish, Herr Major," Canaris said harshly. He turned to Meitner. "You are hereby detached to Headquarters Berlin, Amt/Ausland."

"My position, sir?" Meitner said, obviously pleased.

"My aide-de-camp," Canaris snapped. He softened. "That is, if you wish to accept such a dangerous assignment."

"With pleasure, sir, with pleasure," Meitner said, clicking his heels.

"Now," Canaris said, turning back to Loetz. "There are certain details that you will have to attend to. I will be much too busy over the next few weeks to do it myself. But I'm sure you will do a fine job."

It would tie Loetz up for weeks.

"I see," he said. "Will you leave me Captain Meitner to help?"

"No," Canaris said. "I'm taking him with me this afternoon. I have several pressing jobs for him to start on immediately."

By morning they had reached the Rhein-Main Luftwaffe Base at Frankfurt, where Canaris sent his railway car back to Berlin and commandeered a Dornier Do 17F reconnaissance aircraft with little difficulty. He still was chief of Amt/Ausland Abwehr, no matter what Walter Schellenberg and his SD were doing behind his back. They had to stop to refuel and to repair a minor problem with a fuel pump at the Luftwaffe Depot in Lyon, France, and then continued over the Pyrenees into Spain, finally coming in for a landing in Seville that afternoon.

"The situation is difficult here in Spain at the moment," Canaris explained as he and Meitner changed into civilian clothing. "Franco has become touchy."

"Why are we here, sir?" Meitner asked. He was uneasy.

"Our Führer has his Berghof, Himmler and the others their Bavarian retreats, while I have Spain. Leave me do the talking if any is necessary."

But there was no trouble. The crew of the Dornier, in uniform, were required to remain within the confines of the airport, and Canaris and Meitner were both given handbills prepared by the Guardia, in Spanish, German, and English, that activities of any sort that could be construed as having even the remotest connection with any phase of the war were expressly and strictly forbidden.

They each signed a document that testified they had read and understood the handbill, and would comply; their bags were then stamped by the customs people without being opened, and they were waved through.

"Have a pleasant and safe trip, Señor Guillermo," the official said.

They hired a car, Meitner totally mystified now, and they headed south toward the seacoast. When they had cleared the airport and the city of Seville, Meitner asked Canaris about their reception.

Canaris smiled tiredly. "I was here years ago as a young lieutenant. We were looking for supply depots for our submarine operations in the Mediterranean."

"And you went by the name Guillermo?"

Canaris nodded, the memories coming back in full force now. Those had been the very best of days.

"They still remember you?"

Canaris shrugged. "I have been a friend of Spain."

Meitner shook his head. Everyone knew that the Admiral was an amazing man. In the past twenty-four hours he was coming to learn just how true that was.

They skirted north of Cádiz before they headed south along the coast through Chiclana and later Tarifa, which was directly on the Strait of Gibraltar. The view was magnificent, and Canaris felt almost as if he was coming to his ancestral home after a very long absence.

It was only a few kilometers farther when they rounded a curve in the road and came down the long hill around the western shores of Algeciras Bay; they drove into the resort town itself as the sun was setting. And it *was* like coming home for Canaris. He had worked here; he had played here; he had loved here since before the War to End All Wars, as it had been called. Every time he came back like this, he had to ask himself why he had ever left.

Meitner read at least part of that on his face. "What is this place, sir?" he asked.

"Algeciras."

"I know, sir. I meant, have you friends here?"

"Yes," Canaris said, his voice barely audible. Was it a lost youth, he had to ask himself? Or was it something else? Something even more fundamental that brought him back here time after time?

He directed their driver to drop them off in town at the Hotel Reina María Cristina, but Canaris did not go in. Instead, he instructed Meitner to register for them.

"Tell them it is Señor Guillermo, and I would like the little house next door if it is available."

"And you, sir?" Meitner asked, looking around the square. It was getting dark now, and there were a lot of people here. Tourists escaping the winter and the war. The climate was perfect; it was warm with a light breeze up from the sea, and dominating the eastern shore of the bay was Gibraltar, the huge key to the Mediterranean.

"I'm going to church," Canaris said, and he turned and walked away, leaving Meitner standing there open-mouthed.

He crossed the square, waited for traffic, then went around the corner past a small row of shops: a tobacconist, a leather goods store, a silversmith, and the tiny rental library, where he ducked through a courtyard, out a rear gate, and across a narrow avenue into the Church of the Little Saints.

On the square there had been the noise of traffic and lights spilling from open doorways and windows. Here in the church it was cool and quiet, the only light coming from the votive candles beneath the statue of the Virgin on the left of the altar and a few dim lights hanging from fixtures above.

Canaris dipped his fingers in the holy water at the door, crossed himself, and then went forward to a pew halfway to the altar. He knelt, clasping his hands on the seat back in front of him, and looked up at the wooden crucifix.

"Dear God," he murmured. He knew in which direction his fate was taking him as surely as he knew Germany's eventual fate. He did not want it to be so. But he didn't know what it was he could do to prevent any of it.

Germany was lost. But there was still the possibility for an honorable peace. At least there could be. But he was afraid of what Dieter Schey was sending them from Oak Ridge. In the agent's coded messages he had told them about the new secret weapon involving nuclear energy. The Führer had called it "Jew science," but the scientists at Peenemunde were ready to build it, and the mathematicians at Göttingen paled when he mentioned the possibility.

One of them, reasonably certain that Canaris would not turn him over to the Gestapo for making defamatory statements, breathed the pronouncement that: "Only God has the right to tamper with such things. Man certainly has no right."

A side door opened and a woman dressed in black, a veil covering her face, entered the nave, crossed herself, and came around to the center aisle between the pews.

Canaris' heart began to accelerate as the woman genuflected before crossing in front of the crucifix; then she turned and glided back to where he was kneeling.

He moved over, and she knelt beside him. She lifted her veil, and Canaris' pounding heart skipped a beat. She was beautiful, in the classic Spanish aristocratic fashion. Her skin was olive, her complexion flawless. She had wide, dark eyes, high cheekbones, and full sensuous lips.

"Hello, Wilhelm," she whispered, her voice like gold. "Welcome back."

"Dona Marielle Alicia," Canaris said reverently. He lifted her hand and pressed his lips to her fingers. She stroked his hair with her other hand as the tears fell from his eyes to the sleeve of her dress.

4

Dieter Schey rinsed his coffee cup in the sink and put it on the drain. He stared out the window at the snow blowing in long streaks past the streetlight at the end of the block. The plows hadn't been back here in the neighborhood yet, but the buses would still be running from Administration out to the plants. The main roads were always the first to be opened after a storm.

Maine was going to stay with him for a very long time. All the way back on the train he kept seeing a vision of the coastal watcher's face . . . the dead man staring up at him. He kept hearing Lieutenant Voster telling him about conditions at home. Berlin was being bombed by the Americans as well as the British. Berlin!

And he worried about the submarine making it back to Germany. It would take nothing more than a simple malfunction aboard the boat to send the film canisters to the bottom of the Atlantic. All his work would have been for nothing.

He gripped the edge of the counter hard enough to turn his knuckles white. The film would get home—it had to! His work here at Oak Ridge was finished. Or very nearly finished. Very soon he was going to have to move on. A new project. A new location. A new identity. Robert Mordley would cease to exist. Two years of his life would be gone . . .

"Do you want me to fix you some breakfast?" Catherine asked.

Schey spun around as she came into the kitchen and put a half-full baby bottle in the refrigerator. She was still in her nightgown, her feet bare.

"How is he? Any better?"

"No," Catherine said. She brushed her hair back. She looked very tired. "He's still running a slight fever and he just doesn't want to eat."

38

"Call the doctor this morning; see if he can come over."

Catherine nodded. "I'll wait until eight. How late will you be?"

"Just until noon. Riley has some tooling he wants me to get right on. Shouldn't take more than three or four hours."

"Now, do you want a couple eggs?"

Schey looked at her in amazement. Eggs. She was wonderful. But he shook his head. "I'm going to walk over and catch the early bus."

"Don't tell me you're coming down with something, too," Catherine said. She came across the kitchen to him and touched his forehead with the back of her hand.

"I'm fine," he said, and he drew her close. "How about you?" He kissed her, then laid his cheek against her forehead. It was cool.

She was much shorter than he; her hair was a light brown, her eyes hazel, and her figure pleasant but very plain. From the first she had been flattered that someone so ruggedly good-looking as Schey would give her anything more than a glance. She had always been grateful to him, and her gratitude had always made him feel embarrassed—like he was a heel.

It was going to be very hard to leave her and the baby—very hard, because he had committed the sin of sins for a deep cover agent in enemy territory: He had fallen in love with one of the natives.

He shuddered.

"I don't blame you," Catherine said. "I wouldn't want to go out there this morning." The baby started to cry again, and she looked toward the bedroom door. "Have a cup of soup or something, at the canteen. Promise me?"

"All right," Schey said, looking deeply into her eyes. She read something in his look, because her hand went to her mouth. But then Schey turned and went to the back door where he took his coat down from its hook and pulled it on. The baby was crying louder now, and he was coughing.

"I'll be home a little after noon," Schey said to Catherine, and he went out the back door, leaving her standing in the kitchen, a strange look on her face.

She knew, Schey told himself as he hunched up his coat collar and headed up the street toward the bus stop in front of Administration. Damn. She had read it in his eyes. She knew that he was going to leave soon. She probably thought it was another woman.

During his training and during the first months here, he had never given this moment a thought. He had been caught up in the excitement of his job and of meeting Catherine, in New Jersey, where they both worked in the shipyards. It had been an altogether heady experience, courting her, marrying her, and then getting this job at Oak Ridge. Everything had fallen into place for him, exactly as his instructors said it would if he would remember his training.

But this part now—the hurt deep inside him—he had not foreseen.

In the past few days he had come up with any number of wild schemes to convince Catherine and the authorities that the man they knew as Robert Mordley was dead. An automobile accident and fire; a boating accident; an accident at the big TVA dam. But for that he'd need a body. One that wouldn't be missed. So far he'd drawn a blank on that score. But he did have the car parked in a rental garage in Knoxville. When the time came, he'd get down there and drive to Washington, D.C., where his contact would be waiting for him.

He stopped. Was there a balance between all that and Catherine and the baby? Or was he being pressed into a corner where he'd have to make a choice.

They had congratulated him when he got married. And they had been ecstatic when Robert, Junior, was born. He blended perfectly into his environment. The perfect cog to fit the perfect gear.

All along he had told himself that someday Catherine would understand him when he explained to her about the Thousand Year Reich. He could tell her about the beauties of his home: about the Lorelei along the Rhine; about the Tiergarten or the Zügspitze; about Ünter den Linden or the castle at Heidelberg. Christ! When it was over, they could have an apartment in Berlin, perhaps even a small cottage in Garmisch-Partenkirchen for the summers. They could even spend an occasional Christmas there.

But whenever Edward R. Murrow reported the latest offenses in the war, reported the latest Wehrmacht defeat, Catherine would shudder and look at her husband, her eyes round, liquid.

"We're not like that, Bob, are we?"

"What do you mean?" he asked carefully, not trusting his own emotions.

"I mean about the concentration camps they're talking about," she said. She sat forward, the Knoxville newspaper she had been reading falling to the floor. "They've rounded up the Jews and they're putting them in concentration camps. It's possible they're even being murdered. Innocent babies . . . just like ours."

"Katy," Schey started, but he could not go on for a moment. There was so much he wanted to tell her, to explain to her, but he hadn't gotten it all straight in his own mind yet. In the first place, it was almost certain that the radio and newspaper reports were grossly exaggerated. There were concentration camps all right. For enemies of the state. Just like Roosevelt's Japanese camps out in the desert. That wasn't widespread knowledge, but it was happening. And he also wanted to explain to her how the Jews had strangled the German economy for years—the economy as well as the white man's strain. Couldn't the world see what had been going on for the last two thousand years: It was so clear.

"Bob?" Catherine asked in a tiny voice. Something in his look had frightened her.

He smiled sadly. Once again he was in control. "It's not what you think, Katy," he said.

"But it says in the paper."

"I know. But governments have a way of exaggerating things to make their own side seem much better and free of sin." He heard his own words and thought about Goebbels.

"None of us are . . . are we?"

"What?"

"Free of sin?"

Schey had to smile at the innocence of the remark. He shook his head. "Only you and the baby."

Administration was housed in a large building called the castle. It was lit up, and several dozen people stood between the street-lights out front, waiting for the early buses that would take them over to Y-12, the electromagnetic separation plant; to S-50, the thermal diffusion operation; to X-10, the graphite reactor; or to gigantic K-25, the gaseous diffusion plant where Schey worked. Each operation had been designed to separate an isotope of uranium from its ore, which in turn could be used to build a bomb. Germany could never have mounted such an operation;

the entire Reich did not have the resources. It was the reason Schey's work here was absolutely essential.

The Americans themselves had not known which method would produce results—or, indeed, if any method of separating the bomb material would be effective. Yet the plants had all been built. Tens of thousands of workmen were employed here and at a place called Hanford in Washington state. In addition, there was a laboratory somewhere near Los Alamos, New Mexico.

Schey held toward the back of the group, anonymous in the dark, snow-blown morning, until the big buses appeared and pulled up with a hiss of their air brakes.

K-25. The Americans were now pinning their hopes on the gaseous diffusion method. It would work. Everyone was confident.

A fast-moving gray sedan flashed past the Administration building and turned down Schey's street.

For several pregnant seconds he stared at the car, trying to catalogue exactly what he had seen.

"Come on," someone behind him complained. He was holding up the line. He stepped aside.

Government plates. There were two men. Hats, overcoats. Gray car. Some kind of a shield painted on the door . . . Security!

"Damnit," Schey said, looking up as the last of the workmen hurried across the street and boarded the bus for K-25. He smiled sheepishly. "I forgot my lunch."

"You comin' or not, fella?" the driver said down to him. His right hand was on the door lever.

"Can't go without my lunch," Schey said, and he turned and strode down the street toward his house, his pounding heart steadying as he fought for control. Catherine and the baby were innocents. He hadn't wanted them involved in this.

There were no reasons for him to suspect that security was on its way to his house. On its way to see him. No real reasons. Yet lately Schey had been getting that between-the-shoulder-blades feeling that someone was watching him, that someone was dogging his every move. Riley had not been the same toward him ever since the Maine trip. Some of that Schey had put down to his own feelings of paranoia after what had happened up there. But Riley was different toward him.

It didn't matter, though, what he suspected or didn't suspect; he was going to have to find out for sure. If they were after him, he'd have to deal with it. Better here than at the plant.

Already his mind was racing forward to Knoxville and his car. He'd have to retrieve the radio transmitter, if there was time, and then he'd have to get to Washington, D.C., and his contact. All before the general alarm was sounded and an effective dragnet was begun.

Schey seldom if ever carried a weapon. His instructors at Park Zorgvliet had warned against it: "If you find yourself in a situation where you need a weapon, it will no longer matter what you do, for your cover will have been blown. But if you don't have a weapon on you, there will always be that element of doubt: Is he a spy or is he innocent? Where there is doubt, there certainly is hope."

Only at this moment Schey wished he had a gun.

It took less than five minutes for him to make it to the end of his block. His tiny prefab house was on the upper side of the block in a long row of nearly identical structures. His house was lit up. The gray sedan was parked in front of it.

So this was it, after all. Whatever plans he had been making for moving on were now forced upon him. He resented it, almost as much as he was frightened and sad for Catherine and the baby.

There were lights on in a couple of other houses on the block, but everything else was dark and silent, the snow muffling all sounds. From each chimney came a plume of white smoke bent over with the wind. It was very cold.

He had three choices. He could take the bus into Knoxville right now; chances were, no alarm had been sounded. Or he could steal a car if need be. Or if the circumstances warranted it, he could walk; he knew the route through the hills, past the security posts, out of here. That would be the most extreme. But it all depended upon what security knew, why they had come here. If it was merely on some suspicion for one thing or another, he'd be safe for at least a little while. But if they had found his transmitter or if they had somehow connected him with the thing in Maine, he'd have trouble getting out of here. Before he made that decision, he'd have to know.

Keeping to the shadows, he made his way up the block, to a spot across from where the government car was parked. The curtains on all the windows in his house were drawn, so he could not see what was going on inside.

Ducking low, he hurried across the street and looked in the

car. The keys were in the ignition. The Americans always had such supreme confidence. He smiled.

There was no one coming. No traffic on the street. No one on the way to work. No one out on a porch or in a window watching what was going on over here. The neighborhood could have been deserted.

Schey hurried around the front of the car, across his snow-covered lawn, and around to the backdoor that led into the back hall and kitchen.

He mounted the two steps, scraped the frost off the one small window at eye level, and looked inside. The kitchen door was closed, as he hoped it would be. He opened the back door, stepped inside, and softly closed it.

For several seconds he stood in the darkness, breathing shallowly, listening for sounds from inside. Someone called from upstairs. Schey couldn't quite make out the words, but it was a man's voice. The hairs at the nape of his neck bristled. A man was in his house. An intruder. He felt a sense of righteous indignation.

A door closed somewhere near (a closet?) and he could hear a man's heavy footfalls on the stairs.

There had been two of them in the car. One of them had called from upstairs. The other had just gone up.

Schey pulled off his coat so that he would have more freedom of movement, hung it on a hook, and eased open the kitchen door.

Catherine, still dressed only in her nightgown, was seated at the kitchen table. She looked up, her eyes going wide, her mouth open. He shook his head urgently and hurried across to her.

"What do they want?" he whispered.

He was bent over her, and she was looking up into his eyes. Her lips were working; she was trying to form words, but she could not.

They were moving around upstairs. It sounded as if they were in the front bedroom. Probably going through his things. But there was nothing up there. Or elsewhere in the house.

If they were merely Oak Ridge security people, it would be one thing; if they were FBI, it would be totally different.

He turned back to his wife. "Listen, Katy, did they have a warrant? Did they show you a piece of paper?"

Catherine was frightened. "What . . . what's happening, Bob?" she stammered. "Why are they here?" She was too loud.

There was a silence upstairs. "Mrs. Mordley?" one of the men called.

The color left Catherine's face.

Schey straightened up and hurried into the living room as one of the men started down the stairs. He flattened himself against the wall next to the opening to the stair hall.

"Mrs. Mordley?" the man called again, just around the corner. Then he stepped into view.

Schey reached out, grabbed a handful of the man's coat, and pulled him the rest of the way around, his arm encircling the agent's head, his hand clamped powerfully over the man's mouth and nose.

The agent grunted, his eyes bulging nearly out of their sockets as he tried to reach inside his coat for his gun. But Schey was much stronger, and he had had the advantage of surprise.

"Jerry?" his partner called from the head of the stairs.

The agent's efforts to free himself increased when he heard his partner's voice, but then subsided, and slowly the man's eyes rolled back up into his head, and his body went slack.

"Jesus H. Christ, what the hell is going on down there," the agent upstairs shouted, and he started noisily down the stairs.

Catherine had come to the kitchen door and saw her husband as he pulled the agent's body aside.

The baby cried out and Catherine screamed, her tension and fear bubbling suddenly to the surface.

She leaped forward, and before Schey could do a thing to stop her, she was across the living room when the second agent came around the corner, his pistol drawn.

She charged him, and reflexively he fired, the single shot catching her just to the left of her breastbone, shoving her backwards over the coffee table.

"No!" Schey screamed in rage, and he was on the agent before the man understood what was happening. He batted the pistol away with one hand, chopped at the bridge of the man's nose with the other, then rounded the heel of his left hand to the tip of the agent's nose, driving the broken bone and cartilage directly into his brain, killing him instantly.

The baby was screaming as Schey threw himself down beside Catherine's body. Her eyes were open. There wasn't much blood. The bullet had evidently pierced her heart, killing her at once.

She was dead! There'd be no bringing her back. There'd be no explaining to her about the Thousand Year Reich. The Americans had killed her.

Still the baby cried and coughed as Schey knelt beside his wife's lifeless body and rocked back and forth. He was a professional. Time now was of the essence if he was going to have any chance at escape. He would have to go now. He couldn't help Catherine. Dear God, she was beyond his help. But he still had a job to do.

Slowly he got to his feet and went through the pockets of the two dead men, shuddering when he touched the body of the man who had killed Catherine. They were both FBI agents: Jerry Pote and Thomas Chastigin.

He was not surprised. Not really. They had evidently been on to him for some time now. But why had they picked this morning to come after him?

He looked again at Catherine's body lying on the floor, and slowly the baby's crying entered his consciousness, and he turned and went up the stairs to the back bedroom.

The baby's diaper was soaking wet, and he was warm with fever. He had lost his bottle.

Quickly but gently Schey changed the baby's diaper, speaking to the boy all the while in soothing tones. Then he covered him up again and propped his bottle up for him.

At the door he looked back, his eyes filling with tears. It could have been so different. It should have been so different. After the war they were supposed to have taken up their lives again.

He turned away and went into his room where he packed a single bag. Then he went downstairs as Robert, Junior, began to cry again. He picked up the phone and dialed the operator, asking to be connected with the hospital at Knoxville. When he had them on the line, he left a message for their doctor to come out this morning as soon as possible.

"It's my son," he said. "I think he has pneumonia."

The baby was still crying when Schey got his coat. He let himself out of the house, climbed into the gray government sedan and drove off without looking back.

5

Deland crouched just within the protection of the thick forest at the crest of a hill several miles to the northwest of Wolgast and watched the army truck rumble past on the highway in the valley. The wind was raw and blew snow in long plumes across the open field below.

When he was certain the truck was not coming back, he ducked back into the woods and glanced up at his wire antenna tossed up into the tree branches, then sat in the snow in front of his radio set.

The cold air was very hard on the warm tubes, but just lately Wolgast had become far too dangerous a place for him to transmit his weekly messages to Allen Dulles in Switzerland. Radio detection squads had been randomly driving around the streets of Wolgast. It was something happening in many cities, he had learned.

He tuned the radio, picked up the microphone, and flipped the transmit switch.

"Paris, this is Brussels. Paris, this is Brussels. Come in," he radioed. The reference to those two cities remote from Bern and Wolgast served not only as code names but as an additional confusion for listening Germans.

Deland held one hand to the earphone on his right ear and he heard the faint acknowledgment to his transmission.

"Brussels, this is Paris. We have you. Go ahead."

Deland had pulled a single sheet of notebook paper from his pocket on which he had written a series of numbers in rows and columns. He keyed the microphone and began reading in a clear, distinctly enunciated voice, but he spoke as rapidly as he could. His transmissions were being recorded, so they'd miss nothing. They had to keep these things short to avoid being pinpointed.

He was finished in less than ninety seconds, and Bern was back.

"Acknowledged. Copy?"

Deland had his notebook and pencil out. "Ready."

The operator on the top floor of a four-story hotel in Bern read the series of numbers slowly and distinctly. The list was short. When the operator was finished, he signed off.

"Acknowledged. Brussels out."

He cut the power to the radio set, pulled the wire antenna down out of the trees, coiled it up, and stuffed it in the back of the case that contained the small, oddly shaped radio.

A cover went over the radio itself and a handle fit into the side, transforming the electronic machine into a mechanical machine—an advanced calculator of the type used by engineers and mathematicians. Some of the functions even worked. It was a marvelous machine.

The calculator went into a leather case, which Deland buckled, then slung over his shoulder by a long strap.

He checked the road again, then trudged back through the woods, down the far side of the hill to the woodcutter's road that connected with the highway a few kilometers to the southeast. He retrieved his bicycle from where he had hidden it behind a pile of cut logs, then headed back into town.

Among other things, Deland had sent information to the OSS on the next V2 test firings, as well as Rudy Schlechter's work on high speed pumps for corrosive fuels.

The code was a simple one-time address method based on the *Berliner Zeitung*. The first set of numbers in the message gave the date of the newspaper. Thereafter, pairs of numbers gave the line and word. The first row corresponded to the last page, the second row to the first page, the third row to the second to the last page and so on.

In addition to its simplicity, the beauty of the code was that its numbers roughly corresponded to the types of figures Deland dealt with in his study of trajectory mathematics. So if and when he was ever stopped and searched, and his notebooks and papers examined, the messages would appear to be nothing more than his work.

It took him almost fifteen minutes to reach the highway and another half-hour to make it back into town. It was just past one in the afternoon when he pulled up behind his rooming house on the north side of the town and leaned his bike up against the woodshed. He threaded a thin chain around the bike's frame and through a heavy metal ring in the side of the building, and locked it.

Then he trudged up the back stairs, through the pantry and into the back hall between the kitchen and the landlady's office. The old woman was seated behind her desk. When Deland passed, she rose.

"Herr Dorfman."

Deland stopped and came back. The house seemed almost too hot after being outside. His nose was running. "*Guten Morgen*, Frau Gardner," he said pleasantly. He took out a tissue and blew his nose.

The old woman looked at the watch pinned to the front of her dress. "*Guten Nachmittag*, Herr Dorfman. It is afternoon, not morning. You have again missed your lunch."

"It is all right, Frau Gardner," he said placatingly. Despite himself he had grown fond of the old woman over the past months. She looked after him as a mother might care for a recalcitrant son.

"Where have you been all morning?"

"Working."

"Working?" she sniffed. "At the island?"

Deland smiled. "Why, Frau Gardner, I am surprised by such an indiscreet question."

"I only ask because of the man who was here for you," the old woman said. She was portly, and she always wore dark clothing with a crisply starched white apron. It made her seem severe. Almost as if she were a nun.

Deland's heart skipped a beat. "A man? Did he leave a message?"

"He asked to wait in your room until you returned. I refused him, naturally. But he left no name or message."

"Was he in uniform? S.S.? Wehrmacht?"

"Civilian clothes," she said. "Quite sloppy, I might add."

The relief began. "Tall? Graying, perhaps? Distinguished looking?"

The woman nodded begrudgingly.

"He's a friend, Frau Gardner. A co-worker. Rudy Schlechter," Deland said. But what the hell had Rudy been doing here? On a Saturday morning? Both of them would normally have been at work, but the test firing had been canceled and only the maintenance crew were out there in force today. He figured Rudy would be with his girl. He had talked enough about her.

"Will you be wanting some lunch, Herr Dorfman?" Frau Gardner asked.

Deland could smell the potato dumplings and what was probably a chicken stock. It made his mouth water. But he shook his head. *"Nein, danke,"* he said. "I am going out again."

"As you wish," the woman said, and Deland hurried upstairs to his room.

Schlechter had never been here before. But it really didn't mean a thing, he told himself. The man had introduced him to Katrina. Perhaps now he wished to socialize even further. So far as Deland knew, Schlechter's only friend was Maria Quelle. He was not close to anyone on the island. Perhaps his coming here was nothing more than a gesture of friendship.

Nothing had been disturbed so far as Deland could detect. His pillow lay at a slightly odd angle; the left door of his *Schrank* was slightly ajar and the small brass key in the right door, cocked to the left. Nor had any of his clothing or his papers been bothered.

No one had been up here. He was certain of it. He locked the door and set the calculator up on his desk, as if he had been working with it. Then he pulled off his coat and tossed it over on the bed.

Seated at his desk, he opened his notebook and unfolded yesterday's *Berliner Zeitung* to the back page. The first pair of numbers after the date were for the forty-seventh line and the fifth word: *Erforden*, German for REQUIRE. The second pair was for the third line, second word: *Studenplan*, SCHEDULE.

Within ten minutes Deland had the brief message from his control officer translated.

REQUIRE SCHEDULE OF OPERATIONAL
TESTS VICTORY THREE THROUGH NINE—
MOST IMMEDIATE—EVIDENCE YOUR
POSITION SUSPECT—TAKE CARE

Deland suddenly saw himself as he had been with his parents at the University of Wisconsin Mathematics Research Center in Madison. Donovan had flown out from Washington to speak with him. Matter of the gravest national importance we have a man like you in position. But you will be in constant danger. You have to understand that right up front. The Germans will always suspect there'll be someone like you in place. Be on your guard. There'll be support, of course. But in the end it'll be up to you. You will have to make the final decisions to hold or run. It won't ever be easy.

He got up from his desk with the translated message which he carefully burned in the large floor-stand ashtray near his chair by the window. When the paper was completely destroyed, he mixed the ashes with his pencil, breaking them into a fine powder which he dumped into the lower body of the big ashtray. Not even the mighty scientists of the Third Reich could put that message back together, he thought bitterly.

He looked out the window and shivered. He took a cigarette from a small wooden box and lit it. He rarely smoked, but this seemed to be the time for it. The schedule for the V3 rocket tests as well as the tests for the more advanced models would be relatively simple to come up with. There were several operational readiness manuals floating around. His section security supervisor, Major Preuser, had one. There were others.

But the other matter. That was something completely different.

His position here was suspect, Bern had radioed. By whom? Major Preuser, who was so obvious, or by Rudy Schlechter, who was slightly less obvious but a no less likely candidate, or by someone else?

Deland smoked as he stared down at the narrow cobbled lane. Someone in the parlor began playing the piano. A Liszt tone poem, he thought, and whoever was playing it was very good. The warm music was a fine counterpoint to the cold, wind-blown scene outside (it had begun to snow again and the wind had risen). He himself was caught somewhere between the two. He was doing something positive about the war; he was making his contribution. When it was all over, he wouldn't have to hide his head. It gave him a warm feeling to know that he'd be returning home a hero: It was a feeling he'd never confide to anyone else, of course. He'd be too embarrassed. Nevertheless, he had that feeling of pride in himself that was like a warm brazier on a chill day. That would come later. For now he was here in Germany, and his position was *suspect*. He didn't feel much like a hero. Nor did he feel even particularly grown up. He felt more like a lost, frightened boy. He wanted to go home, or at the very least be with someone who cared.

He stubbed out his cigarette, grabbed his coat, and left his room, after first making certain he was leaving it exactly the way he wanted it left.

Frau Gardner was not in her office when he left the house, but whoever was playing the piano was still at it. Outside, he could hear the music halfway down the block as he strode into town, and for some reason it made him very sad.

The square was busy and Deland looked into a few of the shops that had any goods before he finally crossed to the far side and entered the Hansa Haus Bierstube.

There were still quite a few people inside having late lunch, but it wouldn't be until after four, Deland suspected, that the work crowd would fill the place.

The beer hall was dark, closed-in, warm—a safe haven from the cold outside. A few of the patrons looked up and Deland smiled and nodded as he went around and took a seat at a small table in one of the tiny front windows. The small panes were thick and very old, yet he could make out people coming and going on the street.

A young girl dressed in a neat dirndl took his order for a *Bier und Bröt mit Kase*, and when she was gone, he went up to the counter in the front and bought a small packet of four cigarettes and a few matches.

Back at his table he lit one just as his beer came.

It had been several days since he had been here last. When Schlechter had dumped him unceremoniously with Fraülein Mueller. All week nothing had been said about the incident. But each time Deland had seen Schlechter, the man had had an impish grin on his face.

His hand stopped in midair as another, an uglier thought crossed his mind. His position here was suspect. If not by Major Preuser, then perhaps by Schlechter . . .

Deland had missed her when she had skipped across the street, so when he finally saw her by the front counter, he was surprised. At first he sat stock-still as he watched her. She was purchasing a newspaper. Katrina Mueller. The words rolled off his lips. Even her name was lovely.

If Schlechter was suspicious of Deland and if he had picked a handmaiden, it would be Maria Quelle, not Katrina Mueller. Deland could not believe that of someone so beautiful and so young.

Yet, he told himself, he was young and innocent-seeming. And he was a spy.

Even if it was her, however, he rationalized, it would be necessary for him to discover the extent of her knowledge. It was his duty.

She turned away from the counter, and Deland jumped up and waved. When she spotted him, she smiled and came across the room. His heart was thumping nearly out of his chest.

6

The stars shone brightly from a perfectly clear but moonless sky, providing only a scant illumination for the two long black Mercedes super sedans that pulled off the narrow coastal highway from Huelva. At this point they were only a couple hundred yards from the border with Portugal. Down a gentle hill the guard huts on both sides were lit up—an oasis in the middle of the very dark countryside.

Canaris climbed out of the rear of the lead Mercedes. He glanced nervously at his watch. He was a few minutes early. Thank God for that. If their man was coming across tonight (and their intelligence unit out of Lisbon indicated he was), he'd be showing up at any time now. The penetration window was from 0130 until 0330.

A second man, this one much larger, much heavier, but also dressed in civilian clothes, got out of the big car after speaking with the driver and the other three men who scrambled out of the opposite side.

He looked down toward the border posts, then handed Canaris a pair of powerful night glasses.

"Try these, Herr Admiral," he said, his German very precise, definitely a Berliner.

"*Danke,*" Canaris said in a coarse Bavarian drawl, barely concealing his dislike for the man. He took the binoculars and brought them up to his eyes. At first he could not get the powerful glasses in focus, but then the profile of one of the Spanish customs men jumped into view, illuminated by the light within the hut.

The guard lit a cigarette, scratched his nose, and then stepped outside around to the side of the hut, where he undid his trousers and relieved himself.

Canaris felt like a voyeur and he was having trouble holding the binoculars steady. He was tired. and extremely nervous. He felt burned-out. Too much was riding on what was about to happen tonight. For the past month Meitner had been back in Berlin making sure that the transfer of Hamburg Radio to Zossen went smoothly. At the last minute he had cut the captain out of this operation. The man was too vulnerable. When the hell came, he would not be able to protect himself. Besides, Canaris thought, he wanted one relatively pristine man in Berlin. If and when the end came for the Abwehr, his own movements might very well be restricted. He wanted someone with the freedom of the city.

He went to the front of the car, and leaning over the broad, still warm hood, his elbows propped up, he again trained the glasses on the frontier crossing, conscious of his own heart beating and his shallow breathing. Careful, Willi, he told himself, trying to slow down. He had been having a lot of trouble with hyperventilating lately. There was a lot of pressure, and the loneliness with Erika down in Bavaria and with the children spread over Europe was great. They were out of harm's way, and yet . . .

The Spanish guard went back inside the hut when he was finished, and Canaris shifted his gaze to the Portuguese border hut. If there was going to be trouble, it would come there.

At first he could see no one. Just the glassed-in hut lit by what looked like a single bulb. But then there was a movement. Both guards suddenly came into view. One of them raised a wine bottle to his lips, drank deeply, then passed it to the other.

Major Rheinhard Whalpol came back from where he had been speaking with the men in the second car. There was a pinched, disapproving expression on his round piggish face. Typical of the new order, the thought crossed Canaris' mind.

"Are your people ready?"

"Yes, but I don't like this," Whalpol snapped. He too appeared nervous. A tiny Brandenburger Division pin in the lapel of his dark suit glinted dully in the starlight. Against regulations on these sorts of operations, but Canaris found he no longer cared about such trivial details. Especially not this evening. Lately he found he was losing his stomach for that kind of a fight.

"What exactly is it that you don't like, Major?" Canaris asked.

"It's you, sir, with all due respect. If there's an incident here tonight . . . if anything should develop, and your presence is discovered by the Guardia, there will be hell to pay.''

Canaris smiled at the irony. "This is war, Herr Major, or had you forgotten?'' The night air smelled deliciously fragrant. Algeciras was not far away. He wished he could just turn around, drive down there, and wait out the end.

"I must insist that you remain out of sight until the delivery is made.''

"You're not in a position to insist,'' Canaris said. Whalpol was a fool.

"I see.''

Canaris glanced again toward the border. He was exhausted, mentally and physically, from the rigors of his position, from the incredible tension he had been under lately (Reitlinger's and Schellenberg's names came immediately to mind), and from the extraordinary pressures created by the Führer's recent tactics and the Allied bombing raids.

Curious, he told himself, to think of the last two pressures in the same vein.

Whalpol was still coming at him, like an irritating insect.

"I think we should withdraw, away from the border. We should meet the courier, as scheduled, in Madrid.''

"We will intercept him here.''

"I could pick up the film and hand-deliver it to Maybach II.''

Canaris stared into the man's eyes. Whalpol was almost certainly reporting to the RSHA, perhaps even to Schellenberg himself. Christ, it was becoming impossible to operate. With Oster gone and Dohnanyi all but out of the picture, he had hoped things would finally calm down. But they had not. The SD was after his blood. They wanted complete control of the Abwehr. It was only a matter of time before Whalpol and scum like him took over.

Canaris left the binoculars on the warm hood of the car, brushed past the major, who was fuming, and got his briefcase from the back seat. He pulled out his silver flask of cognac and took a deep drink, the liquor warming a path through his insides. The cognac and his cigars were his only comforts now. His only companions, his dogs—Kasper and Sabine. The animals had all of man's good qualities without possessing any of their failings. They were loyal, no matter what. They never told lies. And when they loved, it was open, very clear, and always honest.

He thought too about Erika and the children. They'd come out of this all right. There'd be no taint on them. They'd all but divorced themselves from him, in any event. It was for the best.

No comfort there, he thought, taking a second drink, then replacing the flask in his case and straightening up. But Algeciras . . . His thoughts were interrupted when one of the Brandenburger men watching the frontier crossing called out softly but urgently.

"Herr Admiral!"

Major Whalpol was watching the border post through the binoculars. But Canaris could see that a small gray car, its headlights on low beam, was stopped on the Portuguese side. Two guards stood back as someone got out of the car. It looked like a large man.

"Is it Kurt?" he asked.

"I think so," Whalpol said, handing over the glasses.

Canaris raised them to his eyes, steadying himself against the hood. The man from the car was turned away, but then, as he handed over his papers, he showed his profile. He was the right size and shape. But it was hard to tell from this distance.

"Ready your men, Major," Canaris said without lowering the glasses.

"Is it Kurt?"

"We'll know soon enough."

Canaris could hear the men shuffling into position in the darkness behind him. Brandenburg Division troops, they were. There weren't many of them left. Most of them had been bled off into the SS, and what few were left, he hated to admit, were of doubtful loyalty. It wasn't like the old days, when a cadet's word was his ironclad bond. The entire fate of Germany rested solidly and four-squarely upon the shoulders of the officer corps. If there hadn't been honor, then where would they have gotten?

The irony of that line of thinking at this moment struck him.

The Portuguese guards were questioning the man. The two Spanish guards had become curious, and they had stepped out of their hut and walked over to the striped turnpike barrier to watch and listen.

"Come on," Canaris breathed. Dieter Schey had indicated by encoded number that Kurt would be bringing two film canisters across. By submarine from the coast of Maine to a deserted Portuguese beach above Aljezur. From there it would be taken to Lisbon, then back down here to cross the border. His destination, the Abwehr headquarters in Madrid. Only he was not going to get that far.

Normally, the film would be processed at Madrid for an immediate spot analysis. It served to speed things up. But in this case that could not be allowed to happen. Whalpol had found out about the film, somehow (Canaris had his suspicions which one of his staff had leaked the information), so had insisted on coming along. There hadn't been much Canaris could have done that would not have created too much attention.

Now that he was here, however, Canaris found that he was becoming increasingly wary of any confrontation. The information coming over tonight, from all the indications Schey had given them, was perhaps more important than anything else they had ever gathered. At once devastating and frightening. He had not wanted to believe it was possible, but their own scientists were sure, and Schey had been providing them with enough hints over the past few months to make him a believer and to make Schey himself a national hero.

The courier took off his hat, his well-oiled black hair glistening in the lights from the border post.

For several long moments no one seemed to be doing much of anything, until at length the guards handed the man his papers and he got back into his car. The Portuguese barrier was lifted, and the courier drove the few yards into Spain where he stopped just short of the barrier and got out, his hat still off. Again papers were handed over for examination.

Whalpol touched Canaris' shoulder, and he looked up, his heart hammering like a pile driver in his chest.

"There may be some shooting, sir," the major said. They were out of earshot of the others.

"Are you planning to assassinate the man?"

"He may not stop. I wouldn't want you to get hurt."

"Reichsführer Himmler would never forgive you," Canaris said dryly.

"Nor would our Führer," Whalpol snapped, recovering nicely. In the next moment he stiffened. "Here he comes."

Canaris turned back. The near barrier had been raised and the gray car was coming up the hill toward them. The Portuguese guards had gone back into their hut, and the Spanish guards were doing the same, their backs to the highway.

Canaris tossed the binoculars on the front seat of the car and put his right hand in his coat pocket, his fingers curling around the grip of his short-barreled Walther PPK.

Whalpol's men, dressed in Guardia Civil uniforms, had placed a road barrier across the highway. They stood shoulder-to-shoulder, their hands on the butts of their weapons.

The car ground its way up the hill, and when its headlights flashed on the barriers and the troops, it slowed down almost to a complete halt. The driver stuck his head out the window.

"What is it?" he shouted in Spanish, the car still moving. It was Kurt.

Canaris raised his hand in greeting and started forward onto the road, but Whalpol leaped past him, his right arm raised, a pistol in his hand. He fired two shots before Canaris could react, at least one of them hitting Kurt. The car swerved to the opposite side of the road and down into the ditch. The engine immediately died.

Whalpol and the others scrambled across the road and down into the ditch, where they yanked Kurt's body out of the car.

Canaris glanced down toward the frontier crossing, his breath constricting in his throat. The customs men had to have heard the two shots. But no one had stepped out to investigate.

He looked again at the car. Whalpol had shot Kurt in cold blood. But why? What had he hoped to gain by such a senseless killing of a mere courier?

His fingers still curled around the grip of the Walther in his pocket, he hurried across the road to where Whalpol's men were searching Kurt's body and his luggage in the back seat. One of them was looking under the hood; the other had opened the trunk.

The major was hopping from one foot to the other. He was very agitated.

"It's not here," he shouted. "It has to be!"

"Why did you do this?" Canaris asked, trying to keep his voice even.

Whalpol just looked at him.

"Orders, Herr Major? From Colonel Hansen? Or perhaps even Brigadier Schellenberg?"

Still Whalpol held his silence, although Canaris could see that the man wanted to blurt out something.

Canaris walked around the car, watching what the men were

doing. Whalpol had gone back up to the road to look down at the border posts.

At the rear of the car, out of Whalpol's sight for just a moment, Canaris got down stiffly on one knee and with his left hand groped up beneath the fender, his fingers searching a small area at the top of the wheel well. He found a section of thick tape, which he pulled aside and opened a small hole into the well, giving access to a dead space in the body. There were two film canisters wired to a short cross member. He quickly undid the wire, withdrew the canisters, and pocketed them as he stood up.

Whalpol was there above him. "You found them, Herr Admiral," he said. He still had his Luger in his right hand. Although it was pointed down, the threat was unmistakable.

"Yes," Canaris said. His throat was dry. He wondered how much of his inner turmoil was showing on his expression. "We have to get away from here now, before the real Guardia shows up."

"If you will just give me the film, I will make sure it gets to the laboratory for processing."

The men had stopped what they were doing, and they all watched the drama. Twenty years ago creatures such as Whalpol would never have advanced this far. And for his actions this evening, against a superior officer, he would have been shot. Canaris considered it, but he was not a murderer. And although Schellenberg was a reasonable man at times, there were others who were not. He was skating on very thin, very delicate ice at this moment. Except for the killing, he had expected Whalpol to act the way he had this evening, and he had come prepared.

He stepped away from the car. "Take the man's money, watch, and ring," he said to the men. "We'll make it look like a highway robbery." He turned back to Whalpol, pulled out a pair of film canisters from his pocket, and handed them over. "I want these developed by 1G's chief himself." He stepped up to the road and hurried across to the car, Whalpol coming after him, a huge grin on his face as he strutted across the road.

It was very cold in Berlin by contrast to southern Spain, and a wind-driven snow stung Canaris' cheeks as he climbed down from the Junkers at Gatow Luftwaffe Base and trudged across the tarmac to his waiting car. The Allies had come through again last night on a bombing raid. From the air this morning he had seen hundreds of fires below. What the Luftwaffe had done to London months ago, they were powerless to prevent now . . . not only here in Berlin, but elsewhere. Hamburg, Kaiserslautern, Dresden, a dozen cities. Disasters on every front.

Until recently, however, most Germans had held up well. But the latest humor going around was different: "What's the shortest joke in the world?" "I don't know, what is it?" "We're winning!"

Treason, but the gallows humor tended in a small measure to alleviate the helpless frustration they all were feeling. When Canaris had heard the joke, he had thrown back his head and roared to keep from crying.

Major Whalpol and his troops got off the aircraft and hurried away in the opposite direction; the troops climbed into a waiting truck, and Whalpol into his own Mercedes.

Canaris smiled tiredly as he climbed into the backseat of his car. The ruse would not last very long, so he was going to have to work rather quickly.

Sergeant Brunner, his driver for the past three years, looked wan and tired. He managed a smile, nevertheless. "Did you have a good flight back, Herr Admiral?" His voice was guttural.

"Tolerable. Looks as if you didn't get much sleep last night."

"No, sir. The bastards were at it until just before dawn when the front moved in and clouded us over." Sergeant Brunner pulled away from the lee of the hangar where he had waited. "Home, Herr Admiral, or back out to Zossen?"

"Is Captain Meitner working out?"

"Yes, sir," the driver said. He looked into the rearview mirror. "A good man, sir."

"Take me to the office," Canaris said, sitting back in his seat. He pulled a cigar from his inside pocket, lit it, and then stuffed his left hand in his coat pocket, reassuring himself once again that the film canisters he had taken from beneath the courier's car were still there. The film in the canisters he had passed to Major Whalpol was blank, as if it had been accidentally exposed to light after the photos had been snapped.

Of course, some of the blame would fall on the major's

shoulders, and Canaris' would be the most strident. But it would not take the SD lab long to put things together.

He closed his eyes against the bomb damage. Senseless, he thought. On the very morning they had crossed into Poland—it seemed a century ago, but incredibly it had only been a few short years ago—he had foreseen this end. Yet the Führer had been so certain, so assured of victory, of the Thousand Year Reich. God in heaven, where would it all lead? And what had happened to his own resolve so many times before when he had decided to go along with Oster and the others, to get rid of Hitler?

The memories were painful to him, and frightening. There were still too many loose ends. If and when Schellenberg and the Gestapo ever got hold of even one of those threads, they'd follow it until the entire spider web was exposed. At the center of any of those investigations, of course, was the Abwehr. Admiral Wilhelm Franz Canaris. Fifty-eight. Sick to death of the destruction. Frightened of what he was seeing around him, and even more frightened by what Schey's report indicated would be in the photographs.

"We are being followed, Herr Admiral," Sergeant Brunner said, breaking into Canaris' thoughts.

Canaris opened his eyes, but he did not sit up and turn around. "What kind of a car?"

"A Mercedes, sir."

"How many men?"

"A driver, a passenger."

"No one in the back seat?"

"No, sir," Sergeant Brunner said. This had been happening with increasing frequency over the past few months. They had not followed him to Spain, but of course they had had Whalpol to do their work for them.

"Recognize either of them?"

"No, sir. Haven't seen either of them before. But they are Gestapo."

"Oh?" Canaris said. "How can you tell, Karl?"

"Their license plate. I have a friend in Abteilung III. She looked up the Gestapo's special numbers for me."

"A very dangerous game."

"Yes, sir," Sergeant Brunner said glumly. "But what do the *Schweinhunds* want with you? What in Christ's name do they expect from you that you haven't already given them or done for them?''

His sergeant's loyalty touched him, yet Canaris could not help but make a quip. ''Probably walk on water, Karl. I haven't done that yet.''

7

Canaris' office was in Maybach II at Zossen, which was an outer ring of steeply pitched A-frame buildings built of thick slabs of reinforced concrete to withstand bomb blasts. Army headquarters had been moved out of Berlin last year, in the spring, and most of the Abwehr's functions had followed soon after.

The building was dark, very closed-in, and cold—like a tomb, Canaris thought, fingering the thick cardboard envelope on the desk in front of him.

Someone knocked at the door and he looked up as his aide, Captain Meitner, poked his head in.

"There is an Obergruppenführer here to see you, Herr Admiral," Meitner said softly.

Canaris got to his feet, his mouth suddenly dry. "From the SD?"

"No, sir. He is from the Reichs Chancellery. Reitlinger."

Canaris opened the top drawer of his desk, shoved the stiff envelope inside, and closed the drawer. "Show him in."

Meitner started to withdraw, but Canaris held up his hand, and Meitner came back.

"Give us five minutes; then interrupt us. Something important," Canaris said. He winked.

Meitner smiled. "Yes, sir," he said, and he was gone.

Moments later the door opened again, and Meitner stepped in. "Herr Admiral—Obergruppenführer Reitlinger."

Reitlinger was at least five inches taller than Canaris, but he was very slight of build. He looked very much like a banker or a very stern schoolmaster with steel-rimmed glasses and very short-cropped white hair. He was in his early fifties, Canaris guessed, and from what he had heard, the man had been a simple shop-keeper in a suburb of Dresden before the beerhall *Putsch*.

He was wearing a black SS uniform, twin lightning bolts at his collar. He saluted crisply, his heels clicking. "Heil Hitler."

Canaris made a vague motion with his right hand and waved for the man to sit down.

Meitner withdrew, softly closing the door.

"Coffee, Obergruppenführer? Or something a bit stronger?"

Reitlinger wasn't smiling. "Neither, Herr Admiral. This is not a social visit." His voice was somewhat high-pitched. He took a seat.

Canaris poured cognac, then sat back. "What brings you all the way down here this afternoon, then?" he said, forcing nonchalance into his voice. It couldn't be the photographs. Not this soon. Yet he could not help but think of the thick envelope in his desk drawer. Not inches away from his right knee.

"It's a delicate matter that I've been told to personally attend to."

"I see. By whom?"

"The Führer!"

Canaris could feel his bowels loosening. He felt as if he was losing his grip on everyone and everything around him. He no longer ran the Abwehr. It ran by some mysterious outside force. Unseen hands, just outside his peripheral vision, were pulling the levers and manipulating the controls that made it all run. Agents outside the country or countermeasures here within Germany were mostly alien to him now. He was losing his control. At the same moment, however, at the same time he could blame Hitler for the debacle, he loved his Führer. Loved and feared and respected the man and what he stood for.

A sly smile came over Reitlinger's features, and Canaris hated the man very much at the moment. Even before he heard what he was going to be told.

"Your wife Erika and the children. They are well?"

The question was totally unexpected. "They are fine," Canaris answered without thinking.

"You are devoted to them, I am told," Reitlinger looked at him slyly.

Canaris shrugged, trying to hold himself in check. "What exactly is this about?"

"Just this," Reitlinger hissed, sitting forward. "The Führer is becoming increasingly perplexed about you, Herr Admiral. Perplexed about your work, perplexed about your . . . loyalty. But that is nothing besides the hurt he is now feeling. He feels he has been betrayed by you.''

The atmosphere in the room was very thick. Did they know about Oster and Dohnanyi and everyone else? About the conspiracy? The diaries in the safe here at Maybach?

"In what way have I betrayed my Führer?'' Canaris asked. His voice came from a long way off.

Reitlinger reached out and turned Erika's photograph around so he could see it. He smiled as he looked up. There was a gold cap on one of his teeth.

"Has Erika ever been to Spain?''

"A few times.''

"Algeciras?'' Reitlinger asked, a note of triumph in his voice. Canaris drew a blank.

"I believe the lady's name is Dona Marielle Alicia.''

Canaris leaped up, spilling his drink. He reached out across the desk and grabbed a handful of Reitlinger's black tunic. A row of ribbons came off as Canaris hauled the man to his feet. "You bastard! You miserable little sneaking son-of-a-bitch!''

Canaris wasn't a strong man, but he had Reitlinger up on the desk and his hands around the man's throat when Meitner burst into the room.

"Herr Admiral!''

Reitlinger was struggling wildly, all the while mewling like a frightened animal.

Algeciras. It was the one important secret of his life—the one thing sacrosanct from the German High Command, from even the Führer—but they knew about it. The bastards had trampled all over it; they had handled it, fondled it like perverts, looked at it like dirty voyeurs.

Meitner was there, and although he wasn't much stronger than Canaris, he managed to pry Reitlinger away. They both fell back, spittle drooling down Reitlinger's chin, his eyes wild as Canaris remained hunched over his desk, his entire body shaking.

"You're insane!'' Reitlinger cried, finally getting his voice. "You're certifiable. You are crazy.''

Canaris straightened up and came around the desk. It was a real effort just to walk. There was a constriction around his chest that made him breathe shallowly. He knew he was hyperventilating, but there was nothing he could do about it.

Reitlinger stumbled against Meitner in an effort to back away from Canaris.

"If you show your face around here again, Herr Obergruppenführer, I will have you shot."

Meitner had grabbed Reitlinger's arm to keep the man from tripping over his own feet. Canaris had stopped in the middle of the room, and when the Reichs Chancellery officer realized he was no longer in any immediate danger, he straightened up, pulling away from the captain.

"You have made a mistake, treating me this way," Reitlinger said.

Canaris' heart was hammering, but he forced himself to slow down. To measure his words. "It is you who have made the mistake. You and your contemptible little bunch of voyeurs." He turned to his aide. "I want you to call the Führerbunker. I wish to see the Führer this evening, or at the latest by morning."

"*Jawohl*, Herr Admiral," Meitner said, coming to attention. He was playing the game perfectly. Thank God for that much at least, Canaris thought.

Meitner turned and marched out of the office. He left the door open so that Reitlinger could hear him on the telephone demanding a circuit to the city.

"You have overstepped your bounds, you bastard," Canaris said. "Whatever you may have heard, I am still the chief of the Abwehr. You have played a little game with my private life. Wait until you see what I can do with yours."

Reitlinger sidled to the doorway. He didn't look as certain as he had when he had first barged in.

"Leave Zossen now, Herr Obergruppenführer. You and I will be in touch again. I assure you."

"You'll soon be cut down a peg or two . . . you aristocrat," Reitlinger said, puffing up. He turned and scurried through the outer office, barely glancing at Meitner who was still on the phone, and then he was gone.

Meitner put down the phone and came into the office with Canaris.

"Close the door, Hans," Canaris said tiredly. He went to the curtains behind his desk and pulled them open. There was a mural on the concrete wall depicting a Spanish mountain scene. It was not a very good painting, but Canaris could imagine that his office was in the summer mountains.

"There wasn't time even to get our own operator," Meitner said. "Bomb damage . . ."

Canaris didn't turn around. "There is a lot to do now, Hans, but none of it will be much fun." His voice was soft, his lisp more pronounced than usual. He felt very old. "None of it is much fun any longer, you know. Like in the old days."

"What is it?" Meitner asked. He had a real feeling for Canaris.

Canaris turned around. His color was shocking, almost cyanotic, and there didn't seem to be any muscle tone in his face.

Meitner rushed across to the sideboard, where he quickly splashed some cognac in a fresh glass. He looked over his shoulder at the admiral. He expected the man to collapse at any moment.

He brought the drink over. Canaris sipped it, his hands shaking so badly that Meitner had to help him hold the snifter.

"The war is lost, you know," Canaris said.

"I know that, Herr Admiral. We all know it."

Canaris looked up at him. "Save yourself. Your family. Go to Switzerland, or Portugal. It won't be long before it's over."

Meitner shook his head.

Canaris smiled sadly. "You, too?"

"No matter what has been done, it still is my Germany. And you are still my admiral."

"The Abwehr will probably be dismantled before long. Schellenberg and his people have become very powerful."

"Why don't you return to Algeciras?"

"No. There is too much to do here."

"The war is lost. You said so yourself. What else is there to do?"

"Make sure it's not prolonged."

"Sir?"

Canaris had gotten control of himself. He straightened up, put his drink down, and adjusted his tie. His dark uniform looked bedraggled. The cuffs and collar were threadbare, and there were several undefinable stains on the lapels.

"Have Sergeant Brunner bring my car around, would you, Hans?"

Meitner looked at his watch. It was a little before 5:00 P.M. "You're not going into Berlin, are you, sir?"

"Yes, of course."

"It'll be dark soon. There almost certainly will be another bombing raid this evening."

"There was one around noon, I'm told. What difference does it make?"

"It will be too dangerous, sir."

Canaris smiled. "Our beloved Führer remains in the city to personally direct the war. And you are worried about me taking an evening drive?"

"May I come with you?"

Canaris had gone around his desk; he opened his briefcase and began stuffing reports into it. "No, Hans," he said, looking up. "I have a lot of work to do tonight. I'm going to get something to eat, then go over to my house. There are some items I need."

"And if there is an Allied raid tonight?"

"They hardly ever come as far south as the Grosser Wannsee or Zehlendorf."

"But you will take shelter?"

"My house has received only a minimum of damage. I promise you."

Meitner held his ground.

"If we're attacked tonight, I promise to scurry beneath the streets like a rat in a sewer."

"Thank you, sir."

"Call Sergeant Brunner for me, please."

"Yes, sir," Meitner said, and he went out to his own office.

As soon as he was out of sight, Canaris opened his desk drawer, extracted the stiff envelope with the photographs, and stuffed it into his briefcase. He closed and locked the clasp.

Dieter Schey was better than any of them expected him to be. Far better. The drawings, technical readouts, and installation photographs were superb. It could leave no doubt whatsoever that the Americans were on the verge of actually constructing a new, powerful weapon. Worse than that, however, the pages of formulae would surely help the Reich's scientists with their own research. Canaris had heard a lot of frightening things about Peenemunde up in the Baltic.

He glanced at the mural, then retrieved his greatcoat from the rack and pulled it on. He put on his hat and gloves.

Before he got his briefcase, he stopped a moment and looked out the door. Meitner was perched on the edge of his desk. He was speaking on the telephone. Beyond him, out in the busy corridor, young people scurried back and forth.

Data still flowed into the Abwehr from agents and listeners all over the world. The material was still collated, its contents and meaning analyzed, and reports were still written and submitted to the Führerbunker three times each twenty-four hours. At 0800, at 1600, and at 2400 hours. Seven days a week. The information flowed in, and the reports flowed out. To a bottomless pit. Meaningless.

How many dedicated men such as Schey were out there with their lives on the line in a futile effort to win this war? Dozens. Hundreds. Thousands, in addition to the hundreds of thousands, millions of men and women in the Air Force, Navy, and Army.

It was a lost cause, he thought. A terrible lost cause.

He got his briefcase, then went out to where Meitner was just hanging up.

"Your car will be out front in just a moment. They had to come up with some gasoline."

"Our supply was pilfered?"

"Requisitioned, sir," Meitner said glumly.

Canaris put his hand on Meitner's shoulder. "I may be gone for a few days, Hans. I don't want you to worry. I'm not deserting the ship. No matter how fast she's sinking."

"Spain?"

"Yes," Canaris said. "I think everything will be all right. I mean, I'll try to make it back. But if something does come up . . ."

"Yes, sir?"

"Good luck, Hans. I will see you in a few days. By Wednesday or Thursday."

8

Everything seemed to be going to hell in a handbasket for Schey, and he was becoming increasingly upset.

For three days in a row he had made the rendezvous that had been set up for him. To no result. Either his contact had not checked the letter drop or his contact was no longer in operation.

Either way, he told himself, he was dead without further instructions. Or papers. A cover. His A-ration coupons would soon run out; he had used almost all of his gasoline coupons on the five-hundred-mile trip to Washington, D.C., from Knoxville. His remaining money and coupons would all be gone within thirty days. From that moment he'd be a doomed man.

His initial cover here in Washington was that of a discharged soldier with debilitating wounds. He walked with a limp, slightly hunched over, as if he had been hit in the spine. There were enough scars on his back and on the backs of his legs from boyhood to convince anyone but a doctor that he had been in a war. A war of a different sort, he thought whenever he looked at himself in the mirror. His father had been a harsh disciplinarian.

The rendezvous had been set up for him before he had come over, and that was several years ago, so anything could have happened in the interim. But it was supposed to have been guaranteed safe. His bolt hole. A long-term safety net for him to use if things got bad at Oak Ridge.

He kept seeing Katy's body lying on the floor. She had been so confused. Her entire world had turned suddenly topsy-turvy. She had charged blindly at windmills. Only she hadn't merely been knocked from her horse. She had been killed by a nervous FBI agent who had been too quick on the trigger.

Schey wore a long overcoat, threadbare and somewhat dirty. A slouch hat was pulled over his eyes, and he wore buckle overshoes, the buckles undone. They jangled when he walked.

He turned away from the frozen Reflecting Pool and went back up the stairs to the drive that encircled the Lincoln Memorial. He stopped at the top and looked back as if he was contemplating some inner message while gazing toward the Washington Monument and the U.S. Capitol building at the far end of the mall.

It was a little past six and dark already. A light snow had fallen for most of the afternoon, putting a glistening coat on the old, dirty slush and snow. The world seemed quiet and clean, at peace. The radio broadcasts and newspaper headlines said otherwise, but for the moment here, there was beauty.

It reminded Schey very much of Munich with its monuments and Greek-inspired buildings, which served all the more to make him feel like the alien intruder he was. Germany never seemed so far away, so unattainable to him as it did at this contemplative moment.

The contact window was from half past five until six every evening, once the indicator was placed at the letter drop. That was nothing more than a short chalk line, a check mark actually, of the kind an inspector might make, on the far southeastern piling of the Frederick Douglass Bridge from the Naval Annex. Perfectly visible day or night from a car appoaching on Anacostia Drive.

He had made the mark Monday morning. When his contact hadn't shown that evening, he had not been overly worried. The mark could have been missed. He was still thinking more about Catherine and the baby than anything else. It hurt so terribly.

He went back to the bridge on Tuesday morning, to make sure his mark was still there. It was. But again that evening his contact did not show. Nor had he shown this evening.

There had been a man and woman down by the Reflecting Pool. They joined Schey at the head of the stairs, and they too stopped to look east toward the Capitol.

He glanced at them. They had been deep in earnest discussion when he had shown up a half an hour ago. He hadn't thought they were aware of his presence. But the woman looked at him and smiled.

"Do you have the correct time?" she asked. "In England?"

Her escort turned around. "If you hadn't been so clumsy with my watch, I'd have the time for you," he said to her.

Schey was startled. What the woman had said. It was the code. Christ! A woman!

"I think it's late," he said, fumbling with the sleeve of his coat.

"Of course it's late," the man said.

"Just how late, can you even guess?" the woman asked.

Her lips were red and moist. She wore a version of a tricorn hat with a feather. Her escort, a husky older man, didn't seem too happy.

"I have just a bit past twenty-three hundred," Schey said.

"Greenwich time?"

"Yes, Zulu time," Schey said, using the military term for GMT. And then he stared at her. She was his contact. Her escort, who seemed about ready to take a poke at someone, apparently was just a cover. But now what the hell was he supposed to do?

"Thank you, sir," the woman said, and she turned, her arm still linked in the man's. "Come along, Bernard," she said.

They headed up toward Bacon Drive either to catch a bus or cab or to retrieve a car.

Schey let them get halfway around the circle; then he started after them. Almost immediately he spotted the matchbook in the snow. He stooped to pick it up, then held it up to the street lamp.

The message on the front cover was for the Sutherland Apartments: "Where the elite gather." There was an address well out on Fifth Street. But there was no name. He had no idea who she was.

He looked up as they rounded the corner. He didn't get more than a few steps before they climbed into a cab and were gone.

Schey stopped and watched the cab disappear up toward Constitution Avenue. He had made his rendezvous. He knew where his contact presumably lived. But that was it. He turned away in frustration. He'd go there, of course. Maybe she was more professional than he gave her credit for being. Maybe there'd be a setup there for him. Maybe she'd be watching for him. Maybe a dozen possibilities.

There were only a half-dozen people waiting for the bus, and forty-five minutes later he was climbing the back stairs to his under-the-eaves room in a three-story house just off E Street, near Christ Church. The house was slightly down at the heels, but it suited Schey's needs just perfectly. The landlord had told him, when he showed up in reply to the ad, that they were God-fearing Christians who minded their own business and expected the same of the folks who lived under their roof.

Schey cleaned up, put on another coat, the one he had worn up from Oak Ridge, and left by eight o'clock. It took him just ten minutes to walk to the parking garage he'd rented for his car, and he headed back up Eighth Street toward Galludet College. He took Florida Avenue around the B&O Interchange, finally cutting back to Fifth on the other side of St. Vincent's Home and School.

The Sutherland Apartments turned out to be half a dozen three-story brown-brick structures in two rows back off the street. There were a lot of trees and a cobblestoned driveway on two sides that led to a long, narrow parking area in the rear. The apartment complex looked like a military barracks. It made Schey nervous.

He drove around back and parked behind the center pair of buildings, and shut the engine off. It was a '33 Hudson—huge, heavy, and very comfortable, but not very good on gasoline.

He hunched up his coat collar and lit a cigarette. If there was someone here watching for him, they'd have seen him come in. Smoking a cigarette would make no difference.

She had dropped the matches so that he would know where to come. She'd be expecting him this evening. And she'd also understand that he would have no idea which apartment was hers. If indeed she even lived here.

He looked up at the windows. Only a few of them were lit. The blackouts were no longer enforced in Washington. It made him think immediately of Berlin. The newspapers and radio commentaries were filled with stories about the bombing of Berlin and Dresden and Köln—Cologne, they called that city. It was horrible, the news. But here, except for Pearl Harbor, there had been no suffering.

Ten minutes later he had finished his cigarette. He cranked down his window, tossed it out, and cranked the window back up before he got out of the car.

No one had come in, or out, of the apartments. At least, not the back way. And as far as he could tell, there was no one obviously watching him from any of the windows. If she was any good at all, though, he'd never be able to detect her in the darkness.

Back here in the parking lot, there was very little light. The street lamp just out front was burned out, and the one up the street was too far away to provide much in the way of illumination this far back.

There were two buildings to the left, two straight ahead, and a pair to the right. She had called her escort Bernard. Perhaps that had been his clue.

Schey went up the snow-covered walk and entered the nearest building. He had to go down the corridor to the front of the building before he found the mail slots. There were a dozen nameplates. Johnson, Appleton, Jankowski . . . no Bernards, first or last name. He slipped out the front door, hurried up the walk, and entered the second building straight ahead from his car.

He found what he was looking for almost immediately, although at first he simply could not believe his own eyes. It was a monstrous out-of-kilter joke. So terrible, so almighty obvious, that no one would ever suspect. It was like playing the childhood game of hide-the-thimble.

The nameplate for apartment 3D was in the name of Eva Braun. The Führer's girlfriend. The one German name recognizable anywhere in the world.

He went to the stairs and listened. The building was very quiet, but from a long way off, possibly on the second floor, he thought he could hear faint talking. Or perhaps a radio. But the harder he listened, the less certain he became of what he was hearing, or if he was hearing anything at all.

Schey took the first flight of stairs two at a time, silently gliding up to the second floor, where in the dimly lit corridor he looked left, then right. The voices had faded so that he could not hear them at all.

A toilet flushed somewhere as he started up, and then a second later a door closed. He froze, holding his breath to listen. But there was nothing. The building was quiet.

He started up again, when a man appeared on the stairs above him. Their eyes met, and for an instant Schey read puzzlement there. It was his contact's escort, the man she had called Bernard.

Schey immediately lowered his head and continued up as if he belonged here, passing the man two-thirds of the way up, then rounding the corner into the corridor at the top.

He stopped and listened. There were no sounds on the stairs for a moment or two, but then he heard the man say something to himself and head down.

Did he recognize me, Schey wondered. He tensed, waiting for the sounds of the man turning around and coming up again. But the sounds gradually faded, and Schey thought he heard the front door open and close, and then there was silence.

He breathed a sigh of relief, then turned and went to the end of the corridor where, at apartment D, he put his ear to the door.

He could hear music very faintly. But nothing else. He knocked. The music stopped.

"Yes?" a woman called from within. "Bernard. Is that you?"

"I'm looking for the correct time. In England," Schey said, keeping his voice low.

"Greenwich time?" the woman asked.

"Yes. Zulu time."

The lock snapped and the door opened. The woman from the Reflecting Pool, the one who on the nameplate downstairs called herself Eva Braun, stood there looking up at him. Her eyes were wide, her nostrils flared, and her lips pursed. His first thought was how good-looking she was, and then she was pulling him into her apartment.

She closed and locked the door, then spun around. "Did you see Bernard?" she asked urgently.

She was wearing a black dress with a Navy collar and a pleated bodice. "We passed on the stairway."

"Goddamn . . . oh goddamn," she swore. She was evidently trying to think it out. "I saw you pulling up and waiting down there. I was in the bedroom for a minute. Bernard was out here. But he'll be back. Damn!"

"Who is he?"

"Bernard Montisier. He works in the War Department, over on C Street. He's a jerk, but he's been good cover. He's jealous as all hell."

"Give me my papers and ration books and money and I'll be gone, Fraülein . . ."

"Eva Braun. It's on my birth certificate," she said with a laugh. "But you're not going anywhere. Bernard will either be back up here or he'll wait outside until you come out. And then he'll beat hell out of you."

Her speech was colloquial. She looked American, or perhaps Swedish, with her light hair, lovely large pale eyes, round face, sensuous lips, and full figure. He found himself comparing her to

Catherine. Plain Katy whom he had loved against all the rules and odds.

"And if I don't leave? Won't he eventually become suspicious and come up here?"

"Yes, he will. And I'll let him in. And he can look around . . . a little. And we'll argue, but he won't find you. With any luck," she added. She was listening at the door. "Did he recognize you?"

"He might have."

"You're all he talked about all evening. He thought we were having a secret rendezvous. He thought we were lovers."

"Any chance he's an FBI man?"

She looked sharply at him. "You're on the run, aren't you?"

Schey nodded.

She shook her head after a moment. "Bernard's too stupid. Even Hoover doesn't pick them that dumb."

Schey let his gaze wander around the apartment. It was a good size and reasonably well furnished. Whoever this woman was, she was definitely well connected. These apartments, contrary to the matchbook advertisement, may not have been where the elite gathered, but the poor didn't congregate here either.

She stiffened. "Here he comes," she whispered. "In the bedroom. Crawl back into the closet. I'll stall him to give you time."

"Any chance he suspects you?" Schey asked. "He might put it together if he does."

"No," she said, shaking her head. "Now get the hell out of here."

Someone pounded on the door. "Eva, it's me!"

Schey slipped into her bedroom, which was just off a short corridor that led back to a bathroom. He closed the door most of the way, then went around the bed to the closet.

"I saw him coming up here," Montisier bellowed.

"You saw who?" Eva asked tiredly. She was a good actress.

"Don't lie to me, damn you!"

"I'm not . . ."

"Bitch," the man shouted, and Schey could hear the sharp sound of a slap. Eva cried out and a table or something fell over.

Schey turned away from the closet and went back to the door. He peered through the crack. The husky man stood over Eva, who had fallen over the coffee table and lay sprawled in a heap on the floor. She was sobbing. There was blood trickling from her mouth and nose.

"Bitch," the man hissed again. He turned. His overcoat was open, his fat belly gross. "You've got him in your bed, I'll bet."

Schey stepped back away from the door, his muscles bunching up into knots. He kept seeing Catherine lying in the middle of the floor. Dead. Blood over the front of her nightgown.

Montisier was charging the bedroom door as Eva was struggling to her knees.

"Bernard . . . no," she cried.

The door slammed open, and the husky man stumbled in. Schey hit him very hard in the solar plexus; then, as he went down, Schey brought the side of his right hand back in a vicious chop to the man's throat, crushing his windpipe, cutting off his air and any sound he might make.

He hit the floor in a limp, crumpled heap, but immediately he began thrashing around, clawing at his throat, trying for oxygen he would never get.

Eva was at the door, the entire side of her face filled with blood. "Oh Jesus," she said.

The man bumped his knee against the door frame; his entire body stiffened, and with a slight gurgling sound in the back of his throat, he lay back, his eyes open and his struggles ceased. He was dead.

"Oh Jesus," Eva said again. "Oh Jesus H. Christ."

Someone pounded at the door. "Hey, you! Eva Braun, you bitch, what's going on in there?"

Eva shoved Schey back into her bedroom, shut the door on him, and rushed across the living room.

Schey opened the door a crack and looked out as Eva yanked open her front door.

"What the hell is going on up here?" a fat woman in a print dress shouted. "You're disturbing the entire building. I warned you time and again about this. Damn. I warned you I'd kick you out of here."

"You're jealous because you don't have a man of your own, you fat slob!" Eva screeched.

The fat woman stepped back a pace, her mouth opening in a perfect circle.

"Get out of here before I have Bernard kick your fat ass up

around your shoulders," Eva shouted. "He's in the mood, let me tell you."

"Oh . . ." the fat woman said in a suddenly small voice, and she turned and hurried off. Eva slammed the door, locked it, then turned around and leaned against it.

Schey came out into the living room. "I'm sorry," he said. He had ruined everything for her.

"Don't look so tragic, sport."

9

Deland knew damned well what the brief message was without having to decode it, and it made him angry to think that he was being dismissed just like that. They wanted him out. The message was only three words: GET OUT NOW or GET OUT IMMEDIATELY, or something to that effect. But he wasn't ready, damnit. Not yet.

For a long time he sat, his back to the tree, listening to the hiss and static in his earphones. Waiting for his control officer to continue. But there was nothing.

Schlechter had been feeding him a lot of information lately. Good things on fuel systems. Von Braun himself had moved in with Schlechter's section. They were light years ahead of anything Dulles had guessed.

Just two nights ago, Rudy and his girl, Maria, had invited Deland and Katrina Mueller to their apartment for dinner. Rudy had quite a bit to drink, and as the evening progressed, he had begun bragging.

It wasn't like Schlechter, or at least like nothing Deland had ever seen. But as the night progressed, Deland began to get the feeling that he was seeing the real Rudy. The man was exceedingly lonely, it seemed. His jokes, and finally his bragging, were his means of attracting and holding friends. Deland felt sorry for the man, but he did not stop him. Schlechter had provided him with a wealth of information.

Besides, he had not wanted to break the spell of the evening. Had he, it would have meant Katrina would have gone home.

Deland shivered. He raised the microphone to his lips and spoke a single word: *"No."* Then he flipped the set off, got stiffly to his feet, and pulled the wire antenna out of the trees. He repacked the radio so that it once again looked like a scientific calculator.

It was very cold. Two days ago the weather had cleared, and the temperatures had plunged. Last night it had reached to below zero. It hadn't gotten much warmer today.

Deland hooked the radio's leather strap around the handlebars of his bicycle, pulled on his mittens, and walked his bike out of the protection of the narrow stand of trees above the road that led north from Wolgast along the river.

About nine miles out, at the headland, was the Germans' new radar station. He had been told specifically to stay well clear of the place. Bern was saving it for something. Either they had another man in here or they were planning on bombing it soon. In any event, it wasn't Deland's problem.

It was just a dirt road, but a lot of the fishermen lived out this way. They would take their boats out the channel and into the Baltic. Coming in, they'd go all the way up to Wolgast where they'd sell their catch, then turn around and let the current take them home.

Church bells were ringing in the distance back toward town. The morning was pretty, in a way, despite the intense cold. Sounds were crisp and carried a long way. The bells reminded him of when he was very young.

He got on his bicycle and began slowly pedaling back toward town. His cover was Katrina Mueller's parents. They lived on this road. Her father was a fisherman. If he was stopped, his story was that he had started to go out to Katrina's parents' home, to talk to her father, but the cold made him turn back.

The cover was a weak one, but he found he didn't care at the moment. They'd probably ask him what business he had with the girl's father. His only answer would be that he wanted to ask the man for Katrina's hand in marriage.

That was impossible, of course, in all but his daydreams. But it was pleasant to think about. She was German, but she wasn't a part of the war, not really. His earlier concerns that she was working for Schlechter and Maria Quelle were unfounded.

He made it back to his rooming house where he put his calculator away and quickly translated the message from Bern. It was exactly as he had supposed it would be. They wanted him out of here, now.

As he lit a cigarette, he looked at his reflection in the mirror above the dresser, and it dawned on him that he could not simply ignore such an order. They wanted him out. For his own safety.

Perhaps they had another assignment for him. Something different.

His escape route was from Berlin, where he would pick up new papers, to Dresden, and finally down to Munich, where he would make his way across the border into Switzerland, going the last few miles through the mountains on foot.

It would be very dangerous. The original plan was for him to remain in Germany until the end of the war—to go into hiding at the last part and stay low until the shooting had stopped.

But his route out through Switzerland was set up for him as a last-ditch stand—as an escape hatch, should things get really difficult for him.

He would have to do it now. He simply could not refuse. If he remained, he would be dead. Either way it was over between him and Katrina. Christ!

He went to the window and looked outside. They wanted him out. The message kept running through his mind, and he had to force himself to think it out. There was the night train to Berlin. He'd be in the capital city with new identification by midnight, before anyone here would miss him.

The evening train. It gave him the remainder of the day.

There were quite a few people downtown despite the cold weather, and a small crowd had gathered at the station for the noon train. No one really noticed Deland as he went up to the ticket clerk, handed over his identification book and his travel pass (of which he had several), and bought a round-trip ticket to Berlin on the train which left at 8:30 this evening, returning late tomorrow.

"A little business in the city, Herr Dorfman?" the clerk asked pleasantly. He was an old man.

"Nothing official, I'm afraid," Deland said. He paid for his ticket, and the clerk handed it through the slot along with Deland's papers.

"Bring your own supper with you, young man. There'll be little to eat on the train." The old man shook his head.

"*Danke,*" Deland said. The old man just shook his head again and looked away. Deland was sure the man wanted to say something about the war, but he was afraid to open his mouth.

A train was coming in as Deland turned and left the depot, the two police officers stationed at the doors not in the least bit interested in him.

Just outside he stopped and pulled up his coat collar. The depot was just three blocks off the central square. He had walked down from his rooming house. The thought struck him that he was simply leaving his life here. No fuss, no apparent bother. He was just going to hop aboard a train and leave. There was nothing to be done on the island. He had no notes there. And he would not take much more than his radio and a few items of clothing with him when he left. Any more than that and too many early suspicions would be raised. If he left his clothing, there'd be one day of indecision on the part of the authorities. Was he merely off for an unauthorized holiday? His clothes were here. Wouldn't he be coming back soon?

The only dangerous time would be in Berlin. As soon as he got there, he'd telephone his contact. If the person was still there and could get to Deland, he'd have new papers immediately. Until that moment, however, he'd be vulnerable. Any spot check on the street would reveal him as a Peenemunde worker with no good excuse for being in Berlin.

He walked up to the square and went into the Hansa Haus Bierstube. There were a few people seated at the tables having their Sunday lunch. Deland didn't see anyone he knew. He went up to the bar, ordered a stein of beer, and then stood there drinking it. He lit another cigarette. He was smoking a lot more than usual just now. He had an excuse.

He looked around again. He supposed he had really come here to see Katrina. They had met three times here, in addition to the dinner with Rudy at Maria's apartment. He knew where Katrina lived with a couple of young women from her same section, but so far he had been too timid to go there.

And now it was too late, he thought, although he toyed with the idea of going to see her. But that was too dangerous. In the very short time they had known each other, Katrina had developed the uncanny knack of reading what he was thinking. She'd be able to read him very easily today.

"There you are," a familiar voice boomed behind him. Deland turned around as Rudy Schlechter, all smiles, came up to him and clapped him on the shoulder.

"Hello, Rudy," Deland said.

"Don't look so glum," Schlechter laughed. He ordered a beer for himself and another for Deland.

"It's the weather."

"Nonsense, the weather is beautiful. Have you been outside . . . I mean, outside of town? It's beautiful, I tell you." Their beer came and Schlechter took a huge drink. "But listen to me, Edmund. The girls are at church. They'll be back after late mass. About two, I think. They sent me to find you. The old bag at your rooming house told me you went out this morning, then came back and went out again. I'm glad I found you. Where've you been?"

"I took my bike for a ride," Deland said. His heart was beginning to accelerate.

"Hell of a day for a bike ride, if you ask me. It's pretty, but it's damned cold. Where were you off to?"

Bern had warned him that his position was suspect. They wanted him out now. He glanced toward the front doors. Were the Gestapo just outside, waiting for the signal from Schlechter to come in and arrest him? Had he been followed?

"I took the river road out of town."

Schlechter's eyes narrowed. "Out toward the Würzburg Reise?" he asked, referring to the radar station.

"No," Deland said, hanging his head. "Much closer than that. But . . ."

"But what?"

"I couldn't do it. I turned around and came back."

"You couldn't do what, my old friend? What were you up to so mysteriously this morning?"

"It was Herr Mueller," Deland said after a hesitation. His heart was really hammering now.

Schlechter just looked at him, incomprehension on his face.

"Herr Meuller. Katrina's father. I . . ."

Suddenly Schlechter's face was split with a broad grin. "Oh, my God, Edmund! What a surprise! Don't tell me you were going there to ask . . . for her hand?"

Color came naturally to Deland's cheeks. He nodded. "But I just couldn't."

Schlechter slapped him on the back. "We are going to be with the girls this afternoon. I thought we'd drive somewhere for dinner. Maybe Greifswald." He laughed out loud. "But I'll tell you what. We'll pick up the girls and go over to Maria's apartment.

There'll be no one there. We'll make some excuse, and Maria and I will go on to dinner. You two can be alone. We won't return until late.''

"But," Deland started.

"Nonsense.''

"Katrina . . . she isn't that kind of a girl.'' He was more than frightened now. He was embarrassed and excited all at the same time.

Schlechter smiled indulgently. "This is 1944, Edmund. You are a big boy, and Katrina is a big girl. Besides, this is war. You can never tell when one of us will leave for work in the morning and never come back.''

It was like a splash of ice-cold water. But if Schlechter had noticed Deland's reaction to his comment, he gave no indication of it.

"Come on, drink up. We've got just enough time for another, and then we'll pick up the girls.''

Katrina was happy to see Deland, but she was a little shy at first. She and Maria sat in the back and Deland looked straight ahead as Schlechter kept up a running commentary on his efforts to find the "wayward boy.'' He did not directly mention Deland's story about trying to see Katrina's father, but he kept alluding to a big secret. It made Deland very nervous.

Maria's apartment was above a dentist's office, so there was no one around at this hour on a Sunday. When Schlechter pulled up and parked, Maria sat forward.

"Why are we stopping here, Rudy? I thought we were going over to Greifswald?''

Schlechter turned around. He was grinning. Deland's mouth was dry. "Give Katrina your key.''

"What?''

"Give Katrina your apartment key. Edmund has something he wants to ask her. I think they should be left alone for a while. It is something very important.''

It was quiet in the back seat. Deland was afraid to turn around. Finally, Maria laughed. "I think that's wonderful, Edmund,'' she said. She reached forward and kissed him on the cheek.

The move was unexpected. Deland turned around. Katrina was smiling, her cheeks glowing, a wisp of blonde hair peeking out from beneath her wool cap. There was a large ache inside Deland's chest. She never looked more beautiful to him.

"Are you two going to Greifswald after all?" Katrina asked, breaking the spell. But her voice sent shivers through Deland.

"Yes, we'll be late. Very late," Schlechter said.

"There's plenty of food to eat, and there's some wine and beer on the back stoop," Maria said. "You know where the records are, and I think there might be some schnapps left in the cabinet by the plant stand." She gave Katrina the key, then kissed her friend on the cheek. "If I had children, they would be like you," she gushed.

Deland, thoroughly embarrassed now, got out of the car and helped Katrina out. Maria climbed in the front seat. She smiled, and she and Schlechter both waved and then were gone.

"It's cold out here," Katrina said. She turned and Deland followed her up the stairs to Maria's apartment, where she unlocked the door and they went inside.

The apartment was very warm. Before she had gone out, Maria had evidently stoked the small heating stove in the living room. There was a bucket of coal beside the stove. There weren't many people in Germany with that kind of luxury at the moment. Coal was almost impossible to find. It had probably come from Rudy.

Katrina took off her hat and coat and laid them over a chair. She wore a knit dress and heavy woolen stockings that on anyone else would have been totally shapeless. But on her the outfit was beautiful.

"Are you hungry? Have you had your lunch?"

Deland shook his head. "I mean, yes, I am hungry."

She stood looking at him, an odd expression in her eyes, her lips half parted. "Rudy said there was something you wanted to ask me," she said softly.

It was very hot. He didn't want this to happen, and yet he did. In a few hours he would be gone. Any complications at this point would be exceedingly dangerous.

She smiled. "Take off your coat, Edmund; it's dreadfully hot in here. I'll find us the wine." She turned and went into the kitchen.

Deland pulled off his coat and tossed it on the chair; then he peeled off his sweater and tossed it aside, too. He went into the kitchen. A bottle of wine and two glasses were on the tiny table.

"Open the wine, would you?" Katrina called from the bathroom.

"Right," Deland said. He went to the back window and looked down at the back storage lot of an old lumberyard. It was empty. There was no one there, but he checked the back door. It was locked. He knew the front door was locked too. He went back to the table and opened the wine. He was pouring it when Katrina came out.

She had let her hair down, and she had taken off her boots and heavy wool stockings. Seeing her bare legs was almost more than he could bear at this point, and he nearly spilled the wine as he handed her a glass.

She took it with both hands and drank it half down while looking at him over the rim. He took a sip of his own wine, but then she handed her glass back, turned, and glided out of the kitchen.

Deland put the glasses down and followed her as she went into the bedroom. He stopped at the door. She turned down the bed, then turned around to him. She looked very frightened, but determined.

"Katrina . . . I . . ."

She shook her head. "Not now, Edmund," she said softly. "It's not time for words." There was a quaver in her voice. She reached around to her back and did something with the fasteners of her dress. Then she pulled it off. She was wearing nothing beneath it. She had evidently removed her underclothing in the bathroom. "Edmund?" she said.

He came to her in a rush and crushed her against his chest. She smelled of soap and cologne, and her skin was incredibly soft and wonderful.

"I love you, Katy," he said softly.

She looked up at him, her eyes filling with tears. "I'm frightened."

They kissed. He could taste the saltiness of her tears and feel her shivering against him. When they parted, he kicked off his boots and took off his clothes. She watched him, wide-eyed, breathing hard.

He was already erect. Her eyes traveled down and her lips parted. "You're hard," she said.

Deland reached out and touched her breast. She flinched. He

eased her down on the bed, then got in beside her. The apartment
had been too warm before. Now it was just perfect.

He kissed her again, and her lips parted as she returned his
kiss, her hands tentatively on his shoulders, the touch of her skin
sending electric shocks through him. He pulled her closer, her
breasts against his chest, her lovely legs entwined with his.

Deland could feel himself nearly at the bursting point. He had
to slow down, and yet he knew he could not. It had been a very
long time since he had had a girl, and then it hadn't been
anything like this. In San Antonio, Texas, where he had taken
some of his basic military training, a bunch of his friends had
taken him to a whorehouse. He had gotten very drunk, and the
young Mexican girls—some of them not much older than thirteen,
with very tiny breasts and only a slight dark wisp of pubic
hair—had sat on his lap, playing with him while they bargained
on a price.

Katrina was kissing his face, and his neck and his ears, as her
fingertips explored his back. She was panting, her entire body in
motion.

At one point he pulled away and looked down at her. Katrina's
eyes were wide, her nostrils flared. "Edmund?" she asked. "Is
there something wrong?"

"You are so beautiful," he said. He caressed her breasts and
she moaned loudly, arching her back, her legs spread, her heels
dug into the mattress.

Her pubic hair was blonde. Deland reached down and touched
her there. She nearly jumped out of her skin.

"Now," she breathed. "*Gott in Himmel*, now!"

He kissed her breasts, then slid down, his tongue exploring her
navel, and finally lower. She reached down for him and pulled
him up.

Somehow he was inside her, and he climaxed almost immediately, her body coming up to his, her legs wrapped tightly around
his waist as she continued in motion for a few seconds.

He felt a sudden deep sense of shame. "Oh damn, I'm sorry,
Katy," he said.

She laughed. "Sorry for what, my darling? We have the rest
of the afternoon and most of the night. There is time."

10

It was well after five o'clock, and already starting to get dark outside, when Katrina got out of bed. She reached back and gave Deland a kiss, then padded into the living room.

They had made love a second time, with Katrina more in charge and both of them slowing down so they could enjoy it more.

At first he had been concerned that he would do the same thing, would come too early. But it was very good. It was as if they were completely in tune, as if they had been doing this together for a very long time.

A few years ago, when he was seventeen, his father had told him a little about sex. No details, of course, but he had said that when the right girl came along and you loved each other, you would suddenly know all that was needed to know to satisfy each other.

At the time he felt his father's advice, though well meant, was terribly old-fashioned. Damned near Victorian. But now he wasn't so sure. He had found his girl. And as bitter as the thought made him feel, he knew that if they remained together, they'd have the life his father had promised.

The toilet flushed, and a minute or two later Katrina returned, wearing Deland's sweater and carrying the wine and both glasses.

She got into bed with him and poured them both some wine. She reached over and set the bottle on the floor, exposing herself.

Deland reached out and touched her inner thigh, and she spun around so fast she spilled her wine.

"What kind of a pervert are you?" she shrieked, laughing.

He looked into her eyes. He wanted so very much to remain with her. But it was impossible. In a few hours he'd be on the Berlin train. After that, there'd be no coming back. Ever.

Her grin faded. "Edmund?" she said. "What is it, darling? I didn't mean what I said."

He shook his head and looked away. "Nothing," he mumbled.

She took his wine and put it down. Then she turned his head so that he was again facing her. "Something is wrong. Something! What is it?"

God, he wanted her. Tell her everything, something inside of him shouted. Take her with you. Get her out of Germany. They could remain in Switzerland until the war was over. It hurt so much. "I . . . have to go, Katrina."

"Go?" she snapped. "Go where? To do what?"

"Back to my room. Tomorrow . . . there is a lot of work yet I have to do."

"No; God in heaven, no, Edmund. Not just like this."

Deland couldn't say a thing. He loved her.

"You just . . . ." she started, and she looked away for a moment. "You just can't do this to me. You just can't come up here, make love to me, then disappear."

"I'm not going to disappear," he lied. The war couldn't last much longer. He'd come back for her, the foolish thought crossed his mind.

"Then stay, please. Rudy and Maria won't be back for hours. They promised. I will make you a nice dinner. You must eat. Afterwards we'll listen to music . . . make love, and then you can go home early."

Deland held his silence.

"Oh God, Edmund, please don't do this to me," she cried. She yanked the sweater off and cupped her breasts. "See?" she said breathlessly. "See?" She jerked the covers back, exposing Deland's nakedness, and threw herself down, kissing his legs and his flaccid penis.

Deland was suddenly angry by what she was doing to herself. He grabbed her shoulders and shoved her back. "Don't do that, Katy."

"Edmund!" she screeched, throwing herself at him again.

Deland lifted her away. Blood roared in his ears. His muscles were bunched. "No," he shouted hoarsely. He wanted to hit something. "Not like this. You're not a whore, Katy. Not like this. I love you. You can't do this."

Then she was on her knees, coming into his arms, and they

were kissing deeply, tears rolling down her cheeks, her entire body shaking, as he held her tighter and tighter against him.

They fell back, kissing and caressing each other, like the starved lovers they were, and Deland could feel himself responding. But then he remembered the time. He had to return to his rooming house to get his things, and then get back to the station— all before 8:30. It would be a long, very cold walk.

He eased her away, then started to get out of the bed, but she was on his back, clinging desperately to him. For a moment he struggled against her, but then he stopped, willing his body to completely relax.

She got out of bed and knelt down on the floor in front of him, her tear-filled eyes wide.

"I'll see you tomorrow," Deland said, hating the lie.

She shook her head. "You just used me. Admit it."

Deland took her hands. "That's not true, Katrina. You must believe that. I love you. I will always love you." It hurt so much to say what he was saying to her, because this part was true.

"There is something! *Verdammt!* I can see it in your eyes."

"It's my work. It's important."

"More important than me . . . ?" She cut herself off. "I'm sorry. I didn't mean that." She buried her head in his knees. "I'm sorry, Edmund," she said, her voice muffled.

Deland stroked the back of her neck for a while, and then he helped her to her feet, kissed her. When they parted, he forced a smile.

"It has been a wonderful afternoon, Katy. There will be others. Many others."

She just looked at him.

"Please," he said, his heart breaking. "I was a lousy lover, but I will get better."

"No . . . oh, no, you were wonderful," she gushed, and then she had to laugh. "I made a fool of myself, didn't I?"

Deland grinned. He nodded. "Yes. But I don't care. I love you all the more."

She reached up and kissed him on the chin. "You must clean up before you leave. If your landlady gets a whiff of you, she'll know immediately you've been a bad boy. In the meantime, I'll make you a sandwich to eat on the way."

She grabbed his sweater and pulled it on. "I'm going to keep this so you will have to come back to me." She turned and marched back into the kitchen.

Deland gathered up his clothes from the living room, then went into the bathroom where he cleaned up and got dressed. He was very confused. Images of his school days in Göttingen intermingled with his days in Wisconsin; memories of camaraderie and student pubs mixed with those of family and picnics by the lake. Overriding all of that, his terribly complex feelings about Katrina. He loved her, and yet he knew that such a thing was impossible for them. She was a Nazi, or at least she worked for them, and yet he felt she was an innocent. In many ways she acted like the whores of San Antonio, yet she fit so well with him that it had to be love. This last was causing him a lot of trouble. Katrina did not fit the mold, his image of how a girl should behave. He knew he was being terribly naive. In Göttingen they'd laugh at him. In Wisconsin they'd turn away. His loyalties tugged him toward Wisconsin, his heart toward what Göttingen represented.

He looked at himself in the mirror over the wash basin. His was a baby face. But his eyes were open and honest, or at least he gave that impression. A cowlick in the front jutted up at an odd angle. His mother was still fond of wetting two fingers with her tongue and patting it down. He shook his head. He hated it. When he was little, she'd moisten the corner of a handkerchief with her spit and use it to wash off a smudge on his cheek or nose. All mothers did it, and he didn't know of any kid who liked it.

He didn't know what to do. He wanted to stay here, but he knew he could not. He wanted help. Someone to make the decision for him. Someone he trusted. He turned away, unable at that moment even to face himself. They *had* made the decision for him. GET OUT NOW. That was the message.

He took a deep breath, let it out slowly to relieve the pressure on his chest, then stepped out of the bathroom. Katrina was there with his coat.

"I know," she said, looking at his face. "I feel the same way, too."

He smiled. Wouldn't it be something, he thought, if he did say the hell with it all and just stayed here.

She helped him with his coat and his scarf, and then she kissed him. "I love you, Edmund Dorfman."

"I love you, Katrina Mueller," he said solemnly.

She gave him his sandwich wrapped in a piece of newspaper, kissed him again at the door, and then began to cry. *"Verdammt,"* she swore. "Get out of here."

There was nothing left to say. Deland trudged down the stairs, then crossed the street; he hesitated a moment. He looked up at the apartment. Katrina was in the window, looking down at him. They waved to each other; then he turned and headed back to his rooming house at a brisk pace, her feel and her odor still lingering with him.

It was nearly six-thirty by the time Deland made it back to the house. He snuck in the back way and made it up to his room without encountering anyone. Once he was safely inside, he flipped on the light. Almost instantly he knew someone had been here.

The pillow on his bed was straight! Both doors to his *Schrank* were closed! And the things on his desk were ever so slightly rearranged!

Someone had been in here! Either an amateur or someone who did not care that Deland knew about it.

With shaking hands Deland opened the calculator case, pulled the calculator out, and pressed the correct sequence of numbers and operations so that the bottom cover would drop off. He looked inside, but there was no way of telling if they had found the radio. It did not appear to be tampered with.

He quickly closed it again and buttoned it up in its leather case. Then he grabbed the smaller of his two bags and stuffed a few items of clothing into it.

At the door, just before he shut out the light, he looked around the room that had been home for more than nine months. They were on to him. It was not surprising that they had searched his room. Except for the radio, however, there was nothing incriminating here. It was the room of a bachelor mathematician. Nothing else.

He reached inside his coat to his breast pocket to make sure he still had his train tickets, and at first he thought he was dreaming. The tickets were not there.

He put the calculator and overnight bag down and reached

deeply into the pocket. It was empty. He unbuttoned his coat and frantically searched his other pockets. There was nothing!

His heart was thumping. It was hard to catch his breath. He forced himself to slow down and to carefully search all of his pockets. But the tickets were simply not there.

Still forcing himself to slow down, he searched his room, inch by inch—the bed, his *Schrank*, the desk. There was nothing. No tickets. They were gone.

Christ! He must have lost them on the way here. Somewhere out in the snow . . .

Another thought struck him. Maria Quelle's apartment. He had taken off his coat and had tossed it on the brown easy chair in the living room. Later, Katrina had picked up his coat.

They were there. The tickets were there! If Katrina had found them, she'd know he was lying. Or would she? He had bought *round-trip* tickets. If she had seen them, she'd think he was coming back tomorrow evening.

He grabbed his bag and the calculator, shut out his light, and managed to get out of the house without anyone seeing him.

He lingered in the shadows at the back of the large house for a minute or two until his eyes adjusted to the darkness. There were no strange cars parked on the road. There was no one here. No one watching for him, yet he hesitated still another moment. He was frightened. They knew about him. They had searched his room. If they talked to Katrina, they'd know he was on his way to Berlin. They shot spies, or hanged them. But he just couldn't close his eyes and make it go away. He couldn't turn around, go back up to his room, get a good night's sleep, and show up at work tomorrow. It just didn't work that way. He was here; it was up to him to get out.

Mindless of the cold now, Deland hurried down the street. He had to leave his bicycle. He could not park it at the railroad station. It would be a dead giveaway.

An Army truck passed him, but then turned at the corner before the square. The town was alive. He could hear the sounds of laughter from the Hansa Haus, but there were no lights. It was another blackout.

He hurried around the square, then out the opposite direction from the railroad station. It was going to be complicated, coming back to her like this. She'd be thinking all sorts of things. But it would be less complicated if she hadn't found the tickets. If somehow he could distract her and find them. He could say he just came back . . . to see her again.

Christ. He knew he was fantasizing. It was possible, though. It was even possible that the tickets weren't there, after all. They could be lost in the snow. It wouldn't matter then. No one would connect the tickets to him. At least not until it was too late. He could return to the station, buy another ticket, and be off.

The thought stopped him in his tracks. He looked back toward the square. It was tempting. Yet if the tickets were up in Maria's apartment, he'd have to get them.

He hurried the last few blocks to the apartment, left his suitcase and radio in these shadows, then tromped up the stairs and knocked loudly on the door.

"Katrina," he called. "It's me. Edmund . . ." His voice died in his throat as the door opened and Rudy Schlechter stood there, smiling, a Luger in his right hand, the tickets in his other. He held them up.

"I believe you are looking for these?"

Without thinking it out, Deland batted the Luger out of Schlechter's hand, and it hit the door frame and went sliding across the living room floor. He charged forward like a bull, knocking the unsuspecting German off his feet.

Deland got the briefest of images of Katrina and Maria by the kitchen door, but Schlechter had gotten his balance and was pounding his fists into the side of Deland's neck and head.

Schlechter had more experience, but Deland was younger and much stronger so that he was able to roll over. He brought his right knee up into Schlechter's groin.

The breath whooshed out of the German. Deland reared back and slammed a right hook into the man's face, breaking his nose, blood gushing everywhere.

Still Schlechter would not give up. With a powerful thrust of his body, he managed to shove Deland aside; then they both went crashing into the coffee table.

Deland twisted around and managed to get his fingers around Schlechter's throat. He began to squeeze, his powerful hands crushing Schlechter's windpipe.

The German's face began to turn blue as he continued to pummel Deland's ribs with blows that quickly lost their strength.

Katrina and Maria were both screaming something, but Deland hung on, even after Schlechter's body went limp. A few seconds later, the German shuddered, and then he lay totally still, his eyes open.

Slowly Deland released his grip and got off the man. He started to get to his feet, when Maria snatched up the Luger and started to swing around.

Deland lunged toward her, the distance impossible, when Katrina raced out of the kitchen, holding a large butcher knife over her head.

"No," Deland shouted, but it was too late. Katrina swung downward, her face screwed up in a grimace, and she buried the blade to the handle in Maria's back.

The woman fell forward without a sound, and lay absolutely still.

Katrina stepped back. "Oh, my God," she cried. "Oh, God . . . oh, what have I done?"

11

Schey went back to the bedroom and looked at Montisier's body. He had been a big man. Six feet or better, and something over two hundred pounds, with a gut.

"We're going to have to get him out of here," Eva said.

Schey turned to her. Their faces were inches apart. "How many people know that you two were . . . together?"

"In this building tonight or in the city?"

"Anywhere."

"A lot of people. Hell, he told everyone we were going to get married."

It was curious, Schey thought. But she didn't seem worried about any of this. If anything, she seemed merely vexed, perhaps inconvenienced. "Were you and he . . . in love?"

"What do you take me for?" she said indignantly. "He was nothing but a big Palooka."

"You'll have to leave as well," Schey said. "They'll find his body sooner or later. And even if they don't, you will be the first person the Missing Persons Bureau will ask questions of."

She shook her head. "I knew this was going to come sooner or later. But it's just been a big game to me, until now." She looked at Schey. "I got nowhere to go."

"Where you from?"

"Milwaukee. Jones Island, actually. My grandfather was a fisherman."

"Go back there."

She shook her head. "My name *really* is Eva Braun. If they start looking for me, they'll trace me there easy," she said. "Besides, my folks and relatives are all dead or gone. There's no one back there."

"The Bund here in Washington?"

"Was dissolved more than a year ago," she said. "Where the

97

hell have you been? In isolation?" She shook her head again.
"I've got nowhere to go, except maybe South America."

"How about back home . . . to Germany?"

She laughed. "We're losing the war, in case you hadn't
heard."

"You can't stay here," Schey said, raising his voice in
frustration.

"No shit, Sherlock," Eva said. She looked down at the body.
"Why'd you have to hit him, anyway? Why didn't you stay
in the closet like I told you?"

There was a nagging thought at the back of Schey's mind. He
didn't want to dwell on it, but he knew he was going to have to
deal with the issue now. She had seen his face. She knew him.
What's more, she would be providing him with a new identification.
If and when she was picked up for the murder of Montisier, she
might cave in. It was only a game to her, she had admitted.

"You'd better pack a bag," he said.

She looked sharply at him. "Where am I supposed to go?"

"With me."

"And where's that?"

Schey bent down and flipped the big man's topcoat open.
"You'll see when we get there," he said without looking up.
"Now go pack a bag. We'll pull his body out around midnight.
Everyone in the building should be pretty well settled down by
then." He glanced up at her. "Don't forget to pack the ration
books and anything else that might be incriminating here."

Eva hesitated a moment.

Schey unbuttoned Montisier's suit coat and flipped it open. He
was wearing a gun. A .38 Police Special in a well-worn shoulder
holster. Instantly a dozen grim possibilities crossed through his
mind.

Eva sucked her breath. "Jesus . . ."

Schey pulled out the man's wallet and opened it. A driver's
license in the name of Bernard Montisier, a few business cards
with notes scribbled on the back, a couple of newspaper clippings
about a World Series game six years ago, and about sixty dollars
in cash.

There was a soiled handkerchief in another pocket, a package
of Lucky Strikes and a battered Zippo lighter in another, and in
one of his side pockets a small leather wallet. The moment Schey
pulled it out he knew what it was.

"What's that?" Eva asked looking over his shoulder.

Schey flipped it open. Inside was a shield and an identification card signed by J. Edgar Hoover. FBI.

"He knew," Eva said, stunned. "All this time . . . ."

They either knew or suspected that she would be making contact with someone. Otherwise they would have arrested her by now. Schey did not think the agent had had time to report seeing Schey here. He had merely gone downstairs, thought it over, and then had come back up.

But it was just possible that the man had looked through the apartment and had found the spare identifications that Eva was keeping. It was possible his cover was ruined.

Schey stuffed the wallet back in the dead man's pocket and started to close his coat, but then hesitated a moment. They were on to him down in Tennessee, and they were on to Eva here in Washington.

He'd been lucky to get free from Oak Ridge and lucky here with Montisier. His luck would not hold out forever.

He pulled the pistol from Montisier's holster and pocketed it. Then he got up. "We've got to get out of here immediately."

"But where can we go?"

"Leave that to me. But first I have to see where you've kept the spare identifications."

Eva's gaze went immediately to the dead government man. Her hand went to her mouth. "Do you think he . . . found them?"

"It's possible."

Eva turned, hurried down the hall, and went into the bathroom. Schey was right behind her. She got down on her knees, grabbed the toilet bowl in both hands, and started to shove it to the left.

"Wait." Schey stopped her. He too got down on his hands and knees. "The things are under here?"

"Yes," she said.

He looked closer, his nose inches from the floor. "Who taught you this?"

"The Bund in Milwaukee, then later in Chicago. It used to be a game."

There was a line of talcum powder and dirt around the base of the toilet bowl. It had not been slid aside for a long time. He looked up. "How long have you known Montisier?"

"A few months."

Schey nodded. Carefully he eased the toilet bowl to the left. It swiveled on the soil pipe. Beneath it a hole had been cut in the floor, opening into the space between the floor joists. A large package wrapped in yellow oil cloth with a flower pattern, tied with some old brown twine, lay just beneath. Schey looked very closely at it. Dirt lay around the package. There were mouse droppings littered on and around it.

"When was the last time you were in here?"

Eva shrugged. "I've never been in it. I put the stuff in there a couple of years ago, and I haven't opened it since."

Schey breathed a sigh of relief. Montisier had not found this. Sooner or later he might have, but it was still safe. He pulled the package out, careful to make sure all the dirt fell into the opening, then carefully shoved the toilet back in place. He cleaned up the skid mark across the floor with his handkerchief, then got up, helping Eva to her feet.

"Pack a bag; we're going to leave right now. With any luck we can be out of the city before they miss your friend."

"We're just going to leave him here?"

"It doesn't matter. He worked with the FBI. They knew about you."

"We're not going to make it, are we?" Eva said. Her composure was starting to crumble.

"They haven't got us yet."

"I mean, the war is lost. There's nowhere for us to go. It's all so useless."

Schey took her by the shoulders. "Listen to me, Eva. The war isn't lost until the armistice is signed. And our Führer will never sign such a thing. Do not forget the humiliation of Versailles. The German people will never go through that again."

"But they're bombing Berlin, for God's sake . . ."

Schey shook her once, hard, and she hiccoughed. "There's more to do. But you must hold yourself together."

"They hate us, you know. Because of the . . . Jews."

"That's mostly propaganda," Schey said. It had been the same with Catherine. All she talked about was the bombing of Germany and the business with the Jews. Perhaps it was he who was missing something.

He took her firmly by the arm and pulled her back down the hall and into her bedroom. They had to step over Montisier's body. "Get your suitcase and pack it. Hurry, please."

She looked into his eyes. "Are we going to make it?"

"If you hold yourself together."

"You're right," she said after a moment. She seemed to draw strength from him. She nodded. "You're right, of course." She squared her shoulders, then went to the closet and pulled out a cheap cardboard suitcase. She opened it on the bed and began stuffing clothes into it from her closet and bureau.

Schey watched her.

"Go into the bathroom and get my cosmetic case," she said without stopping. "And on the shelf is a pair of scissors somewhere. Pack those."

"Anything else?"

She looked up. "Yeah. In the medicine chest is a bottle of henna rinse. Throw it in."

"What is that?"

She smiled. "By morning I'll be a short-haired redhead with long, thin eyebrows and thick ruby lips. My mother wouldn't even know me."

He found the things in the bathroom, and ten minutes later she was ready. There was no one on the third-floor corridor as they headed down the stairs. Nor were they met by anyone coming up.

On the ground floor they hurried out the back door and across the parking lot to Schey's Hudson. He tossed Eva's bag in the back seat and climbed in behind the wheel. When the woman was in and the door closed, he started the car, backed out of his slot, and headed slowly around to the street at the same moment a black and white police cruiser slid up to the front door of the building they had just left.

"Down," Schey said. He kept going. He turned onto the street toward the cruiser as its doors opened and two uniformed police officers got out.

As Schey passed them, they were going up the walk and entering the building.

"It's clear now," he said when they turned the next corner.

Eva got up and cautiously looked back the way they had come. Then she turned to Schey. "It's that fat bitch Leona, from down the hill."

"The one at the door?"

"She called the cops. I know damned well she called the cops on me. She hates me."

The police would go up and talk to the woman. Then they'd knock on Eva's door. He didn't think they'd break in. Not simply for a call of domestic troubles, of excessive noise. Eva shattered that notion, however.

"Leona is the housemother. She's got the keys. She'll let them in when I don't answer."

Schey turned north again and headed up toward the Walter Reed Army Medical Center. The car's gas tank was nearly full; he had a few dollars and some ration coupons in his pocket. The radio and most of his things were in the trunk. And presumably the package he had fetched from beneath Eva's bathroom contained more money, ration booklets, and identifications. There was nothing holding them in the city. Nothing to return for.

By the time they connected Montisier's murder and Eva Braun's disappearance with him, if they ever did, he and she would be long gone.

"We can't go back," she said forlornly, something of her earlier uncertain mood coming back to her.

"What did you forget?" Schey asked sharply.

"Nothing," she said. "Nothing. It was all in the package under the toilet." She looked out the window. "Nothing but a job and friends and a life."

They passed the medical center, then crossed into Maryland, in Silver Spring, where Schey took the highway around to the northeast, finally picking up Maryland 190, which roughly paralleled the river.

As he drove away from the city, out into the dark countryside, he got the overwhelming sense that now his life with Catherine was really over. Seeing her lying on the floor of their house in Oak Ridge, blood down the front of her dress, simply had not been real to him. Nor had his run to Knoxville, and then here to Washington. For some reason all of that had been blanked out of his mind. Or rather it had unfolded like a motion picture on a screen—representative of reality, but nothing more.

Now, however, driving through the night, heading to the southwest and whatever lay there, he felt as if he were beginning a new life.

They were on their honeymoon.

Around six in the morning they crossed into North Carolina

from Danville, in a blowing snowstorm that had been cutting their speed for the past three hours.

Schey knew he could not go on much longer. He was exhausted.

They were well out of what he considered to be the danger zone around Washington, D.C. And no one would recognize Eva, in any event.

He looked at her. She had fallen asleep again. Her hair was very short and was colored a deep reddish brown from the henna rinse. Sometime in the night she had crawled into the back seat, where she had carefully cut her long golden hair, tossing it out the window as she clipped.

Later they had stopped beside the road, and in the cold she had wet her hair with snow, had applied the rinse, then had cleaned her hair again with the snow and dried it with a reasonably clean rag from the trunk.

At first it had looked awful, but as it finally dried in front of the car's defroster vent, she had managed to brush it out and it didn't look so bad.

She redid her eyebrows and her lipstick at a gas station somewhere in Virginia. Now she was a different woman. Evelyn Baker, her driver's license, Social Security card, and Red Cross blood donor card all said.

He had become Robert Stromberg, 4F because of a heart problem. His occupation was journalist with the War Information Bureau in New York. No such bureau actually existed, of course. But if he was asked, he would tell anyone who wanted to listen that his job was to report on the attitudes of the country.

The cover was ingenious. It allowed him a logical reason to travel across the country.

This evening he had a second reason to be traveling: He and Eva (Evelyn) had just been married. They were heading south for some sun.

A couple of miles south of the Virginia border they passed slowly through a very tiny town. The signboard identified it as Pelham, North Carolina. Just at the edge of town was a gas station, a diner with its lights on, and a half-dozen tiny cottages in the back. A couple of trucks were parked around the side.

They couldn't go on any longer, Schey figured. If he fell asleep at the wheel and they had an accident, it would be all over for them. It was better to stop here and continue after they had had a few hours of sleep.

Eva stirred when Schey pulled in and parked in front of restaurant. She sat up, blinking.

"What is this place?" she mumbled.

"We're stopping here for some sleep."

"Something to eat, too? I'm starved."

"Sure, why not," Schey said. He got out of the car, came around to the passenger side, and helped her out. The wind was very strong, and it was cold.

They went into the diner. A couple of truckers were seated in a booth, platters of fried potatoes, bacon, and eggs in front of them. An old black woman was behind the counter, and a burly white man was in the back at a grill.

Schey and Eva sat down at the counter. The waitress brought them mugs and poured coffee.

"Lordy, lordy, you two look like death warmed over," the woman said.

Schey smiled. "I don't feel *that* good," he said.

"Is it pretty bad out there this morning, buddy?" one of the truckers called out.

Schey turned around. "We just came down from New York. It wasn't so bad until the last couple of hours, though. Now it's pretty rough. We just had to pull over."

The trucker shook his head and said something to his friend, who turned around. He had a sour look on his face. "What the hell you doing out in this shit?" he asked. His buddy punched him across the table. "If you don't mind me asking, sir."

Schey grinned. "We're on our honeymoon."

"You'll be wanting a cottage then," the black waitress said. She was grinning ear to ear.

"First I want some breakfast," Eva interjected. "I'm practically starved out of my mind here. The brute doesn't feed me."

"Go on now," the waitress said laughing. "Hush your mouth and we'll fix you two lovebirds right up."

12

Katrina had stumbled back, away from Maria's body, and she stood swaying in the kitchen doorway, a look of incredible surprise on her face.

"Go," she said. She sounded out of breath.

Deland straightened up and started for her. "Katrina . . ."

"Don't come any closer . . . spy!" She shrank back against the door frame. "Get out of here. Leave me."

For a moment Deland had no idea what he could say or do. His trainers had told him that a spy's likelihood of survival in the field was firmly linked with his adaptability. But God in heaven, what was he supposed to do now, kill the girl?

His train would be leaving very soon. He was going to have to decide whether he should be on it or whether he was going to have to remain here to take care of this.

He tried to weigh the possibilities. The authorities already knew about him. Schlechter was no doubt Gestapo. It meant there were reports on him. On his movements. On his activities.

Or were there?

If they had been certain he was a spy, wouldn't they have already arrested him? He glanced down at Schlechter's body. Was it possible that he was only suspected and Schlechter was merely here to watch for a mistake? The ticket would have been his mistake. They had evidently found nothing in his room. Had Schlechter, or whoever had searched his room, suspected the calculator was a radio, wouldn't they have taken it?

Katrina was watching him, almost the way a cornered animal might watch its attacker. It made his heart ache to see her like that.

But then he steeled himself to the thought that she was a loyal German, after all. Killing Maria had been a dreadful mistake on

105

her part—a knee-jerk reaction that she was already coming to
deeply regret.

It was not likely Schlechter had made any report about the
ticket. Not yet. So in that respect nothing here had changed.
Deland could find no regret in his heart for killing the man. This
was war. If there was no report about the ticket, he thought, he
could take the train to Berlin for his new identity as planned. He
could be on his way to Switzerland before the bodies were found
here. By the time the alarm was sounded, he'd be long gone.
There'd be no problems at this end.

All except for Katrina.

Her complexion was pale, her hair in disarray. She had gotten
dressed. Beyond her, in the tiny kitchen, he could see his sweater
lying over a chair. Her coat was on the floor beside it.

"I'm sorry this had to happen, Katrina," he started. She
flinched.

"It's true, isn't it," she said. "You are a spy." Her voice was
hoarse.

Deland looked at her for several seconds. He was very conscious of the passage of time. He nodded. "Against the Nazis, not
the German people."

"What are you talking about?" she cried.

"I'm in the military. I'm fighting your military."

"Are you British?"

"American," Deland said. Why was he telling her this?

"I killed for you, Edmund . . . or whatever your name really
is. Do you understand that? I killed . . ."

Deland didn't think she understood what she was saying. Or
rather she didn't understand the implications of what she had
done.

"No, you didn't," he said. "I killed Rudy, and then I stabbed
Maria to death. They were both Gestapo, you know."

As she watched him, he picked his train ticket off the floor and
pocketed it. Next, he went to Maria's body, hesitated a moment,
then firmly grabbed the knife, smudging Katrina's fingerprints
and putting his own on the handle. Some blood got on his
fingers; his stomach churned. He straightened up and looked at
his hand. He turned; Katrina shrank back even farther as he
crossed the room and deliberately placed his hand on the back of
the easy chair, as if he had used it for support. He left bloody
fingerprints.

He wiped the rest of the blood from his hand on the arm of the chair, then turned to face Katrina.

"They were going to get married," she said.

Deland shook his head. "No, Katrina. They were partners. They worked together. They used you as bait to make me talk."

"Lies," Katrina shrieked, holding her hands to her ears.

He advanced on her. She backed into the table in the kitchen. He took her in his arms, but she was stiff, her head down.

"You must listen to me, my darling. I am leaving now. I must go. But when it is over . . . the end of this year, or sometime next year, I will be back." There, he had said it. What's more, he meant it.

She tried to push him away.

"No, Katrina, I never lied to you. I never used you. I told you the truth when I said I loved you. I still do. More than ever."

She looked up finally, tears streaming down her cheeks. "You're a spy."

"I'm a soldier."

"Where's your uniform? Where's your gun?" she said. She pointed vaguely toward the southwest. "The soldiers are down there."

"The fighting is everywhere. Hitler has to be stopped. Too many people have been killed."

"I don't care! I don't care!"

"I care, Katrina. It's why I'm here."

"In my country. Killing my people."

"They're not your people . . ."

"They are! They're Germans!"

"Listen to me, please," Deland said, taking her hands. She was trying to pull away from him, a crazy, trapped look in her eyes. "The Nazis are not your people," he said. He took a shot in the dark. "What does your father think about Hitler?"

She stopped dead. An expression of incredible grief came over her. Suddenly she had no more fight. Her shoulders sagged.

He took another guess, this one a little wider of the mark. "You have a brother in the service?"

She shivered. "Helmut," she said in a very tiny voice. "He was killed at Stalingrad. Just before Christmas, a year ago."

"Did he write home while he was out there? Did he tell you about it?"

"He was proud . . ."

"Was your father proud?"

"What do you know?" she bridled, but there wasn't much conviction in her voice.

"My father knows where I am. He's proud of me." It was a dreadful thing to say to her.

"Then go back to him and leave us alone," she sobbed.

He drew her close. "That's exactly what I'm going to do. But that means when the Gestapo comes looking for Rudy and Maria, they'll find you." Only in the last few seconds had Deland realized what he was going to do. He would be taking a monumental chance. But there was simply no helping it.

"I'll tell them anything they want to know," she said, her voice muffled against his shoulder. "I'll tell them I killed Maria."

"No. I killed them, and I nearly killed you. But I didn't because I loved you."

She looked up.

"You can tell them that. Tell them you didn't know."

"Oh, Edmund, I do love you. God help me, I do."

"Then you must stay here, Katy, and tell them the truth about everything except Maria and where I am going. Tell them everything else."

She was shaking her head.

"Yes. They'll want to know about how we made love, here on Maria's bed. They'll want to know all of the details. It's the only way they'll be satisfied."

"I can't. Not that," she said.

"You'll have to, or else they'll know about this. And then they'll stop at nothing to make you tell them everything." He looked into her eyes, steeling himself for what had to come next. "Tell them everything, Katy. Every little detail, about how I kissed your breasts. How we kissed each other . . . there, below . . . All we did."

"I'll go with you."

"That's impossible." He stepped just a little bit back from her. She tried to move closer, but he held her off. "I'm going to leave Germany. You won't be able to come."

"I can't stay here," she cried.

Deland's heart was breaking. "You will have to stay with your mother and father. They are going to need you."

"No, Edmund. I love you . . ."

Deland stepped back at that moment, shifting his weight to his left foot, and he clipped her neatly on the jaw with a right hook.

She said, "Oh . . ." as her head snapped back, but before she went down, he grabbed her in his arms.

He eased her down on the floor. His blow had knocked her unconscious. Her eyelids were fluttering, but she seemed to be breathing all right. His blow had loosened one of her teeth, and a small amount of blood trickled from her mouth as well as her right nostril.

Her chin was turning a bright red. He kissed it as he laid her head on the floor. "I'm sorry, Katrina," he whispered, his throat constricted, his eyes stinging. "I'm sorry. I'm sorry." He sat back on his haunches and looked down at her. He didn't think he had broken her jaw, but Christ, he could have killed her. She was so fragile by comparison to him.

He looked away. There was nothing but destruction here. Ever since he had come to Germany, he had participated in nothing noble, nothing of any worth, nothing constructive. He had worked for just the opposite. Now two people were dead, and the woman he loved lay unconscious and possibly faced arrest and even death at the hands of the Gestapo.

He wanted to strike out at them, hurt them for what his life had come to.

He stumbled back and got to his feet. He was frightened for Katrina, deeply fearful for her safety now.

Deland turned resolutely and left the apartment, making sure the door was locked behind him. At the foot of the stairs he retrieved his suitcase and his radio from the shadows in the corner, then stepped out across the street and headed back toward the square.

He looked back after he had gone half a block, but the blackout curtains in Maria's apartment were tightly drawn, so he couldn't see a thing except the blank windows.

After a bit, he turned and continued into town, around the still busy square, and then three blocks to the railroad depot.

Inside, he had to show his ticket to pass through the boarding gate, but his hat was low, the light not particularly good, and several last-minute passengers crowding behind him, so the guard didn't get a good look at him.

His ticket was for ordinary third class. The car wasn't too crowded with people, although there were a lot of crates and burlap sacks filled with goods and piled at one end. Deland found a hard wooden seat toward the middle, shoved his suitcase and radio beneath, and settled back, his hat low over his eyes as if he wanted to sleep.

He kept seeing Katrina lying on the floor in Maria's kitchen. Mingled with that was the look on Schlechter's face when he went down. What had they said or done to Katrina from the time he had left until he had returned? That's what bothered him most. She had been dressed only in his sweater. Had they forced her to disrobe in front of them, and then dress? Had they used her for their own little perverted sideshow?

He had never really gotten to know Maria, but Rudy Schlechter had been a nice man. At least he had been outwardly warm and friendly. Deland had never been able to trust him, of course, but he would have been happy if it had turned out that Rudy was not Gestapo.

The train whistle blew, and they moved slowly out of the station.

The blinds were closed on all of the windows, and only a few dim red lights were lit in the car, making it impossible for anyone to look at a newspaper or to read a book.

There hadn't been an Allied bombing raid in these parts for some time now, but Berlin was hit regularly. Trains coming in and out of the city were often favorite targets.

They gradually built up speed, the car swaying rhythmically, and Deland settled back. No one else was seated with him, so he put his feet up. The car was very warm, but there was a small, very cold draft coming through the window frame where he laid his head. It felt good, although he knew that if he fell asleep with the cold on his head, he'd awaken with stuffed sinuses.

For a long time he lay there like that, not moving, listening to the sounds of the train, listening to the other passengers talking.

They passed a crossing, and a bell rang, the Doppler effect raising the pitch of the bell until they passed it, and then lowering it.

Most train schedules, and all train routes through the Reich were classified, to thwart men such as Deland from making their way easily across the country. But it was a simple matter to do as Deland was doing. Take a train from city to city with no mind for the time or the exact route.

From Berlin he would travel to Leipzig. From there to Nuremberg, then on to Munich, and finally across the old

Alpenstrasse to the Swiss border near Radolfzell, where he would cross on foot.

He could visualize the route. It would be very dangerous in Berlin, and again in Bavaria, not only because of the German authorities—civil as well as military—but because of the Allied bombing raids, too.

Wouldn't it be ironic, the thought crossed his mind, to have come this far only to be blown to bits by an American bomb.

A blast of cold air swept through the car and Deland looked up sharply. The conductor and two men in dark overcoats and wide-brimmed hats had come into the car. They stopped at the first seats. The passengers handed up something which the conductor took. Tickets, probably, Deland figured. But then the passengers also handed up something to one of the civilians. Even in the very dim red light Deland could see they were identification booklets. Probably travel passes and work cards as well.

The Gestapo could not have discovered what had gone on in Maria's apartment. Not yet. It was impossible. His heart sank. Impossible, unless Katrina had awakened and had called them. If she had, they were looking for him. And they'd know exactly where to look.

He was going to have to get off the train. Now! He sat up slowly, so as not to attract any attention, and using the toe of his boot, he slid his radio out from beneath the seat. He'd leave his suitcase, he didn't think he could get out of here unnoticed with it. There was nothing incriminating in it, in any event. But the radio was simply too important to leave.

The conductor and civilians, who were probably Gestapo, had moved up a couple more rows. Deland started to get up, when someone shouted something.

One of the Gestapo agents reached down and pulled a young man to his feet, then shoved him out into the aisle.

The other civilian punched the boy in the chest, sending him sprawling. The first man kicked the boy in the ribs.

None of the other passengers dared to look.

"Traitor," one of the Gestapo shouted. "It'll be to the East for you."

He and his partner dragged the young man down the aisle and out the door. The conductor followed them.

Gradually the hum of conversation increased in the car, and

Deland, whose heart was hammering, sat back in his seat and once again closed his eyes. But there'd be no sleep for him, he suspected. Not this night.

Berlin had come under attack. Thirty miles away, the passengers on the train could see the flash of the bombs going off—even through the blackout shades on the windows. And twenty miles out they could hear the pounding of the bombs and the heavy thump of the anti-aircraft guns.

They had been stopped well north of the city's suburbs in Oranienburg for about an hour, until the bombs began to subside. Then they were allowed through Reinickdendorft and Wedding, then into the heart of the city itself.

The train stopped again; this time the rear door opened and the conductor came aboard. It was after midnight.

"Stettiner Station," he called. "Stettiner Station." He ducked back outside.

Deland got off the train with the other passengers, the odors of smoke and plaster dust very strong. There were a lot of people milling around, most of them apparently waiting to board the trains leaving the city.

Shouldering his radio and hefting his suitcase, he pushed his way through the crowd at the ticket barrier and started into the depot itself, but barriers had been erected, blocking the way in. Several civil police officers were directing the people.

"Around this way, sir," one of them said to Deland as he approached.

"What happened?"

"Go around! There are a lot of wounded inside!"

"The bombing raid?"

"Yes. The bastards hit the station when it was full," the policeman said, full of disgust.

Deland shook his head, and followed the crowd along the trackside boarding area to the far side of the building and finally out onto Invalidenstrasse.

The entire front of the railway station had collapsed inward. There was no roof left. A lot of ambulances and Army trucks were blocking the streets, and fire units were spraying water somewhere inside the far end of the building.

Deland could hear people crying and screaming, men shouting.

Rubble was everywhere. Big craters pockmarked the street. Glass littering the streets sparkled like a million blood-red rubies in the fires.

He turned away and headed slowly up toward the Museum of Natural History, parts of which were also on fire, conflicting emotions raging in his head.

When he was studying mathematics at Göttingen, he and his friends had come to Berlin as often as they could. Several of his classmates had families or girlfriends here, and he'd got to know the city pretty well.

It was all different now. Horribly different. It made him sick to his stomach. And yet the Germans had brought this on themselves.

God, what a waste, he thought. What a terrible waste.

Two Army trucks filled with troops rumbled up Friedrich Strasse, and Deland ducked into the doorway of a mostly bombed-out building until they passed. Then he continued across to the Museum, and twenty minutes later he found a telephone booth near the Lehrter S-Bahn Station.

The phone lines were all underground, and if the telephone and postal building hadn't been hit too hard, there was a very good chance he'd get through.

He dialed the number he had memorized in Switzerland during his final training before he had been sent over.

It took a long time to get through, and Deland almost hung up before the connection was finally made. It rang, and a man's voice answered cautiously.

"Yes?"

"It's David."

"I don't know anyone by that name."

"Perhaps you know my cousin. Edmund Dorfman."

"He is a first cousin, or what?"

"My third, actually."

"You're lucky there was a raid tonight. I'll come get you. Where are you?"

13

There were only a couple of times in his life when Canaris had actually admitted to himself that he was frightened. The first was in 1915 in the harbor at Valparaiso, Chile, when he managed to escape from the light cruiser *Dresden* despite the blockade by the British. The second was January 2, 1935, the day he took over the Abwehr. And the third was at this moment.

A warm late-afternoon breeze off the Atlantic ruffled the long grasses in the rough along the golf course fairway. A foursome of German officers were finishing play just ahead as Canaris walked his dogs, Kasper and Sabine. He paused and looked back toward the villa outside Biarritz where he had stayed the last couple of days.

He had tried everything within his power to get back into Spain. But the German ambassador, Hans Dieckhoff, had blocked his move with a flurry of cables to Berlin. KO Spain was having a lot of trouble. The Spanish government was upset. All hell would soon break loose.

"Not a propitious time for the head of the Abwehr to be visiting Spain," the ambassador had wired the Reichs Foreign Ministry.

Not a propitious time indeed! Spain was and always would be open to him.

The dogs whined and barked, bringing Canaris out of his daydreams. He bent down and the dogs came to him, their entire bodies wagging as he scratched behind their ears and looked into their eyes.

"Yes," he said puckering his lips. "If they all were like you, we wouldn't be in this mess."

The dogs loved the attention, and when Canaris stood, they were filled with energy and enthusiasm. They tried to bound off, straining against their leashes.

Canaris was following the golf course. It had been a lovely day. He could appreciate that, even though the meeting with Dieckhoff's deputy, Minister Baron Sigismund von Bibra, and the others from the KO's in Spain and Portugal had gone badly.

They had ostensibly gathered to review intelligence problems, but Canaris had merely probed for a way to reenter Spain. Once there he had planned on going immediately down to Algeciras, where he would remain.

Even as he had planned out his moves, he had known deep inside that such a maneuver was outside the realm of possibility for him. As much as he might want to, he could not simply sit idly by while Germany was brought to total ruin by a madman.

Yet the alternatives to sitting out the rest of the war with the only person on this earth who really meant anything to him were deeply frightening.

He had brought everything with him that he would need for his alternative plan. It was all back in his room at the villa under lock and key. No one would have disturbed it. There were no Reitlingers here.

"Admiral Canaris . . . Oh, Admiral Canaris, sir," someone called from behind him.

Canaris stopped and turned back as Major Kremer von Auenrode, the chief of the *Kriegsorganisation* for Portugal, came hurrying up from the lake.

The dogs came to Canaris' side and sat.

Von Auenrode, a tall, thin, good-looking man, was out of breath. He seemed very troubled. One of the dogs growled.

"It's Cartagena," von Auenrode said heavily. He was trying to catch his breath.

Something cold clutched at Canaris' heart. Cartagena was a principal port in Mediterranean Spain—supposedly neutral. British ships called there for fresh fruit. So long as the Germans in Spain did not interfere with the British, the Spanish government turned a nearly blind eye to German intelligence operations. On more than one occasion, however, the local Abwehr operatives had struck against the British in their enthusiasm for the war. It had become a pet peeve of Hitler's. If Canaris could not control Cartagena, how could he control the Abwehr?

"What has happened, my friend?" Canaris asked.

"It just came on the teletype from Zossen."

"Another bomb?"

Von Auenrode nodded. "Another British orange ship. She blew up in the harbor. The Spanish authorities have one of our people in custody."

Canaris turned away. He could feel himself shrinking inside. This was it, then. It was truly all over. Reitlinger and Brigadier Schellenberg and all the others who had been after his scalp for the past year and a half would finally have their way.

"Sir?"

Canaris turned back. The dogs were confused. They could sense their master's disturbance. "It's all right now," he said, reaching down and petting first one, then the other.

Von Auenrode seemed confused as well.

"How could they do such a thing?" Canaris said, looking up. He could feel some anger deep down. He knew what this meant. What it really meant not only for himself personally, and for the Abwehr, but for Germany. "This is quite impossible—now of all times!"

"We should go back," von Auenrode said. "Most of the others have already left."

Canaris shook his head. "Go if you want, Herr Major. But there is no hurry any longer."

"Sir?"

"Has von Bibra left yet?"

"He left just after lunch. They all were asking about you."

"Leissner?"

"He left as well. They felt that under the circumstances they should return . . ."

"They knew about Cartagena?"

"No . . . no, sir. That just came. They left because they felt there . . . was nothing to be accomplished here. The real work is back in Spain now."

"Switzerland," Canaris said under his breath.

"Herr Admiral?"

"Nothing. Perhaps I should return to Berlin, after all."

"Yes, sir."

"Perhaps I will leave this afternoon," Canaris said. He had come to Biarritz with two alternatives in mind. He would either find a way to get into Spain, by which he would be running away, or he would turn and fight with the only weapon he had left at his disposal. "Yes," he said, shaking von Auenrode's hand. "It is time we all get back to work."

*   *   *

Frau von Auenrode, a slim beauty, was at the villa, but everyone else had left by the time Canaris and Major von Auenrode returned. Upstairs in his room, Canaris packed his two bags, called the houseman to fetch them, called for his car, and telephoned out to the airfield in Bayonne for his aircraft to be made ready. He was dressed in civilian clothes. He had not bothered to change.

The houseman came for his bags and the dogs, and Canaris followed him downstairs, but not outside. Instead, he went down the back corridor, past the kitchen, and beyond the receiving dock and service entrance to the small communications room that had been built in what once had been an ice storage room.

Bread and vegetables were being delivered from a horse-drawn cart. The old Frenchman did not look up as Canaris passed.

The teletype machine in the communications room was silent. Bitner, the KO communications man, was gone. They all had had a busy night. He was probably sleeping.

Inside, Canaris shut the heavy door and relocked it. Then he stood stock-still, listening to the absolute silence of the narrow, very thickly insulated room. The walls, ceiling, and floor were all rough-hewn cedar. It smelled good.

He had ten or fifteen minutes at the most before someone would begin to wonder where he had gotten himself to. Von Auenrode was upstairs with his wife; they'd be packing. Everyone else would be sleeping, except for the staff. The houseman would wonder, and so would the chauffeur when he didn't show up.

The telephone in this room was secure from the others in the house. No one would be able to listen in on any conversations. Yet Canaris found himself reluctant to pick it up. Once he did, he would be committed to a very dangerous course.

Treason, it would be called—because treason it was.

He sat down at the desk and lit a cigarette. He stubbed it out almost immediately, picked up the telephone, and dialed for the operator in town.

"Operator."

"This is 87.443," Canaris gave the telephone number. "Please connect me with the Berlin operator."

"I am sorry, sir, but the circuits are restricted to priority traffic at this hour."

"This is a Reich war effort priority."

"Yes, sir. Your name, sir?"

Canaris took a deep breath and involuntarily glanced over his shoulder at the locked door. "Auenrode," he spoke into the phone. "Major Kremer von Auenrode."

"Yes, sir," the operator said. "It will be just a moment or two; will you hold?"

"Of course," Canaris said. He lit another cigarette. It tasted terrible. He wished for a drink of schnapps, or perhaps some cognac.

The *Forschungsamt* would trace this call sooner or later. Schellenberg would see to it. If Auenrode were ever arrested and charged with treason, however, Canaris would make sure he got off.

"This is a Reich war effort priority call," the operator was saying.

"Yes. Your number please?" the Berlin operator replied. Her voice was very far away, and scratchy.

Canaris gave the number he had memorized before coming here. One of Dohnanyi's staff officers, who supposedly had contact with the German underground, had given it to him. The number belonged to the chief of Berlin operations for the American OSS.

It took a while for the connection to be made, but then it was ringing, and a man answered.

"Yes?"

For a long second or two Canaris could not bring himself to speak. He just held the phone to his ear, listening to the hollowness of the long-distance line.

"Yes?" the man said again, with no inflection in his voice.

"I want you to listen very carefully to me," Canaris said.

"Who is this?"

"That is what you must determine. You must recognize my voice. You must know who I am. I will not identify myself to you."

There was silence.

"There is no one coming for you; this is not a trick. I must meet with a certain party who is your superior in Bern. I must meet with him this very night. Before morning."

"Are you defecting?"

"Do you know who I am?"

"I know."

"I am on my way to Lyon. From there I shall proceed by air to a small airstrip near the town of Portarlier. There will be a full moon so no lights will be needed. I will wait there until one hour before dawn."

"Impossible. You will have to cross the border."

"I cannot. I will have no access to a car. Our border patrol there is very lax. The Swiss are not."

"How do we know this is not a trap?"

"You do not," Canaris said. "But I give you my word, I merely must talk with . . . him. This is of extreme importance to us all. Of the highest importance. I cannot emphasize it strongly enough."

"It cannot be done so quickly . . ." the man started, but Canaris hung up. His hands were shaking, his heart pounding, and he was having trouble catching his breath. It seemed as if the walls of the old ice storage room were closing in on him.

He jumped up, remembered to stub out his cigarette, and left the room, making sure the door was locked before he made his way again to the front of the house.

"Ah, there you are, sir. Your car is waiting," the houseman said.

Von Auenrode appeared at the head of the stairs, and he hurried down. "Herr Admiral, you are leaving so soon?"

"Yes. It's time to get back to work," Canaris said, forcing a calmness to his voice. Despite his extreme anxiety, his palms were warm and dry. He and the major shook hands. Canaris looked into von Auenrode's eyes. "You are doing a good job for the Reich."

"Thank you, sir."

"I just wanted you to know that," Canaris said. "Have a safe trip back."

"You, too, sir," von Auenrode said.

Canaris turned, left the house, got into the back seat of his Mercedes, the dogs all over him, and the big car pulled around the circular drive and headed down the long road out to the main highway. Von Auenrode was joined by his wife on the front veranda, and they both waved.

* * *

It was well after six by the time he made it to the Luftwaffe airfield just outside the Basque seaport of Bayonne, where, if his memory served him correctly, the bayonet was invented. His driver brought him around to operations, where the officer of the day, a young lieutenant, came out and saluted, looking askance at the dogs. A Dornier Do 17F, which had been used as the Germen's chief reconnaissance aircraft until the advent of the faster Junkers 88, was warming up on the field.

"They are ready for you, Herr Admiral," the lieutenant shouted over the noise.

The driver had climbed out of the car with Canaris' bags. He handed them to the officer who carried them out to the plane. The navigator was waiting by the hatch to receive the bags. When he had them, Canaris hoisted up the dogs, one at a time.

"We hope you enjoyed your stay here, sir," the lieutenant said.

"Immensely," Canaris replied with more levity than he felt at the moment.

The navigator helped him climb up into the belly of the aircraft, and he crawled forward and strapped himself down in one of the observation seats just behind the pilot. The dogs were tethered aft.

"Good afternoon, sir," the pilot said. He was a twice passed-over captain. Too old for combat. At least for the moment, though Canaris suspected that if the war continued to go as badly as it was, his pilot would be taken as well. "We should be in Berlin in time for a midnight schnapps, unless there's a raid tonight."

"We'll put down at the depot in Lyon for the evening and continue on to Berlin in the morning," Canaris said.

"Very good, sir," the pilot said without blinking. "It'll be a hell of a lot less dangerous if we wait." His name was Erich Hewel. He had been detached to Abwehr service fourteen months ago. Of the pilots Canaris knew, he liked Hewel the best. The man knew how to keep his mouth shut.

"Let's go then, Erich; I haven't had my dinner yet."

"Of course, sir," Hewel said. He and his crew busied themselves with the plane.

Within five minutes, their preflight checks completed, they

were hurtling down the runway and lifting off, the dark Atlantic rising off to the west, his beloved Spain to the south, and the war—his war—to the northeast.

When they were settled at altitude, Canaris went aft to check on the dogs. Kasper had piddled, the urine running farther aft in a long stream. The dogs were leashed to a bulkhead. An old greatcoat had been laid down for them. They were wild with excitement that their master was with them.

He smiled indulgently at his animals as he petted them. "If you were the Führer," he said to Kasper, "you would not have done such a naughty thing." He smiled. "Or you, Sabine, you would have had him before a firing squad." He laughed out loud at his own joke.

After a while he strapped down in one of the camera operator's positions, laid his head back, and closed his eyes. But sleep was a long time coming. His gut hurt from anxiety, and his face and neck were so warm that he began to sweat. The doctor had said he was having trouble with high blood pressure.

The technical details of Schey's report were beyond his grasp. But overall he well understood what he carried with him.

The Americans were going to win this war with or without their new super weapon. There was absolutely no doubt of that. Within a year, perhaps two, the war here in Europe would be over. It could take another five years to defeat the Japanese with normal methods. But if the atom-smashing bomb were perfected and used, it would end the war immediately.

The bomb was the guarantor of an immediate and decisive victory for whoever possessed it—Roosevelt and Churchill, or the Führer.

14

The weather was very bad across the Texas panhandle. As he drove, Schey thought about the honeymoon cottages he and Eva had stayed at. During the day, on the road, it wasn't so bad, but at night, sleeping on the floor beside the bed, he couldn't help but see Catherine's body and hear the baby crying upstairs. It was a nightmare.

It was the afternoon of their fourth day out of Washington, D.C. They were taking Route 66 the remainder of the way out to Albuquerque. Schey hoped only to make Amarillo tonight, before it got too bad.

Great plumes of snow blew across the highway, slowed here and there to pile up where snow fences had been erected.

The Hudson had performed very well for them. The car was heavy, and it plowed through all but the deepest snowdrifts with apparent ease. The only problem it had developed was with its heater, which seemed to give less and less heat the farther they traveled.

At a service station near Oklahoma City, a mechanic had looked under the hood, but he came out shaking his head.

"Mister, not only shouldn't your heater work; this car shouldn't even run. If I were you, I'd count my blessings and just keep on going. After all, it is wartime."

"You can't fix it?" Schey had asked.

"No, sir; don't believe Professor Einstein could fix it."

The heater hadn't gotten any worse, but it was so cold in the car that at times Schey could see his own breath. It dominated their thoughts.

"It's cold enough in here to freeze the balls off a brass monkey," Eva said. They hadn't spoken for at least an hour, and Schey was startled, but he had to smile. Her language was expressive.

"We'll be getting into Amarillo pretty soon," he said.

"We're going to stop there?" she asked. She was bundled up in Schey's old overcoat, the one he had worn in Washington. She looked small and defenseless in it. Her nose and cheeks were red.

"We'll get something to eat and then find a room."

Despite the weight of the car, it was difficult driving. The highway was very slippery, and often the big car would lurch sickeningly. He was constantly playing the wheel, his nerves coming to the raw edge, his eyes burning.

They were silent for a long time. There had been no other cars or trucks on the highway for the past hour and a half. It was spooky.

"You know, I was just thinking," Eva said. She glanced over at Schey.

"Yes?"

"Why don't we just keep going? Let's not stop in Albuquerque or Santa Fe. Let's just say the hell with it and head down to Mexico."

"And do what?"

"Stay there until the war is over. We could live. We have plenty of money, at least for starters. We could get jobs." She looked out the windshield and scraped away some of the frost with a mittened hand. "At least we'd be warm."

Schey could understand her. What she was asking was tempting, in a way. But every time he thought about it, he couldn't help but see himself walking along Ünter den Linden in Berlin, or at the beer halls with his friends in Munich, or a dozen other favorite places back home.

"No," he said, shaking his head. "I have a job to do."

"The war is lost, you know that."

His anger rose. "Don't say that!" he snapped.

"It is, goddamnit, you stubborn Kraut."

It took Schey a moment or two to frame his answer. He didn't want to come back at her in anger. In the four days they had been together, he had come to respect her. At times she could be a very strong woman.

"Whether or not the war will be lost, it is not over yet. I have a job to do, and I will do it."

"It's useless, Dieter . . ."

"Robert," Schey corrected. "Robert Stromberg."

"Sorry, Bobby, but it is useless."

"If we all quit now, it *would* be useless."

"Christ," Eva said, shaking her head. "What are you going to get for them in Santa Fe? A new *Wunderwaffen*?"

Schey's instinct was to lash out at her, but once again he held himself in check. What bothered him more, however, was his reaction—or rather his overreaction—to her. It wasn't like him, he decided.

He had not told her about his work in Tennessee, although she knew, of course, that he had been spying on a large government installation up there. She also knew about his radio transmitter concealed in a suitcase in the trunk of the car. But it was better that she didn't know everything, although if they were captured, they'd both almost certainly be hung as spies.

In the distance he spotted a large water tower with a light on top of it. He scraped some frost from the windshield so that he could see a little better, and as they got closer, he could see that they were coming to what appeared to be a small town. There was a diner off to one side and a couple of gas stations farther on.

They passed the sign that said: MCLEAN POP: 879, and went slowly through the pleasant-looking town. There were a lot of cars at the diner, and a number of cars and trucks angle-parked in front of two bars on Main Street. A neon sign was lit on the front porch of a very large house. It said: ROOMS. Several cars were parked in front of the house.

Some Christmas decorations, still up on the streetlights downtown, were being whipped around by the increasing wind. It would be dark within half an hour or so, and then driving would become very difficult.

"Why don't we stay here tonight?" Eva asked. "It looks like a nice place."

They came around a sharp bend, the snow piled up high on either side of the street. "Maybe we should," Schey said. He glanced in his rearview mirror, although there wasn't much to see because of the thickly frosted rear window.

"Christ," Eva shouted.

Schey's eyes snapped forward. A single police car, its lights flashing, was parked across the highway just at the city limits sign! A uniformed police officer got out and held up his hands as Schey fought to control the car. His first instinct was to speed up. But there was no way the authorities could have traced them here, he told himself. Eva sat white-faced and rigid. Roadblocks were not put up in the middle of nowhere, and small-town cops were not sent out to stop German spies.

Pumping the brakes, Schey finally managed to bring the car to a complete stop. His muscles were bunched up. He thought about the pistol he had taken from Montisier's body. He cranked down the window, the car instantly filling with the icy wind.

The police officer came up to them, first glancing at the New York license plate.

"What's the trouble, officer?" Schey asked.

"Long ways from home," the cop said.

"Yes, we are. We're trying to get to California."

"You won't make Amarillo. Not tonight. Haven't you been listening to the radio?"

"Not for a while," Schey said. The cop was staring at Eva, his eyes narrowing.

"We've got us a big storm coming. Your missus not feeling well?"

Schey leaned a little closer to the cop. "Truth is, officer, she's frightened half out of her mind."

"Frightened?"

"Yes, sir. By this weather. She's a Florida girl. Never has seen much snow."

"Well, tonight's not the night to be showing it to her. All the roads out of here are closed."

"Even 66?"

"Even 66. So what I want you to do is just turn right around and get yourself back into town. Perkins will find you a room."

"Perkins?"

"The rooming house. Big place right on Main Street. You passed it on the way through."

"We saw it," Schey said.

"Don't believe I caught your name," the cop drawled.

"Bob Stromberg," Schey said. "This is my wife, Evelyn."

Eva looked up at the cop and smiled weakly. "We just got married, and this ain't my idea of a honeymoon," she said, a slight southern accent in her voice.

The cop grinned. "Newlyweds. Tell that to Mrs. Perkins, she'll fix you two up right. Try Danny-Joe's on the corner. Best eatin' place in town."

"Thank you," Schey said. He cranked the window back up as the cop went back to the cruiser.

"I thought . . ."

"You did fine," Schey said, looking back as he made a U-turn. The cop was standing by his cruiser, watching them. He hadn't quite bought their story. Schey was almost sure of it.

"I don't know if I'm cut out for this . . ." she said.

"Don't fall apart on me now," Schey said absently. What was it they had done wrong? Why had the cop been skeptical? Or was he that way naturally?

"What's wrong?"

"Nothing. I'm just tired. We'll get a room, get something to eat, and get a good night's sleep. Everything will be better in the morning."

"Nothing will be better in the morning. It'll all be the same!" Her voice was rising.

Schey held his silence until they were parked in front of the rooming house back in the middle of town. Then he turned on her. "If you're going to be with me, you're going to have to help. I don't need an anchor. It could kill us both!"

"Fine. We'll split the money and I'll go my own way."

"That's right," Schey said. "When we get into New Mexico, I'll put you on a bus for Mexico City."

"Fair enough," she said stubbornly. "At least I won't have to put up with your Nazi spy bullshit!"

Schey looked into her eyes for a long time. She was frightened. He would have to kill her, of course. He couldn't let her go off by herself. If she was caught, which was likely, she would be made to tell everything. She knew Schey would be in Santa Fe. It wouldn't take them long to run him down.

He wanted to reach out at that moment to touch her cheeks, her lips. He didn't know, sometimes, how he could go on. There were instances like now when he felt very lost and very much alone.

"Crap," she swore. "I'm not going to sit out in this deep freeze arguing all night." She tossed off Schey's old overcoat and got out of the car.

Schey hopped out after her, getting their bags out of the trunk. He looked at the suitcase containing the radio transmitter, then glanced up the street toward the west. He took it.

Together they crossed the street to the rooming house and rang the doorbell. A short, thin—almost emaciated—woman came to the door.

"Get in out of the cold before you catch your death," she twittered, letting them in. "I suppose Willis stopped you on the highway and you'll be needing a room."

"Yes, we will," Schey said, pulling off his hat.

"We're newlyweds," Eva said sweetly.

"Land o' Goshen," the landlady said, clapping her hands. "We'll just be putting you two up in the front bedroom." She leaned forward. "A little more privacy that way. Not so far to the bathroom."

They followed her upstairs where she showed them into a tiny room on the third floor. From one small window they could look down on their car parked in front, and to the west, Schey could see over the tops of the buildings to the highway where the police car was stationed. Beyond that the highway was blotted out with blowing snow.

It's going to be a real screamer out there tonight," the landlady said. "But you'll be snug up here."

They ate dinner at a packed Danny-Joe's, and from Danny's private back-room stock, Schey bought a pint of bourbon and a pint of vodka.

Back in their room Eva refused a drink; she was still angry. Instead, she crawled into bed and pulled the covers up around her shoulders.

"If they get the snow cleared off in time, we'll be in Tucumcari by tomorrow evening. You can be on a bus for Mexico first thing Monday morning," Schey said.

"Suits me," she snapped. "Now turn out the light."

She didn't want to go, and he didn't want to let her go. He turned out the light, and she was soon asleep.

That had been an hour ago. Schey was now in the darkness, smoking a cigarette, sipping a small bourbon, as he stared out the window, down at the sleeping town and at his car.

The wind was really blowing now, whipping the snow around. Two snowplows kept going back and forth up the main street, out to the city limit where they would turn around and come back. The cop was no longer parked there.

As they had each evening, Schey's thoughts drifted back to

Catherine and the baby. So far he had been able to resist the nearly overwhelming urge to telephone the doctor and find out about his son by keeping himself busy, by pushing toward Santa Fe, although getting any information out of Los Alamos would be difficult, if not impossible. He had set his mind to the task, all but blocking out thoughts about his child, except at times like this. But to call back there would be suicide for him.

He sipped his drink.

Catherine and Eva were two totally different women. Where Catherine had been meek, Eva was brash. Where Catherine had been dull and on the frumpy side, Eva was definitely a big-city girl, smooth and good-looking. Where Katy was soft, Eva was hard . . . or was she?

A snowplow came by again, and a minute later the police cruiser went slowly past and stopped in front of the Hudson.

Schey put his drink down. The cop definitely suspected something. He stubbed out his cigarette, grabbed his coat where it was tossed over a chair, and went back to the window.

The cop had gotten out of his car. He went back to the Hudson and looked in one of the windows. He opened the door.

There was no one with him. He was alone. And except for the snowplows, there was no one out on the streets.

"Hmm?" Eva said, opening her eyes. She sat up. "What's happening?"

"Nothing. Go back to sleep."

"Where are you going?" she said in sudden alarm. She reached for the light.

"No! Don't turn on the light. It's the cop; he's looking at our car."

Eva jumped out of the bed and came to the window. The cop was in the back seat of the Hudson now. She swore softly. "What's he looking for?"

"I don't know. But I have to find out."

"And then what?" she asked, looking up into his eyes.

"I don't know," Schey said grimly.

"Don't go. Please, just stay. He's not going to find anything."

"He's suspicious. We can't just go to sleep and wait until morning. He could have the FBI up here. It means our lives."

"In this weather?"

"They'd get here sooner or later," Schey said. He pulled

away from her. He hesitated at the door. "Get dressed. We might have to leave in a hurry."

She came to him. "I'm frightened, Dieter . . ."

"Robert," he said automatically. "And so am I."

"What are you going to do?"

"I'll be back," Schey said, and he slipped out the door, silently went downstairs, and let himself out the front door, the house dark and still.

The wind was blowing very hard. It seemed like another planet outside. Schey reached inside his coat pocket, his fingers curling around the grip of the .38, and he crossed the street.

The cop saw him coming and got out of the car. He was half a head taller than Schey and fifty pounds heavier. He put his hand on the butt of his gun at his side. He looked frightened.

"I saw you down here going through my car. Can I help you with something?" Schey asked. He was going to have to get the cop off the street as fast as possible. Every moment they stood here out in the open increased the risk that someone would spot them.

"Where's your missus?"

"Asleep. Say, can we get in the car and talk. It's damned cold out here."

"In my car," the cop said. They went up the street and climbed in the cruiser. It was warm.

"Now, what's this all about, officer?" Schey asked.

"I want to see some identification."

"What for?" Schey asked. If he could not get past a small-town cop, how in the hell would he be able to operate in Santa Fe which would be crawling with FBI?

"Because I asked for it, son," the cop drawled, a dangerous edge to his voice.

Schey slipped out the pistol, cocked the hammer, and pointed it at the cop, whose eyes went wide. The man started for his own gun.

"I will kill you the instant your hand touches your weapon," Schey said softly.

The cop stiffened.

"Now. Turn around there. I want you to drive out to the edge of town where you stopped me this afternoon."

"What have you got in mind?"

"Just do as I say."

The cop put the car in gear and headed down the street. His Adam's apple was going up and down.

"Why'd you search my car?" Schey asked. "What were you looking for?"

At first the man said nothing. Schey raised the pistol to the man's temple.

"I'll blow your brains all over this car."

"It's a stolen car. I got the report on my desk. There was supposed to be radios and things like that . . ."

"What?" Schey asked incredulously.

"It was stolen last week in San Antonio. A Hudson with New Jersey plates. Or Connecticut or someplace out east like that. It belonged to a salesman. RCA Victor."

Schey could not believe his ears. It was all a mistake! The cop had made a mistake! He could have checked and found that out in the morning. There would have been no trouble. After the storm cleared up and the highways were plowed, he and Eva could have continued.

But now it was too late.

They had come to the city limits, and the cop slowed down.

"No," Schey snapped angrily. "Keep driving."

"We'll get stuck . . ."

Schey prodded him with the gun barrel, and the car lurched forward. Almost immediately they bogged down in a snowdrift. It took them several minutes of rocking the car back and forth before they got free.

Another couple of hundred yards and the road was impossibly blocked by a long, sweeping drift. The cop pulled up.

"We can't go any farther. You can see that, can't you?"

"You're right," Schey said. "Out of the car."

"What are you going to do?"

"Out of the car," Schey snapped. He hated this, but there was nothing else he could do. His back was against the wall. He could not simply turn and walk away. Not now.

The cop opened the door and got out. Schey slid across behind him and got out, slipping the pistol in his pocket.

"Here . . ." the cop said, reaching for his gun when Schey hit him in the face, knocking him back, blood flying from his nose.

Schey came at him again, driving one hammer blow after the other to the cop's mouth and nose, driving him down to his

knees, and finally leaving him unconscious on his back in the
snow.

A particularly violent gust of wind rocked Schey on his feet as
he turned away and threw up in the snow. The cop had been
doing his job, nothing more. But he had screwed up. He had
come looking for a stolen car by mistake.

The man was out, and would be for several minutes at least.
Schey thought about the coastal watcher up in Maine and that led
him to think about Catherine again.

There were times when he was certain he could not continue,
or that he even should continue.

He switched off the cruiser's ignition, unlocked the trunk, and
pulled out the spare tire and jack, which he brought around to the
front.

Getting down on his knees by the front left wheel, he un-
screwed the cap on the air stem, and using his thumbnail, his
fingers nearly freezing, he let out most of the air from the tire.
Then he replaced the cap.

He set up the jack, pried off the hubcap, and loosened the lug
nuts. Then he jacked up the car. The cruiser was very unstable in
the wind and on the slippery road, and as Schey worked, he kept
thinking about the people who would find the cop in the morning.

He pulled the wheel off and laid it aside, then took a deep
breath and went back to where the cop was lying, still unconscious.
Schey's stomach was heaving again.

This was war, he told himself. There was nothing he could do
differently. It was for the Reich. For the Führer.

He dragged the cop back to the car and positioned him so that
his battered face was directly beneath the jacked-up wheel. Then
he stood back, his throat constricting, sweat running down his
chest beneath his coat despite the cold.

The cop's eyes were fluttering as Schey slipped around to the
front of the car and kicked the base of the jack outwards.

The car fell, the wheel instantly crushing the cop's head.

It was a long walk back to the rooming house in the cold
blowing snow, but Schey was surprised when he looked up and
realized he was there.

He made his way up to their room without waking anyone.

Eva was waiting for him, her hands clasped together, her eyes wide. She had been crying.

"It's all right now," he said. He pulled off his coat, then poured himself a stiff drink which he tossed back.

"You left with the policeman. I thought you were arrested. I thought we were both . . . dead."

"It's all right now," Schey said again, realizing he was sounding stupid, but not able to help it.

Eva came into his arms, tears pouring from her eyes as she kissed him. "I'm not going to leave. I'll stay with you. Oh, God . . ."

"It's all right now, Katy," Schey said, the sound of the cop's head being crushed by the wheel of the car reverberating over and over in his ears.

15

The countryside along the French-Swiss border above Lake Geneva was very hilly. There were a lot of dairy farms in the region. The neat checkerboard squares of the fields followed the irregular contours of the landscape. The full moon, very nearly overhead, illuminated the land almost like day.

Canaris sat in the rear tandem seat of the Fiesler Storch light spotter plane they had commandeered from the Luftwaffe depot at Lyon. Captain Hewel was flying.

It was nearly one in the morning when Hewel pointed down to the east, along a fold in the hills. "It is there, Herr Admiral," he shouted.

Canaris spotted the airstrip almost immediately. He had seen photographs of the place, and it was easily recognizable. A small trout stream bordered the field to the west, while along the south end were two falling-down hangars and a small stone house.

There were no planes in sight, either on the grass runway or in the open-front hangars. Nor were there any cars or trucks, or any other sign of habitation.

The town of Portalier was a few miles farther to the north. Nothing seemed to be moving in the town either, although Canaris was able to pick out a few lights.

Hewel came around the strip twice, judging the wind as he brought the light plane lower, finally paralleling the runway on his downwind leg.

When he was opposite the end of the runway, he cut back on the throttle, and gradually they dropped as he turned gently onto a base leg and then entered his final approach, the runway lining up perfectly.

They touched down smoothly and within a minute or so had taxied back to the far end of the runway, where Hewel powered the plane off to the side, then turned it so they could see the landing approach.

Hewel cut the engine, and for the first few seconds the silence was deafening.

"There is no one here, Herr Admiral."

"We will wait until just before dawn. Then we will return to Lyon. I must be back in Berlin by noon."

They were silent for a bit.

"May I get out, sir? I'd like to stretch my legs."

"By all means," Canaris said. "But during the meeting I want you to come back here and stand by to take off at a moment's notice."

Hewel had opened the door flaps. He looked back. "Will there be . . . some danger, sir? Shall I have my gun ready?"

"I don't think so. But it wouldn't hurt to unbutton your holster flap and make sure your Luger is loaded."

Hewel nodded, then stepped down out of the plane. Canaris unstrapped his seat belt, shoved the seat back ahead of him forward, and Hewel helped him climb out.

The plane was black with a lot of windows and struts and with very tall, spindly landing gear. Standing away from it, the machine looked like some sort of gigantic prehistoric insect. The swastika was painted on the tail.

Hewel walked away from the plane and stood looking down the runway. Canaris joined him and lit a cigarette.

"It is very well maintained," Hewel said. "Is there a caretaker?"

"From what I understand, no. He is no longer here. Someone from the town comes out on a regular basis."

"Strange . . ." Hewel started, but they both heard the sound of a light plane overhead at the same time.

Hewel spotted it first on its downwind leg. He pointed.

"I see it," Canaris said, stubbing out his cigarette. "Stick close to the plane," he added. He went back to it and pulled out the cardboard envelope that contained the photographs Schey had sent over from the United States.

Hewel had taken out his Luger and he checked to make sure it was loaded. His face seemed pale in the moonlight.

"This is a very delicate operation, Erich. I don't want anything to go wrong."

"I understand, sir."

"It is of utmost importance to the Reich that I convince these people what I'm giving them is real. Do you understand that?"

Hewel shook his head. "No, sir, I don't think I do. But it doesn't matter; I'm just the pilot, and I can do that for you."

"Very good," Canaris said, patting the man on the arm. The other plane was on final and was dropping for a landing.

Hewel's eyes widened slightly. It was a Piper Cub with Red Cross markings. But he didn't say a thing. Nor would he, Canaris knew.

"Steady now," Canaris said. "Keep your eyes open. If anyone else shows up, we must leave here immediately."

"Yes, sir."

The plane touched down just in front of them, then breezed past, the wind ruffling their hair.

Canaris stepped out into the middle of the runway and headed after it, getting about ten yards when the Piper Cub stopped and turned.

For a moment the plane just sat there, its prop turning over. But then its engine died and the door flaps came open.

Two men got out of the plane; one of them headed up the runway. Canaris started walking again. The night was very still. There were no insects, no sounds at all from the countryside. Canaris felt very much alone.

Allen Welsh Dulles, chief of OSS activities for Europe, was in his early fifties. He was somewhat taller than Canaris, with gray hair and glasses. He stopped a few feet away and looked beyond Canaris to where Hewel stood by the Fiesler. Then he came closer and stuck out his hand.

"It is a unique experience meeting you like this, Admiral Canaris," Dulles said. His voice was soft.

Canaris shook his hand. "But not a pleasure?" he asked, his English a little rusty.

"A rare pleasure, sir."

Canaris nodded. The other man seemed much younger, much more vital and energetic than he would have suspected. There had been a spring in his step. There were even laugh lines around his eyes. Of course, they were winning; Dulles had every right to be happy.

"I trust you kept knowledge of this meeting to a minimum?"

"There are others who know. But the list is not large. And they all are to be trusted implicitly."

Canaris bit off the obvious rejoinder. Instead, he said, "You telephoned Washington? There was time."

Dulles just stared at him, a flinty look coming into his eyes.

"What if I came here to discuss terms of ending the war?"

"No. You are not here for that."

"If I were?" Canaris insisted. He didn't know why he was doing this, playing this game.

"We would refuse. Unconditional surrender and the total dismantlement of your military forces is the minimum we will accept."

Canaris sighed. The butterflies were back in his stomach. The night was warm. "Your government is in the process of constructing a new weapon, Mr. Dulles."

Dulles shrugged. "We, like you, are constructing many new things."

"This will be a new type of bomb. One in which atoms will be smashed."

Dulles held his silence.

"The work name for this bomb is the Manhattan District Project. It is the Army Corps of Engineers, I believe, who are making it."

"I have not heard of such a project."

"I have," Canaris said; he slapped the cardboard envelope against his leg. Dulles' eyes were drawn to it. "In a place near Knoxville, Tennessee, there are gigantic factories for the distillation of a pure isotope of uranium. Near Hanford, Washington, at another large plant, work is being done to extract a material called plutonium. And somewhere near Santa Fe, New Mexico, in the mountains at a place called Los Alamos, there is a laboratory at which many of your chief scientists are at work."

Dulles was thunderstruck. He could not hide it. Still, he said nothing.

"Shall I continue?" Canaris asked.

"All that is there, in the package?"

Canaris nodded. "At your Tennessee operation, your engineers are trying several methods to separate the uranium isotope. The gas diffusion method, at a plant which you call K-25, seems to be the only one that will work."

"My God," Dulles said, his shoulders falling. "Oh, my God . . . you . . ."

Canaris held out the cardboard envelope. For a moment Dulles made no move to accept it. "No one else in the Reich has this information. Just me."

Dulles took the envelope. "Why?" he asked.

"Why am I being a traitor to my country?"

Dulles nodded.

"This is a very important bomb. It will end the war for whoever possesses it. My country is morally . . . bankrupt."

Dulles' eyes widened. "Strange of you to say such a thing."

Canaris ignored the slur, incredible considering the circumstances. "This information was sent to me by one of my people in the States. He has worked at the Tennessee plant."

"Yes?"

"His name is Dieter Schey. There he was known as Robert Mordley. He was an engineer. Married, with one child. A son."

"We will arrest him."

Canaris shook his head. "It will be difficult. He is no longer there, in Tennessee. From what we understand he has fled."

"Our FBI . . ."

"Your FBI is not good enough. Our man is very good. He will not stop with this material. He will gather more. The next time it comes across, I may not be in a position to intercept it."

"What are you saying to me?"

Canaris looked away. This was the part he dreaded most. Schey wouldn't have a chance. "In the package are photographs of Schey. He has a contact in Washington, a woman with money and ration books and identification. Her name and description are there as well."

Both men were silent for a long time. Dulles finally broke in. "What do you want, Admiral? I don't know if I can give it to you."

"No, you cannot. I want peace. I want happiness . . ."

"We all do."

"Your agents in Germany . . ."

"I will not betray them," Dulles said.

"I knew the procedure for contacting your man in Berlin."

"By now he is long gone."

"I cannot believe he or the others have left the city. They will remain. But very soon now, the purges will begin. Anyone with knowledge will pose a serious threat to you."

Dulles stepped close. "Kill him," he hissed.

Canaris was rocked back by the nearly physical impact of the words. "Kill whom?"

"Hitler. Assassinate him. You have the people dedicated to such an end. We know you do."

Canaris shook his head, aghast. He had not thought it would come to this. "I have handed you your atom-smashing bomb on a platter."

"Once Hitler is dead, your general staff will listen to reason. Your soldiers will lay down their weapons. The war will be over."

Canaris stepped back. "No," he said. "What do you take me for?"

"That has already been established, my dear admiral," Dulles said without sensitivity. "We will make it known what you have done here this morning, if necessary."

"How do you know I was not lying, Dulles? How do you know I don't have a copy of the bomb documents?"

"You would not have come here."

"Don't be so smug. If our positions were reversed, could you do for your country what I have done for mine?"

"The war will be over sooner or later. Why prolong the suffering?"

"Why do you think I have come here?"

Dulles said nothing.

"Could you return to Washington and assassinate Roosevelt after coming here and turning over the greatest secret your country could possess?"

Dulles reached in his coat pocket and pulled out a pistol. "I cannot let you go away from here, Admiral. Not with what you know."

Canaris found that he was no longer frightened. The thing he had dreaded most, he had already done. Nothing else was threatening. "So you will shoot me now?" He shook his head.

"If need be."

"Then perhaps my pilot will manage to kill both you and your pilot, and like a good, loyal German soldier, he will return with the package I have given you. And then what?"

"You are in an enemy country at the moment."

"You are in an occupied country," Canaris snapped. "I have given you your guaranteed victory in Japan. That's all I came for." He looked deeply into Dulles' eyes. "You are a good man. Capable at your job. But I do not believe you will shoot me."

For a long time they stood there in tableau. Finally Dulles lowered the pistol. He shook his head. "No, I cannot shoot you, even though you are the enemy." He put the pistol back in his pocket. "Where do you go now?"

"Back to Berlin."

"It must be . . . very difficult there now."

"It is. For my people as well as yours."

"How much longer will you be able to hold on?"

"As chief of the Abwehr?"

"Yes."

Canaris managed a very slight, wry smile. "The Abwehr as an independent service is finished. The SD will take it over very soon. I suspect I will be fired as soon as I return."

"And then what?"

Canaris thought a moment. "Whatever fate brings me will be better than the Abwehr," he said, and he really meant it.

He and Dulles shook hands again, and Canaris turned and headed back to Hewel and their plane. He did not turn around until he got to the end of the field. Dulles had already reached his own plane, and he and the pilot were climbing in.

Hewel had his Luger out. Canaris smiled. "That won't be necessary, Erich. The meeting went well. They swallowed everything I had to tell them."

"Now what, Herr Admiral?"

"Now we return to Lyon for the rest of the crew and then back to Berlin in time for lunch."

The Piper Cub's engine started, warmed up, and then the tiny plane taxied up to the end of the runway, opposite where Canaris and Hewel stood watching.

Dulles waved, and then the American plane was bumping slowly down the runway, gathering speed, and easing up into the night sky.

The jeep bearing the high command devices on both front fenders stopped at the security gate leading into Maybach II at Zossen. The guard commander approached the jeep, but when he saw who the two officers were in the back, he came to ramrod-straight attention and saluted. The barrier came up, and the two officers mechanically returned the salute as their vehicle continued into the compound.

Neither of them had spoken very much on the trip out from the Führer bunker near the Tiergarten in the city.

They did not like what they were about to do, but they were good soldiers, and they would follow their orders.

The jeep pulled around to one of the bunkers and stopped. First out was Field Marshal Wilhelm Keitel, who strode up the walk, his tall boots gleaming. Colonel General Alfred Jodl, who was head of the armed forces operations staff, followed closely behind.

Inside, they were immediately escorted into Canaris' office. The admiral stood.

"Wilhelm," he said pleasantly. "Alfred." He knew what was coming.

Captain Meitner closed the door on them.

"Hello, Willi," Keitel said. "Did you have a good trip to Biarritz?"

"Tolerable," Canaris said. "At least the weather was fine."

They all shook hands. Canaris poured drinks. They sat down.

"We have some . . . disturbing news, Willi," Keitel began.

Jodl sat forward. "Our Führer sent us. The military situation is, as you well know, at the moment, critical. There is talk . . ."

"The Führer wants to streamline our intelligence services," Keitel said.

"By abolishing the Abwehr?" Canaris asked, his voice surprisingly strong.

"No, not by that. But by merging the Abwehr and the SD under the command of the Reichsführer-SS."

"There has been too much duplication of effort," Jodl tried to explain, but Keitel had opened his briefcase. He extracted a single document which he handed over to Canaris.

It was stamped, top and bottom, *Geheime Reichssache* (secret Reichs document), and was signed by the Führer himself.

It read simply:

Führer Headquarters
February 12, 1944

I direct:

1. A unified German secret intelligence service is to be created.

2. I appoint the Reichsführer-SS to command this German
   intelligence service. Insofar as this affects the German
   military intelligence and counterespionage service, the
   Reichsführer-SS and the head of the OKW shall take all
   requisite steps by mutual agreement.

Adolph Hitler

Canaris looked up. "And me?"

Jodl looked away. But Keitel did not. "Our Führer sends his
regards. He will decide your future employment in due course."

"And in the meantime?"

"You're to leave within the hour for Burg Lauenstein, where
you will hold yourself in readiness."

"House arrest," Canaris said. "I see. May I take Kasper and
Sabine?"

"Of course," Keitel said, flustered. "Of course."

—That's lyrical. I mean, fucking far out!

The older man didn't know whether the kid was referring to his story so far or to the young woman up on the tiny stage. They had turned off the jukebox, and instead, a stereo system was blaring a brassy melody by Herb Alpert or someone like that, while a young, bony woman took off her clothes. There weren't many people in the place paying attention to her.

The young man was smoking a joint. He offered it to the older man, who declined. But he ordered another beer.

—I mean, Nam wasn't so elegant, man. Half the time the guys were trying to figure out how to frag one of the officers.

—How about your heroes?

—You mean Terry, and Major Fisher, and guys like that?

The older man nodded. He was very tired, although it wasn't terribly late yet. In fact, it was on the early side for a Friday night. But the week had been a pure, unadulterated bitch. And all the while, somewhere at the back of his mind, he kept thinking that he knew the guy across from him. I mean, really knew him from someplace. Like they had lived together, or fought together, or something. But that was impossible.

The kid took another hit and shrugged. He glanced up at the stage and at the thin woman whose tiny breasts were sad.

—They were always in another platoon. Up the road somewhere, you know.

—You read about them?

—Hell, no. They were there, all right. As big as life. Bigger than life. We all knew about them. Everybody talked about them.

—But you didn't know them. Personally. The older man didn't know why he was pressing the kid.

—What the fuck are you trying to do here, call me a motherfucking liar?

142

—I'm trying to understand.

—Understand, shit. What the fuck do you know?

—Not a lot. I never was in combat.

—You weren't even in the service, you cocksucker.

The older man shook his head. He could feel tears coming to his eyes. It was as if the entire world was dumping on him.

He clearly remembered going out to Truax Air Force Base, outside Madison, Wisconsin . . . it was back in the mid-sixties, before the base had been closed. It was an open house.

The University of Wisconsin was just across town, with better than thirty thousand kids, most of them rebels who went around in those years throwing rocks, draping themselves with the U.S. flag, and chanting: WAR, WAR, FUCK THE WAR.

The base commander decided to have what he naively called "Friendship Day." The entire town was invited out to the base to look around, to meet the officers and men.

The entire exercise was aimed at the college kids. Show them we were the good guys, not some bug-eyed monsters who loved to napalm babies.

It backfired, of course. There was a huge demonstration by late afternoon, and the military police, along with the civilian cops, had a hell of a time clearing them out.

—Hey, look, man, I'm sorry. I didn't mean to fuck with your head.

He decided that the kid sitting across from him wouldn't understand the story. Wouldn't understand how he had managed to remain hidden until retreat was sounded from all the speakers and the base flag came down.

All across the base GI's were turning toward the flag, coming to attention and saluting.

Christ, but it gave him goose bumps thinking about it now. Those guys were the real heroes that day. Not some son-of-a-bitch climbing to the top of Bascomb Hall, ripping the American flag off its staff, and then tossing it down to his spaced-out friends.

Yet the kid across from him had been in Vietnam. He had met the enemy on the battlefield.

—I want to know what happened next. Son-of-a-bitch, don't leave me hanging.

The older man sipped his beer. For all he knew, the kid himself was a hero. But if that was so, he guessed he didn't really know what the word meant.

PART TWO
HEROES
July 1944

16

Wilhelm Canaris showed up for his new job at Eiche, in Potsdam, on Saturday, July 1st. It had been a warm, almost sultry evening. This morning the atmosphere smelled of a combination of moist growing things and the ever-present plaster dust. The Allies had come through again during the night on a bombing raid. There were many fires across the city to the southwest of Berlin proper.

It had been strange for him to get back to the city after his four months above the Loquitz Valley in Burg Lauenstein. There, he had had Kasper and Sabine, as well as a driver, Hans Lüdecke. There, he had had no worries, no concerns, no duties. The war had gone on without him. The dismantlement of the Abwehr had happened without him as a witness.

Lieutenant Colonel Albrecht Focke had been a formal but not unkind jailer, allowing his honored guest the full run of the castle and its grounds—*inside* the walls, unless an escort accompanied him.

There were a few official letters and communiques during the first weeks, the most brutal coming on March 10th—from Dönitz himself. The Commander-in-Chief of the Navy informed Canaris that as of June 30th, he would be removed from the active list of Naval personnel. On March 21st, the Navy Personnel Office sent him a brief notice that he would be placed at the Navy's disposal as of that date, but that no reemployment was contemplated.

He had gone into a funk then. It was over. He would not be participating in Germany's downfall or her rescue. He'd spend the remainder of the war as a prisoner in a gilded cage. It was bitter, after all that had gone on since the days of Valparaiso so many years ago.

Burg Lauenstein, in its secluded spot, housed the experts who forged passports and other documents, as well as the scientists and technicians who developed secret inks, microdot techniques, and other equipment. Canaris was the only prisoner.

For weeks on end he saw no one, spoke with no one, and did little more than roam the extensive grounds with the dogs, or sleep.

During those times he was not at peace. Instead, his mind ranged over his career, forwards and backwards, and most painfully, over the future of Germany.

He wondered then, too, about Dieter Schey, if he had been caught, or if he had been killed, and what the outcome of the contact with Dulles had produced.

Erika came down to visit him, but he went through the visit in a daze. For a week afterwards he had fallen deeper into his depression.

Canaris showed his papers to the guards at the door before he entered, then went down the long corridor where he stopped at a tall door with a frosted glass window that bore the officious title: *Handelskrieg und Wirtshaftliche Kampfmassnahmen* (Mercantile Warfare and Economic Combat Measures). The HwK, it was called.

He smiled wanly. From the Abwehr to this. He shrugged. It was better than Burg Lauenstein. Anything was better than isolation.

He reached for the doorknob, but the door suddenly opened, and he found himself staring into the eyes of a much taller, but very old man, wearing an out-of-date threadbare uniform, his eyes bloodshot, broken veins crisscrossing his cheeks. He was a second lieutenant. For several long seconds he stood rooted to his spot, staring into Canaris' eyes, but then he blinked several times, swallowed hard, and snapped to attention, raising his right hand in salute.

"Heil Hitler!" he screamed, spittle flying everywhere.

Canaris started to raise his hand in salute, when the lieutenant bellowed: "Admiral on the deck! The Admiral is here!" He shuffled aside.

With a sinking heart, Canaris stepped into the large office. A dozen old desks had been stuffed into the room. Behind each was an old man in about the same condition as the one who stood more or less at attention now. All of them had gotten up and were holding out a salute.

Canaris returned it.

The office was in shambles. Nothing was new. Nothing was even in good repair. The windows were cracked and dirty, several of them boarded over. And it looked as if the floor had not been swept since before the war.

Canaris stood there for a long time, taking in the scene. The cracked plaster walls. The section of ceiling that had fallen, laying bare the plaster lath. The faded maps on the walls. The incredible litter everywhere.

He could have the senior man present sweep the floor. Immediately. In front of the others. It would put them all in their places and would instantly establish his authority.

But there was no use, actually. By tomorrow the floor would be dirty again. And these men no longer cared about such things as authority. Had they cared in the first place, none of them would be here now, like this. These were the dregs. Worse than the dregs; these men, he realized, were not even fit to be used as cannon fodder. Young boys and very old men were on the battlefields these days. But not these men. And he was their leader.

"If you would be so good as to show me my office, Lieutenant . . ." Canaris peered at the lieutenant's nametag. ". . . Bender."

"*Jawhol, Herr Admiral,*" the lieutenant shouted.

"And please, Bender, I am not deaf. Do not shout."

Several doors led off the main office. One of them opened now, and an officer, his tunic open, charged out. He was fuming. "What in God's name is all the commotion out here . . ." he began, but then he stopped.

Canaris was thunderstruck. It was Meitner. Hans Meitner.

"*Gott in Himmel,*" Meitner breathed. "*Meiner Admiral.*"

"What are you doing here?" Canaris asked. He had not moved from his spot.

"They sent me to this office to shape it up for the next man. I never dreamed . . ." Tears had formed in Meitner's eyes.

Canaris smiled. "Well, from what I can see, you've done a wonderful job, Hans."

Meitner was startled. But then he understood the joke, and he smiled. "You should have seen it last week, sir."

Canaris came the rest of the way into the office, and Meitner met him halfway across. They shook hands.

"Between us this will not be so bad," Canaris said. He felt that an impossibly heavy burden had been lifted from his shoulders. Meitner's next words dashed that.

"I'm sorry, Herr Admiral. My orders were to stand by until my replacement showed up, and then I will be reassigned back to Zossen. Either that or to a field command."

"I see," Canaris said. He fought the urge to slump. "At least if you get to Zossen, we will not be so far apart. From time to time we could get together."

"Of course, sir."

Canaris stepped closer and lowered his voice. "There are a number of things I'll need you to do for me, Hans. Things that only can be done by someone who has an unrestricted access to informational sources. If you understand what I mean."

"I understand, Herr Admiral," Meitner said. He was disappointed for some reason. It was obvious from his expression. Canaris caught it, but he didn't know why, nor did he feel it necessary at the moment to ask. This was wartime.

Canaris turned to the others in the office, who had all remained standing and were watching, some of them open-mouthed. He noticed for the first time that all of them, except for Bender, were either enlisted men or civilians. A pretty sad collection.

"I assume, Bender, that you are my adjutant?"

"Yes, sir."

"You've had your people working six days a week?"

"Oh no, sir," Bender said, puffing up. "We have been working seven days per week."

"I see," Canaris said. He let his eyes roam around the office. "You may take the remainder of this day, and all of tomorrow, off."

Bender said nothing. But his mouth dropped open.

"The rest of you as well," Canaris said. He wanted to laugh and cry at the same moment.

No one moved.

"I will expect you all back here first thing Monday morning, ready to get back to work. Now get out of here. Move! Now! *Macht schnell!*"

Bender was the first to come out of it. "*Jawohl, meiner Admiral,*" he said. He actually clicked his heels.

Within moments everyone had swung into action, and within two minutes flat Canaris and Meitner were alone, laughing so hard the tears were rolling down their cheeks, though neither of them thought what they had just witnessed was funny.

"I'm sorry, sir," Meitner finally said. "I didn't mean to laugh at those poor wretches."

"I understand," Canaris replied. They *were* poor wretches. But no matter which way the war went, their lot would remain essentially the same. In a small way Canaris envied them. They had no troubles with conscience, with duty, with honor . . . or was he being too harsh? He thought not. Theirs was the simple, unfettered existence.

They went into the inner office—Canaris'. Meitner had been using it, he said, for the past three weeks. It was the only room in the entire HwK suite that was clean and in any kind of order.

Meitner poured a cognac for him from a bottle in a desk drawer. Canaris looked at it pointedly.

"It was the only way I could cope here at times."

"I understand."

"Pardon me for saying this, sir, but *I* don't understand. I no longer have any faith in the OKW. How in God's name could they send you to such an operation as this?"

"In God's name, Hans?" Canaris asked with irony. "No, in our Führer's name." He looked around. "But even this is preferable to Burg Lauenstein." He shook his head. "Did you know that Dönitz pulled me from the active officers list? Said I was unfit for duty."

Meitner said something under his breath that Canaris couldn't quite catch. The meaning was quite clear, though, and it was not complimentary to the high command.

"But here I am. Back in the fray, so to speak."

Meitner looked toward the window. Only the bottom panes were whole. The top half was boarded over. "It certainly will not last much longer."

"No," Canaris said.

"The Russians are coming at us from the east, and on Tuesday Cherbourg fell."

"Cherbourg?"

"Yes, *meiner* Admiral."

"Then it is true, it *will* be over soon."

"By Christmas, perhaps."

"Our madman will not give up so easily, you know," Canaris said. He took his drink over to the window. He looked down at the street, then over the top of the one-story building across. A smoke pall hung over the city.

"I tried to come to see you," Meitner said. "But I was ordered not to."

"By whom?"

"Colonel Loetz."

Canaris' eyes narrowed. "From Hamburg Station?"

Meitner nodded. "He managed to worm his way in with General Schellenberg himself, and had himself transferred to the SD. He's in charge of all communications for the entire Reich."

"I see."

"He and Brigadier Reitlinger are fast and famous. All they can talk about is you."

Canaris smiled. "They are like jealous old women."

"Yes."

"So, Hans," Canaris said, bucking up. "Tell me about the HwK. What are we doing here? What does the future hold for us?"

"There isn't much left, I'm afraid, sir. At one time this was a very important operation. But no longer."

"No?"

"No, sir. No one wants to deal with us any longer," Meitner said. "Nor can I say that I blame them. We no longer receive chrome from Turkey, and no wolfram has come from Spain or Portugal since last month."

"We still have Sweden and Switzerland."

"Probably not for long, *meiner* Admiral."

"Then there isn't much left here for us."

"No, sir. Tuesday and Thursday we brief the Luftwaffe and the Navy. On Wednesdays we present our reports to the Foreign Office, and on Friday mornings we're with the Ministry of Economic Affairs. But no one listens any longer."

"The weekends and Mondays are free?"

"Not actually, sir. On those days we make ready for our briefings. It's why Bender and the others were reluctant to leave. It'll put us very short come Tuesday."

"No one pays any attention, you said, so it won't really matter."

"No, sir."

"We could tell them anything. Give them any set of numbers. It would not matter."

"Practically speaking, that is correct, *meiner* Admiral. I am sure that the information we provide is not used, and it certainly is never checked."

"Which leaves us all the time we need for other, much more important activities."

"I don't understand."

"No, you don't, Hans. But you will. You will."

Meitner was very loyal. "If there is anything I can do, sir. Anything at all."

"I know," Canaris said. "There will be a lot you can and must do for me."

Meitner waited.

"My movements, of necessity, will be somewhat restricted."

"The Gestapo?"

Canaris nodded. "You will act as my eyes and ears. So it is very important that you be reassigned to Zossen, even if it means going back to work for Loetz."

"Yes, sir."

"First off, I need to be put back on the Summary Line List."

"There are so many copies coming out of Schellenberg's office that no one knows where they all go. We can get you included, through this office."

"At least that way I will have some understanding of what is happening to us. Next, I will need communications. Probably the Class A line to my home could be reactivated."

"That can be accomplished with no real problem."

"Finally, I want to set up a meeting with two old friends. But it will have to be done here, in the open, for all to see, and therefore not to be suspected. Our little meeting will have to be set up so that anyone who observes us will believe that I am being granted a sympathy call. A visit to the invalid's bed." Canaris grinned.

Meitner was heartened by the apparent turn-around in his chief's attitude. He had seen such rapid changes before. Whenever the admiral began planning some intricate operation, he was most happy.

"Who are these two, sir?"

"They're both lieutenant colonels. Werner Schrader, and Baron Wessel von Freytag-Loringhoven."

"Wasn't the Baron the chief of Abwehr II for a time?"

"The one, but he's changed," Canaris said. "I want them here. Very soon. Certainly within the next week."

The night had come. Canaris was alone. He had managed to lever the bottom section of his office window up a foot or two. He sat with his legs crossed, facing the window, smelling the damp, earthy odors of the night.

No lights shone in the city of Potsdam. The sky was clear, which meant there would almost certainly be an air raid this evening.

On some nights, when the Allied planes came overhead from the west, they would unload their bombs on Berlin proper, then peel off back to England. On other evenings they would drop their loads here, over Potsdam. It was like the macabre game of Russian roulette.

The Führerbunker would be busy. Communications would be coming and going. Command decisions would be in the process of being made. Exciting things would be happening throughout the night.

God, but he missed it. His entire life had been dedicated to the bitch-goddess military and her ideals and systems. At times he wondered: Had it all been a waste? But mostly, such as at this moment, he felt a great sense of adventure.

A military man studied the past and had a very firm understanding of the present. But it was to the future that his life was directed. When the battle was won or lost, the warrior was expected to comport himself in a manner befitting honorable men.

After all, men worked for honor for happiness' sake, but not for reward, because that would be ambitious. Camaraderie. Admiration. Even medals. But never monetary gain, to put a finer point on it, though the differences were slight.

The air raid sirens sounded, their mournful wail drifting over the city. Canaris got up, crossed the dark office, and looked across the outer office with its rows of shabby desks.

He shook his head, turned back, poured himself another cognac, then sat down again in front of the window as the first of the evening's Allied bombers droned in from the west.

17

It was hot up in the mountains. Much hotter than Schey ever imagined it could be.

These were the Sangre de Cristo and Jemez Mountains. At the lower elevations they rose in gentle slopes that were covered sparsely with scrub pine, low mesquite grasses, and goat droppings—everywhere, goat droppings. Higher up, the slopes became sharper, more angular with large outcroppings of rock.

He reined in his horse, scanned the bleak countryside, and then whistled once, twice, three times. Afterwards he cocked his head to listen for chance sounds on the breeze. But there was nothing except for the distant call of some large bird.

There were stray cattle up here, animals that had either cut out of the herd or had gotten lost on their way down to the valley around Jemez Springs. It was his job to find them. Now that beef was at a premium, even one or two head of cattle were worth going after.

He followed the natural fold between two hills, the land rising up toward the distant Redundo Peak at more than eleven thousand feet. The snow-capped mountain was still a long way off, at least three or four miles as the crow flew and twenty miles on horseback. He had not been up this far since he had begun his search.

The Romero family had been overjoyed to hire him and Eva as ranch hands. Because of the war, there was no one left except for very old people and drunken bums. Even the bums were beginning to disappear.

An able-bodied man and his strong, willing-to-work wife were blessings that simply could not be questioned.

He and Eva had moved into one of the out buildings behind the old bunkhouse, and they had managed to fix it up so that it was habitable. They took their meals sometimes with the other hands, most of whom were illegal Mexicans, and other times alone in their own place.

From Santa Fe, at the end of February, they had simply checked around with the ranchers in the general direction Schey thought the American atomic bomb laboratory called Los Alamos might be located, finding their jobs with the first ranch they called at, just north of Jemez Springs.

At first he had figured it would be fairly simple to follow the traffic to the laboratory or listen to the rumors that an installation had been constructed in the mountains.

But it had been easier than that. The location of the lab had been published in the newspaper. A local citizens group was convinced that a gigantic submarine repair facility had been constructed in the mountains. How they ever expected the subs to be transported to the sea was anyone's guess, but they had pinpointed the installation and had even gone up to picket the main gate.

Another group was convinced that the government was running a home for pregnant nuns in the mountains.

Still another organization argued that the flying saucers they believed had been landing in the mountains for years were operating from a secret base that only Roosevelt and the government knew about.

The rumors were ridiculous, of course. The American people were so naive and gullible that they'd believe almost anything.

Still, the base had been difficult to get to overland on horseback. He had come across the newly constructed dirt road in his wanderings, but he could hardly ride a horse on it right up to the front gate. Too many questions would be asked. Nor could he take a car up there. Their Hudson had finally given up the ghost and died. It was parked behind the machine shed. One of the Mexican hands tinkered with it whenever he got the chance.

Following the road on horseback, overland, the way the countryside rose and fell, was very difficult. He had been picking his way around the mountains for weeks now, trying to find a way up to where the installation was located.

Survey maps were no longer being sold, at least for the duration of the war, and asking one of the locals to act as a guide was totally out of the question. It would bring too much suspicion down on him.

For a time Schey had thought about joining one of the citizens groups that had picketed the place, but he had decided against that approach as well. The FBI watched those groups very carefully. If someone new showed up, they'd take a great interest in him.

After his work up in Oak Ridge, the FBI would almost certainly be looking for him down here. They'd have to suspect that he would either come down here or out to Hanford, in Washington, where another large atomic plant was located. If he became visible by joining a group or getting stopped for questions, they'd nail him immediately.

Nothing had been in any of the national newspapers about him or about Eva and the dead FBI agent back in Washington, D.C. That hadn't really surprised him, of course. The authorities could hardly advertise that they were looking for spies. It would tip them off, and it would create panic in an already nearly hysterical public.

The path he was on ended within a narrowing box canyon. He wheeled his horse around, worked his way back out of the canyon, and then cut back toward the northeast.

This area was at once desolate and beautiful. There was nothing like it in all of Germany, and most Germans seeing this would be damned glad of it. This was mostly nonproductive land. Huge tracts were needed to support even the smallest of cattle herds. Only the rattlers and mule deer and goats thrived here. And at times, he was told, even they were at risk.

As hot as he was, he did not feel sweaty, but he was very thirsty. He stopped and drank sparingly from his canteen. The water was warm and tasted metallic.

He looked at his watch. It was well after four in the afternoon. He turned in his saddle and looked back the way he had come. The valleys in the distance were tinged with blue. It would be at least a half-hour's hard ride back to where he had left three stray cattle he had found, then another hard hour and a half back to the ranch.

He gazed up toward the ridge that overlooked the box canyon. It was early yet, he told himself. Somewhere very near the base. He could feel it. Just a little farther. Just to the top of the ridge, and then, depending upon what he found up there, he'd head back.

The horse jumped as he jabbed his heels into its flanks, and they started up. As a young man, his uncle had taught Schey to ride. He had been on the team in his *Gymnasium*, and finally he had been in regional competition in the one-year prep school he had attended in Switzerland.

Eva, who had never been near a horse in her life, except for the police horses in the park in Chicago and once in Central Park when she visited New York during a Bund rally, was amazed at his skill.

At first he had had difficulty with the western saddle. The tall horn was disconcerting. He had learned on the much smaller English riding saddle. But very quickly he got used to the working leather, and after a long day on it, he was glad for its width and bulk.

Just to the top of the ridge, he promised himself, coming to the top and then raising up and reining in short, his breath catching in his throat.

Below, in a flattened valley, was a large installation, its buildings, for the most part, aligned in streets and avenues like a well laid-out town or a military base. He hurriedly backed his horse down so that he would not be outlined against the horizon. Now that he was this close, he wanted to minimize the risk as much as possible.

The first time he had set eyes on the vast buildings and huge machinery at Oak Ridge, he had been awed. But here they were putting the super weapon together. Here was the distillation of all the work being done at Oak Ridge and at Hanford, and some sports stadium in Chicago.

There was only one step remaining for them—that of testing the bomb in the desert south of Albuquerque. He was going to have to find out how close they were to that stage. Once that happened—once the Americans successfully tested their first bomb—the war would be over within a matter of weeks, perhaps days, unless the Germans could beat them to it.

Schey dismounted and secured the horse's reins to the branch of a low pine, then scrambled back up to the edge of the rim with his camera.

Starting at the far end of the installation, he took a series of photographs, each overlapping the other, that when put together would provide a panoramic view of the entire valley.

Back in Oak Ridge he had received several sets of instructions for the time when he would come here. First on his list of priorities was to secure photographs of the entire installation, and then to shoot close-ups of its individual components. Its buildings; its machinery, if possible; its electrical generating facilities; its personnel—anything, in short, that might help the Reich's scientists to duplicate the effort would be useful.

The main road was just below him, and he could see the front gate from where he lay on the rock outcropping.

Several cars and two large trucks were stopped at the gate. Armed guards were checking them, searching each vehicle before it came in.

As he watched, a car approached from the inside. The driver and passenger were made to get out, and they, as well as their car, were searched before they were allowed to proceed.

Schey lowered his binoculars and rubbed his eyes. Security was very tight. He suspected there would be high density perimeter patrols, probably outside the fence as well as inside. There might be other security measures, too. He would have to use a great deal of caution in his approach.

He eased down from the ridge to his horse, where he took another drink from his canteen. He ate one of the sandwiches that Eva had packed for him.

There was no question about him returning before dark. This was a marvelous opportunity that he simply could not afford to ignore. He would remain until after sunset, and then he would make his way down and, if possible, into the installation so that he could take the close-up photographs his people wanted.

While he waited for darkness, he fed and watered his horse, finished the sandwiches, and loaded a roll of high speed night film into his 16 mm camera.

The moon had not come up yet, but the bright stars directly overhead would provide plenty of light. Below, the installation was well lit, which would work to his advantage, he figured. Those inside or anywhere near the lights would have no night vision. They would not be able to see much of anything out in the darkness.

Schey made his way down the hill, being extremely careful not to dislodge any stones that might give him away.

He angled toward the north, away from the main gate, and when he came to within fifteen yards of the tall, barbed wire-topped steel mesh fence, he stopped and lay flat on his stomach.

There would be guards coming along. He had to know when and in what fashion they would pass.

Within minutes of the time he had settled down, a jeep slowly ground its way up the hill, along the outside of the fence, two guards plus the driver. All armed.

They stopped just down the fence line from where Schey lay. He held his breath as a spotlight came on and flashed across the hillside just above him.

He looked over his shoulder, but there was nothing to be seen up there other than the rocks and brush. His horse was still concealed behind the ridge. The jeep would not be able to make it up that far, and he did not think the guards would walk up. It was their duty to guard the laboratory, not to explore the countryside.

The spotlight was doused, and the jeep continued along the fence, passing below where Schey lay, and then disappeared into the distance.

Inside the compound there was a lot of activity around what he took to be a dining hall. The trucks that he had watched come through the gate earlier were parked in what appeared to be a supply depot. Several men in uniform were busy unloading big crates.

Electrical wires seemed to run everywhere. From somewhere across the installation Schey could hear the sounds of large diesel generators turning over. Whatever they were doing in their laboratories, they were using a lot of electricity.

To the far southwest of where he lay was the housing section, lights in nearly every window.

It made him think about Dresden and Berlin and other German cities being bombed day and night by the Allies. Those cities were not lit, save for the fires that, he read, raged almost continuously.

Here, there was no fear of a bombing raid. Here, they were secure. Perhaps smug in their relative safety?

In one respect Schey had the terrible urge to enter the compound and wreak havoc. Blow up the generators. Locate and identify the laboratories and destroy them. Find the key scientists and kill them.

Yet another part of him, a saner, more rational part of him that surfaced these days whenever he begun to think about Katy and about his son, urged him to turn around and leave. He should take Eva's suggestion and get down to Mexico City, only a hundred miles or so from here—not so far, actually—and sit out the remainder of this terrible war that could only end in victory for the Americans.

Twenty minutes after the jeep had passed, two soldiers on foot marched down a path on the inside of the fence. They were talking. Schey could hear their voices, but he could not make out what they were saying. Gradually they disappeared into the darkness.

He made his way down to the tall fence, scrambled to the top, threw his jacket over the three strands of barbed wire, and crossed over, disentangling his jacket, then dropped down to the path.

For a moment or two he remained there, listening for any signs of an alarm, but all was quiet except for someone who beeped a car horn somewhere within the installation.

He scrambled away from the fence, off the path, down into a ditch and along it for several hundred yards until he came to the electrical distribution center.

Schey lay upon the bank of the ditch and took two photographs of the electrical equipment, then continued along the ditch, which was used to control flash flooding during the infrequent but very heavy rainstorms.

Three more times he stopped to take photographs of interesting-looking buildings. One of them had all of its windows boarded over, yet he could hear the sounds of some kind of machinery running from within—a high-pitched sound, not like a generator, but more like a centrifuge, Schey thought.

Another five hundred yards farther on, the ditch ended at a narrow culvert that he could not follow, forcing him to either return the way he had come or to climb up.

He chose the latter, scrambling silently up on the bank, then across it between a row of long, low barrackslike buildings.

Schey could hear music coming from one of the barracks, and soft yellow light spilled from the windows, although most had curtains covering them.

He approached one window that was open a crack. The slight breeze ruffled the curtains, and he was able to catch a glimpse of the inside.

It was a barracks. It was filled with at least fifty men, some of them in bed, some of them lounging, drinking, or reading. Five men in skivvies were playing cards around a foot locker at one end of the barracks. At the other end, a tall, thin red-skinned man, a portable radio perched on his shoulder, the speaker directly against his ear, was doing some kind of loose-limbed shuffling dance.

All the clothing he could see hanging on rods behind the bunks and lying around were civilian. These were not soldiers. They were civilians. Probably engineers and perhaps even scientists. Bachelors, or men whose wives had decided not to come along.

Schey stepped away from the building and looked down the row of similar buildings, all the windows lit. If each was a bachelor barracks and the housing across the base, which he had seen earlier from above, was presumably for married couples, and if all were filled, then there were at least five thousand people here. Perhaps more.

The effort of the Americans to produce this bomb was at once staggering and frightening. Germany was under a siege at the moment, and that seriously hampered her war efforts. Even at peace, however, her factories and laboratories working at full capacity, her people as dedicated to this as they were to their Führer, Schey did not think they could match the Americans.

There were too many people in this country, too much industry, too vast a pool of natural resources for Germany to possibly match it.

And yet the war was not over. Not yet. Not by a large measure.

Schey continued taking photographs of the buildings across the wide dirt street that ran in front of the barracks. Many of them looked like laboratories. Some of the individual buildings were isolated within their own separate enclosures, with signs warning passersby that special permits were required for entry.

He made his way back to the ditch that paralleled the fence, then back away from the well lit buildings toward the area of relative darkness where he had come over.

Even before he got back to his starting position, he could hear a jeep's engine, and he could hear someone talking.

He crouched down and went the last dozen yards, finally flattening himself against the bank and peering over the side.

The two foot soldiers who patrolled inside the fence were speaking with the soldiers in the jeep on the other side of the fence.

At first Schey could not tell what they were talking about. Had they discovered that someone had breached the security of the base? Perhaps someone had found his horse up above the ridge. Or perhaps they had spotted his trail down the hill. Maybe he had ripped his jacket and a patch of material was stuck on the barbed wire.

But then one of the men laughed. Another stepped away from the fence and urinated not ten feet from where Schey lay.

A few minutes later, with a parting word or two, the jeep headed west and the foot soldiers went east. Soon they were out of sight, and Schey quickly made his way over the fence and up the hill, his horse whinnying softly in the suddenly very cool evening.

18

Deland and Bernard Dannsiger walked together along Wilhelm-strasse, the Reich Chancellery and Foreign Office in the park across the broad avenue from them. They were both large men, Deland somewhat fairer of skin and more Nordic-looking, if anything, but Dannsiger much older and obviously wiser.

The late afternoon was warm, and although there wasn't much vehicular traffic, other than the occasional Army troop truck or open Mercedes staff car, there were a lot of pedestrians out and about.

Allied raids had come every night and morning for seven days in a row. Last night there had been peace as there had been this morning because of a low, humid overcast that was supposed to last for several more days.

"It's a rare pleasure to be outside without having to maintain an awareness of just where the nearest air raid shelter is located," Dannsiger was saying. He had been a lecturer in Latin and South American history at the University of Berlin until three years ago when his post was declared "superfluous." He ran the under-ground now.

"At least it's not cold. We don't have to worry about overcoats," Deland said.

Dannsiger, along with a dozen others in the underground, provided identification, clothing, and some limited transportation for downed Allied fliers. In some respects their job was much easier now that it was summer. At least they didn't have to worry about a man freezing to death.

But Deland was chafing at the bit.

"This winter will probably be the last," Dannsiger said firmly.

"You think so?"

"He can't hold out much longer."

They both glanced instinctively over at the Reich Chancellery building. Dannsiger had learned that Hitler was spending a lot of time in his specially constructed bunker beneath the building. He had his staff with him. Practice, they all supposed, for when the siege came, although it was likely that when the end did come, the Führer would head south into Salzburg where he could more easily be defended.

"He'll probably hold out a lot longer than I will," Deland said. It was time to get out. Something at the back of his head had been telling him that for weeks now.

Dannsiger stopped him at the corner. "Don't you think I know what you are going through?"

"I want to go home. I'm tired, Bernard."

"We're all tired, Helmut," Dannsiger said reasonably. (Deland's cover name here in Berlin was Helmut Schmidt. He posed as a voice teacher. At home he had been on the church choir and had a surprisingly good tenor voice.)

"None of this matters to me anymore. I find I don't give a damn."

Dannsiger smiled indulgently, like a father might with a son who was trying to find his way. "Don't you think we know?"

"About what?"

"Katrina Mueller, of course. Up in Wolgast."

Deland could feel the blood rush to his ears. "How?" he managed.

"Before anyone joins us, we must know their background. Everything about their past. But if that wasn't enough, you talk in your sleep very often."

They went across the street, then started across the wide square in the middle of which stood the Brandenburg Gate, the Four Horsemen of the Apocalypse rushing off the top of the arch.

"I'll come back when it's over."

Dannsiger looked at him not unkindly. "I keep forgetting that you're not a German. You are so very much like my . . ."

"Don't say that," Deland snapped. Dannsiger's son had been killed in France.

They had to wait for half a dozen trucks to pass, then they went through the gate, and headed up Chausse Strasse. There was a lot of bomb damage just here. Many craters pockmarked the street; many buildings were down, rubble piled very high, some of it still smoking.

Deland was perspiring. He didn't feel well. "I could just go."

"The frontier is not particularly safe at this moment, so if that is what you really want to do, and intend doing it, please let me know."

"Yes?" Deland said hopefully.

Dannsiger smiled and nodded. "Yes. I will see what I can do for you, although it will not be much."

"I'm not looking for a first-class ticket out."

"No. But what about Fraülein Mueller?"

That really hurt. "I'm coming back for her as soon as hostilities cease."

"Do you think she will be there, waiting for you?"

Deland stopped the older man. "Do you know something? Have you heard some news?" His heart was hammering.

At length Dannsiger shook his head. "No, Helmut, I know nothing about the girl, except that she is there in Wolgast. Nothing more. There are other things more important at the moment. I just wondered if you were disgusted with all Germans, or just those of us here in Berlin."

Deland said nothing. He was visualizing Katrina the last time he had seen her in Maria Quelle's apartment. Rudy and Maria were both lying dead on the floor, blood everywhere. That memory, that vision, had stayed with him day and night through five months. More than once he had almost gotten on a train and gone back up there. Daily he reached out for the telephone to call her where she worked. He'd pretend he was an official from Berlin. He needed information.

Each time, of course, his own better sense stayed his hand. Something so reckless would endanger not only himself and the underground here in Berlin; it would place her in grave danger as well.

But he did not know if she had survived the suspicion that must have fallen on her. Did she still hold her job? Was she still living in her own apartment or had she moved back with her parents?

They got on a trolley and rode the rest of the way down to Berliner Strasse in the vicinity of the Forschungsamt building, where they got off and walked a half-dozen blocks north into a run-down, all but bomb-destroyed neighborhood of three- and four-story apartment buildings. The Spree River, stinking like the open sewer it had become, was directly behind the row of buildings that they approached by a circuitous route.

They did not speak. Each was alert to their surroundings. Each building, each burned-out car or truck, each overturned handcart, each pile of rubble could possibly present a grave danger. Each could conceal a watcher. Someone who would turn them in to the Gestapo for nothing more than suspicious behavior, for a reward of food. Perhaps two eggs. Perhaps a quarter kilo of pork or a small chicken.

They ducked through the gate of what once had been a girls' finishing school, then in to the burned-out building. The top three floors were gone. But the first floor and the basement were more or less intact.

This building had been selected because of its room—it was a very wide and long building—and because of the fact that a storm sewer emptying directly into the Spree ran beneath the building.

A hole had been punched through the concrete floor in the basement, and through to the eight-foot-diameter sewer pipe. It provided an escape route for Allied fliers dressed in civilian clothing, with Polish worker identification, to relative safety outside the city.

From there they were on their own, with sketch maps, counterfeit money, and ration coupons sufficient to last them until they reached the frontier where the fighting was going on. From there it was anyone's guess how many got through. They were never officially informed, although some of the fliers they interviewed seemed to think the underground system in Berlin was very good.

There were no guards or even lookouts on the entrances to the building. They would have been a useless waste of time and manpower. If the authorities came, there would be little any of them could do to save themselves. It would mean that they had been observed. Their faces and their methods of operation would be known.

Besides, in Berlin these days, no one strayed into strange places. It simply was not healthy. So there was little risk that they would be discovered by accident.

Marti Zimmer, a young woman from Westphalia, with the pale look of the Dutch, whose husband had been shot as a deserter one year ago when he had been too sick to fight, appeared in the corridor. She stopped, doe-eyed, on the verge of scurrying away, but then she managed a very slight smile.

"All but two went out early this morning," she said, her voice barely a whisper.

"Was there any trouble?" Dannsiger asked.

Marti cocked her head, as if she were trying to listen for some faint far-off sound, and then she shrugged. "There was shooting. But we don't know what it was. Karl went out, but he said he saw nothing. He was gone for nearly an hour."

"I see," Dannsiger said. "Where is Karl now?"

Deland felt somewhat uncomfortable around the girl. There was no one else here in the shelter even remotely her own age, except for him and, of course, some of the fliers. She was very lonely. It made him nervous.

"He is with the others."

"Are the new workbooks completed?"

"They are just finishing them now," the girl said.

"I'll go downstairs and check on their progress," Dannsiger said. He turned to Deland. "In the meantime, find out what is needed in the way of supplies. We'll have to take care of it this evening or first thing in the morning."

"Of course," Deland said, and Dannsiger went down the corridor and down the stairs to the basement where most of the shelter's work was done.

The remaining two fliers were both Americans from a B17 shot down five days ago. They were bunked in the basement in a room adjacent to the opening into the sewer. If all else failed and the building did come under attack, they would at least have a chance of escape.

Deland had talked at length to both of them, as he had with many of the Americans who came through, getting news from home.

He could not identify himself, of course, or send messages back home. If the escapees were picked up and interrogated, it would give him away. For the same reason the downed airmen were brought into the shelter only in the middle of the night, and they were sent out in darkness as well. They'd never be able to find their way back—or lead their captors back here.

Marti turned and started up the corridor. "Come," she said.

Deland followed her to her office-bedroom. She had become the requisitions and supply officer for the shelter. It was she who figured out what they needed to continue their work: everything from ink and pen-nibs to material for clothes and the sewing machines to make them with.

The room smelled of lilacs. There were three large bunches of them in vases around the large room. Tall windows overlooked the river. From here the Spree was pretty.

Deland went to one of the windows and looked outside. Several children were playing some game in a large bomb crater in the narrow strip of yard between the backs of the apartment building and the muddy river banks. A lot of debris was laying around.

"I watch them often from here," Marti said.

Deland turned to her. She stood in front of her desk. The room was furnished with a bed and a small *Schrank*. A tattered old throw rug lay in the middle of the spotlessly clean wooden floor. A bullfight poster from Spain was tacked on the wall. On the opposite wall was the standard-issue photograph of Adolph Hitler.

"For inspiration," she always said. "He is what we are fighting against."

"It always make me nervous," Deland said.

"What, the children?" she asked in surprise.

He nodded. "I'm afraid there will be an unexploded bomb. Or some glass, or something that they might hurt themselves on."

Marti laughed. "You Americans are all alike."

He smiled with her, although he wasn't quite sure he understood, or even liked, the inflection of her remark.

"You're all little boys. The bombs are raining down every day and every night, and yet you are worried about the children playing in the leftovers."

She had been working with a German first aid unit outside of Paris until nine months ago when a group of French Resistance fighters had ambushed her one night. Five of them had raped her and had left her for dead.

The German command had returned her home, and then she had come here to Berlin after she had recovered. Instead of turning her against the Resistance, it had opened her eyes to what war was doing to people. She was on a pension now for full disability. As far as the German military was concerned, she was above suspicion, although Dannsiger was her uncle.

"It doesn't make any sense, does it?" Deland said looking again down at the children. An overwhelming sense of frustration and sadness welled up inside of him.

"It won't last much longer, Helmut," she said. "And then we will be able to begin rebuilding our lives. All of us will be able to pick up the threads that were torn from us."

"We'll never be the same."

Marti laughed again, the sound light, almost musical. "No, of course not, but maybe we'll be able to get sane again."

"In the meantime . . ." he began.

"In the meantime we live our lives. At the moment we need India ink. Black and blue."

"India ink?"

She nodded, then picked up a piece of paper and held it out to him. "Along with a few other things."

Deland took the list from her. It was long, and included everything from buttons (all sizes) to wallets, eyeglasses, and German Reich marks.

Deland chuckled at the last. "We should have gold."

"That, too, if you can come up with it."

He looked up. She was smiling at him. Whereas Katrina was short and full-bodied, Marti was tall and somewhat willowy for a German. But her hair was blonde, her eyes blue and her manner very Nordic. She was definitely German or Dutch.

She came around her desk, but stopped in the middle of the room. She was wearing wool trousers and a thick, long-sleeved flannel shirt. "We shouldn't be fighting this war, you know."

It was his turn to smile. "No."

"It's turned everything upside down."

"I'm sorry . . . about your husband," Deland said. Dannsiger told him that she had loved her husband very much. She had been pregnant when he had been killed. She had had a miscarriage.

"I'm sorry about your Katrina in Wolgast."

"What?" Deland asked, suddenly very frightened. "Has something happened to her? Have you heard?"

Marti came a few steps closer. "No," she said. "I meant I was sorry that you could not be together. You must miss her very much."

"Christ," he said, his heart hammering. He went back to the window. The sun was setting. The haze was thickening across the city.

Marti followed him. She touched his shoulder, and he jumped as if he had been shot. He turned.

"I . . ." he sputtered.

She looked up into his eyes. Then she put her arms around him and drew his lips down to hers. He had no resistance left.

Marti was thin, and very bony after Katrina, and yet it was comforting to hold a woman. Boys began with their mothers and ended with their wives. In between were difficult lonely times.

She led him to the bed where she pulled him down. Blindly he had her shirt off, and then her bra, and he was kissing her breasts, taking her nipples in his mouth, her back arching against him.

For just a moment he pulled back, thinking about Katy, thinking about the way it had become for them in Maria's apartment, thinking about all the hopes and desires he had had for them. For just a moment he thought about how it would be when the war was over and he came back to her. What would it be like, in Wolgast? What would it be like in Germany then, for an American? He shuddered to think about it.

"Helmut," Marti breathed. The name was foreign, as was the voice calling it, but God help him, he was lonely, and cold, and frightened.

They parted, and he stood up and took off his clothes, while she pulled off her shoes, then her slacks and her underpants. The tuft of hair at her pubis was very blonde and hardly visible.

When they were in bed together, lying side by side, Marti propped herself up on her elbow and looked into Deland's eyes.

"I want to say something to you," she said seriously.

Deland was hard. He wanted her. "What?" he said.

"I don't want you to forget about your Katrina," she said. "It may sound strange that I am saying this now, but after the war you must go to her. This between us now, it is just comfort. Nothing more."

Tears began to leak from her eyes. He tried to draw her to him, but she pushed him back, and kissed his chest, his stomach, the inside of his thighs, and then took his full length into her mouth.

The sensation was amazing, wonderful, and yet he wanted more. He had her head in his hands, and finally he pushed her away, over on her back, and he rolled over on top of her, entering her with a great feeling of relief.

"Oh . . . yes," Marti cried at one point.

He slid his hands under her hips and grasped her buttocks, pulling her up each time he thrust, pushing harder and deeper each time, until he couldn't stand it any longer, and he could feel himself coming, everything draining from him, Marti shuddering beneath him as she too climaxed.

They held each other for a long time, until Deland began to feel that his position was awkward and that he was probably too much weight on her. He moved aside.

She clung to him, though, not allowing him to move too far.

"It was wonderful, Helmut," she said. "It was for me. Did you get pleasure?"

"Yes, of course," Deland said, the beginnings of embarrassment rising within him. He couldn't believe they had done what they had just done.

Marti sat up and looked at him. "You're sorry," she said.

He sat up and pushed away from her, getting to his feet.

"What was I, some sort of a leper?" she asked.

Deland hurriedly got dressed. "I am sorry, Marti," he mumbled. He felt like such a fool.

"Sorry?" she shrieked. "Sorry for what? Sorry that we made love? Sorry that there was a little pleasure in the midst of all this death?"

Deland stepped back. His face and ears felt very hot. He kept thinking about Katrina. He was glad that she wasn't here.

"I'm sorry, Marti, this should never have happened."

She jumped up and grabbed a small ceramic cat that stood on the floor at the foot of her bed, and she flung it at him.

He easily ducked aside, although it surprised him. The figurine breezed past his head, striking the wall and shattering into a million tiny pieces.

"You bastard!" she screamed.

He backed away.

"You miserable bastard," she screamed again, and Deland, only half dressed, fumbled his way out of her room.

19

The early morning was very hot and sticky. Deland, stripped to the waist, sweat dripping from his nose and running down his chest and from his armpits, stood in the upstairs corridor of his apartment building, his radio in hand, as he listened to the air raid sirens wailing across the city.

It was late. After four A.M. This was the third raid this night. The weather had broken three days ago, and the Allies had been unmercifully pounding the city day and night.

He went to the end of the corridor and looked out the rear window across the bombed-out courtyard and beyond, toward the Kurfürstendamm. Spotlights worked back and forth, their beams stabbing the black night sky.

There were stars up there. Only he could not see them from here. It gave him a sense of claustrophobia. He thought about Wisconsin: the lakes and the woods, fishing and hunting with his father and his uncles, and then later, as a young man, with his high school friends. In college he had been too busy, but there for a while in high school he had really enjoyed himself in the outdoors. He missed it now for some reason.

The first bombs began falling well to the southwest in Charlottenburg, which meant the raid had a fifty-fifty chance of either coming up here to the Tiergarten area or south to Schöneberg.

Deland guessed he no longer gave a damn.

He turned away from the window, went to the far end of the corridor, and entered what once had been a linen closet but now was a storeroom for buckets and mops.

Slinging his radio over his shoulder, he carefully climbed up on the shelves until he reached the overhead trapdoor which led into the attic and from there up onto the roof.

It was only slightly cooler outside, but from here he could see the bomb flashes and feel the rumbles shake the entire earth each time a big bomb struck.

Deland had been through this before. A hundred times before—so the bombs, the sirens, the night did not bother him. He had aged a lot in the last months.

Quickly he set about rigging his antenna between a pair of chimneys a hundred feet apart, then sat down, his back against a standpipe, and began transmitting his numbers.

Now he used Morse code; the transmissions were more likely to be received and understood that way, and his encryption was a simple grid overlay of the city of Berlin.

Whenever he had the data Bern was interested in, he would transmit numbers which amounted to nothing more than grid references for strategic military targets within the city. Troop billets, supply depots, small factories that had sprung up in mostly residential neighborhoods over the past six or eight months—a host of targets that Allied bombadiers could concentrate on. In effect he had become less of a spy and more of a forward spotter.

In one respect he no longer minded. He had become all but immune to what he was doing, to what was happening here. It was a defense mechanism.

Two days ago a half-dozen British fliers filtered in from the countryside. They had provided the men with food, clothing, money, and papers. Within twenty-four hours the six had escaped through the sewer tunnel. Within two miles downriver of where they had been released, a German shore patrol had spotted them and had machine-gunned them. Karl Körnmeister, one of the men from the shelter, had watched the entire thing, had watched it frustrated and helpless.

He and Marti had been making love on a more or less regular basis now every time he went to the shelter. It meant little or nothing to either of them, although Deland still felt guilty, and so did Marti, he supposed. She still clung to the belief that somehow the reports of her husband's death were wrong, that once the war was over, he would be found in some field hospital somewhere, or perhaps in a prison.

Deland would never go back to Wolgast, and Marti's husband would never return. They both knew that, and yet neither of them could give up the fiction.

The bombs came closer, one striking less than a block away, and Deland shuddered, shrinking down.

A second and a third bomb struck to the north, a block or so away, and then for a few minutes the city was quiet. Even the air raid sirens had ceased.

Deland broke off his transmission, got up and went to the edge of the roof and looked out across the city. Fires burned here and there, and there was a great deal of smoke in the air. Smoke and plaster dust. Deland figured that when the war was long over, he would remember it most by the smell of plaster dust which seemed to forever hang in the air.

The searchlights still swung over the city, and it seemed strange to him that no noise accompanied their sweeps.

Then he heard the sounds of the B17's very high up, coming in from the west. A moment or so later he could heard the engine sounds of one or two Messerschmitts, and then distant cannon fire.

The air raid sirens began again, and soon the dull thumps of bomb explosions rolled down from Wedding, accompanied by the sharper crunch of the few antiaircraft guns still functioning in the city.

He went back to his radio and finished transmitting his coordinates. When he had completed the last sequence, the Bern operator signaled him to stand by, which usually meant that they'd want him to send the coordinates of some military target within the city.

The *Berliner Zeitung* was not much of a newspaper these days, but they still were using the old one-time code. The message came over and Deland copied down the numbers, one pair at a time, until Bern signed off.

He pulled his antenna down, repacked his radio, and went again to the edge of the roof to watch the bombing of Berlin.

There were a lot of fires now; far off to the northeast, perhaps as far as Mitte or even Prenzlauerberg, a great fire was raging high into the night sky. Most likely it was one of the fuel depots there. Either that or it was the asphalt production center. Both were targets Deland had pinpointed weeks ago.

The other raids today had lasted less than ten minutes each. This one seemed to go on forever, although when the last bombs finally fell and Deland no longer could hear the drone of the bombers, he looked at his watch and was shocked to see that only nine minutes had passed since the first bomb had dropped. Nine minutes! Eternity.

His apartment was two rooms, actually. It had once belonged to a dentist. The outer chamber had been his waiting room, the inner his office and operating theater combined. Some of the dentist's equipment was still stored in the back. He and his family had lived one floor above. They were Jews and had been taken away long ago, according to the fearful neighbors.

He lay down on his cot with the *Berliner Zeitung* and his message. He quickly translated it, his gut tieing in knots as each word emerged.

HITLER SUSPECTED IN RESIDENCE IN BUNKER BE-
NEATH REICH CHANCELLERY. WHAT ARE CHANCES
OF UNDERGROUND GETTING TO HIM? ALL MEANS
BUT SUICIDE MISSION APPROVED.

                                        BERN

He had not written out the message. He had translated it in his head. He began to laugh. Bitterly.

There had been plots against Hitler's life since day one, although most of them had been amateurish. It would have been relatively easy to have killed him years ago. Now it would be impossible. They said the Führer led a charmed life. There had been recent assassination attempts, but apparently none of them had even come close.

Deland got up from his cot. He was very tired, his eyes burning, his throat raw from the smoke, and he was very hungry. Just now there wasn't much food in Berlin. Most of what little they had been able to gather went to the downed fliers who would need their strength to return to their units and fly other missions. Always other missions.

"The end of the war can be counted by the number of missions it will take to beat Hitler and the OKW into submission," Dannsiger was fond of saying. "For every flier we return to the fight, it means that many less days we will have to endure this war."

But this was another story. Hitler, they suspected, was spending most of his time in his bunker behind the Reich Chancellery building on Wilhelm Strasse.

The place was heavily guarded, of course. There'd be no getting close to it.

No suicide missions, Bern had radioed. There would be no other way. Even if they got into the bunker, even if they could actually get to Hitler and gun him down, there'd be absolutely no hope for escape.

In the small porcelain bowl that was still hooked to the plumbing, Deland ran a small stream of water into his cupped hands, rinsed his face and his mouth, then dried himself off with a dirty towel.

He put on his shirt, his shoes, and a cap, then went out the back way, across the littered courtyard, through the ruins of an apartment building, and finally out onto Taunte Kleist Strasse.

He had no cover, not at this hour of the morning. Anyone out at this time was either on some official duty or up to no good. His only hope was stealth. If he was discovered, he would have to make a run for it through the bombed-out buildings.

Actually he wasn't too worried. Berlin had become a labyrinth of back alleys and rat-maze passages through the blocks of rubble. He had come to know the city in a way he had never dreamed possible in his student days. He knew her sewers, her passageways, and he knew some of her dark wartime secrets: where to buy cigarettes, where to find a woman (though he had no need of that kind of woman), where, at times, even to find liquor. Food was much more difficult, but not impossible.

But he was getting tired of the game. He was burning out on all the death and destruction. He was becoming numb to the constant fear, the ever-present over-the-shoulder feeling that men in black uniforms and jack boots were coming for him.

Bern's message was intriguing though. He cut up across Kurfürstendamm and then Budapester Strasse, past the Auslands-organisation building on Tiergarten Strasse, and finally the park itself, one block west of Wilhelm Strasse, behind the Foreign Office and the Reich Chancellery.

He could hear the animals in the zoo howling and screaming in fear and rage. They were upset because of the bombing. Someone had told him that people were starting to come to the zoo to hunt for fresh meat.

It turned his stomach to think about it. But all the police horses had long since disappeared from the city, as had most of the dogs. Why not the zoo animals? Next it would be the family cats that had escaped and had gone wild, and finally the plump rats by the river.

What would one do to survive, Deland asked himself from the shadows. Assassinate a madman who had brought this once-proud people to absolute ruin?

It took him more than an hour to make it to the area behind the Reich Chancellery by his circuitous route, and yet he was not tired. Less than two hundred yards away, and perhaps not too many feet beneath the garden, was the seat of German power. Adolph Hitler.

There had been a lot of street patrols, but from here Deland could see nothing but the dark back side of the Reich Chancellery building. The entire area seemed deserted at this moment. He knew better. Anyone starting across the open ground behind the building would be cut down before they got ten yards, and certainly long before they got within a hundred yards of the bunker entrance.

Dannsiger had told him about it, though how the underground leader knew about the entrance was anyone's guess.

Was there a chance of getting to Hitler and killing him? Deland kept his eyes on the back of the building, waiting to catch a flash of light, a movement, anything that would signify there was life there. But he saw nothing. Nothing at all, which was frustrating.

Was there a chance, Bern asked. Probably, but it would have to involve Dannsiger and the underground. They were the only ones who knew enough to pull it off. If they would. After all, they were still Germans. It would almost be like planning to assassinate Roosevelt because you didn't like the way the Americans were conducting the war.

He shook his head. He had been here too long. He stepped across the dark street and started back the way he had come, but then he stopped, an overwhelming sense of loneliness rising up within him.

It would be morning soon. He looked back toward the bunker. There was no way of knowing for certain whether or not Hitler was actually there. They'd have to post a watch to see when he came or went. It would be the only way in which to make certain their efforts were not wasted.

He turned in the other direction, heading up Bellevue Allee through the park, instead of down Tiergarten Strasse.

There could be no wasted time. Bern wanted an answer. He would have to speak with Dannsiger immediately. The only way was to return to the girls' school. To the shelter. Marti would know where he was.

By the time Deland made it all the way up to the Charlottenburger Strasse, the dawn had come and people were coming out of the bomb shelters and out of the remains of their homes to congratulate each other that they were alive.

Each time after a bombing raid the streets filled with people—celebrating life over death, Deland supposed. He and the others did not fit. The people out and about this morning were civilians, whereas he, Dannsiger, Marti, and the others were soldiers.

A half-dozen black market shops had sprung up on the corner where Deland turned to head the final few blocks to the school. Quite a crowd of people had gathered to haggle over the few bits of limp vegetables and a couple of bottles of cheap wine at one of the stands.

Deland stepped around the knot of men in front of the tobacco stand when he brushed past a man in rags, who looked up.

Deland saw the face out of the corner of his eye, and alarms began going off in his head like the air raid sirens last night and this morning. He knew the man!

"Deland!" the man behind him shouted.

Deland's blood ran cold. He kept walking.

"Robert Deland!" the man shouted. "*Aye yi yi yi!*" he hooted. It was the unmistakable secret call from their student days at Göttingen. He could not ignore it.

He stopped in his tracks and spun around as Rudy Gerhardt, dressed in rags, his right leg gone nearly to the hip, an Iron Cross around his neck, hobbled up to him.

"*Gott in Himmel*, it is you," Gerhardt boomed. He let his crutch fall and grabbed Deland in a powrful bear hug. He smelled very badly.

It had been the mid-thirties since he had seen Gerhardt last. They had been mathematics students together under Professor Doktor Reichert at the university. They had never been close, but

they had attended the same parties, and there had been the one
girl they were both interested in for a short while.

Gerhardt stepped back, balancing himself on his one leg. Tears
streamed from his eyes.

"*Gott in Himmel*," he said again. "It is so good to see you
here like this, Robert. My God, it's been so many years."

"It's Rudy," Deland forced himself to say with surprise.

"Yes! Of course it is Rudy, you old bastard." Then something
came into Gerhardt's eyes, and his manner. "But wait," he said.
"But wait, you have . . . you are here, in Germany. You
defected?"

Deland smiled as broadly and as sincerely as he could. "Don't
say that so loud, Rudy," he whispered. "*Scheisse,* it's been
years since I was back in . . . America. I am a German now. A
soldier."

"A soldier? What kind of a soldier? Where is your uniform?
Why are you not on duty? *Was gibt, Robert?*"

"I can't tell you. Not like this. Not out here on the street."

Gerhardt just looked at him. He was shivering. His complexion was very pale, and a thin line of sweat had beaded on his
upper lip. He was a very sick man.

"What happened to you?" Deland asked. He felt very much
out of control of the situation. The entire Reich was looking at
him. Everyone in Berlin was looking, wondering who he was,
wondering when he would be arrested by the Gestapo.

"It was in France," Gerhardt was saying slowly. He seemed
to be measuring his words.

Christ, he knew! Deland's heart hammered so hard that his
chest ached. "I'm sorry, Rudy."

"It was just bad luck, that's all. The Resistance set out home-
made mines across the road. I was the only one to come out
alive. I was the unlucky one."

Deland glanced around. Everyone was interested in the black
market shops, especially the tobacco stand. No one paid them the
slightest bit of attention. Yet he still felt as if he were on stage.

"Listen, Rudy, I want us to get together very soon. Perhaps
for supper. Some potatoes and some sausage. Can you make it
for supper?"

"What *are* you doing here in Berlin, Robert?"

"I told you, Rudy; I'm working for the army."

"Doing what?" Gerhardt asked. He grabbed Deland's arm. "Doing what, Robert?"

"Later, Rudy. We'll have supper and I will tell you everything. Promise." He pulled Gerhardt's hand away. "Now, tell me, where do you live? Where can I come see you? I will bring some eggs."

20

It had been four days since he had stumbled on the Los Alamos laboratory in the mountains and had taken his photographs. It had been three days since he had sent his first radio message that he had a batch of films for delivery. There had been no answer that evening, so he had tried again.

He had walked five miles from the ranch, mostly up, so that by the time he was ready to set up his radio, he was at a very high elevation.

The radio signal with Berlin was very weak, the Morse code buried within the static.

"Acknowledged," they had radioed.

But instead of rendezvous coordinates, they advised him that in this instance the photographs would be picked up.

It was very late. Well after two in the morning. Overhead the stars were so bright and seemingly so close that they looked unreal.

He tapped out his acknowledgment signal, then repacked his radio in its suitcase and headed back to the ranch.

He and Eva had been here for several months now with no trouble. She had fit well into the domestic role. At times, lying in bed together in the evening, she would talk to him about saving their money and buying their own spread of land some day. This wasn't so far from Milwaukee, after all.

"My grandfather and my father were fishermen on Lake Michigan. My grandmother and mother tended the house, had the babies, baked the bread. What's the difference here, if you go out to tend the herd and I keep the house?"

At first Schey had reminded her that they were German and this was war. But after a while he let it go. She lived in a fantasy world. Or at least, in that one respect, she did. At the ranch, the war seemed very far away, in any event, except on the nightly news when Walter Winchell or Edward R. Murrow spoke about the latest battles with the Reich, and then Schey would descend into a deep depression.

There was a definite procedure he had been taught for making what was termed "blind contacts," which were meetings with another agent in enemy country when the meeting had not been prearranged.

In each different language the code was, of course, different, but in each language the message which was placed in the local newspaper's classifieds, read: *Berührung,* which was German for CONTACT. In English the ad would read something like: B.E. requests ur honest reply, unloved N.G., the initials of each word spelling out the single German word.

Any combination of words that spelled that word would signal the contact. A phone number would be given, in most cases a public phone booth, and the contact would stand by at ten minutes before ten in the morning, three minutes before three in the afternoon, and eight minutes before eight in the evening, until the meeting was consummated.

Before the war, Canaris had come up with a lot of schemes such as that one, literally hundreds of codes for his agents to use in whatever circumstances they found themselves.

There was no reason to think now that the contact procedure wasn't as valid as it had been when it had first been devised. And yet Schey was nervous about it.

They had told him at Park Zorgvliet that the longer he remained in the field, the more skittish he would become.

"At first your survival will be simply another military exercise. You are in enemy country; you will feel like a soldier on a mission, and you may well act like a soldier on a mission.

"Later, however, once you have been in place months, or perhaps even years, you will begin to better understand the nature not only of your assignment but also the nature of the people you are living with.

"At that point you will discover that your instructions truly were only guides to your performance. The successful field man will adapt to whatever situation he may find himself in. Adapt with a firm feeling for the people he is living with . . . and spying on."

Coming down from the mountains, the early morning air wonderfully cool, he thought about Katy and the baby. Katy had been so grateful to be married that at times Schey had felt embarrassed. At first he told her he loved her and he had *not* meant it. She knew that, but she loved him desperately and she was willing to go along with whatever he said, as long as they could be together.

Later, when he had *truly* fallen in love with her and it frightened him because he worried about his assignment, she began to doubt their relationship.

Poor Katy. She had been out of sync the entire time. Now, thinking about her, it was hard for him not to go completely berserk, take a gun, and indiscriminately kill whomever he chanced upon.

Katy! Christ, he had finally loved her and she had been taken from him. She, along with Robert, Junior.

Schey would meet with his contact when the message came, but the rules had changed now by virtue of the importance of the information he was transmitting home. When the message came, he would devise his own method of contact.

He came within sight of the ranch and stopped. The out buildings were all dark, except for the one he and Eva lived in. A soft yellow light glowed in the single window facing north. She would be waiting up for him. Like Katy, she had become dependent upon him, and it bothered him, mostly because he did not know exactly how he felt about her.

They had been making love, as if they were married, for several months now. But just lately he was getting the strong impression that Eva was falling very much in love with him.

Two weeks ago it had caused him some irritation to realize it. But now, standing several hundred yards off from the ranch, cold, nervous about what the future would bring, he found that he was looking forward to getting back to his home and crawling into bed with Eva. There was a certain comfort in that.

The horses whinnied softly as Schey came onto the property, skirted the corral, and stopped beside the barn. He looked up toward the ranch house set on a small rise. None of the windows showed any light. The Romeros were all asleep. So far as he could see, no one was on the front porch, either. Nor was anyone lurking in the yard. No one to see him return in the middle of the night, carrying his small suitcase. No one to ask questions or to report his strange behavior to the authorities.

Because of the installation up in the mountains and the several military bases down in Albuquerque, people in this part of New

Mexico were very jumpy. They had heard stories about conditions in Europe, and they all believed it was the Germans' fault. Everything in that part of the world was Germany's fault.

Eva was sitting up in bed when he came in, the covers around her neck, the small table radio playing softly, the lamp by the window on. Her eyes were wide, her nostrils flared. They were signs that, Schey had come to know, indicated she was frightened.

He put his radio down. "Are you all right?" he asked.

She nodded. "Did it . . . go well? Did you get through?"

He nodded.

She sucked her breath. "What'd they say? Did they tell you what they wanted?"

"Yes," he said. He took off his coat and hung it up. Then he pulled a chair to the middle of the small room, got up on it with the radio, and shoved open the small trapdoor that opened above to the rafters. He shoved the radio up, replaced the cover, and stepped down.

"Well what'd they say, for God's sake? What are we supposed to do with the goddamned pictures?"

She had been extremely frightened to have the photographs in the house. Anyone could find them, she said. And then it would be the gallows for both of them.

He went to her on the bed. It would be a lot better when he got rid of the photos. She could not go on like this much longer. Sooner or later Mrs. Romero would notice that something was wrong. Sooner or later Eva would make a mistake. She was not cut out for this.

"It might be a few days yet," he said.

She reached out for him, letting the covers fall. She wore a flannel nightgown, the buttons undone. He could see the swell of her breasts which never failed to excite him.

"And then what?" she asked. "Do you put them in a package and mail them? Or put them under a rock? What?"

Schey sat down on the bed, her hands in his. He looked deeply into her eyes. "Listen to me, Eva. You are going to have to be very brave now."

"Oh God . . ." she said. She shook her head. "I don't like this."

"I could lie to you and tell you everything will be all right. But you deserve better than that."

"I don't want to hear this."

"There may be some trouble."

"What is it?"

"They are sending a courier to pick up the photos. I'll have to meet him somewhere. Soon."

"Who will it be?"

"I don't know."

She was getting desperate. "If you don't know, then anyone could come here. The FBI. Anyone."

He nodded. "We will have to be very careful. But it may end up that we'll have to leave."

She pulled her hands away from his and shoved him away.

"I just wanted you to know so that you could prepare yourself," he said. "We promised that there would be no surprises for each other."

"Why can't you just leave this stupid thing alone?" she cried. "The damned war is lost! We're bombing the living shit out of you . . ." She cut it off, suddenly realizing what she was saying.

What she was saying hurt. Mostly because it was true. Germany was losing the war, and the Allies were bombing Berlin and other cities. They had been for some time now. But it was not over yet. It couldn't be. He wouldn't allow it.

He got up and went across to the small wood stove. For the last few nights they had had to make a fire to ward off the mountain chill. It had gone out, though. He contemplated restarting it.

"I'm sorry, Bobby," Eva said from the bed.

He turned back to her. "Don't worry about it. I have a job to do. In that there can be no discussion. You don't have to stick around, though. Mexico might be the place, after all."

She shoved the covers back and jumped out of bed. Her feet were white and tiny. She ran to him, stopping short.

"Look," she said in a small voice. "I'm sorry. I mean it. Whatever you think is best, I'm with you."

He just looked at her.

"I mean it, damnit, Bobby. I got nowhere to go. You're it. And I love you."

He reached out and brushed a strand of hair away from her eyes. Her high cheekbones were accentuated by the poor light which cast hard shadows. Katy had been lovely, beautiful in her own way. But Eva was an exciting woman. Katy had been comfortable; Eva was difficult. At that moment he couldn't honestly say which he preferred, given the choice. But Eva was here and now, while Katy was simply a dull ache in his memory.

"I don't know where I'm going to end up . . ."

"I don't care," she quickly interjected.

He put his fingers on her lips. "Listen to me, Eva. You're right, Germany is losing the war. But it's possible I will have to return home to help with our defense."

"No," she said in a tiny voice, shaking her head.

"Yes. If it comes to that, I will." He sighed. "And it looks as if it will come to that, sooner or later."

"Then I'll go with you," she said.

He smiled. "I think not. You would not fit in Germany. You're an American. It would be impossible for you."

She hesitated a moment, as if she wanted to say something, but wasn't quite sure of it. Finally, however, she blurted it out. "You're still in love with her, aren't you?"

"Who?"

"Catherine."

"What are you talking about?" Schey asked. His stomach was sinking.

"Catherine. Katy. Your wife. She's dead, but you're still in love with her." Tears were coming to Eva's eyes. "If she were alive, you would take her to Germany with you. You'd take her anywhere."

He shook his head in a reflex gesture, unable for the moment to cope with what she was saying. Because she was closer to the truth than she knew, it frightened him. But she took the gesture to mean he disagreed with her, and it gave her some measure of comfort. But only some.

"You talk about her in your sleep. All the time. But I'll come with you, Bobby. I love you. Can't you see that?"

Schey took her in his arms, a great wave of love for her rising in his breast, forgotten for the moment his rendezvous message, and even Katy, his poor dead wife. Eva was here and now. And she loved him.

In the afternoon, after chores, Schey would go up to the main house to speak with George Romero about the day's work, about the next day's projects, and would collect the Santa Fe and Albuquerque newspapers the Romeros had already read. When he and Eva were finished with them, they'd pass them along to the few old ranch hands in the bunkhouse.

It was three days after the message when the contact code appeared in the personals column of the Santa Fe classifieds.

Big Earl Really Understands Henrietta's Rotten Upbringing.
N.G. wants you back. Market 4-4510.

Berührung. CONTACT. Except for the last three words, but they were nothing more than fillers. He was certain of it.

Schey was sitting at the small table by the window. He was drinking a cold beer. Eva was outside taking the laundry off the line. It was just after six-thirty. He memorized the telephone number, then folded the paper and set it aside.

He had missed the morning and afternoon contact times, which left eight until eight this evening. Less than an hour and a half away. It was a Thursday. A little unusual for him to be going into Jemez Springs on this night, but not dangerously so.

He got up and went outside, around to the bunkhouse, where he dropped off the newspapers. The four ranch hands inside were playing poker and didn't pay much attention.

Back outside, he angled up to the main house where George Romero and his wife Juanita were sitting on the porch.

"Hey, George," he called out, pronouncing the name in the Spanish way. "Can I take the pickup into town this evening? Be gone a couple hours."

Romero was a short, very stocky Mexican-American who was jolly when he was drunk: He was almost always drunk now that he had Schey and Eva to help out.

He waved his beer bottle. "Get some gas when you're in town, old friend. Should be a few coupons in the glove compartment." Romero got up and staggered to the porch rail. He winked, and his wife shook her head. "Stay away from Mama Roseros, you know. You come back with the disease, and the little bugs, and I think Eva will kill you."

His Mexican accent was almost comic. Schey grinned and waved, then headed back down the hill to where Eva was just finishing with the clothes.

She looked up when he came. Almost immediately she knew that something was happening, and she nearly dropped the shirt she had just unclipped from the line.

"I'm going into town for a little while," he said.

She looked into his eyes. "Has it come?"

He nodded.

"Oh Christ," she said, looking away. "Oh Jesus . . ."

"It's all right, Eva. I haven't committed us yet. I'm just going to make a telephone call. We'll see what happens after that."

"Where are you going, Jemez Springs?"

"Too dangerous," he said. "I'll get down to Jemez Pueblo, or even San Ysidro. I'm just going to make a telephone call. Nothing more than that."

"Then you'll come right back?"

"Promise," he said.

The battered Dodge pickup truck was parked in the barn. Eva was standing in front of the bunkhouse when he went by and headed down the dirt road to Highway 4. She waved, and he waved back, but then he was down the hill and out of sight.

It took him less than half an hour to make it the ten or twelve miles through Jemez Springs and the rest of the way down to Jemez Pueblo, which was a town of about eight or nine hundred. There were several taverns, a few Catholic churches, one farm implement dealer, a blacksmith, and two gas stations, one of them combined with a diner.

Schey stopped at the diner, had the attendant put in five gallons of gasoline—he had to give the farm ration coupons first—and then he went inside where he ordered a beer.

He took a deep drink, then went over to the phone booth in the corner. He plugged in his nickel and dialed for the operator.

"Number, please," she said.

No one knew him here in Jemez Pueblo. No one would be able to say who it was who had used the phone. At least he didn't think so.

"I'd like a Santa Fe number, MArket 4-4510," he told the operator.

"That will be seventy-five cents for the first three minutes, sir."

He had gotten enough change with his beer. He plugged the money into the phone. Moments later the Santa Fe number was ringing. Once, twice, and then it was answered by a man.

"Big Earl."

"I have something for you," Schey said softly.

"What?" the man snapped.

"Where can it be delivered?"

"Where are you calling from?"

"Where can we meet?" Schey countered.

"You're calling long-distance. Can you get into Santa Fe?"

Schey said nothing. He held his breath as he pressed the receiver close to his ear. He could hear something in the background on the other end of the line. Something he knew.

"Hello?" the man said. "Hello?"

Then Schey had it. He was hearing a radio. Like a police radio in the background. A police radio! At a police station.

"Hello . . ." the man shouted, but Schey hung up.

21

The lovely white Polish-Arabian mare contentedly crunched the sugar cube, then nuzzled Canaris' hand for more.

"No, Motte, you have had enough," he laughed, patting her broad, sleek neck.

She reared back and shook her head, as if to disagree. Canaris laughed again. At that moment he felt a surge both of pride and of bittersweet happiness. Forgotten for the moment, at least, was the disturbing news that Schrader and Freytag-Loringhoven had brought him earlier in the month. Had it really been two weeks ago?

The Arabian, which was often given the run of the property adjacent to Canaris' home at 14 Betazeile, backed off, turned, and imperiously headed off at a gallop, frisky now that she had gotten attention, that she had been given a treat, and that the weather was so splendid.

Canaris had to shake his head. He looked at his watch. It was just a bit after two. Rely on the goodness of animals. It was the one certain thing remaining in this very uncertain world, he thought.

Although it was only a Thursday, he did not feel guilty about being away from his office. Bender had turned out to be a fine, if unimaginative, aide. The office, by and large, ran itself these days. No one on the high command gave a damn, in any event. So why should he?

He started back up toward the house, when an open Mercedes staff car came up the drive. Canaris recognized Werner Schrader in the back seat. He was dressed in civilian clothes. He seemed very agitated.

Canaris angled down toward the road, the car slowing to meet him.

"Hello, Werner," Canaris called from the fence.

Schrader jumped out of the car and came across the road. He was sweating furiously. His face was flushed.

"I tried to get you at your office! That fool, Bender, was there. He didn't want to tell me a thing!"

"What has happened?" Canaris asked. He could feel his heart pounding. Everything Schrader and Freytag-Loringhoven told him at the beginning of the month came back. "Is it Stauffenberg?"

"I think so," Schrader said breathlessly. "I've had three Valkyrie calls, but just as many denials."

Valkyrie was the code name for the assassination of Hitler. Freytag had given Stauffenberg a package of captured British plastique explosives. That had been weeks ago. They all assumed the man would assassinate the Führer. But exactly when or where, no one had been sure. Valkyrie was the code word that was to go out to every Army unit within the Reich, signaling the immediate takeover of political key points, such as town halls, as well as all police stations. The rationale to be presented to all the troops was that civil war was imminent. The safety of the Reich was at stake.

"Well, what is it then, yes or no?" Canaris demanded. "Has the fool actually done it?"

"I don't know, Admiral. I came here hoping that you had heard something."

"I have heard nothing," Canaris snapped. He looked back down the road toward the main avenue. If the Gestapo was there, they were well hidden.

He had told them all that Stauffenberg was a fool. The man had contacted the KPD, for God's sake. He wanted an alliance with the Communists! And he was the one with whom they entrusted the coup d'etat? It made no sense, less than that, it was criminal.

"What do we do?" Schrader pressed.

"Get out of here. Leave me alone. You did not want me included in your plans in the first place; do not bother me now that you do not know what to do next. I cannot answer it for you."

"But what will you do?"

Canaris answered without a moment's hesitation. "Friends are coming over. We shall listen to the piano and talk. Such as we often do in the afternoon. I suggest you return to your office, Werner, where there will be witnesses to your loyal behavior."

"But what if it is true . . ."

"That Hitler is dead?"

Schrader nodded, afraid even here to utter the words.

"Then he is dead, and your Valkyrie shall proceed. But be careful, Werner. Be very careful." Canaris shook his head. He was tired, suddenly. "Now get out of here. It would not do for us to be seen together."

Schrader practically jumped out of his skin when he realized the implications of what Canaris was saying to him. He turned to go back to the car.

"And Werner," Canaris said.

Schrader looked back.

"Don't return here."

Schrader's lips pursed; Canaris turned and continued up the paddock toward the house without looking back. He heard the car door slam and then the sound of the big car turning around and heading back out to the avenue.

Helmut Maurer, his next-door neighbor, was just coming up the walk when Canaris came around from the side. The older man's eyes lit up.

"Willi," he said. "Coffee?"

"Uncle Mau, yes, of course," Canaris said, greeting his old friend. They had known each other for years. Canaris had gotten Maurer a civilian job with the Abwehr III, which these days was under the aegis of the RSHA. He in turn provided Canaris with a lot of day-to-day information about the goings-on downtown.

They shook hands. "What is it, Wilhelm?" Maurer asked, lowering his voice.

"Am I that obvious?"

"Yes, of course you are."

Canaris took a moment to answer. When he did, it was with the greatest of care. "I could tell you what is bothering me, Helmut, and you would be suitably impressed. But from that moment on, should any questions be asked, you would not be able to plead ignorance."

Maurer regarded him through widened eyes. "Is ignorance so dear?"

Canaris nodded. "Just now it is."

Maurer sighed. "Then, Willi, we shall go inside and I shall play the piano for us. Perhaps Vladi will join us this afternoon."

"Perhaps," Canaris said, and he and Maurer went inside.

Mohammed, Canaris' manservant, met them at the door with a huge grin.

"Herr Kaulbars is here, sir," he said, bowing deeply.

"Thank you," Canaris said. He went into the conservatory, Maurer directly behind him. Baron Vladimir Kaulbars was there, gazing out the French doors.

Canaris had known the old Russian since the early twenties when the former staff captain in the Russian Imperial Army had first surfaced in Berlin.

Kaulbars had worked, on and off, as an interpreter in the Abwehr, and from time to time he played at giving Canaris Russian language lessons. His real usefulness, though, were his British and East European contacts which he maintained through Colonel Juhlinn-Dannfeld, the Swedish military attaché in Berlin.

He was much taller than Canaris, and huskier, too. He turned when he heard the two men enter.

"Ah, Willi, I wondered if you hadn't climbed on your horse and, like a good Cossack, gone for the hills," Kaulbars said. His German was deep and rich, with a marvelous courtly accent.

"The thought has crossed my mind," Canaris said, lightly. "Can you stay for coffee?"

Kaulbars nodded. "Of course. If Helmut will play a little Tchaikovsky instead of Mozart, today."

"Oh, I think that can be managed," Maurer said.

Mohammed brought in the silver coffee service as they were settling down; Canaris sat in the large overstuffed easy chair across from the French doors, while Kaulbars perched, as usual, on the edge of the couch and Maurer sat at the baby grand piano.

When the coffee had been poured and small snifters of cognac had been passed around, Maurer began to play a cutting from Tchaikovsky's Piano Concerto in D, and Canaris slid back into his own thoughts.

For a time now he had thought it possible that he could ease into a state of semiretirement. He had almost, but not quite, divorced himself from the day-to-day events of the Reich, except what he came directly into contact with through his office.

Maurer still brought his tidbits of gossip from time to time. And Major Meitner (his friend had recently been promoted—only through attrition, he claimed) brought him news from Zossen. Still, one part of his mind was able to shunt such details into a netherworld in which, although he was conscious of the facts, they were no cause for reaction.

In the mornings he went down to Eiche where he presided over his fools' court. He had gotten through, finally, to Lieutenant Bender on three counts: The man no longer shouted as if everyone around him were deaf; the man made sure the office was tidy; and he had rapidly become very facile at coming up with lengthy reports on the barest of data.

Four mornings a week he presented his departmental briefings. At first his presence caused quite a stir. But in the incredibly short period of only a couple of weeks, a torpor had seemed to settle on anyone who listened to him.

It was exactly the effect he had worked toward. He was more successful than he had hoped he could be.

That left him the entire weekend, as well as every afternoon, free. It was as close to retirement as he could be and yet still have a hand in the war effort.

Tomorrow, the 21st, he would have been at it exactly three weeks. And already he was beginning to get bored.

Valkyrie. Even the word was electrifying. He had been less than honest with Schrader. He hoped with all his might that Stauffenberg had been successful. He personally disliked the baron. He thought the man was a fool. But fool or no, Canaris hoped that Hitler now lay dead on the floor of his Wolfsschanze near Rastenberg.

Maurer's music flowed around him—a fine, calming counterpoint to his thoughts. He had a sense of fatalism. What would come would come. Events seemed to be propelling him forward without any effort on his part.

At first it had been easy to drift with the current. But just lately the tide had seemed to grow very strong, and he was being accelerated faster than he wanted to be toward a fate he had no knowledge of.

". . . asked, more cognac, Willi?" Kaulbars was saying over him.

Canaris looked up out of his thoughts. "I'm sorry, Vladi; I guess I was drifting."

Kaulbars poured some of the fine French brandy, then poured some for Maurer, and finally some for himself.

Kasper and Sabine, the two dachshunds, raced into the draw-

ing room, their entire bodies wagging in delight that Mohammed
had finally let them free.

"Ah, there we are, my little darlings," Canaris beamed, forgetting his dim thoughts for just a moment.

The telephone in the stair hall rang; once, twice, and just at the
third ring, Mohammed answered it. Maurer had turned back to
the piano and was about to resume playing, but Canaris held him
off with a gesture.

Kaulbars seemed very deeply concerned, but Canaris didn't
really notice.

They could hear Mohammed speaking, but they could not
make out the words. After a moment or two he appeared at the
door.

"It is Herr Sack, Admiral."

Canaris jumped up, his heart suddenly racing. Karl Sack,
besides being an Army judge, was involved with the conspiracy.
In fact, it had been Sack who had intervened on Stauffenberg's
behalf when Canaris wanted the man certified as insane.

After what news Schrader had brought, Sack could only be
calling for one reason.

"What is it, Wilhelm?" Kaulbars asked, getting up.

"Nothing," Canaris mumbled. "Nothing." He hurried out of
the drawing room, Mohammed stepping aside for him. In the
hall, he snatched the telephone from its alcove. "Yes?" he said.
"This is Canaris."

"Herr Admiral, this is Karl Sack."

"Yes, Karl. What is it?" Canaris said. He glanced over his
shoulder. Maurer had come to the door.

"It is the Führer. He is dead. It was a bomb. It exploded
during a meeting near Rastenberg."

Canaris said nothing at first. So many thoughts raced through
his mind. It was actually so. Hitler was dead. He felt the
profoundest sense of relief, mixed with that of a terrible loss, and
a feeling of dread.

Maurer stood in the doorway watching him. Just as the Gestapo were probably watching . . . and listening.

"Our Führer," he stammered softly. "He is dead?"

"Yes, Wilhelm. I just learned of it."

"Dead? Good God, who did it . . . the Russians?"

There was a long pause on the line. Canaris could almost hear

Sack thinking. The man knew exactly what Canaris had said, and why he had said it.

"It may be a rumor," Sack said.

"God, I hope so!"

"I don't know for sure. It is what I have heard," Sack said.

"Where will you be later this afternoon?"

Canaris' mind was moving rapidly. "My office, I think," he said. "Try here first, and then my office."

"I understand. I'll see what else I can find out. If you hear anything . . ." Sack let it trail off.

"Of course," Canaris said, and then there was a click on the line as Sack hung up.

Slowly Canaris put the handset down and he turned. Maurer was white-faced. Kaulbars was behind him.

"What is it?" Kaulbars asked.

"It was Karl Sack."

"Yes," Kaulbars said impatiently. "What news does he have?"

"It was our Führer. Someone has evidently assassinated him. In his Wolfsschanze near Rastenberg. A bomb, he said."

"My God," Maurer said softly.

"Has it been confirmed?" Kaulbars asked. His eyes were wide.

"Karl thought it had been."

The three men stood looking at each other. Mohammed, who had gone back to the kitchen, stood with the Polish cook looking out the door. They, too, were open-mouthed.

"What will you do, Willi?" Kaulbars finally asked.

"I think I shall go to my office. I may be needed there."

"One cannot tell in which way fate will fall," Maurer said vacantly, almost as if he were in a trance.

"Thank you, Uncle Mau, I think you are most certainly correct. At this moment it is Deutschland I am thinking about."

"*Über Alles*?" Kaulbars asked gently.

"*Nein*," Canaris replied. "*Für uns, nur für uns*—only for us."

Canaris' driver, Hans Lüdecke, drove him down to Eiche as the sun got lower in the summer sky. It would be a while yet before it was dark, but already there seemed to be a strange chill in the air.

"Shall I remain, Herr Admiral?" his driver asked at the office building.

"No, you may return home. I shall call when I am ready."

Lüdecke nodded. But he did not immediately drive off. Instead, he remained there for a long moment. Canaris looked at him with impatience. There was a lot to do tonight. Many decisions to be made. All before dark.

"What is it, Hans?" he asked.

"Is it true, Herr Admiral? About our Führer?"

"I don't know," Canaris said. At that moment he had a very sharply defined sense of history. In one sense he felt somewhat melodramatic, but in another he felt that he was in the midst of a great historical event in the making. Chroniclers would be marking his words, even the simplest of his pronouncements. "We can only pray to God that the right thing for Germany has occurred."

"Yes, *meiner* Admiral," Lüdecke said. He drove off.

Canaris turned and went into the building, the guard saluting.

Lights shown from all the HwK offices, and just inside, Lieutenant Bender was holding court with about three-quarters of the staff. They all jumped to attention when he came in.

He returned their salute, then charged directly through to his office, Bender right on his heels.

"We just heard an hour ago," the lieutenant said.

"Who told you?"

"Colonel Schrader telephoned, asking for you. He told me. I told the others . . . naturally."

"Naturally," Canaris said dryly. "Get me Major Meitner on the telephone. I imagine he will be at Maybach II."

"Yes, sir," Bender said.

Canaris left the office as Bender was on the phone. He stepped next door to the office of Economic Adjustments, and went in. Captain Marks, whom he had gotten to know quite well over the past weeks, was there with his secretary.

"Herr Admiral," the captain said.

"Donni, I need to use your telephone for just a single important call. All my lines are tied up just now."

"Of course, Herr Admiral, of course," Marks said. He jumped up and went into the outer office. Canaris dialed the Zossen operator. "Major Meitner," he said when the connection had been made.

"His line is busy."

"Break in on him; this is a Reich Priority call."

"Of course, sir."

Meitner was out of breath. "Yes?" he asked.

"Is it true?" Canaris asked, keeping his voice low.

Meitner sucked his breath. "No. It is not true. Do you understand?"

"You are certain?"

"Yes."

Canaris hung up. He had had a feeling about it. A hunch, if you will. Again he had curious feelings at cross-purposes; on the one hand, he was sorry that the madman was not dead, while on the other he was deeply relieved.

He thanked Marks, and back in his own office he took the phone from Bender, told Meitner, who was still holding, that his reports would be late this week, and then he hung up.

"We will send a telegram now," Canaris said to his adjutant.

"Sir?"

"To our Führer. A telegram congratulating him on his miraculous escape."

"Our Führer is alive?"

"Oh yes," Canaris said. "Did you ever doubt it?"

22

Schey knew it was time to leave.

The authorities had evidently picked up the man he was supposed to contact, and they knew that someone would be calling. They had been waiting for him. Which meant they knew he was here. Which meant they may even have picked up his radio transmissions. It had only been bad luck on their part that the police radio had been going when he called. Bad luck or poor planning.

The FBI would, of course, know his face from his employment file at Oak Ridge. They also knew something of his method of operation. In fact the more he thought about it, the more he realized that they may have been monitoring his radio transmissions all along.

He had to go. There was no question about that. He had gotten most of what he had come for. Now he was going to have to get the information back to Germany.

The question was: What about Eva? He did not want a repeat of Catherine. At this moment he knew, at last, that he loved her. Even more than he had loved poor Katy. Eva was a stronger, brighter woman. And yet she, too, had her frailties, her weaknesses. She, too, for all her sometime bravado, needed protection.

It was dark, and only the bar in Jemez Springs showed any lights as he drove through the tiny town and continued up to the ranch.

It came down to three choices. He could leave her here; he could just slip away in the night—this night—and never return. She would not go to the authorities, of course. But if the FBI was on to him, they'd be on to her as well. Leaving her here would be tantamount to guaranteeing her arrest.

He could take her with him. On the way down from Washington,

D.C., having her with him had not been so bad. But now he was going to be on the run, having her along would be like carrying excess baggage. She would not fit. She would get them both arrested, and they'd end up at the end of a hangman's rope.

There was a final option. If he could not leave her here and he could not take her with him, he would have to . . . kill her.

Driving the last mile or so through the night, he turned that final option over in his mind. He could not kill her, of course. Which meant he was going to have to take her with him. At least part of the way, just until he could figure out what to do with her. But she could not come to Germany with him. That was totally out of the question.

If he survived, then they'd see what came next, when the war was over. But they were going to have to get out of here tonight. There was no telling how fast the FBI would close in.

He increased his speed, the old pickup truck wheezing up the final hill, the dim green light on the broken speedometer casting an eerie glow in the cab. He had a sudden, terrible sense of urgency. As if he was running out of time and he was going to have to hurry to save his life.

A few minutes later he turned onto the ranch road, went through the gate, and headed up to the barn, a great sense of relief coming over him when he saw that everything appeared to be normal.

He hadn't known what to expect, but he was happy that nothing seemed to be out of the ordinary. No one was here. There were no flashing red lights. No policemen. No soldiers.

He parked by the barn, left the keys in the ignition, and walked back down to his place. The lights were on. He took a deep breath, held it a moment to relieve the tightness in his chest, and then let it out slowly.

At the cabin he glanced back up at the ranch house. There was a light on in the kitchen. George had probably gotten up to have a drink and a cigarette. He often did that.

Schey opened the door and stepped inside. Eva, still dressed, was sitting at the kitchen table. She was drinking a glass of wine. She looked up and shook her head.

"What . . ." he started to say.

A large man stepped out from behind the door. "Robert Mordley? You are under arrest," he said. He was wearing a large hat.

Another man came from outside and pushed the door all the way open. He hung back, though. He had a big pistol in his left hand.

The entire situation was crystal clear in Schey's brain. They had not been worried enough about his telephoning to make sure the police radio had been switched off, because at the moment he was calling them, they had their people on the way out here.

It must have given them fits to know that he was on the loose. But there would be reinforcements on the way out here now. So he did not have much time to defuse this situation and get the hell out.

"Evelyn? . . . Who the hell are these guys?" he demanded. He took a step forward. The man from behind the door stepped aside. Schey ignored him. "Are you fuckin' around on me again? Goddamnit!"

"Bobby . . . I," she said.

The man inside the shack pulled out his pistol, and he brought it up to bear on Schey. "Hold it right there."

Schey turned on him, ignoring the gun. "All right. Just who the hell do you think you are, anyway, coming in here like this? My wife alone."

"How long have you lived here, Mordley?"

"A long time, but my name isn't Mordley, you stupid son-of-a-bitch. It's Stromberg."

"Is that your latest alias?"

"Alias? Christ. Check with Romero up on the hill."

"We already did," the man from outside said.

Schey glanced over his shoulder. The man had come to the doorway. He looked very nervous. They evidently had a fair idea of who they were up against. Either that or they were very green. Schey suspected it might be a little of both.

"And what did George tell you? Probably that I was a god-damned German spy direct from Berlin!"

The door to their shack opened inward. Schey figured that if he could get the man in the doorway to come inside just another foot and if he could distract the second one, he might have a chance.

He wheeled around toward Eva, shaking his fist at her. "You miserable slut!" he shouted.

She jumped up, spilling her wine and screeching. It was exactly what he had wanted her to do. From the corner of his eye he could see that the inside man had turned toward her, bringing the barrel of his pistol around. The one from outside stepped farther into the cabin.

Schey reached back and slammed the door, catching the outside man full in the face. He shifted his weight to the left, away from the inside man's gun as it came around, and he charged. His left hand went out to deflect the pistol; his right went to the man's face. The pistol went off, the roar huge in the tiny space, and Schey's right hook connected, snapping the man's head back, his hat flying.

The outside man had just started to regain his balance, when Schey tore open the door and was on him, his right hand behind the man's neck, his left on the man's forehead, and he shoved with all of his might. The man's neck broke with a loud pop. He fell to the dust as Schey spun around.

The inside man was up on his knees, shaking his head. The pistol was still held limply in his right hand.

In three steps Schey was on him, shifting his weight to his left foot and kicking out with his right. The toe of his heavy boot caught the FBI agent square in the chin, sending him backwards, his head bouncing off the floor.

Eva had gone to the bed. She was fumbling beneath it to where Schey kept the pistol he had taken from the FBI agent in Washington, D.C.

She turned around, the pistol in her shaking hands.

"It's all right," Schey said, holding his hands out.

Her eyes flicked from the man in the dust outside the door to the man lying flat on his back across the room.

"Oh Christ," she whimpered. She looked at Schey, the gun lowering. "Jesus . . . they're from the FBI."

"I know," Schey said. "We have to get out of here." He pulled the outside man back into the cabin and closed the door. Then he turned to the other man who was beginning to come around. He grabbed the pistol, checked to make sure it was loaded, and then pulled the man's wallet from his inside pocket and flipped it open.

Hubert Swanson, his ID read. Albuquerque. Federal Bureau of Investigation.

Swanson's eyes began to flutter. Schey looked up at Eva, who had remained crouched by the bed.

"Get me a blanket," he said.

"Bobby?" she whispered.

"Now!" Schey roared, and she jumped as if she had been slapped. She brought the blanket over. Schey spread it out on the floor, then rolled the FBI man onto it. He brought the muzzle of the long-barrelled .38 to the bridge of the man's nose and cocked the hammer.

"You will answer my questions, without hesitation, or I will immediately kill you," Schey said.

Swanson's eyes were open. He realized he was lying on a blanket. He knew what it meant. He voided in his trousers, a sudden stench rising from him. Schey ignored it. He knew that the man was convinced.

"Are there others on the way out here?"

The FBI agent nodded yes so violently that the back of his head banged against the floor.

"Police? More FBI? Soldiers? Who?"

"The Bureau," Swanson squeaked, barely able to talk.

"Christ," Schey swore. "How long have you known I was out here?"

"I . . ." the man said, but then he stopped.

Schey jammed the pistol hard against the bridge of Swanson's nose. "How long?"

"Just a day. We picked up your radio transmission the other night."

That was it then, Schey thought. There wasn't the slightest hope that they might have made a mistake. That they might not yet be a hundred-percent convinced. There was only one thing left for him to do now. It was purely a matter of survival. For the Reich.

The FBI agent read Schey's thought from his eyes. His eyes went wide and he started to raise his right hand, as if to ward off a blow, when Schey pulled the trigger.

The gun bucked in Schey's hand, blood and bits of bone splattering outwards from the hole in the agent's head.

Eva cried out. Schey got to his feet and turned around, the smoking pistol in his hand. Eva shrank back.

"It was him or us," Schey said. "If you don't understand that, then you can remain here."

She stood her ground. One of their suitcases lay open on the small bed. The other was on the floor beside it. She held a pile of clothing in her arms.

Schey shoved the pistol in his belt and went to her. She shrank back for just an instant, and then fell into his arms, the clothing falling to the floor.

"Oh . . . Bobby, what have we done," she cried.

"It was either them or us. And more of them are on the way. We have to leave. Now."

They parted and looked into each other's eyes. She was frightened, and very sad.

"It was nice here for a while, wasn't it, Bobby? We had a good life."

Schey forced a smile. "It's nothing compared to the life we're going to have when this is all over."

Eva looked at the dead men. "Did we have to kill them?"

"Pack," Schey said.

He turned away and went to Swanson. He kneeled beside the body, and went through the man's pockets. He found the car keys in a jacket pocket. He flipped the blanket over the body.

"I'll bring the car down," he said, and he slipped outside.

He had not seen their car on the way in, which meant they must have parked it behind the barn. Which also meant the agent had not lied; they had talked to Romero.

Schey looked up toward the ranch house. The kitchen light was still on. George was up there waiting. Waiting to find out the outcome.

Schey trotted up to the barn, all his senses alert for the slightest out-of-place sound. A small, gray two-door Chevrolet was parked behind the barn. It looked like a '37 or '38, and it had government plates.

On the back floor was a riot shotgun. A box of shells was beside it.

Schey pulled out the gun, loaded five shells into it, then got behind the wheel, started the engine, and drove back down to his cabin. He opened the trunk.

Inside, Eva was just finishing packing. Schey pulled the first man out the door and heaved his body up into the trunk of the Chevy. Back inside, he dragged the second man out; he stuffed his body on top of the other. Then he closed the trunk lid. The stench was terrible.

He took the suitcases from Eva, shoved them in the back seat, then pulled a chair out into the middle of the floor, opened the ceiling trapdoor, and brought down his radio. He reached back up into the attic and fumbled around in the insulation until he found the license plates from the Hudson. There was still two months on them.

He grabbed a screwdriver from the cabinet, went outside, and quickly switched plates. Eva came out when he was finishing.

"What about the Romeros?" she asked.

"What about them?" Schey asked, looking up.

"Are you going to kill them, too?"

Schey threw the screwdriver in the back seat, then took Eva in his arms. "Listen to me, and listen to me good," he said.

She hiccoughed.

"We're in a war. I'm a German. I love my country. I'll do whatever it takes to ensure we win."

"Oh . . . Bobby."

"No, listen to me, Eva," he said, shaking her. "We don't have a lot of time. We're going to have to get out of here. But unless you're with me one hundred percent, you'll have to stay behind."

"Then you'll kill me?"

"Stop it!" Schey shouted. "Stop it." He shook her again. And then they were in each other's arms, kissing deeply, the sensation so terribly strange—from danger to murder to this. Schey was confused.

"I don't understand anymore," she said when they parted.

"That doesn't matter. For now we have to get away. There'll be more FBI out there. And if we get caught, they'll hang us."

"I know," Eva said. It was all she could do to keep from crying.

"Have you got all our things?" he asked.

She nodded vacantly.

Inside, Schey grabbed the agent's hat, and jammed it on his head; then back outside, he climbed behind the wheel and started the motor. Eva got in. Schey flipped on the lights, pulled the hat low, and slowly headed up past the ranch house on his way out the front gate.

George Romero came out onto the porch. Eva looked up at him. Romero raised his right hand to wave at her, but then dropped it.

Schey raised his right hand and waved. Romero hesitantly waved back.

23

The Chevy's engine ticked over slowly as Schey looked both ways up State Highway 44. He tried to decide which direction he should go.

Within the next fifteen to twenty minutes, perhaps sooner, the FBI reinforcements would be coming up this highway from Santa Fe in the east. If he turned that way, he would run the risk of meeting them. They'd recognize the car. But to the northwest was nothing . . . mountains, the tiny towns of Cuba and Counselor, and eventually the Colorado state line. If he turned that way, they would gain a couple of hours, perhaps more. But by morning, if they had not been found, planes would be put up from Kirtland Field down in Albuquerque. It would not take very long to find the small gray Chevrolet with a man and a woman.

Eva was staring wide-eyed at him. She was frightened nearly out of her mind. But she was still functioning. She hadn't given up.

"Are they coming?" she asked.

"Not yet. But it won't be long now," he said. There was nothing to the north, he kept telling himself.

He put the car in gear and turned toward the east, working his way up through the gears. He reached up and twisted the rearview mirror over.

"Watch in the mirror for lights behind us," he said.

She practically jumped out of her skin. "Are they coming that way?" she asked. She turned and looked out the rear window. "Christ, Bobby, have they got us surrounded?"

"I don't think so, but I want to know the moment you see anyone back there. I don't want any surprises."

"Okay," she said after a moment. She adjusted the mirror, then sat there staring up into it, her hands folded on her lap.

At that moment Schey felt a great wave of love for her. He knew that she would follow him to hell and back if he told her to. She'd even follow him back to Germany. But that was totally out of the question. This was not her fight. Despite her protestations to the contrary, she was an American. She had been raised by a German family, but they were all gone now. She had been a member of the Bund, but that was gone too. Everything else in her life had been American.

Eva fell silent as Schey drove. His every sense was at a raw edge. The moment he saw a light on the highway ahead of them, he was going to have to pull over to the side of the road and hide the car. But just at this moment there weren't very many places for him to conceal the car. The ditch at the side of the road was very shallow, the trees sparse.

He began to think ahead. There was a very definite procedure for when it was time for him to get out of the country. His contact this time was in New York City. He had two telephone numbers to call. If both of them were bad, he still had his radio. He could try to get through. Get new instructions. But from now on he was going to have to be very careful. He was going to have to assume that all of his contacts were compromised. After all, it had been a very long time since it all had been set up by Canaris. Nothing lasted forever.

He would still have to do something with the car tonight. It was too easily recognizable, even with the Hudson's plates. Besides that risk, there was the chance he might be stopped for a routine traffic matter and the bodies would be found in the trunk.

He had taken the bodies so that when the agents showed up at the ranch, they'd be slowed down, believing that the other two had successfully arrested Schey and Eva and were on their way back to Santa Fe.

Far away on the horizon to the east, Schey detected a pinpoint of light, and then it was gone. It was a car on the highway. He knew it!

He switched off the Chevy's headlights, the road ahead plunging into darkness. Eva gasped.

"Watch to the rear!" he shouted. There was nowhere to pull off. Nowhere to hide. No trees, not even any brush.

Schey pressed down harder on the accelerator as his night vision began to improve. He caught another glimpse of the lights on the highway to the east. There were three . . . perhaps four, sets. It wasn't just some farmer returning home after a night in town. They were coming after him and Eva.

Well off to the south, outlined against the ridge of a hill, Schey spotted what appeared to be an old ramshackle barn or storage shed. Even from here he could see by its outline that it was half fallen-down. He sped up, the accelerator pedal jammed to the floor, and the little car surged forward.

It was going to be very close, he figured. He'd make it to the road up to the barn before the headlights, but he didn't know if he'd make it up the hill in time.

At length he slammed on the Chevy's brakes as they came to a deeply rutted dirt track that led up to the building. They slid on two wheels around the corner.

The headlights of the approaching vehicles were getting uncomfortably close now. If they spotted the Chevy making its way up the hill, they'd know—or at least suspect—what was happening. Someone would come up to investigate.

The car was bottoming out on its springs, and sweat began to pop out on Schey's forehead. It would be too damned close. Eva was shouting something as she held on, but Schey was too busy to make any sense of it.

They careened around the back of the falling-down barn, and Schey stood on the brake, the Chevy slewing to the left and finally sliding to a halt.

He jumped out of the car and hurried back to the corner of the barn.

Below, on the highway, the lights raced past the dirt road and continued, their tires whining on the asphalt, their red taillights visible for a long way in the night.

Schey hurried back to the car.

"Are they gone?" Eva asked fearfully.

"They're past," Schey said. He spun the car around and raced down the dirt track, back to the highway.

They drove another five miles to U.S. 85, which led south to Albuquerque and north to Santa Fe. It was only ten or twelve miles down to Albuquerque, but nearly forty miles back up to Santa Fe. The FBI agents had come from the north. There would be others. Certainly, when they finished at the ranch, they'd head back to Santa Fe. It was not the direction to go.

A truck passed, heading south. Schey turned south and headed after it.

"Where are we going?" Eva asked.

A car passed them, going in the opposite direction, its headlights momentarily illuminating the interior of their car.

"To Albuquerque," Schey said absently. He reached up and twisted the rearview mirror back so that he could see.

"They'll find us there," she said, panicky. "They'll know this car. We'll be arrested. Christ, they'll hang us." She grabbed his arm.

Schey pulled away from her. "They have to catch us first. And they won't do that."

"How can you be so sure?"

Schey had been going on nervous energy now for hours. He snapped at her. "I'm bloody well not sure, goddamnit! But I'm not going to lie on the side of the road, crying my eyes out, waiting for them to come get me!"

"Oh sure . . . you can say that. You've got somewhere to go. You've got yourself a goddamned cause. What the hell do I have?"

"You've got me! If I'm not good enough for you, then the hell with it!"

They had been shouting. Eva choked off her next words as she gazed at him in wonder. Another car passed, going the opposite way, and it made her face seem white, her eyes very large and very dark.

"You operated in Washington right under the nose of an FBI agent. You didn't fall apart then. If you're coming with me now, you're going to have to hold yourself together."

She nodded. "Do you mean that, Bobby? That I'm coming with you?"

"It's up to you," he said. "But I'm not going to beg you. It's not going to be easy getting out of here, and it sure as hell isn't going to be a piece of cake back home."

"I don't care. I'll go anywhere you say. I love you. Don't you know that? Haven't you got that figured out yet, you big ape?"

Schey had to laugh, not so much at the colloquial English, but at the situation. It was very likely they would never get out of the New Mexican desert alive, and he was worrying about how difficult it would be for them in Germany with the war ending and all. Eternal optimism, or just plain stupidity? He wondered.

"If that's funny, then I've been way off all along," she said peevishly.

Schey glanced over at her. He was smiling. He could not help himself.

"Jesus," she said, looking away momentarily. "Jesus H. Our backs are against the wall, and you're grinning like a coon eating shit."

Schey laughed out loud. His stomach convulsed, which struck him even funnier, and he laughed harder.

"Bobby?" Eva shouted alarmed.

He couldn't stop. It was nearly impossible to see the highway through the tears in his eyes and even harder to control the car.

A part of him understood that there was absolutely nothing humorous about their situation, and yet it felt good to let go now that the immediate crisis was past. He could not remember the last time he had laughed.

Eva finally laughed, then looked away, her right hand to her mouth. She was fighting it, but at last she too succumbed, and she began to laugh very hard, tears rolling down her cheeks.

The highway ran straight as a ruler down out of the high plateau on which Santa Fe was located, to the desert flats where Albuquerque sprawled. The temperature rose at least ten degrees within as many miles, and as they came into the city, the Atchison, Topeka & Santa Fe railroad line was off to their right.

The speed limit changed from 65 down to 45 and finally to 30 as they came into the city.

Ahead, and far off to the right, Schey spotted a railroad depot. A passenger train had pulled in. They came to the access road, and the sign said: HAHN STATION: A.T.&S.F.

They drove down the road, coming into the station's parking lot. The depot itself was nothing more than a long, low wooden structure. A dozen cars and two trucks were parked in front. Schey drove around to the far end of the uneven row and parked well in front of the largest truck so that the Chevy would not be so noticeable from the highway.

"We can't take a train from here," Eva said. "What's the matter with you? They'll spot the car, and then they'll have us."

Schey got out, and making sure no one was watching, threw the keys across the tracks well out into the brush.

Eva got out of the car. "What are you doing?" she demanded.

Schey reached in the back seat and grabbed their bags. "We're

Mr. and Mrs. Veltman. Karl and Elizabeth. Our car broke down. We're trying to get to Denver. We both have jobs waiting for us.''

He shut the door, handed one of the bags to Eva, and started across the graveled parking lot back to the dirt road that led out to the highway. Eva bounced after him. She wore a white blouse, long black skirt, and low tie shoes with medium heels. Her hair was done up in a bun with a scarf around it. She looked typically middle-American.

''Hey, wait up,'' she puffed, catching up with him. But he did not slow down, and she finally fell in with his pace.

It was several blocks around to the highway, across a broad, grassy field. There were houses and streetlights across the tracks from the station behind them, but ahead there was nothing but the highway, although well to the southwest, at least a couple of miles away, they could see the green and white flashes of an airfield.

She asked him about it.

''It's the Cutter-Carr Airfield,'' Schey said. He had studied maps of the entire area. ''It's called Number Two.''

''So where's Number One?''

Schey shrugged. ''You got me.''

It took them nearly ten minutes to get back out to the highway, and Schey was hot. It was very much warmer down here than it had been up in the mountains. Of course, it was high summer, and he should have expected this.

A big truck lumbered up the highway from town, and Schey stepped up onto the edge of the pavement and stuck out his thumb.

The truck rumbled by, its wake hauling a great gust full of dirt over them. Eva jumped back, coughing and rubbing her eyes.

''Christ, don't you know nothing?'' she snapped crossly. She bodily shoved him aside. ''Go sit on the suitcases.''

Schey moved back off the side of the road. For just a minute or so the night was exceedingly quiet. Even more silent than the high country where night birds screeched and where the insects whined. Here it was absolutely still.

Eva stepped back as two cars, a truck, and a bus came by from the north, their tires whining on the pavement, audible even before they were visible.

A pair of headlights came their way from the south, and Eva

stepped out onto the edge of the highway and lifted her skirt well above her knees, exposing the tops of her nylons and a lot of her thighs.

The car flashed by, but screeched to a halt just beyond where Eva stood. It was a big four-door Pontiac. A '39.

"Wait here," she shouted back to Schey, and she hurried up to the car, her shoes crunching on the gravel.

She leaned into the driver's window and hung there for a long time. Schey stepped up onto the roadway. He couldn't see her head and shoulders, only the white blouse at the small of her back and the curve of her bottom.

He was about to go to her, when she pulled away and looked back. She was smiling. She waved him on.

Schey hurried down into the ditch, grabbed their bags, and rushed up to where she had gone around to the passenger side of the car.

Schey threw their bags in the back seat after Eva crawled in, and then he climbed into the front seat. A very fat man sat behind the wheel which rubbed his bare belly where his pullover shirt had hiked up. The man had stuffed a large red and black handkerchief between the bottom rim of the steering wheel and his belly to avoid chafe. He was smiling uncertainly.

"This isn't what it looks like, believe me," Schey said, sticking out his hand and smiling.

The fat man just looked at him for a moment, but then he reached out and shook Schey's hand. "I saw the girl . . . the . . ."

"My wife," Schey said. "I'm Karl Veltman. My wife's Elizabeth. Our car broke down." Schey looked out the windshield. "Hell, the mechanic said it'd take weeks, maybe forever, before we'd get the parts. And a hell of a lot more money than we've got."

"We're headed up to Denver," Eva said from the back seat. She leaned up over the back of the front seat, between Schey and the fat man. "We both got jobs up there." She grinned. "Course, the jobs don't do us a bit of good unless we can get to 'em. You headed up that way?"

"I'm going over to Tucumcari. Route 66. 'Fraid I'm going in the wrong direction for you," the fat man said. His voice was gentle and pleasant.

Shit, Schey thought. He reached leisurely into his pocket for the gun, but then decided against it. He was not a common murderer. If he did kill this man, his body would be found and the chase would be on.

"Hell," Schey said.

Eva said something in the back, but he ignored her. "Tucumcari. We might be able to get over to Amarillo and get a ride up from there easier than from down here."

"The Raton Pass is open, if that's what you're worried about," the fat man said. They still had not moved. Several cars and a truck had passed them on the highway. Schey felt very exposed here. But he also had the feeling that the man was lying to them.

"No, it's the traffic. Can't get a ride if there's no cars on the highway."

The fat man shook his head.

"Look," Schey said, taking a chance. He reached for the car door and opened it. "Thanks, anyway. But if you don't want to help us out, we understand." Schey half turned toward the back. "Don't we, honey?" he said.

"Sure," Eva said on cue. "It'll be morning before too long."

"Close the door," the fat man said after a moment's hesitation. "Damnation, ain't nobody going to accuse me of leavin' someone to camp out all night on some stupid highway."

Schey looked at the man. "You sure now?"

"Yeah, sure," the fat man said. "Close the door."

Schey closed the door. The fat man pulled away from the side of the road, accelerated through the gears, and then looked in the mirror at Eva.

"If you don't mind me saying so, ma'am, you sure got a nice set of gams."

Schey had to laugh. Eva did too. "Why, thank you, Mr. . . ?" Eva's voice trailed into a question mark.

"Shamus. Burt Shamus. I work for Westinghouse. We just shipped a big load into Albuquerque. It's headed up to Santa Fe someplace. I had to ride along to make sure no one swiped it."

"Whose car?" Schey asked. Westinghouse was one of the prime contractors for the Manhattan Project.

"Company car," Shamus said.

"So, what're you doing heading over to Tucumcari?"

Shamus shook his head. He seemed embarrassed. "Ain't so," he said. He glanced over at Schey. "I was lying."

"Where you headed then?"

"Denver," Shamus said. "Denver, Colorado, and you and your missus are welcome to ride along."

24

"They've killed him! The generals have killed him in Rastenburg," Marti screamed as she raced down the broad corridor.

Deland looked up toward the stairs. Dannsiger and the others seated around the long, narrow table in the basement of the girls' school looked up as well. It was late.

Marti's voice echoed off the corridor walls. She kept screaming. They listened as she clattered down the stairs.

"They've killed him! My God, they've killed him!"

Deland jumped up and met the distraught woman at the open steel door. Her hair was disheveled, her eyes wild, her complexion pale. She was out of breath as she fell into Deland's arms.

"Oh . . . God, Helmut, they're talking about it on the street. They say it's on the radio."

"Did you hear an official broadcast?" Deland demanded, grabbing her shoulders.

They had worked for the past three days on a plot to get to the Führer at his bunker. They knew he was gone at the moment (although they had no idea where) by the fact security around the Reichs Bunker was so lax.

"Everyone is talking about it! Don't you believe me?" She squirmed out of his grasp and ran to Dannsiger. "It's true," she shouted, looking into his eyes. "There was a bomb at his bunker in Rastenberg. It exploded and he was killed. The war is over!" There was a joyous, though oddly pitched tone to her voice.

Deland suspected she was finally on the verge of cracking up. It was a wonder they weren't all crazy by now. Over the past few days Marti had hung on their plot to kill Hitler. For her, it symbolized the end of the war, although she understood that peace would not be quite so easily obtained. She, like the others, knew that there would be a lot more suffering in Berlin before they began the long road back.

"Let's hope it's true," Dannsiger said. He sent two of the others up to see if they could find out for sure. Then he turned to Deland. "I'm glad it happened now. There isn't a chance of success with this, Helmut." He glanced at the sketch diagrams of the bunker. "You understand that, don't you?"

Deland nodded. Their own plot to kill Hitler *was* impossible. They had known it from the beginning. Only now were they willing to face it.

Tonight he would radio Bern and tell them that they had thought it out, but that the job could not be done. They would order him out then. But now he wasn't at all sure he wanted to leave.

Marti was looking from Dannsiger to Deland and back again. At this particular moment she seemed so tiny, so frail. Like all of them, she had not been getting enough to eat. She had been thin in the first place; now, when she was undressed and they were making love, Deland could see and feel her ribs, and her pelvis jutted out from her pale, nearly blue skin.

"What are you talking about?" she screamed. "Didn't you hear me? He is dead! The generals have killed him!"

Dannsiger took her shoulders. "Listen, Marti, it may not be true. We have heard this news before."

"No!" she screeched. She backed off.

"If it is true, then the war will soon end, although it will be very difficult for us in Berlin," Dannsiger said, glancing at Deland. "If it is not true, if they tried to kill him and failed as they have each time before, then it will still be very difficult here in Berlin. For all of us."

"No," she whimpered.

"You will have to hold yourself together a little longer, my dear."

"It'll be all over, in any event, very soon," Deland said.

She looked at him, her eyes very wide, and doelike. "You're both in this together," she said. "This is a big game for you. Men love to make war. It is they who start them, they who fight them. It is us women who must suffer." She was nearly irrational now.

"It's not true, Marti," Dannsiger said gently.

She backed farther off.

Stay or go, Deland thought, watching her. He did not love her. Or at least he didn't think he did, but he felt so damned responsible for her well-being. He could not simply desert her. No matter what happened.

He glanced at the sketches. That project was out. But there was the other thing he had been avoiding. If he remained here in Berlin, it would have to be attended to immediately. His own survival was at stake.

Deland stepped around the table and went over to Marti, but she shrank back to the doorway.

"You're no different," she said. "You don't want it to end. You enjoy this."

Stay or go, he asked himself again. The question was like a metronome in his head. If he was going, it would have to be very soon, now that their own plot to assassinate the Führer was scrapped. And if he was staying, he would have to deal with Rudy Gerhardt.

"Why don't you go upstairs to your room?" Deland said.

She didn't move.

"We will tell you when we find out for sure."

Someone came down the stairs, and Marti shrank away from the steel door.

One of Dannsiger's people came in. He was holding himself stiffly erect, as if he had been hurt. There was a terribly pained expression on his face, deep in his eyes. It took Deland's breath away.

"What is it, Karl? What has happened?"

"It is on the radio. The bomb . . . failed to do the job."

"Hitler lives?"

Karl nodded. "The Führer lives. He wasn't even hurt, the announcer said. They are playing marching music." He lowered his head, held it there for a moment, and then raised his hands to his face and began to weep bitterly, his shoulders heaving. But he made no noise.

Marti stared at him for a long time. She shuddered, then rushed out of the room and raced upstairs.

For a long time Dannsiger and Deland stood in embarrassed silence as the other man cried. Deland was the first to move.

"Destroy our sketches. I'll radio and tell them it's a no-go."

"You don't want to . . . try?" Dannsiger asked.

"No."

"Are you going to leave us?"

The question was really hammering inside Deland's skull now. He shook his head. "No," he said. "I'm staying." He had not told anyone about Gerhardt. But how could he? The man wore the Iron Cross. His leg had been shot off. He was a hero of the Reich. How did you plan to kill a German hero and tell other Germans about it? Dannsiger and the others hated Hitler, not Germany.

"Are you all right?" Dannsiger asked. He sensed something was wrong.

"Yes," Deland said. "I'll send the message now."

"Will you be back this evening?"

Deland was about to say no, but then he looked toward the stairs. Marti would be needing him. And he knew that he would be needing her. He nodded. "Later," he said.

He thought about taking a gun, but decided against it. The noise would be far too loud, unless another bombing raid was going on at the exact moment he needed to use it.

He also thought about a knife, but in his mind's eye he could see the gruesome mess it had created in Maria Quelle's apartment in Wolgast.

He was being a fool. On several counts. It would not be easy to run now. In fact, it would be very difficult merely to get out of Berlin. But that was nothing in comparison to what he knew he would have to do tonight.

If it ever got out that he had killed a hero of the Reich, his life in Germany would be forfeit. Even Dannsiger and his people would have no use for him.

Gerhardt lived to the north, just within Wedding. It was very dark outside when Deland left the girls' school, hesitated a moment within the gate, and then hurried up the street.

A low overcast was beginning to move in again. There would be no air raid tonight. In the distance he thought he could hear martial music, but then it faded as the gentle breeze switched directions.

Gerhardt had given him his address only after Deland had promised to bring some eggs. "Eggs, my God, it has been so long since I have had an egg."

"Are you married yet, Rudy?" Deland had asked. "Children?"

Gerhardt shook his head sadly. "I had a girl. But afterwards . . . after my leg, she went away."

"How about your parents?"

"They're dead, Robert. Their apartment building got a direct hit. They were on the top floor . . . American bombs . . ."

"I'm sorry," Deland said, touching the man's arm.

Gerhardt smiled wanly. "Eggs. Even if you could only get one from the quartermaster . . . tell him I would trade for this . . ." He held out his Iron Cross.

"That's all right," Deland said. "I will bring you some eggs."

"Soon?"

"Very soon."

Deland kept seeing Gerhardt's hopeful eyes as he continued across town through the quiet night. The city would be in shock from the news about the Führer's near assassination and weary from the constant air raids over the past few nights. This was not a night to be caught out. Yet he did not think there would be many people on the streets. Even the soldiers would be sticking close to their posts. Everyone would be on full alert. But if a chance patrol caught him, he would be shot on sight.

It was just midnight when he made it to Wedding, and three blocks later he reached Gerhardt's apartment building in an area of shattered buildings, piles of rubble making many of the streets all but impassable and garbage piled in heaps.

He could smell wood smoke, and something else, some sickly sweet odor of cooking. He did not want to think just what it was someone was cooking as he passed. The people of Berlin were becoming desperate.

He stopped in the shadows at the corner and studied the street. He did not want to be caught in any kind of a trap. Gerhardt might just as well have contacted the Gestapo. They could be waiting for him.

He turned and worked his way around to the far end of the street, then went through a debris-choked courtyard and along the narrow alley behind the buildings.

It was pitch-black. Every few yards he had to stop and look up toward the overcast sky in order to get his bearings.

Once he stopped and almost turned around and left. He was suddenly feeling very guilty about Gerhardt and about the promised eggs.

Everything depended upon this night, though. If Gerhardt was not dealt with, sooner or later the man *would* go to the authorities (if he hadn't already) and tell them about Deland, his old Göttingen school chum. He'd tell them where he had seen Deland. They'd close in on the school. So it wouldn't be his own life that would be forfeit. At risk now were the lives of Dannsiger, Marti, and the other underground fighters, as well as the Allied crewmen processed through the basement.

He had to climb over a pile of rubble beneath several thick wood beams that lay across the alley before he came to the back of Gerhardt's building.

Most of the rear of the apartment complex had been shattered by a near miss in some bombing raid. Deland picked his way carefully through the jumbled piles of brick and wood and glass and bits of furniture, finally crawling around a canvas curtain that covered the opening into the front portion of the first-floor stair hall.

The building smelled of urine and human feces. Water dripped from a section of ceiling that was half falling down.

Deland stepped around it and started up the stairs. Gerhardt said he lived on the third floor, just to the left of the stairwell. He lived alone.

At the first landing Deland stopped and held his breath so that he could listen for any sound. There was nothing, only the overpowering odor in his nostrils that made his stomach churn. He was certain that everyone in the building could hear his pounding heart.

In school Gerhardt had not been a bad sort. Somewhat aloof, if Deland remembered correctly, superior that he was a German—a true Aryan—and Deland simply an American. Gerhardt used to make jokes about the Polacks and about the dirty Frogs, but he was condescending about Americans.

Deland continued up a step at a time, careful not to trip over the garbage that lay everywhere.

At the third-floor landing he could hear the sound of dripping water again. Toward the back of the corridor he could see the roof of the building across the narrow alley. Suddenly he realized that there was a gaping hole in the building. The third floor corridor ended at the hole. Most of the ceiling and back wall were gone.

Something felt very wrong to Deland. He could almost sense it in the air. He felt as if a million eyes were watching him from the darkness. Suddenly he had a terrible sense of claustrophobia, of frustration with what he was doing. One more death in the midst of all this death and destruction: Could it mean anything toward the final outcome?

He stepped away from the stairs, crossed the narrow, filthy corridor and reached out to touch the door. It was the only one on this side. He realized that Gerhardt's apartment fronted on the street. He listened a moment longer, but hearing nothing he tried the door. It was not locked.

Deland pushed it open, a terrible stench coming from inside, making him gag. When his stomach settled, he held his breath again to listen. Someone was inside the pitch-black room. He could hear the regular breathing.

He stepped inside and closed the door. The odors were of human waste, of a long-unwashed body, and of some rotting, putrescent wound; the last smell was cloyingly sweet.

"Rudy?" he called softly. There had to be blackout curtains on the windows.

The breathing across the room was interrupted.

"Rudy?" he called softly again.

"*Wer ist*?" Gerhardt said. Deland recognized his voice.

"It is me: Robert. I have brought you some eggs," Deland said, hating the lie. He was shaking.

There was a shuffling. A match was struck. Rudy Gerhardt, sitting up in the middle of a pile of filthy rags and blankets beneath the curtains at the window, reached with the flame toward a candle. "Robert," he said, smiling. "You've finally come."

It was all wrong! Gerhardt didn't give a damn about the eggs, after all. But he had been waiting for Deland to show up.

Gerhardt reached up for the blackout curtains. Deland leaped forward, slamming into the man's chest, knocking him back away from the window, his fingers seeking and finding Gerhardt's throat.

The lit candle fell over as Gerhardt struggled against Deland's powerful grasp. But he was a sick man, undernourished and very weak. His single leg thrashed; a horrible smell came from the rotting stump of his blown-off leg.

"Oh God." The cry choked in Deland's throat, as he squeezed harder, his powerful grasp crushing Gerhardt's windpipe. Tears streamed down from Deland's eyes. This was a nightmare from which he knew he would never be free.

Gerhardt had only wanted eggs. He had wanted food. Nothing more.

Gerhardt's struggles rapidly diminished, and in the end he lay still.

A corner of the blackout curtains had caught fire from the candle, the flames growing at an alarming rate.

Deland released his grip and fell back away from Gerhardt's corpse. His stomach heaved, and he vomited, his entire body shaking as he was wracked with terrible chills.

The flames continued to grow, licking the ceiling now, and Deland fell farther back toward the door.

"Rudy," he said. "I'm sorry, Rudy . . ."

For a second or two he contemplated tearing the curtains down and trying to put out the fire. But it was already too late. It would be better this way. The fire would cover the murder.

Sirens sounded from outside. Very close. Deland scrambled to his feet in the corridor as the downstairs door crashed open. Someone shouted orders, and there was the sound of boots pounding on the stairs.

Deland spun around, the flames in Gerhardt's room building into an inferno, choking smoke filling the corridor. He raced to the jagged hole at the back of the building.

It had been a setup, after all! Gerhardt had recognized him! He had gone to the authorities! They had been waiting for him to show up!

Any second the Gestapo troops would be here. There was no other way out. He stepped back, and then sprinted forward, leaping out through the shattered back wall, out into the darkness, down to the debris-choked alley three stories below.

He landed very hard on the roof of the building, rolled once, and then barely knowing what he was doing because the breath had been knocked out of him, he scrambled around the corner of a shed, through a steel door, and down the stairs into the dark interior of the partially destroyed building.

This one smelled of boiled cabbage and onions, and he could hear a baby crying.

Careful to make as little noise as possible, although he must have made a terrible racket landing on the roof the way he had, Deland hurried down the stairs to the ground floor.

Outside, there were a lot of sirens and sounds of shouting. Flames from the burning building were reflected on the corridor walls from the backdoor.

Deland made his way to the front door, opened it, peered outside. The block was empty. He stepped outside and without a backward glance hurried down the street, back toward Tiergarten. His mind turned around the only question that mattered any longer.

Stay or go? Or did he have the choice?

25

Berlin seemed more forbidding than ever. The increasing overcast assured there would be no Allied air raids tonight, but it also plunged the city into almost complete darkness.

Deland kept looking over his shoulder as he hurried through the rat maze of rubble and downed buildings, back into Tiergarten. For a long time he had been able to see the fire rising. But now he was too far away.

Gerhardt had called the Gestapo. They had been waiting!

Deland stopped on a wide avenue, across from a row of dark apartment buildings. He wasn't sure, but he thought it was Augsburger Strasse. The big cathedral on K'Damm would be just to the northwest. Sometimes it was hard to be certain about the streets.

There was absolutely no traffic. Nothing moved in any direction for as far as he could see. Nor were there any lights to be seen. It was as if the city had finally been deserted.

Evidently the Gestapo had not expected Deland to come the back way. They had missed him, although when Gerhardt lit his candle, he had smiled, evidently confident that help was on its way.

Deland's insides were quivering. He kept seeing Rudy's face; his eyes were bulging, a blue cast coming to his skin, his thick tongue protruding. Deland knew that he would smell the terrible odors in that room for the rest of his life. He would feel the thin bones and cartilage of Gerhardt's neck being crushed.

Three-quarters of a block to the north, a very large building had been knocked down into the street. Deland walked up to it and crossed the broad avenue within the protection of the maze of brick and huge sections of walls. The street seemed deserted, but he was very jumpy. He didn't want to take chances.

There was absolutely no question now about his remaining in

Berlin, or anywhere else in Germany, for that matter. He had come to that conclusion as he walked. In some respects he was glad it had come to this. He had been losing his nerve now for months. He did not think he could take much more of it. And there was no way the business with Marti Zimmer could be worked out to any degree of satisfaction.

He was not German. When the war was actually ended, life in Germany, and especially here in Berlin, was going to be very difficult. It would be a nightmare. He did not want to get caught in the final hours of the struggle.

It was going to be difficult getting out now. But they got fliers out. Dannsiger certainly could help get him to Switzerland.

It was well after two by the time he made it to within a block of his apartment building. He turned the corner and pulled up short. There were an Army troop truck and two civilian automobiles parked at an angle in front.

He ducked back against the building as someone shouted an order. A half dozen soldiers and three civilians emerged from his building. One of the soldiers carried something. He handed it to one of the civilians. For just that moment Deland was able to catch a glimpse of what it was the soldier had handed over. It was illuminated in the beam of the truck's headlights. It was his calculator-radio in its leather case. He recognized it by its shape and by the long shoulder strap.

The soldiers scrambled into the truck, and the civilians climbed into their cars. Deland turned and hurried back the way he had come, crossing the street where the collapsed building had blocked it.

They had his radio. He was cut off from any communication with Bern.

He was going to have to warn Dannsiger and the others. The Gestapo had found his apartment. But how? Gerhardt had gone to them and told them about his old school chum. An American, here now in Berlin. And they had waited for him to show up at Gerhardt's apartment. That he could understand. But how had they known about his place?

He passed again through Tiergarten, hurrying but still taking great care so that he would not be spotted. But the city remained as if deserted. The more he saw of it, the more he became nervous. It wasn't natural. It had to be because of the assassination attempt on Hitler. The city was frightened. Everyone was staying indoors.

He heard the guns three blocks away, and he knew exactly what was happening. He also suddenly knew how the Gestapo had found out where he lived. They had followed him from the girls' school. They had been following him, and probably the others, for several days now.

Gerhardt had told the Gestapo about his encounter. More importantly, he had told them exactly where he had seen Deland. They had evidently posted surveillance people there.

Deland cut through the shell of a building where the black market shop was located, the sound of gunfire much louder now. He crossed through the adjacent empty building, and finally from the basement through a cellar door, and up a service entrance stairway which was only three buildings from the girls' school. Alicia had shown him this escape route against the day the sewer tunnel was blocked off.

The shooting was very close now, and very fierce. He could hear the bullets ricocheting off the pavement.

Someone screamed. A man shouted for a medic. An instant later an artillery shell went off with a shattering roar that broke windows in all the buildings on the block and nearly knocked Deland down the stairs.

He regained his balance and eased up far enough so that he could see over the lip of the stairwell.

The entire block had been cordoned off. There were dozens of SS troops, and on the far side of the school a tank. Its 88 mm cannon, smoking, was pointed at the school.

Soldiers were barricaded behind piles of rubble, and behind their trucks and the tank itself. They were laying down a heavy screen of small arms fire into the building.

From where Deland crouched he could not see much of the front of the school, but he could hear that someone inside was firing back.

Evidently they hadn't had the chance to get out through the tunnel. Either that or a few of Dannsiger's people had elected to remain behind to cover the others' escape. It was a safe bet that no one still in the building would come out of this alive.

The tank fired its huge gun again, and Deland ducked as the explosion shook every building in the block, dirt and plaster raining down into the stairwell.

Marti was in there. Poor, confused Marti. She should have been the wife of a schoolteacher, or perhaps a college professor at a small university, living her life amid teas and weekend trips to the forests, not in this hell.

The German 88 fired a third time, a piece of the cornice above Deland breaking free and crashing down on the head of the stairs, a large piece of the concrete just missing him. He scrambled the rest of the way down the stairs and through the cellar door.

He could not remain here. It was all over for the underground. At least for the moment. Sooner or later the SS and the Gestapo would begin searching the buildings in this block, probably for several blocks on this side of the river.

He could not stay. He could not find out from here what happened to Dannsiger and Marti and the others.

He crossed through the basement, went up into the shell of the building, and cautiously emerged behind the black market corner.

Several more 88 rounds were fired in rapid succession as Deland hurried away in the opposite direction, his head down, but all his senses alert for danger. It would be difficult getting out of the city, but once free it would not be impossible to make it south. In his mind he could see a picture of Germany. Berlin was in the northeast, while Bern was directly south of Basel, across the Swiss border, in the extreme southwest. He would have to avoid the bigger cities—Leipzig, Frankfurt am Main, Stuttgart. But most of the military traffic he would have to fear traveled on the *Autobahn* system. He would not be on those roads in any event.

He had his work card and identification. But he had no travel permits with him. They were all back at the school, being re-done for the new month—which meant he would not be able to take a train.

He stopped and looked back the way he had come. It was possible that he could gain access to the basement by the river entrance. For a moment he considered it, but realized just how foolish that was. The Gestapo had had the building spotted for some time now. They certainly knew about the sewer outfall. And very soon they'd be inside anyway.

He did have some money, a couple hundred marks. It wasn't

much really, but then he wasn't going to be able to take a train, nor was he going to be eating in fancy restaurants, even if there were any.

He continued walking south until he crossed the Berliner Strasse bridge over the Spree to the west, and then he turned south again toward Charlottenberg.

A truck rumbled by, and a second later another truck ground its way up through the gears, and Deland shrank back. Suppliers and workmen were beginning to move about. The bakers would be at work now, with what little flour was available. The farmers would be straggling in for a pitifully meager market day. The morning railway people and trolley conductors would be showing up for work soon. Slowly the city was coming alive.

It was amazing, Deland thought, that despite the way the war was going—the Allies had invaded France—and despite the bombing raids, despite the shortages, life essentially went on as normal. Or at least it had a semblance of normalcy, although there wasn't enough food in the city and water and telephone service were often interrupted. The joke went that the only thing more unreliable than the electricity was a husband with four children who had two mistresses.

He crossed Kürfurstendamm, and an hour and a half later he was within the park at the edge of the Grosser Wansee in Zehlendorf.

There were many fashionable homes on the western shores of the lake, many of them belonging to high party officials. Security over there would be tight, so Deland stayed well away.

To the south and east of the lake were lesser residential areas, as well as the park and the railway line. It would be so convenient to merely board a train. But without travel permits—and money—it was impossible.

He stopped just at the edge of the park and peered out across the still well-tended lawns of the big houses. The railroad depot was not lit up, of course, but he could make out its bulk. The tracks ran out of the city to the southwest, across Dreilinden Strasse. Within a mile from the lake the city gradually gave way to farmlands, where there wouldn't be so many prying eyes.

How long would it take for a train coming out of the Grosser Wansee depot to accelerate to the point where it would be impossible to jump aboard? Within the city they would have to keep speeds low for fear the tracks would be blocked with bomb debris. They would not actually come to speed until they were well away from the danger.

He looked back across the park. Within the city there were plenty of places for him to hide. Out in the country he would be exposed. It would be more difficult. He shook his head. Berlin was impossible for him now. At least his mission to help downed Allied airmen out of the city was impossible for him.

Deland stepped out of the park, crossed the Wanseebad West, and went down to the lakeshore walkway. The air was much cooler near the water, and it smelled wonderful. Very soon the sun would be coming up, ruining his chances of escape for this night. Before it was light, he would have to be out of the city and aboard a train. Short of that, he would have to find a place to hide himself for the day.

He looked back again as he walked, but from here he could no longer see the depot. There might not even be another train until daylight. In that case he'd have to keep going on foot. He'd end up having to hide himself in the woods or perhaps in a farm field.

Around the west shore of the lake, Deland left the path and took the broad stairs back up to the main square, which branched to the north around a low marshy ground and to the southwest out toward the open countryside. A truck loaded with lumber rumbled along the southwest road, and Deland followed it, his stride long, his body leaning into the effort.

There had been roadblocks at several spots back in Berlin proper. But out here there didn't seem to be any military activity of any kind. It was peaceful. As he walked, he kept looking over his shoulder, as if he expected someone to be sneaking up on him. But besides the lumber truck, he saw no other traffic for a long time.

Deland pulled his coat collar up against the cool air. The residential areas gradually gave way to scattered vacant lots, and finally over a hill was a thick stand of trees, beyond which were the open fields, the railroad tracks to the left disappearing into the woods.

Deland went another half-mile before he crossed the highway, scrambled across the ditch beside the road, and climbed up into the woods. The railroad tracks ran through a clearing fifty yards from the highway, just below a sharp hummock. He leaned up against a tree above the track bed. From where he stood he could make out the tracks in both directions, as well as the highway half a mile back toward the city.

Normally, he thought, the night sky toward the northeast would be ablaze with the lights from Berlin. But this night the sky was dark. No lights shone from the city. It was as if Berlin were a gigantic ocean liner whose power had failed. She was adrift now in a very dark, very dangerous sea. All her passengers were doomed. It made him very sad.

Half an hour later the eastern horizon did seem lighter. Only it wasn't the city lights. It was the sun. Very soon it would be daylight. Deland could feel panic rising up inside of him.

This was no place for him to spend the day. It was too exposed. Anyone could come along and spot him. Yet there was no train.

He almost missed the single headlight coming up from the city. He had been staring down the tracks. But then the bobbing motion caught his eye, and he straightened up.

One headlight stabbed through the predawn darkness, coming around a curve in the road and disappearing in the shallow valley below the hill for just a moment.

At first Deland suspected it was a car or a truck with one of its headlights gone out. But as he watched, he could see that the headlight flashed back and forth too fast for that, its motion too erratic, and he understood it was a motorcycle.

A courier, possibly. With a uniform. With a travel pass. A legitimate reason to be out on the highway, day or night.

Deland shoved away from the tree and raced through the woods back to the highway, desperately searching, as he ran, for a downed tree limb. A branch. Something he could use as a club. But the woods had been scoured clean. Every scrap of firewood had been picked up.

The motorcycle topped the rise about three hundred yards away as Deland hesitated beside the ditch. There wasn't going to be a thing he could do about it. The motorcycle would pass and that would be the end of it.

Deland's eye finally lighted on a pile of loose rocks around the opening of a drainage culvert that ran beneath the road.

He could hear the sharp roar of the motorcycle now as he

scrambled down into the ditch, grabbed a fist-sized rock, then crouched low, ready to spring.

The headlight flashed high on the trees and then the bike was passing.

Deland straightened up, bringing his arm back, and he threw the rock, leading the helmeted driver by several feet.

Deland got the impression of a pair of goggles turning toward him just before the rock struck the driver in the side of the head. The man's left leg went up into the air; the bike went straight for about ten yards, but then it swung sharply to the left, bumping over the edge of the road at the same moment it fell over on its side and skidded into the ditch with a tremendous crash, sending the driver tumbling end over end into the ditch.

The motorcycle's engine raced wildly for a second or two before it suddenly sputtered and died. The silence encompassed everything.

Deland was on his feet, racing up the ditch toward the courier, the night suddenly too still.

The courier lay on his back, his right arm twisted impossibly beneath him. Deland pulled the man's goggles up. The driver's eyes were open. His tongue lolled out of his mouth. Blood covered the side of his face. His neck was broken. He was dead.

Deland looked both ways down the highway. No one was coming. Yet. But the sky was definitely getting lighter in the east.

He dragged the driver along the ditch back to the culvert. There he stripped the man's leather jacket, leather trousers, and boots, then put them on.

When he was finished, he stuffed the body deep inside the culvert. Certainly no one from the road would be able to spot the body. And only someone down on his hands and knees directly in front of the opening would see a thing.

All that had taken less than ten minutes, but as Deland hurried back to the downed motorcycle, he knew that he was seriously pressing his luck. Sooner or later another vehicle would be coming along the highway.

He lifted the bike and with great difficulty managed to get it back up onto the highway.

The front fender was bent into the spokes. Deland pried it away and carefully looked over the machine. There didn't seem to be much damage. Some dents, paint scraped off, and the handlebars slightly askew. But the odor of leaking gasoline was very strong.

The motorcycle started on the third try, its engine roaring into life, its headlight coming on.

He adjusted the rearview mirror, pulled the goggles down over his eyes, and slowly accelerated down the highway.

The courier's orders were to deliver a dispatch to the commander of the air base at Luckenwalde, directly south of Berlin.

Deland skirted the ruined sections of Potsdam and stopped beside the road twenty miles away, to go through all of the courier's papers. Besides Luckenwalde, the courier also had travel passes for bases and supply depots covering half of Germany.

South, beyond Erfurt, Deland figured his risks would rise. But no one stopped couriers who obviously were in a hurry on a very important mission.

Once south of Stuttgart, making it the rest of the way to the Swiss border and then across would be fairly simple. He hoped.

By morning he would be in Bern, he thought, putting the bike in gear. Definitely, he would be having a Swiss breakfast. And for him the war would be at long last over.

26

It was late morning, only a few minutes before noon, Canaris suspected. There were no clocks in his bedroom. He would not allow them. Here is a place for sleep, he maintained; for rest, where time does not matter.

He still wore his dressing gown as he paced back and forth while sipping his coffee.

He stopped at the window and looked out across the paddock. Motte and one of the other Arabians were romping along the fence line. They seemed happy. Unconcerned.

Canaris let his eyes lift to the sky. During the night the weather had turned sour. An overcast had blotted out the stars, threatening to bring rain. It was cooler now, too.

There was a strangeness to the very atmosphere, he decided, that could not be entirely explained by the overcast. When Jesus Christ had been hung on the cross, the afternoon was said to have turned odd. The radio was comparing the Führer's escape with the resurrection. And in a way Goebbels' people were right. Adolph Hitler was the God of the German peoples. It was right that he should rise, Phoenixlike, from the terrible flames and ashes of Rastenberg. It wouldn't be long before they'd be calling his Wolfsschanze Calvary.

Someone knocked at his door, breaking him out of his thoughts. He turned as Mohammed came in.

"Good morning," Canaris said. His voice sounded weak, even to his own ears. It had been a long, trying night at his office in Eiche. There had been so many telephone calls.

"Major Meitner is downstairs. He says it is urgent."

"Send him up. And bring more coffee."

"Yes, sir."

Canaris knew exactly why Meitner had come. And he knew

exactly what he was going to say to his old friend in reply. But there was still work to be done, loose ends to be picked up.

He put his coffee down and took a cigar from the humidor on the fireplace mantle. He had just snipped the end and was lighting it when Hans Meitner, in uniform, came in.

"Good God, I thought you would be ready to leave by now," Meitner said. He looked as if he hadn't slept in a week. There were circles under his eyes, and his skin was sallow.

"You should get more sun, Hans. Really, you are looking terrible."

Mohammed came with more coffee, and poured Meitner a cup. He withdrew, closing the door behind him.

"All hell is breaking loose, you know," Meitner said.

"All across Germany, I suspect."

Meitner nodded. "There has been a steady stream to Prinz-Albrecht Strasse. It will grow."

"There will be many arrests before it's over, Hans. I know that."

"Yours?"

Canaris shrugged. "One can only hope for the best."

Meitner hit the side of his leg with his hand in impatience. He was enough of an old school officer not to say something impatient. "Then you are planning on leaving? Will you go to Algeciras?"

At the mention of the city Canaris' heart clutched. "Algeciras," he said the word half to himself. He would never see Algeciras, or his love . . . never. He had known that for some time now. He shook his head.

"What, then? Surely, *meiner* Admiral, you are not going to remain here and simply do nothing?"

"That's correct."

Meitner seemed relieved, but Canaris' next words dashed any hopes he might have had.

"I am staying, of course, but there is plenty to do. And of necessity, you are going to have to run my errands."

"But, sir . . ."

Canaris had to smile indulgently. "Let's have no double standards here, my old friend. If I were to tell you to leave, would you?"

For a moment Meitner resisted. Finally he shook his head. "No, *meiner* Admiral. I will remain to the end. And beyond."

Canaris nodded. "In the meanwhile, there are two things you must try to do for me."

"I will try, but it has become very difficult now with all the arrests. Everyone is being watched."

"Do what you can," Canaris said.

"Yes, sir."

Canaris put down his cigar and went to his small writing desk in the corner by one of the windows. He wrote a series of four numbers on a slip of paper. He turned back and handed it to Meitner.

"It looks like the combination of a safe," Meitner said.

"Exactly," Canaris said. "Start left."

"Where?"

"Behind my old office at Maybach II. There is a central storeroom."

"Yes, I know it. The place has become a scrap area for discards."

"The safe is there. Inside, on a middle shelf, are three leather-bound volumes. Black. No markings."

"What are they, sir?"

"Diaries."

It took a moment for the significance to strike Meitner, and when it did, he turned very pale. His hand shook. *"Gott im Himmel*! Why did you leave them there, *meiner* Admiral?"

A mistake, Canaris thought. A blunder. "There was no time," he mumbled, turning away. "And I naturally thought I would be returning." He turned back. "Don't ask what is in the books. Don't look at them. Just remove them from the safe and bring them to me."

Meitner nodded heavily. "Yes, sir." He looked at the combination.

The diaries contained everything. The business with Schrader and Freytag-Loringhoven had only been the end-result of years of discussion. Names. Dates. Places. But the books had always had an aura of history to them that fascinated Canaris. He realized now that the aura had been more like the open flame, and he the moth. Deadly.

"There is another thing you must do for me," Canaris said, shaking off the darkness.

Meitner looked up.

"Do you remember our friend Dieter Schey?" Canaris had been thinking about him a lot just lately.

"In America? At Oak Ridge? He sent the ruined film over."

Canaris had to smile. He nodded. "The one. I must know what has happened to him."

"I have heard nothing, Herr Admiral."

With luck, Schey was dead or captured by now. But Canaris had to know for sure. Schey was the one man who had the potential knowledge to change the course of the war. He was, perhaps, the most dangerous man on earth.

Meitner put his cup down and pocketed the safe combination. "I don't know what I'll be able to find, but I will try."

"That is all I ask, Hans. That is all," Canaris said. He walked him to the door and then downstairs.

"There can be no delays, Hans. The diaries first, then information about Schey. When you have both, return here."

They shook hands at the front door. Meitner was very tense.

"There is nothing I can say to convince you to leave, *meiner* Admiral?"

"The same argument you would have me use on you."

A faint smile passed Meitner's lips, and he shook his head. "With luck I will return this evening."

"Then good luck and Godspeed, Hans."

Meitner paused on the front step, then turned back. "I'm stepping out of bounds . . . but I was wondering if you would like me to get a message to Algeciras?"

Canaris shook his head. "Under no circumstances." He would not have her name tainted.

"I understand, sir," Meitner said. He turned and left.

Another car was just coming up the drive when Meitner left in his. Canaris' stomach tightened, until he realized it was Helmut Maurer.

The car pulled up and parked at the foot of the stairs. Maurer got out and came around.

"Uncle Mau," Canaris said when his very old friend and neighbor came up the stairs.

"You look terrible, Willi."

"Is that why you came so early? To tell me that?"

"No," Maurer said. He was dressed in civilian clothes. Like

Meitner, he appeared to have gotten no sleep last night. He seemed very harried. "Nor can I stay. I must get right back."

"What is it?" Canaris asked, alarmed now.

"They've arrested Georg Hansen. He's at Prinz-Albrecht Strasse this very moment."

Hansen had been chief of AMT/Ausland Abwehr, Section I. But more importantly, he had been one of the chief conspirators planning Hitler's death. He was mentioned prominently in Canaris' diaries. Conversely, he was in a perfect position to mention Canaris' name and have his story believed. This was terrible.

"I thought so," Maurer said, reading much of Canaris' thoughts from his face. "You are going to have to leave. Immediately. They will almost certainly arrest you. Today, perhaps tomorrow. But very soon."

He heard a horse whinny—it sounded like Motte—in the back, and his heart went out to his animals. To all of them.

"Do you hear me, Willi? Or has something struck you deaf and dumb? You must leave!"

Canaris shook his head. "No, Uncle Mau, I will not leave. I did not plan to assassinate our Führer, and I am glad that the plot failed. Do you understand that?"

"It will not matter! Don't *you* understand?"

"You must do something for me."

"I am trying! *Verdammt!*" Maurer said with great feeling. They still stood on the porch. He came closer to Canaris and lowered his voice. "There already have been executions. There will be more. Many more."

Canaris was outwardly unmoved.

"In the name of God, Willi, you must save yourself."

Canaris smiled, and reached out and touched Maurer's arm. "I am more interested in saving Germany."

Maurer started to say something else, but he clamped it off. Instead, he looked deeply into Canaris' eyes and sagged as if some of the air had been let out of him. He shook his head.

"That's better," Canaris said. "Now, I need some information."

"Yes?"

"There is an underground group in Berlin. Run by a man named Dannsiger. They help Allied fliers, I believe."

"They were smashed last night."

Canaris had been prepared to go into much greater detail so

that Maurer would understand what he was talking about. This revelation stunned him.

"What is it, Willi?" Maurer said, alarmed. "Good God, don't tell me you were involved with them as well?"

"No," Canaris said. It meant there was no longer any sure way in which to contact Dulles in Bern. At least no way which Canaris was aware of. The RSHA would perhaps know some of the conduits. But he could not ask Maurer that. He simply could not ask the man to betray his country.

"What about Dannsiger's group? What's your connection?"

"One of my people infiltrated it some years ago. I wanted to get him out. I don't suppose anyone survived?"

"There may have been one or two escapes, from what I gather. One of our people who acted as an informer, then as a lure, was killed. He claimed an American spy was in the group. We think he may have murdered our man. He's still at large. But he'll be found. Unless he has help."

Hope had flickered for a moment, but then it had died. One or two men on the run could offer no help. Even if one of them was an American spy.

"I can arrange to get you out of the country," Maurer was saying. "I spoke with Kaulbars. He believes we can get you to Sweden. But you would have to leave now, this afternoon. Before light tomorrow you would cross."

Canaris shook his head. "No, Uncle Mau, I will not desert Germany."

"Then you will die here," Maurer said in frustration.

"As so many others have and will. It will not be unique."

A tear formed in Maurer's eyes. "Willi, is there nothing I can say to you?"

"Are you my friend? My comrade?"

"Yes. Of course."

"Then that is enough," Canaris said. "Now you must return to your office before you are missed."

Maurer wanted to say more, but he suddenly turned, went back to his car, and moments later was heading down the driveway.

Canaris watched until the car was out of sight, then stepped off the porch and ambled around to the back of the house as Motte came galloping up from the paddock and Kasper and Sabine bounded from the backyard.

*   *   *

Hans Meitner did not return until well after two in the morning.
The house had been settled down for several hours. Canaris was
seated in darkness in his study, which faced the long driveway up
from the street. The dogs were asleep on the Persian rug at his
feet.

Kaulbars had come this afternoon to add his plea to Maurer's,
for Canaris to run. But he had not stayed long.

There had been a few telephone calls later, but very few. The
taint was on him now. Anyone associating with him would
probably fall as well.

He spotted the flash of headlights in the trees before he actually saw the car. For a few seconds his entire body went rigid
with the thought that they were coming for him so soon. It was a
favorite Gestapo trick to come for their victims in the middle of
the night. He had once heard an officer boast that midnight
arrests accounted for an eighty-seven percent increase in immediate confessions. The man had laughed out loud, then added that
the statistic included confessions people made for crimes they
hadn't even committed.

The car came into view and parked. Meitner got out.

Canaris met him at the front door and led him around to the
study. Once he had the door closed and the heavy curtains drawn
over the large windows, he turned on his desk lamp, which threw
a soft glow downward, leaving the upper half of the room in
shadows.

Meitner looked frightened.

"Bad news, Hans?" Canaris asked.

Meitner nodded. "*Meiner* Admiral, I . . . ."

Canaris held him off. Now that he knew the flavor, he decided
he could wait for a moment or two before he listened to the
details. At the sideboard, he poured cognac for both of them.

"Sit down, Hans."

Meitner sat heavily on the wide couch and tossed his drink
back. Canaris refilled his glass, then perched on the edge of his
desk.

"Now tell me first, what news of Dieter Schey?"

Meitner seemed surprised by the question. "There is very little
news, from what I can gather. He radioed for a rendezvous

someplace in New Mexico . . . that is in the Southwest, I believe.''

New Mexico. The implications were electrifying. Schey had evidently eluded capture in Knoxville and in Washington, D.C., and had somehow made it all the way across the country. That, in spite of the fact the American authorities had his description.

''Was the rendezvous made?''

''No. That is the difficult part. We believe Schey's contact was arrested some time ago.''

''Then if Schey did make his rendezvous, it would have been a setup. He would be taken.''

''Presumably. But there is no way of verifying it.''

''Why was he given rendezvous instructions in the first place?''

''It slipped through. It was a mistake.''

It took a moment or two for the significance of Meitner's earlier statement to sink in. When it did, it provided another shock. ''We have no one left in the United States?''

Meitner shook his head. ''No one reliable. There are one or two in New York. But that's it.''

Canaris leaned back and closed his eyes as he thought back to the hundreds of contingency plans he personally had worked out for his field agents. Schey had been his special case.

If he could somehow make it clear of New Mexico, and was on the run, he'd come to New York to try to make contact. The New Mexico contact had been a trap. Schey would be wary now. Yet New York was his only way out of the country. From there, Newfoundland, then Greenland, and finally home. If the contacts hadn't been compromised. If the airstrips were still intact. If the planes and personnel were still in place.

Schey had to be stopped. But there was so little time. He had given Dulles all the information the OSS needed. *Verdammt*, were they all bungling fools?

Another thought struck Canaris. If Schey had been trying to meet a contact, it meant he had more information. Most likely from the bomb laboratory at Los Alamos. It meant that if Schey did make it back to Germany—somehow, if he pulled that feat off—he'd have the immediate and sympathetic ear of the Führer himself. Germany needed heroes just now. Schey would be perfect.

Meitner was saying something else. Canaris focused on him.

''They've moved the safe, *meiner* Admiral.''

"What are you saying?" Canaris asked, something very cold clutching at his heart.

"The old storeroom behind your old offices is empty. There is nothing there any longer. I could not ask about it for fear of raising suspicions. But your safe is simply gone."

27

It was well past eleven o'clock by the time they had quit the desert plateau and had begun to seriously climb the switchback road toward the Raton Pass at nearly eight thousand feet. Eva was asleep in the back seat, and Schey had nodded off for about an hour.

Burt Shamus had turned out to be a glad-hand sort, who before the war had been an industrial equipment salesman. Because of the manpower shortage, he had been made a special courier and escort for classified equipment produced by the Westinghouse Corporation. Most of the time, he told them, he traveled alone. The war had made him jumpy (which is why he had lied about going to Tucumcari), but his lonely job had also served to make him garrulous, and he had told Schey his entire life story, all the tense way through Santa Fe and across the desert through the night.

Now he seemed tired. Schey lit a cigarette and held it out.

"Care for a smoke, Burt?"

Shamus glanced over. He shook his head. "Nope. I got heartburn that won't quit. My eyes feel like someone's poured hot sand in 'em, and I gotta piss like a racehorse. Don't need a fag."

Schey had to laugh. "How about if I drive for a while, and you catch some sleep?"

"You mean it?" Shamus asked. "You wouldn't mind?"

"Pull over, Burt. You're givin' me the creeps the way you've been driving." It was hard for Schey to speak so colloquially. But even as hard as he tried, he could see that Shamus, who had a flat midwestern accent, would look at him oddly every now and then.

Shamus slowed the car down and pulled over to the side of the road. He cut the lights, then got out, careful not to slam the door so as not to wake Eva, and he walked around to the passenger side where he urinated in the ditch.

Schey scooted over to the driver's side, and for just a moment he considered driving off without the man. But he decided against it. Sooner or later a car or a truck would come by. Shamus would flag it down and they would get to a police station, probably down in Trinidad, on the Colorado side of the pass. From there it would be a matter of telephones and radios that no car could outrun.

Shamus got back in the car, Schey flipped the headlights on and pulled out onto the highway.

"Wake me up if you feel yourself gettin' sleepy," the fat man warned, lying back, his head against the doorpost.

"Sure thing, Burt," Schey said.

Shamus was sound asleep within a few minutes.

They crossed over the pass, some snow still in the higher mountains around them, and then they descended onto the Colorado high plains, the rolling hills like high waves on the ocean.

They went through the town of Trinidad, then Ludlow and Aguilar—all very small, all predominantly Mexican—the well-maintained highway rising and falling through the grasslands that paralleled the awesome wall of the Rockies close in to the west.

By now the FBI would have figured that something had gone wrong at the ranch. Romero was there to tell them he had seen the FBI agent with the large hat driving off the ranch. The agent even waved. But they would not be fooled by that for very long.

By now the search would have already spread outward from the ranch. North along Highway 44 to Cuba and Counselor, of course, and then back to U.S. 85 up to Santa Fe and down to Albuquerque.

If they hadn't found the Chevy by now, they would very soon. Certainly, by morning, someone at the railway station would notice that the gray car with out-of-state plates had been there all night. They'd call the police, and very quickly the bodies in the trunk would be discovered.

They passed through the town of Walsenburg around three-thirty, and Schey began to push the car, the speedometer topping seventy much of the time on the long straightaways, and he never drove less than sixty, although he was careful not to wake Shamus.

There was some construction going on in Pueblo and the route was detoured to the west, around the downtown section, but soon they were heading north again.

Shamus woke up about ten miles south of Colorado Springs, needing to urinate again, and then curled up and fell immediately asleep without, Schey suspected, even realizing what he had done or where he was.

The mountains seemed very close through the southern part of the state, and especially through Colorado Springs. Pike's Peak wasn't far to the west, but Schey could not pick it out in the darkness.

There was quite a bit of early morning traffic around the towns. Most of it was ranchers down for early morning coffee, Schey suspected. Then they'd be off to the feedlots or the mills.

Schey realized that they were very conspicuous, traveling like this. They had Colorado plates on the car, but they were obviously out-of-towners—one man sleeping in the front, a woman sleeping in the back. It was gas-rationing time. What were they doing traveling?

The sun was beginning to illuminate the eastern slopes of the mountains a wonderful golden color, and Schey sped up again. The land became dull and uninteresting for a while, but then they began to get signs that they were coming to a much larger city. There were junkyards, mostly empty now that the war was using up most of the scrap metal; small, junky motels that Schey looked at longingly; power lines overhead; little shacks, their east-facing windows lit with the morning sun like diamonds under a strong light.

Eva woke up and looked around. "Where are we?" she demanded from the back seat.

Schey looked at her in the rearview mirror. "Just coming into Denver," he said.

"God, have I slept that long? I feel like hell."

"Son-of-a-bitch, I gotta pee," Shamus shouted, bolting straight up from a sound sleep.

Schey laughed, and so did Eva. The fat man looked around, blinking, confused for the first few moments about where he was and about what was happening. But then it started to come back to him. He smiled sheepishly.

"Good morning, Burt," Schey said.

Shamus yawned deeply. "Why don't you pull over . . ." he started to say, but then he glanced ponderously over his shoulder and saw that Eva was awake. He blushed. "Er . . . it's all right."

"We're almost in town," Schey said. "If you can wait, we'll be there in another half-hour, and you can drop us off and be on your way."

"Hey, no, wait a minute now. I got a little place in town. I use it just when I come through. All the guys on the courier runs do. Christ, it's great. There's always chow, plenty of cold beer, usually a little gin or maybe some scotch. What do you say? I don't have to be back to Pittsburgh until Monday."

"Thanks a lot, Burt, but we've got to be on our way. We were supposed to be on the job yesterday as it was."

Denver was suddenly there, across a broad plain, the mountains gray-blue and golden behind it. Schey unconsciously sped up.

Shamus shrugged. "I thought I'd ask."

They came up from the south on 85 through Littleton, a sleepy little one-tavern suburb, and half an hour later they were through downtown Denver, crossing over the stockyards on the long bridge that turned sharply right at the far end, railroad tracks below, and for a long way feedlots where tens of thousands of heads of cattle were processed for shipping. There was a rich, earthy odor to the air here that reminded Schey very strongly of his home in Germany. Eva had turned up her nose.

"Are you sure I can't convince you to come over to the hideout. We can rustle up some breakfast."

"No, thanks, Burt. Really, you've done enough for us already. We can't thank you enough."

"Well, hell, I guess I want to thank you, too. I don't suppose I would have made it this far without going to sleep, if I was lucky, or running off the road, if I wasn't. Where do you want to get off?"

"Just anywhere here. We've got our friends we'll call. They'll come pick us up." Schey had seen the Union Station down by the stockyards. Once they were off the long bridge, he turned off the highway and pulled up. A Mexican tavern was across the street. It was just a little before seven, yet already there were a number of men seated at the bar.

"This is no place . . ." Shamus started to protest.

"This is fine, Burt. Honestly," Schey said, turning to him. He was very tired. He stuck out his hand. "Really. Thank you, Burt."

Shamus shook his hand. "Well, damn. I thought you'd at least stop by for a drink or something."

"Thanks, Burt." Schey got out of the car. It seemed strange to be on his feet. He helped Eva out of the back and got their suitcases.

Shamus got out and came around. They shook hands again, and the fat man got behind the wheel.

"Best of luck to you, now," he said.

"You, too," Schey called. Eva waved, and they watched until the car turned the corner and was gone.

Eva shivered. "It's cold here," she said. "And I'm hungry."

One of the men in the bar had turned around on his stool. He punched the man next to him and pointed toward Eva.

"Let's go," Schey said. He hefted their suitcases and then headed back under the bridge toward the huge, ornately decorated Union Station. The place was old, but it was different than the old places in Germany. Here, age usually meant disrepair, or old-fashioned, out-of-date. In Europe, old meant tradition, well-built beauty.

"There's a lot to be excited about here, though," Eva had once told him.

"Yes, what's that?"

"You never had cowboys and Indians in Germany."

Schey had laughed. "No, we never had that. We never had anything except dull kings and warrior princes. It was boring."

She had caught the obvious joke, and she had laughed at the time. But now Schey felt what she had meant about the American heritage. With the stockyards and loading pens to the west and the old Union Station straight ahead, he almost expected to see the stagecoach rattle up and cowboys riding by on their horses, six-shooters at their hips.

There was a fair amount of traffic coming and going from the station: buses from town, trucks, people on foot. A lot of them were soldiers, their duffel bags slung over their shoulders.

Inside the vast main hall, Schey left Eva with the bags at the ladies' rest room so she could clean up while he went across to check the train schedules and fares.

They had spent very little of the money that they had dug out of the bolt hole package months ago in Eva's apartment. There was slightly more than five thousand dollars left in the package, so that was no worry for them.

Train schedules were displayed on two huge posters beneath glass that encircled massive support columns across from the ticket counters. One schedule was marked WEST; the second, EAST. Schey approached, slowly studying the rows and columns of names and times.

He began to make sense of the thing, understanding that trains left Denver day and night—some of them for places such as North Platte, Grand Island, Kearney; others, evidently stopping trains, for small towns such as Hudson, Fort Morgan, Brush, Sterling.

Finally he found the train that would take them to Chicago, with connections, the schedule read, with New York Central's Twentieth Century to New York City.

There were two Chicago trains each day. The first left Denver at 10:05 A.M., and the second at 10:05 P.M. The morning train had a one hour layover in Omaha, but arrived in Chicago at 9:30 A.M. the next day, in plenty of time for the noon departure of the Twentieth Century.

Schey bought a pair of first-class tickets, round-trip, scheduling their return for one week hence. If and when the FBI got this far in their search, they'd be checking second-class tickets one-way, not first-class round-trip.

He bought a newspaper at a stand, then went into the men's room where he hired a razor, soap, a towel, and a wash cloth, and he quickly cleaned up. When he was finished, he had his shoes shined, then went back out.

Eva was waiting for him beneath the big overhead clock. She looked greatly relieved and smiled when she spotted him.

"Don't you look handsome," she said.

"You don't look so bad yourself," he said. She had fixed her hair and had put on some makeup.

They went across to the restaurant that Schey had spotted on the way in, and got a seat in a booth. They both ordered coffee. Schey ordered ham and eggs; Eva, ham and pancakes.

"We leave at a little past ten," he told her. "We've got a sleeping compartment to ourselves."

"To where, Bobby?"

"We'll be in Chicago by tomorrow morning, and Manhattan by Sunday morning, early."

"New York?" she said loudly, in surprise. She lowered her voice and leaned forward. "Why New York? Are you crazy? The place is crawling with FBI."

"That's where my contact is located."

"Like your Santa Fe contact? Is it going to be the same?"

"I don't know . . ."

"And if it is, so what then? What's he going to do for us? Give us new identities? Change our faces? Change our finger-prints?"

"I suppose we'll take a car to Canada, and from there an airplane to Greenland, and then home."

Eva's eyes widened. The enormity of what he was saying suddenly struck her. "Home," she repeated softly. "Oh, Bobby. The war is lost. Given half the chance, the Russians will overrun Germany. When that happens, it won't be very nice." She shook her head. "Christ, you said it yourself."

Schey took her hands. "When we get to Europe, I'm going to get you to Switzerland. You can stay there until it's over."

"Switzerland? . . . What the hell do I know about Switzerland?"

"You don't have to know a thing, other than it is very pleasant and you will be safe. No one will hurt you there. And we have plenty of money."

"Bobby, for Christ's sake, what are you talking about?" she said. "I don't want to go to Europe. But if I'm going across with you, I'm not going to run off to the mountains to wait it out while God only knows what's happening to you."

They'd work it out later. Schey knew that when it came right down to it, she would do as he told her. He had been with her long enough to understand that, although from time to time she was able to hold up a tough-guy facade, she was mostly a lonely, frightened little girl who desperately wanted love and direction. He would give her both. In abundance.

They had their breakfast, and Schey read the newspaper afterwards. There was nothing about them. He hadn't thought there would be, but he had to check. They went down to their train by nine-thirty, but before they went through the gates, Schey held back for five minutes, watching the people coming and going, watching the ticket takers.

There were a lot of soldiers around, and pairs of military policemen, with their helmets and armbands, looking for desert-ers and troublesome soldiers. But there were no cops. No suspicious-looking civilians. No one paying much attention to anything at the ticket barriers other than the tickets.

He and Eva went through with no trouble, found their car, and inside, the porter helped them with their bags to their compartment. He was a black man. Short and very squat. He showed them how to use the tiny sink and told them the toilet was down the corridor. He promised that whenever they were ready to turn in tonight, he would be by to pull down their beds and make them ready.

"Lunch is from eleven-thirty until one-thirty, dinner from five-thirty to eight-thirty. The club car opens at noon and closes whenever the last dog dies."

The man reminded Schey of Rochester on *The Jack Benny Show*. But then, all Afrikaners sounded that way to him.

Schey tried to give the porter a tip, but the man turned it away.

"You've never traveled on a train before?"

Schey shrugged. What the hell had he done? "Never first-class," he said. "It's sort of our . . . second honeymoon."

"Well . . . bless my soul. I'll bring you folks back a little surprise later this evening. Just you wait and see." The porter laughed. He glanced at Eva and nodded his approval. "Yessiree. But if you think I deserve a tip, why you just wait until we hit Chi-town; then you do whatever you think is best."

Eva was laughing so hard when the porter left that she doubled over and fell back on the settee.

"Oh Christ," she said through her tears. It was the terrible tension they had been under. It had been released in her. "Spies get caught by porter in Denver," she choked.

Schey did not see the humor; he knew only that he had screwed up with the man. If and when the FBI came around to checking the trains out of Denver, it would be just the kind of thing they'd be looking for.

"Any of your passengers seem to be unsure of themselves? Any of them make a mistake about tickets, or destinations, or tipping?"

28

Schey felt a glow of well-being, although he was terribly tired and understood that the most difficult part of their escape would come in New York City. But he and Eva had had a lovely dinner in the dining car, and later, back in their compartment, the surprise the porter had promised them was a bottle of champagne.

A token for the honeymooners. The champagne was out of the porter's private stock. He was a pro, and probably made more in tips than in salary because of the extra niceties.

Schey lay on his back, his eyes closed, feeling the steady rhythm of the moving train, listening to the soothing clatter of the wheels on the tracks.

They had leisurely finished the wine while they talked, mostly about Eva's past in Wisconsin. She had been raised by her German immigrant grandparents who were fishermen on Lake Michigan. It had been an idealistic life for her, and there were times, she admitted, when she was truly sorry she had grown up.

Schey listened to her with one part of his mind, the gentle words flowing around him, while with another he thought about his own childhood that had begun with hatred for what the Allies had done to Germany after the First World War, then with idealistic hope and expectation for what the future would bring under the leadership of their Führer.

Where had it all gone wrong for them, he wondered now, lying in bed. Eva was washing her face at the little sink. Only the single light over the mirror was on.

For her, the downward path came with the deaths of her grandparents. To fill the gap they left behind, she had joined the Bund in Milwaukee.

For him, it came on the day he joined the Nazi party and began his training at Park Zorgvliet for his infiltration into the United

States. His father wanted him to be a soldier. A moderate. He shook his head.

"What are you smiling about?" Eva asked.

Schey opened his eyes. She switched the light out, but there was enough coming from the open curtains at the window to see that she was nude.

"I was thinking about my father," he said softly. Eva was lovely. Her breasts were large and well-formed, her legs long and straight, and the tuft of hair at her pubis very blonde.

"I never rode first-class on a train like this," she said.

Schey lay on the top bunk. He threw the covers back. Eva grinned, came across the tiny compartment, and climbed up with him, her skin soft and a lovely, clean odor coming from her.

He held her close.

"We've got this night, at least," she said, her voice husky.

He looked into her large, liquid eyes. Her nostrils were flared, her lips wet. Her face was slightly tanned from the New Mexican sun. It contrasted nicely with her blonde hair.

"I love you," he said to her.

Her eyes filled. "I love you, too, Bobby, but I'm frightened."

He stroked her hair. "It'll be hard, getting back. But the war will be over pretty soon. Then we'll be able to settle down."

She wanted to believe him. It was obvious from her expression. But it was also clear that she was very frightened. She shivered, and he pulled her close again, her breasts crushed against his chest, her legs entwined with his.

"Oh . . . Christ . . . I don't want this to end," she cried.

She was kissing him, her mouth exploring his, her hands fluttering over his shoulders and his back, drawing him even closer, holding him so tightly that at times he could feel her heart beating.

Later, he gently pushed her back, kissed her chin, her neck, then her breasts, taking each nipple between his lips, his tongue making a circular pattern on the areola.

She moaned and arched her back as he slid lower, kissing the gentle rise of her belly, his tongue flicking suggestively in and out of her navel.

"Bobby?" she called softly. She reached down and took his head in her hands, and raised him away so that she could look into his eyes.

He smiled at her. This was so good he never wanted to stop.

"I can't wait. I love you. I love you . . ."

He turned and kissed the palm of her right hand, then slid down lower, his lips brushing her inner thighs, and she flinched.

Then his tongue was inside her, parting her lips, making circular motions around her clitoris. She wanted to jump out of her skin. The pleasure was so intense it was nearly painful. But then he took the tiny organ in his lips and drew it in, her entire body rising off the bed, the sensation was so intense.

"Bobby . . ." the involuntary cry escaped from her throat.

He slid it slowly back and forth between his lips, even the tiniest of motions causing wave after wave of pleasure to course through her body. She was coming again and again, each time not quite completely, but each wave more intensely pleasurable than the last.

Suddenly he was on top of her, and inside her, deep inside.

Eva looked up into Schey's open eyes. She could see that he was lost in his pleasure. It was the first time that he had lost himself so completely, and her love for him rose like a huge ocean wave—a tidal wave that could not possibly leave her unchanged. And he was coming; she could see it in his eyes, could feel it in the thrum of his body, and she could sense it between her legs. He *did* love her, and it was all she needed.

It was cold and raining in Chicago when they arrived. They were an hour and a half late because of some delay in Iowa during the night. Instead of a two and a half hour layover for the Twentieth Century, they now had slightly less than an hour.

Their porter helped them with their bags. Schey slipped him fifty dollars. He knew it was far too much, but the man had shown them kindness. At the moment, in the present world situation, it was rare.

They transferred over to the Twentieth Century, a sleek, long train with silver Pullman cars and brisk, efficient, even somewhat haughty porters who installed them in their spacious first-class compartment.

They had coffee, and before they were finished, the train was pulling out for the long sweep around Lake Michigan, then east toward New York, the western hospitality they had enjoyed on the Denver train now replaced with an eastern efficiency that would brook no delays.

Last night they had been tired and had been glad of the inactivity. But as they rolled across the Illinois and Indiana farmlands, Schey was impatient to get on with it.

"How long will it take for us to make contact in New York?" Eva asked at one point.

Schey had been smoking and staring out the window. "That depends," he said absently.

"On what?"

He looked at her. "On whether or not he's been compromised."

"What if he has been . . . compromised? Or what if the FBI has somehow traced us to this train? What then?"

Schey resisted the urge to snap at her. He counted three before he answered. "I don't know, Eva. We'll just have to see."

"Play it by ear?"

He smiled. "Play it by ear." He looked again out the window at the flat and, to him, mostly featureless land. A little farther to the east and they would be passing through the heart of industrial America. It was not so concentrated as the factories and mills in the Ruhr, but it was large, powerful, and considering the vast forces the U.S. had sent into the field, seemingly unlimited.

The train stopped in South Bend for about ten minutes, then headed out again.

Schey was becoming uncomfortable. In the west there had been wide open spaces. Places for them to run, if the need arose. Here, the closer they came to New York City, the more he began to feel a sense of claustrophobia.

It was possible, he told himself, that the FBI had gotten on the train at South Bend. It was an unscheduled stop.

It was even possible that they would wait until New York City. They'd wait until he and Eva got off the train and then take them.

After lunch he lay down for a while to try to get some sleep while Eva read some of the magazines the porter had brought around. But he could not calm down. Every few minutes he would turn his head so that he could see out the window to make sure they were not slowing down again.

He went over and over in his mind the possibilities of escape from here. Actually, they were much nearer to Canada at this point than they would be in New York City. But Canada was not the safety zone. There'd be an airstrip somewhere in Newfoundland, and a plane waiting to take them home. Until they got to Germany, they would be enemies in a foreign country.

Schey got up after a while and went down to the club car where he had a couple of drinks and a cigarette. But some salesmen from Chicago were arguing loudly about the Chicago Cubs versus the Brooklyn Dodgers. They were drunk, and when they tried to involve him in their discussion about batting averages, he left.

He and Eva had dinner early. Although the meal was excellent, Schey had no taste for it. He was extremely jumpy, and Eva picked up on his mood. She too became very tense and nervous.

Back in their compartment, they got ready for bed, but neither of them could sleep, and after a couple of hours, Schey got up, got dressed, and made sure their bags were packed.

"Are they going to be waiting for us?" Eva asked from where she lay on the top bunk.

The compartment was dark. Schey sat by the window, smoking as he watched the lights of the towns pass them.

"I don't know . . ." he started to say, but then he turned toward her, suddenly realizing what he was doing. He shook his head. "I don't think so. They'll trace us to the train sooner or later. But not this quickly. It'll take them time to cover that much territory. It's a long way from Albuquerque to Denver. And then they have to question all the ticket agents." He shook his head again. "It's not even likely anyone will remember us."

"Are you sure, Bobby?" Eva asked.

He wanted to shout that no, he wasn't sure. Instead he nodded in the darkness. "Of course. Now try to get some sleep. Tomorrow will be a busy day."

She was quiet then, and after a bit he put out his cigarette and laid his forehead on the cool window glass. He was asleep almost immediately.

Something was terribly wrong. Schey woke with a start, his mouth gummy, his neck stiff, his head throbbing. They had stopped. There were a lot of people just outside his window. He could hear a public address system blaring something. And there was the smell of a big city.

He realized finally that they had arrived. This was Penn Station.

"Are we here?" Eva asked sleepily from the top bunk.

Schey got up. There were a lot of red caps and porters on the platform, but every second person seemed to be a serviceman. So far as Schey could see, there were no cops, but a battalion of them could have been out there; there was such a crowd on the platform it was impossible to pick out anyone.

"We have to get out of here now," he said.

Eva hopped down from the bunk, splashed some cold water on her face, ran a comb through her hair, and then tossed the rest of her things in her bag.

Schey had opened the door. Their porter came and he slipped the man a twenty-dollar bill.

"Need some help with your bags, folks?"

"No, thanks," Schey said.

Eva was ready, and he took her arm and led her down the corridor and out onto the crowded platform. They headed toward the stairs that led up to the main hall and the exits. As they walked, Schey half expected to feel a hand on his shoulder, hear a stern voice ordering them to stop. But nothing happened, and soon they were upstairs in the main hall.

The station was very busy this morning, although it was a Sunday. Another train besides the Twentieth Century had come in, and one transcontinental train was apparently about to leave. There were soldiers everywhere, and military policemen were stationed, it seemed, at every column.

They stood off to one side for a moment or two, watching the activity, listening to the din of announcements and a thousand conversations all going on at the same time.

"Are we going to get a hotel?" Eva asked. "I'd like to take a proper bath."

"I don't think so," Schey said. He started across the big hall. "I want to be out of the city by noon."

"What? . . . So soon?" Eva sputtered, keeping up with him.

On the far side of the hall, Schey set his bag down in front of a phone box and dug in his pocket for a nickel.

"Are you going to call from here? Right now?" Eva asked, looking around.

"The sooner, the better," Schey said. He slipped inside, dropped the nickel in the slot, and dialed a number he had learned by heart years ago. It rang three times before a man answered.

"Yeah?" There was a lot of background noise; it sounded like a factory.

"Is this Frankel Importing/Exporting?"

The speaker hesitated. "Who wants to know?"

"Uncle Willi asked me to call and say hello."

Again the man hesitated.

"We need help," Schey said. "There are two of us."

"Where are you?"

"Never mind. We'll come to you."

"Is your phone secure?"

"I'm in a booth. It's secure. Can you help us?"

"We're leaving this afternoon."

"For where?"

"Home," the speaker said, and Schey's stomach flopped. He looked up at Eva waiting outside the booth for him. He would have to get her to Switzerland, somehow. He wouldn't leave if that wasn't possible.

"We're coming with you, but there may be a complication," Schey said.

"What are you talking about? Are they after you?"

"The second person is . . . not going home."

"I said, what are you talking about?"

"The second person has to get to Switzerland. Do you understand?"

Schey could hear relief in the speaker's voice. "Is that all? No problem. But your friend will have to cross himself. Sweden first, and from there to Switzerland. I'm not running a courier service there."

"I understand," Schey said.

"How soon can you be in front of St. Bartholomew's?"

"I don't know where it is?"

"Park Avenue and 50th."

It wasn't far. "About twenty minutes. Maybe sooner," Schey replied.

"A brown delivery van with RCA markings will pull up from the south on Park Avenue. You'll have to cross the street."

"RCA, the radio company?"

"RCA . . . the Royal Canadian Army."

"We'll be there . . ." Schey said when Eva suddenly rapped on the window glass. She was highly agitated. Schey hung up and got out of the phone box.

He spotted the men before she had to point them out. A dozen of them in civilian clothes had rushed in the Eighth Avenue doors, and they were spreading out across the main hall. They obviously were in a big hurry, and just as obviously looking for someone. Four of them ran for the stairs to the trains.

Someone in Colorado had gotten to the train station and had discovered that he and Eva were scheduled to arrive here in New York on the Twentieth Century.

"Are they after us?" Eva asked fearfully.

"I think so," Schey said. He took her by the elbow and steered her away from the phone booths, leaving their bags behind. They would no longer matter. They would only slow them down.

He put his hand in his pocket and felt for the .38 he had carried with him ever since he had taken it from the FBI agent in Eva's Washington apartment; it seemed like years ago.

They hurried across the main hall, directly toward the Seventh Avenue exits, keeping within the heavier concentrations of people as much as possible. If they could make it out of the building within the next minute or so, Schey figured they might have a chance of getting free. Much longer than that and the FBI or whoever it was would have had a chance to settle their people into place.

Two men came through the Seventh Avenue doors at the same moment Schey and Eva had reached them. They had nowhere to go now.

For a split second the agents looked from Schey to Eva and back again, the expression on their faces changing from one of curiosity to surprise, and then to fear. They both started to reach inside their coats.

Schey shoved Eva aside, pulled out the .38, and fired two shots, the first hitting the agent to his right in the chest, driving him backward, and the second hitting the other agent in the abdomen, doubling him over.

Someone screamed.

Schey leaped forward, shoving the wounded agent out of the way, and as he hit the doors, he half turned to make sure Eva was coming.

But she had shrunk back. Her mouth was opening and closing, but no sounds were coming out.

"Eva . . ." Schey shouted, halfway out the door, when the side of her head exploded in a mass of blood and bone. She was thrown violently to the left, her legs flying out from under her.

Schey brought the .38 around as a bullet smashed the glass

door just to the right of his shoulder. He fired three shots in quick succession. One man went down, and two others fell back as pandemonium raged in the crowded station.

"Eva!" he shouted again. But she was lying in a bloody heap on the floor, her eyes open. She was dead! There was no question about it!

Schey fired his last shot; the second time he pulled the trigger, the hammer fell on an empty chamber.

He turned, stepped the rest of the way outside, let the pistol fall to the pavement at his side, and hurried across Seventh Avenue, dodging traffic.

"Stop!" someone shouted behind him. Horns were blaring, and someone was screaming; in the distance he could hear sirens. But he did not turn around and look back.

Seconds later he was around the corner, and he ducked into the Statler Hotel, calmly walked across the lobby as if he belonged there, and stepped out the West 32nd Street exit where he got directly into a cab.

"St. Bartholomew's Church," he told the driver, and he sat back so that he could not easily be seen from outside, as the driver took off away from the station area.

"Sounds like some sort of trouble back there," the cabby said.

"Yeah, I guess so," Schey mumbled, as the vision of Eva's body being flung to the floor, her head erupting in blood, flashed into his mind. It began to build and pound, threatening to engulf him completely, but then changing so that her image seemed to meld with the image of poor Katy going down in their house in Oak Ridge.

He thought about his son back in Kentucky. He would never see him again. Never. He had come to this country alone. He would leave it that way. Behind him was death and destruction. Had it been worth it? Had he served as an honorable soldier of the Reich? Would his father be proud of him?

Katy, he cried inside. Eva. What in God's name had he done?

29

Erwin Delbrück poured coffee for Baron Kaulbars, then for his Uncle Willi, and finally for himself. He sat down.

"I can take care of Motte and the other horses out at our place, but what about Kasper and Sabine?" Erwin asked. "Won't you take them with you?"

Canaris sipped his coffee and smiled wanly. Kaulbars knew what was going on, even if Canaris' nephew did not. "I'm not necessarily going anyplace, Erwin," he said. "I merely mentioned it as a possibility."

"But what about the dogs?"

"You would have to take care of them as well."

Erwin shrugged. "It's all right with me, but for how long? Maria will almost certainly want to know that. And how about Aunt Erika? Wouldn't she rather take care of the animals?"

"I don't think so," Canaris said.

Kaulbars had not said much of anything all afternoon. But it was clear he was nervous, on edge. He was very worried about Canaris.

"I miss Helmut's piano playing," he said now.

"He had to be at work this afternoon. They are very busy just now," Canaris said, glancing toward the windows. It was a beautiful day. The sun shone from a lovely blue sky. Surprisingly, there had been no bombing raids this morning. Everyone had been expecting the planes to come. But they had not. He was sure that the beaches at Wannsee would be crowded.

"Did he stop by yesterday?"

"Yes, Uncle Mau was here," Canaris said. Kaulbars had always been very emotional. Canaris watched him closely now. It seemed as if he was ready to burst into tears.

"How is your new job at Eiche?" Erwin asked.

"It's fine," Canaris said. "But tell me, how have you been? How are Maria and the boys?"

"Everyone is in good health . . ." the younger man started to say, when they heard a car pull into the driveway and stop out front.

Kaulbars half rose out of his seat, but Canaris waved him back.

"Mohammed will see to it," Canaris said. His heart was racing, and it was difficult for him to catch his breath.

Someone came to the door, and moments later they could hear Mohammed talking. He appeared at the drawing room door.

"SS-Brigadeführer Walter Schellenberg is here to see you, sir."

This time when Kaulbars rose out of his seat, Canaris did not wave him back.

"Show him in," Canaris said. He stood. "Perhaps you two should wait in the living room."

"Of course," Kaulbars said. He waited for Erwin to join him and they stepped across the stair hall. A moment later the SD chief entered. He was dressed in uniform. He was alone.

"Good afternoon, Walter," Canaris said.

Schellenberg, who was very handsome, a dueling scar on his chin, came across the room and shook hands. "Good afternoon, Herr Admiral. You are in good health?"

Canaris nodded. They looked at each other for a long time. They had been rivals, but never really enemies.

"Somehow, I felt it would be you," Canaris said.

Schellenberg said nothing. It was obvious he had his instructions as to exactly what he was to say and what not to say.

"Tell me, have you found anything in writing by that fool Colonel Hansen?"

Schellenberg nodded. "We think it's possible there was a connection between Georg and Stauffenberg."

Again they looked at each other for a long time. Canaris' heart was still hammering wildly in his chest. He hadn't known how he would react when the time came, but certainly he'd not thought he'd be like this. He felt like a stagestruck schoolboy who has suddenly forgotten his lines for the Christmas pageant.

Schellenberg glanced toward the sideboard. "Do you mind if I pour myself a drink?"

"Please, help yourself."

Schellenberg inclined his head. He went across and poured a small measure of cognac. His back was to Canaris as he drank. "I shall wait here in this room for an hour, and during that time you can do whatever you choose. I shall say in my report that you went to your room to change."

Canaris had never had any personal gripe with Schellenberg. It was other men, such as Reitlinger, who were the thugs. Schellenberg, on the other hand, was a man of breeding. But this now was odd. Were they afraid of him? Was there hope, after all?

"No, Schellenberg, there's no question of my escaping. I shan't kill myself either."

Schellenberg put the snifter down and turned around. "Are you sure?"

"I know what I'm doing."

"I see."

"Just let me pack a few things."

Schellenberg nodded. "We were all surprised. . . . I did not want to do this. But orders . . ."

"I understand," Canaris said. He left the room, crossed the hall, and started up the stairs. Kaulbars came to the living room door.

Canaris stopped and looked down at him. "This is it, Baron."

Kaulbars nodded, not trusting himself to speak. His eyes glittered.

"Tell Erwin that he is to take Kasper and Sabine as well."

Again Kaulbars nodded.

Canaris looked at him for several moments, then smiled. "Goodbye, old friend. Perhaps I shall be back." He turned, went the rest of the way up the stairs, then down the corridor to his room.

He packed a few things, including his toilet gear, in a single suitcase, then changed into his uniform, the Iron Cross in gold around his neck. He went to the mirror and looked at himself. He had lost a lot of weight recently, and his uniform hung sloppily on his frame. There were stains on the lapels, and the cuffs were frayed.

It was of no consequence.

When he was ready, he went back downstairs, leaving the suitcase in the hall by the front door.

Mohammed was with the cook by the kitchen door. Canaris turned to them. "I will be leaving now. I don't know when I'll be back. Baron Kaulbars and Herr Maurer have my utmost confidence. They will instruct you.''

Mohammed nodded. ''Yes, sir,'' he said uncertainly.

''You will be all right here. No matter what happens.''

''Yes, *meiner* Admiral,'' Mohammed said. The cook had begun to cry.

Canaris took a deep breath, let it out slowly, then went into the drawing room. Schellenberg waited by the sideboard. Canaris went across to him and put his arm around his shoulders. ''All right, let's go.''

Schellenberg nodded. Together they left the drawing room. Canaris retrieved his suitcase and they went outside, down the stairs, and across to the big Mercedes staff car.

Baron von Völkersam, who had worked in the Abwehr but had later been transferred to the SD, was waiting at the car. He was in the uniform of an SS-Hauptsturmführer. He came to attention and saluted. ''Good afternoon, Herr Admiral.''

Canaris returned the salute. ''So they sent you as well.''

Völkersam opened the rear door for Canaris. Schellenberg took his suitcase and put it in the trunk as Canaris got in. He climbed in with him. Völkersam got in the front seat. Their driver started the car immediately and they pulled away from the house.

Canaris looked back, hoping to catch a last glimpse of Motte or one of the other horses, but they were down the driveway and out on the street too fast.

He settled back in his seat for the ride into the city, but within a few minutes it was obvious they were not going into Berlin itself. They were skirting around to the north, up into Mecklenburg.

Canaris resisted the urge to ask Schellenberg where they were going. He would find out soon enough. Suffice it that he was not being taken to the labyrinth of cellars at Gestapo Headquarters on Prinz-Albrecht Strasse.

There was hope.

It took them nearly forty minutes to make it to the tiny town of Fürstenberg an der Havel. They pulled up in the courtyard of the Frontier Police College. Maurer had mentioned that a number of the high-ranking officers implicated in the July 20th assassination attempt were being held here in the officers' mess.

Schellenberg got out, and Canaris followed him as a disagreeable-looking officer came down the walkway. He was an SS-Brigadeführer, the same rank as Schellenberg.

The officer came stiffly to attention and saluted. Canaris idly returned it.

"Permit me to introduce the college commandant, Dr. Hans Trummler," Schellenberg said. It was obvious he disliked the man.

Canaris was going to be neutral.

"Are you hungry, Herr Admiral? Have you eaten?" Trummler asked.

"I'm not hungry, but I might have a glass of wine," Canaris said. He turned to Schellenberg. "Would you care to join me?"

Völkersam had stepped out of the car. But it was clear that Canaris' invitation did not include him.

"Of course," Schellenberg said.

"I'll wait here," Völkersam said.

Trummler led Canaris and Schellenberg across the courtyard and into the officers' mess, where they sat at one of the tables. There were a few other officers there. It was early dinner. Some of them Canaris recognized. Most, however, were strangers.

A waiter brought them a bottle of good Italian red wine and poured each of them a glass.

Schellenberg raised his in toast. "I wish you luck, Admiral. Sincerely."

Canaris nodded. "Thank you, Schellenberg," he said. He sipped his wine. "It has been a long time since the thirties."

"Yes, it has. A lot has happened. Much of it has been very good."

Canaris had looked off. "Yes, there was much that was good. Our Führer was so . . . brave, in the old days."

Schellenberg smiled. He too was thinking about the old days.

"When you get back to Berlin, there is a favor I would like you to do for me," Canaris said.

"If it is possible."

"I would like to speak with Himmler."

Schellenberg nodded.

"I believe he owes me an interview. A very brief interview."

"I will ask," Schellenberg said. He sipped his wine.

"Thank you."

"What about your horses? Have you made arrangements?"

"Yes. Erwin Delbrück, my nephew, has agreed to take care of

them . . . if I am here for very long. Otherwise my house staff will see to them.''

''Yes, I see,'' Schellenberg said.

They drank together in silence for a while. Canaris took out a cigar and went through the ritual of lighting it. The smoke tasted excellent at this moment. He only wished that he had been allowed to take his dogs with him, as he had to Burg Lauenstein. But he had not thought to ask. Now it was too late.

''Do you remember what it was you were doing on the first of September in '39,'' Canaris asked suddenly.

Schellenberg did not seem startled by the question. He smiled and nodded. ''Of course,'' he said. ''I was home napping when the news came.''

''Were you excited?''

''A strange question.''

Canaris shrugged. ''I was almost sad. Yet I was happy that it had begun at last.'' He blinked. ''It was a very long road back from Versailles.''

''Yes, it was,'' Schellenberg said. He drank the rest of his wine. Canaris offered him more, but Schellenberg put his hand over his glass, then got up. ''I must get back.''

Canaris looked up at him. ''I love Germany very much, Walter.''

''I know that, Herr Admiral. We all know that.''

Canaris nodded. He felt very odd at the moment. He felt as if he could talk openly to Schellenberg, and yet he knew everything he said could and would be used against him. But it really didn't matter. Nothing could matter if they already had the diaries from the safe at Zossen.

''Be careful to steer clear of the kind of trouble I've gotten myself into,'' he warned.

''I will,'' Schellenberg said.

Canaris got to his feet. He and Schellenberg looked into each other's eyes for a long moment, and then they shook hands.

''I have no animosity for you, Walter.''

''I am happy to hear that, Admiral. I have always admired you.''

''Good-bye.''

''*Auf wiedersehen*,'' Schellenberg said, and he turned and walked off.

Canaris remained standing until Schellenberg was gone; then

he looked around the officers' mess, picked up his wineglass, and offered a silent toast.

Several of the officers raised their glasses in toast, but others turned away. It didn't matter, Canaris thought. From this point on, nothing mattered. His fate was in someone else's hands.

—I think you're out of your fuckin' gourd. I think your head is firmly planted up your ass.

Someone had come by a few minutes earlier and had sold the younger man a small plastic packet of white powder. The older man figured it was cocaine.

—Let me tell you something. You might be a Tom Terrific bullshit artist, but you don't know nothing about your so-called heroes.

Just possession of the coke had made the young man belligerent. The older man shook his head in sadness. He had known in the beginning that tonight would be no use. The kid had no conception.
—Did you know this Terry from South Dakota?

—No.

—How about Major Fisher?

The younger man waved it off. —Fuck, no. But I knew plenty of heroes, and they weren't no saints in shining armor.

—They loved their country, didn't they?

The younger man seemed embarrassed by the question. —I don't know.

—Name me one. Did he or didn't he love his country? It's an easy question. The older man listened to his own voice in wonder. It had been a bitch of a week. Tonight he had drunk too much. But going back like he had, trying to make it clear to this punk, was goddamned frustrating.

The jukebox was silent for a while. The young girl was on break. They could talk more easily now, but they were still shouting out of habit. They had attracted some attention. The bar manager was thinking about calling the cops. These two looked as if they were ready to come to blows. The older one was drunk, and the long-haired freako was higher than a kite.

—He just went in there and did his job, and got the fuck out.

266

—*Was he any different afterward?*

The younger man laughed out loud. He flipped his long greasy hair back. —*Yeah, he was different, all right. Half his kneecap was blown off.*

—*He got wounded. That doesn't make him a hero.*

The young man sat forward so fast he almost fell off his chair. —*Don't fuck with my head, man. I don't appreciate it.*

The older man held up his hands in surrender.

—*I was just trying to tell you something here, if you'll just shut up and listen a minute.*

The older man figured it was about time to leave. Hell, it was long overdue time for him to leave, but there was something about the younger man, something in his eyes, that was compelling. And oddly, so very familiar. Again he got the very strong feeling that he had known this man for a long time; it was almost as if they were brothers. But that was ridiculous.

—*You're talking about heroes, here. In the big war. W-W-Two. But it wasn't like that in Nam. Honest to Christ.*

—*I'm listening.*

The younger man lit another joint. He had a Marlboro box stuffed with them already rolled. He no longer thought to offer the other man a hit.

—*You know, I'm just as American as the next guy. AFL/CIO and all that crap. But I was drafted, man. I didn't give a shit one way or the other about the war.*

The older man ordered another beer. He did not notice that the barman hesitated.

—*A lot of guys were drafted. They went in and did their jobs. Nothin' fancy. No extras. But if their backs were up against it, if they got pissed off, then look out. They'd do somethin'.*

—*Was Terry pissed off?*

—*Shit, I don't know. You're twisting my words.* The young man stabbed a finger at the other man. —*I'll tell you this much for sure: Terry sure the fuck didn't go looking for the slope. It just happened.*

—*Right, but he didn't run away.*

The younger man shook his head. —*Terry was one of the good ones. But they weren't all like that. Just cause some guy's a hero don't make him a saint. I keep trying to tell you that. Some of them were absolutely class one sons-a-bitches.*

Maybe Vietnam *had been* different *from the Second World*

War, the older man thought. Or perhaps his own definitions were off. But what the younger man was saying to him was alien to everything he had been trying to put across here tonight. Duty. Honor. Country. Heroism. Christ, things couldn't have been that much different. This still was the human race, wasn't it?

His beer came, and he sipped it, but then he almost dropped the bottle in his lap.

The kid had opened the packet of coke. He averted his head and held the packet up to his nose. He held one nostril, then sniffed deeply. Almost immediately he rocked back and a slow smile spread across his face. He folded the packet and put it in his shirt pocket. Then he took another hit from his joint.

—Like I said, man, I don't want to fuck with your head; I just want to hear the rest of the bitchin' story. I want to hear how it turns out.

Understanding hovered just around the older man. It was there. All of it. But he refused for the moment to make the connections. It was easier to continue.

PART THREE
PEACE
April 1945

30

The stench of his own fear rose into Canaris' nostrils as he tried to concentrate on the code tapping from the next cell. He was hunched in the corner, on the floor of his cell, in what was called the *Kommandantur Arrest*—the bunker—at Flossenbürg Concentration Camp near the old Czechoslovakian border. His wrists were handcuffed, and his ankles were shackled to the wall on longer chains.

The Allies were attacking Mannheim, and the Russians were crossing the Oder. As unbelievable as the news seemed even now, it gave Canaris some hope.

Their investigation of him had bogged down. He was sure of it. There wasn't a way in which the Gestapo could prove that he had been a part of the conspiracy to overthrow the Führer. At least not by simply questioning him. That fool Josef Stawitzky asked his stupid little questions. Around and around they went, the RSHA criminal prosecutor never even realizing when he was being outclassed, outgunned, and outthought.

It was hard to concentrate on the tapping from cell 21 next to his, and for a minute or so he lost track of the message.

For more than eight months he had endured imprisonment. First at the Frontier Police College in Fürstenberg, then at Prinz-Albrecht Strasse itself, and finally here, since the beginning of February, when the bombing had become too intense in Berlin.

The Führer had barricaded himself inside the Reichs Bunker in the Tiergarten. Fortress Germany, they were calling it.

Such news filtered even here. Men like Mathiesen Lunding, a former Danish military intelligence officer being held in the next cell, had ways of getting such information.

But would the war end before . . .

Canaris glanced toward the tiny window in his cell. It was

nearly morning. The sky had definitely gotten much lighter in the last few minutes.

Unconsciously, his mouth began to water. Breakfast, like supper, consisted only of coffee with two pieces of bread and jam. But it was better than nothing. It was food. As long as it kept coming, it was survival.

He turned back and put his ear against the wall. He could distinctly hear the muffled rapping of the chain against the other side of the partition. He listened for a few minutes, then nodded. Yes, it was Sunday. April first. He had not yet lost complete trace of time, although some days were more fuzzy than others.

The Russians would be in Berlin within two weeks. The Americans would be here in less time than that. Lunding seemed so certain.

The tapping seemed to fade out, then resumed for a few moments, and finally it was gone again.

Canaris tapped. "More news?"

He listened, but there was no reply. He was about to repeat his interrogative when someone was in the corridor at his door, and he painfully hauled himself up onto his narrow cot.

The door opened and the very large, rat-faced corporal who served the bunker came in bearing a tin bowl filled with steaming coffee and a small wooden tray that held two pieces of bread spread thinly with a watery blackberry jam.

Canaris licked his lips, barely able to contain himself. His stomach kept turning over.

The corporal grinned brutishly. He held up the tray. "Ah . . . out little sailor boy wants his breakfast?"

Canaris started to nod vigorously, but then he remembered himself, and he sat erect, his eyes on the corporal's.

For a moment the callous young man was nonplussed, but then he grinned. "The sailor boy perhaps doesn't want his breakfast?" He looked at the bread. "Perhaps it is not fit for his aristocratic tastes?" The corporal laughed. "Is that it, then? Didn't you ever get a meal like this in the Navy mess?"

Canaris wanted to cry. His mouth was filled with saliva, and bile rose up in his throat. God in heaven, he was so terribly weak and hungry.

The corporal laughed again. Carefully he lifted the slices of bread from the tray and deliberately dropped them, jam-side down, on the dirty concrete floor. With a short harsh laugh, he set the tiny bowl down, slopping some of the coffee on the floor.

"Five minutes," he shouted, turning on his heel. He stomped out into the corridor.

Canaris willed himself to wait until the metal door was slammed and locked. Then he waited a little longer, until he was certain that the corporal was not watching, before he crawled off his bunk, scraped the bread from the floor, and willing himself by supreme effort to act human, slowly began to eat.

It was terrible, but it was food. It was life. He kept telling himself that.

Incredibly, the meal was finished. He sat looking at the empty coffee bowl and at the stains on the concrete floor, realizing that he could not remember having just eaten. It was not enough. His stomach was still empty. His teeth ached. Every muscle in his body was stiff and sore.

For a long time he sat where he was, but finally he willed himself to get up and clean himself at the tiny bucket of water in the corner.

Someone would come for him this morning, as they did every morning. Sometimes it was a taciturn lieutenant; sometimes it was the prosecutor himself. The questions continued. In a way he almost looked forward to the interrogation sessions. He was never physically abused like some of the others here. And it was sometimes interesting to exercise his mind.

He put on his reasonably clean white shirt and slowly managed to knot his tie. He was buttoning his suit coat when his door was opened. He turned as his interrogator, Stawitzky, came in.

"*Güten Morgen, Herr Admiral*," the little man said. His official title was *Kriminalrat*—criminal consul—for the RSHA. He was considered to be one of the best Gestapo bloodhounds, but Canaris did not think much of him.

"What little misunderstandings shall we clear up this morning?" Canaris asked, careful to keep his voice calm and nonchalant.

"Oh, I think we shall explore again your relationship with the criminal Hans Oster. A fellow plotter," Stawitzky said. The corporal returned, and the criminal consul motioned for him to release Canaris' chains.

Canaris enjoyed this moment most of all. The corporal had to get down on his hands and knees in front of Canaris to undo the ankle shackles. Canaris always outwardly ignored the man, as if he were not there, although he was aware of every movement.

He knew it infuriated the young man who, after all, had been nothing more than a simple farmer's son before he had been given a uniform. A farmer's son on the Polish border.

"You were fast friends, from what I understand," Stawitzky was saying.

"On the contrary. I had known from the very beginning that Oster was up to something. Up to his neck," Canaris said.

"But, then, why hadn't you reported this . . . behavior?"

Canaris smiled. "To whom, *Herr Kriminalrat*? It was an Abwehr matter."

"But you went along with it."

"Indeed. Merely to find out the true extent of Oster's plans."

"I see," Stawitzky said thoughtfully. Canaris' shackles were undone, and the criminal consul took his arm and led him out of the cell.

It felt good to be able to walk like this every morning, although it was depressing to see the rows of cells standing empty. It seemed that every second or third day there would be one or two more empty cells. He did not want to dwell too long on what had happened to those officers.

"But there were discussions between you and Oster," Stawitzky insisted. "Ongoing discussions, if my memory of the notes serves me well."

"There were many discussions between us. Oster was head of my *Abteilung Z*—Central Section—after all."

"I understand that, my dear Canaris. The discussions I refer to specifically are ones concerning the outcome of the war. You both held dismal outlooks."

Canaris stopped and looked directly into Stawitzky's eyes. He knew damned well what the little bastard was trying to do this time. If the man could find the tiniest of cracks in the wall of self-defense Canaris had built around himself, he would work on it until the tiny fracture became a gaping fissure through which the hearse could be driven.

"We definitely had talks along that line," Canaris said.

Stawitzky's piggish eyes lit up.

"We gave consideration to the difficulties in conducting the war. We tried to seek remedies."

"By plotting against the Führer?"

"Don't be a fool! Oster was a dreamer, but what he had in mind, and I concurred, was changing the entire face of our efforts in the field. We felt that a Commander-in-Chief East should immediately be appointed. That is where our potential problems lay. His staff would be augmented, and any proposals for the conduct of the war on the eastern front could be immediately decided by the CiC-East. There would be no delays."

Stawitzky just shook his head. It wasn't quite what he had expected. Inwardly, Canaris was laughing.

"What about Oster's desire to speak with our enemies . . . both to the east and to the west? To try to work something out?"

Canaris smiled. "Yes, Oster spoke to me about such matters, but I attached absolutely no importance to those remarks. I never thought them to be a product of any serious deliberation. From my own point of view, Oster's dreams were nothing more than that—impractical, and certainly unworthy of discussion."

"I see," Stawitzky said. They continued down the corridor and entered the interrogation room at the far end. The place was furnished with a sturdy steel chair in the middle of a bare concrete floor that sloped slightly toward a drain at one side. There was a water tap and a hose in the corner. A worktable faced the chair. This morning there were only a few file folders on the table. Sometimes, much to Canaris' horror, there were various kinds of apparatuses on the table. Although the equipment had never been used on him, he had heard the screams coming from this room and he could imagine what went on down here.

Canaris sat down, eyes forward, without being told. This was becoming routine.

Stawitzky went to the table and thumbed through the file folders.

Canaris had warmed to his subject and did not want to let it go. Oster was one of the very strongest links between him and the conspiracy. By admitting a little of the truth, Canaris hoped to head off the stronger connection.

"Oster had a lot of wild schemes."

"Oh? Plots, do you mean?" Stawitzky asked without turning around.

"No, just dreams. I was never in any doubt that any change of government during the war would not only be construed as a stab in the back but would also disrupt the home front."

"I see."

"I was also convinced that neither our western enemies nor the

Russians would accept an offer of peace. They would automatically regard any such gesture as a sign of weakness."

"You told this to Oster?"

"Yes. And were they actually to accept one in the first instance, they would do so only for show, in order to submit a ruthless demand for unconditional surrender thereafter."

Stawitzky turned around, a pinched look on his face.

"Don't you see, it would be 1918 all over again, but in a far worse form."

"How about General Pfuhlstein's allegations . . ."

Canaris sat forward. "Pfuhlstein was commander of the Brandenburg Division, so naturally he took certain dim views. He was trying to protect his own territory."

"What are you talking about?"

A warning bell began ringing at the back of Canaris' head. Had Stawitzky actually come up with something new? "The rumor went around that I would not place the Division on the front line. That I was keeping it as my own personal bodyguard. Sheer nonsense."

"I understand that, Herr Admiral," Stawitzky said. He referred to a document in one of the files. "There is a statement by Major General Alexander von Pfuhlstein that: '. . . *Admiral Canaris predicted Germany's certain collapse no later than Christmas. This was in 1943.*' "

"That is a lie," Canaris said.

"The general calls you a disseminator of pessimism."

"Pfuhlstein misunderstood me. It can be the only explanation."

"You did speak with him about the war?"

"Of course. Often, as a matter of fact. And my comments to him were colored by the grave responsibilities we all carried on our shoulders. But there certainly was nothing defeatist in my comments."

"And the Brandenburg Division? Let's return to that. You did not want them sent to the front lines?"

"Of course not."

"When we needed the Division the most?"

Canaris dismissed the objection. "The Brandenburg Division's real task was operations *behind* enemy lines, not *at* them."

Stawitzky looked at Canaris for a very long time. Slowly he put the file back on the worktable. He made a motion to someone behind Canaris, and suddenly the rat-faced corporal was there.

Canaris was startled. He had thought he was alone in the room with the interrogator. The corporal was grinning.

"Oster and Pfuhlstein . . . two totally unreliable witnesses," Stawitzky said.

The corporal bent down and tied Canaris' legs to the chair legs and then handcuffed his wrists to the chair back.

"Thank you," the *Kriminalrat* said. "If you will just stand by here." He motioned to his side.

Canaris' heart was pounding. This was different than the other times. He did not like this. It worried him.

"They misunderstood me, that is all," he said.

"You have never been involved in any sort of a plot against National Socialism?"

"Of course not!"

"Pfuhlstein and Oster—both men your friends—tell us that you are lying."

"I have stated to both of those men that we would eventually emerge successfully from the war, despite our steadily mounting difficulties."

"Our mounting difficulties?"

"We have to realize, however, that such a war, in which our entire nation is giving its all and the people at home are being called on for achievements very different from the first war, will not immediately be succeeded by a golden age. All our resources will be required to rebuild Germany and create fresh openings for her continued development."

The corporal was grinning mindlessly, but the criminal consul was hanging on Canaris' rapid-fire words. Or at least he seemed to be.

"You have to bear in mind—and I told this to Oster and Pfuhlstein—that even after the war we will initially encounter a great internal foreign resistance which will inevitably make it hard for us to rebuild at speed and regain our footing abroad."

"But this we will overcome?"

"Yes, of course. But we will have to attune ourselves to the idea that everyone would have to continue making sacrifices and place himself exclusively at the service of the Fatherland. Everyone would have to accept the need to lead a simple life in order to lay the fundamentals of better living conditions for the rising generation."

"What is this pigshit coming from the sailor boy's mouth, Herr Stawitzky?" the corporal asked disgustedly.

"No, no, he is being consistent. You must give him that," the criminal consul said. He turned and picked another file from the table. He thumbed through some of the documents it contained, finding the one he was looking for. "Here it is. On September 13th of last year, and again on September 21st, you made essentially the very same statements."

God help him, he could not remember. Had he said those things?

"What does this mean?" Stawitzky asked pleasantly.

"I am telling the truth," Canaris said, still racking his memory. He had been taken to Prinz-Albrecht Strasse by then. Oster and Pfuhlstein had been there. Or had they?

"No! You lie!" Stawitzky screamed. "It is all lies!"

The rat-faced corporal went to the hose in the corner and turned on the water. He uncoiled it and began running water beneath and around Canaris' chair. Whatever it meant, it terrified him.

"You still have a chance, Herr Admiral, to save your soul, to confess your sins. Our Führer is a compassionate man. He will certainly forgive you."

Love for his Führer rose in Canaris' breast. "I never plotted against him . . ."

"Lies!" the corporal bellowed, dropping the hose.

Canaris turned toward him as a huge fist seemed to rocket out of nowhere, connecting with a sickening crunch with his nose.

Canaris' head snapped back, and the chair crashed backwards, his head bouncing off the wet concrete floor and the ceiling bursting into a billion tiny shards of light.

31

Berlin was a wasteland.

It was Sunday afternoon, April the first. Dieter Schey strolled through the Tiergarten arm-in-arm with Marlene Helbronn. There were a lot of other Germans out and about today. There had been a twelve-hour lull in the bombing. Like gophers coming out of their holes to sniff the air, the people had come from their hovels to enjoy the brief respite.

Marlene had been a rising young actress before the film industry had been ruined by the war. Now she was a regular at OKW headquarters here and out at Zossen. She clung to Schey's arm as if she were afraid he would suddenly disappear.

Like most Germans these days, her skin had a pallor which resulted from her mostly underground existence. Although the Führer would not have her and the other "sluts" in the Führer Bunker, Schey had found her a reasonably secure basement apartment in Charlottenburg which was safe from all but a direct hit by a large bomb.

"All this madness will stop very soon, will it not, Dieter?" she asked.

Schey looked at her and nodded absently. He had been looking at the animal cages in the zoo. They were empty. Most of the animals were gone. Someone at headquarters had whispered that the people had eaten the creatures. Everyone was afraid to tell the Führer.

"It's very sad," he said.

"The whole thing is sad, you know. What happened to our Germany? What has that madman done to us?"

Schey came out of his thoughts and stopped. He shook his head. "You should not say things like that, Marlene. Not to someone like me who works at headquarters."

She smiled and patted him on the cheek. "You're a nice boy,

Dieter, and your loyalty to the end is touching. But you're not facing the facts.''

''I came back to help.''

''Indeed. That was your first mistake . . .''

Schey turned away. These days he could no longer bring up a clear picture in his mind of Katy back in Oak Ridge or of Eva where she fell in New York City. Instead, he was seeing a montage of them both. It was like double vision. Like what he imagined a schizophrenic might see.

Actually, getting out of New York City had been easy, as had crossing the Canadian border disguised as Canadian soldiers. It had taken nearly two days to make it to the airfield in a remote section of Newfoundland, and two more days from there to their refueling depot in Greenland, then on to Norway, and finally home.

There had been a lot of confusion when he returned. Some of the officers treated him as a hero, while others at headquarters treated him as a big fool. There were even snickers when he was given the Iron Cross, in gold. The Führer himself had hung it around his neck, with shaking hands, in what should have been the highlight of his life.

But Katy and Eva were dead and gone. His parents were killed in a bombing raid more than a year ago, and Berlin had never even bothered to inform him. There was no one else in Germany for him. He could not stand to be alone. Especially not at night, when he would hear his son crying and coughing in the upstairs bedroom of their Oak Ridge home.

''I'm sorry, Dieter,'' Marlene was saying. ''I am truly sorry. I forget what happened to you.'' She looked around at the empty cages and beyond the park toward the smoking ruins of the city. ''God, what a terrible, terrible waste.''

She was blonde and blue-eyed, but there her resemblance to Eva ended. There was a hard edge to her that was never present in Eva, despite Eva's sometime bravado. Marlene wore too much makeup, and she sometimes swaggered when she walked, as if she were a model on a runway.

''What do you think it will be like afterwards?'' he asked.

She turned back. ''There will be no more bombing!''

''It will be Versailles all over again. Only this time much worse.''

She laughed. ''You have been brainwashed. What do you

know of the Versailles treaty? You read it in a history book, just like me. German history books."

"You won't be treated very well," he blurted. He did not know why he wanted her to bend.

She laughed again. "The slut of the OKW? The hero's prize?"

"I'm sorry, Marlene; I didn't mean it."

"Sure you did. How do you suppose we met? Why do you suppose I was so willing . . . at first?"

Schey felt as if he were being backed into a corner. "You don't have to stick around. I'm not holding you."

"Oh no, you don't," she snapped, suddenly alarmed. "You have your little bauble. I have mine."

"I'll give you my rations, if that's what you're worried about . . ."

She stepped back and slapped him in the face. The unexpected blow snapped his head back. His hand went to his cheek.

"You son-of-a-bitch! You *Schweinhund*! You think I want your ersatz coffee and cheap cigarettes?"

None of the other strollers in the park bothered to stop and watch. Berliners were numb to almost everything these days.

He didn't know what to say.

"I want you, *Standartenführer* Schey. I don't want to be alone when the end comes. Misery loves company . . . you have heard the expression, no doubt? Well, it's my misery, and you're the company." She shook her head. "You can continue to run off and play war games in the Reichs Bunker. But you will come back to me in my little Charlottenburg hovel. And when it's over and it's my turn to protect you, I will be there still."

Like so many other civilians, she had no concept of what the end would be like, especially if the Russians got to Berlin first.

"I have to go," he said.

"Oh no, you don't, my hero colonel," she said, taking his arm. "Your appointment is not until four o'clock. You made the mistake of telling me that first. We have two hours together. Back at my place."

She led him out of the Tiergarten, down toward Kurfürstendamm, where he had left his car near the *Auslandsorganisation*—or what remained of the building.

*   *   *

The lingering odor of Marlene was still on him when his driver, Sergeant Wilbur Proknow, dropped him in front of the Kaiserhof Subway Station on Voss Strasse. Damage here seemed to be much greater than in other parts of the city. But the Führer Bunker was just around the corner, and along with the Reich Chancellery, this made for the most tempting of all target areas.

He dismissed the driver, then paused a moment to sniff the air. Berlin smelled like a cross between garbage and plaster dust. Always a haze hung over the city from the bombing. It was a part of coming home that he had not been prepared for.

The SS guards at the main entrance to the subway station saluted Schey as he passed, and then he went down the broad marble stairs to the lower level where he checked his Luger and signed in with an SS lieutenant.

"Just one moment, Herr Colonel, and your escort will be up," the young officer said. His left arm had been lost from just above the elbow. The sleeve of his black tunic was pinned up. Schey had trouble keeping his eyes away from it.

Embarrassed, Schey turned away, slapping his gloved hand against his trouser leg.

"How is it up there, sir?" the lieutenant asked.

Schey turned back. "Lieutenant?"

"The weather, sir. What's it like today?"

Schey shrugged. "Not bad. At least the bombing has stopped for a time. There are a lot of people out walking."

"In the park?"

"Yes, but everywhere else, too."

The young lieutenant smiled, but then a civilian in baggy trousers came up the stairs from the lower level.

"Colonel Schey," the gray-haired man said tiredly. They shook hands.

Schey remembered him from debriefings a couple of months ago. He had been at a place called Kummersdorf East outside the city for the past few weeks. Schey had thought his debriefings, which had been going on for months now, had finally come to an end.

"I don't know if there is anything else I can tell you, sir," Schey said. The man was an atomic scientist, but Schey could only remember his first name. Bertrand.

"Neither do we, Colonel," the scientist said.

Schey followed him down the stairs and along the tunnel into what once had been a maintenance area for subway cars. Desks and a few cots had been set up on the far side, away from the tracks, but in the middle of the cavernous hall some great machine had been set up. Wires ran in every direction from it. Huge blades for cooling jutted out. And above and below a central chamber were what appeared to be huge electromagnets. Ductwork ran off at odd angles. A dozen men were working on it.

The scientist was obviously proud of the contraption. "Well, what do you think?"

"I don't know what you mean, sir."

"You were in the United States. You saw their efforts. Come, man, how does this compare?"

Schey gazed at what amounted to a toy by comparison, and he thought about K25, the gas diffusion plant outside Oak Ridge. It had been only one of four operations. The building was more than a mile long. He shook his head.

"It does not compare, sir."

The scientists grinned, apparently misunderstanding. "I told them," he said. But then he lowered his head. "Still, it is too late for us. The war will soon be over, will it not?"

Schey nodded. "It is only a matter of days, perhaps weeks."

"Who will be first in Berlin, the Americans or the Russians?"

"The Americans probably, but we have some intelligence that Eisenhower may hold Patton back and allow the Russians to come first."

The scientist did not seem overly upset. He glanced at his machine. "It is called a cyclotron, Herr Colonel, but I suppose that means little or nothing to you."

"It is a particle accelerator," Schey said. "High frequency oscillations drive a charged particle in increasing circles as it gathers energy."

The scientist's mouth dropped open. "You . . . amaze me, Herr Colonel. You do understand something of this business."

"Only the smallest amount. I know that the Americans are very close. And I also know . . . ." Schey let it trail off.

"Yes . . . yes?"

"I know that Germany would never have developed the weapon."

"I know that. We all do. The war has ruined our chances."

"No, sir. I mean ever. Even if the war had not come here to

Germany, we would never have managed to come up with the bomb.''

''What makes you say that?''

''We don't have the industrial capacity. We never did have. You have seen my reports.''

The scientist smiled indulgently. ''You could not have been everywhere at once, Colonel. One man in your position could never have properly evaluated something so technical.''

''Sir?''

''You were mistaken.''

''About what?''

''About everything,'' the scientist said in irritation. ''Vast warehouses to store war materials we can understand. Machines that take up buildings nearby two kilometers on a side? . . .'' He shook his head. ''I think not even in America.''

It didn't matter after all, Schey thought. He had been dreading these appointments with the scientists. He wasn't any longer.

''Perhaps you are right, sir.''

The scientist nodded. ''Of course, Colonel, of course.''

Schey took a step closer to the big machine. ''The cyclotron works well, sir? You have sufficient equipment on hand? You have no need of further supplies?''

The scientist almost laughed out loud. ''My dear Colonel, you don't seem to understand something here.''

Schey said nothing.

''This machine is months, perhaps even a year away from actual operation.''

''I don't see then . . .''

''It is a research tool, not a production device. This is a laboratory, not a factory.''

''Then why have I been called here today? What do you want of me? I thought you desired information on the American project?''

''You thought wrong, Herr Colonel. We are proud of our work here, of course. But I called you here to show you at what stage we had come to. We need permission to begin dismantling this equipment before the Americans or the Russians show up. It would not do for such toys to fall into wrong hands.''

''And that is all?''

''Yes,'' the scientist said resentfully.

''Then tear it down!''

"No, it is not that easy. We will need permission from the highest authority."

"I'm on the Reich Chancellery staff, I can . . ."

"The *highest* authority, Herr Colonel," the scientist insisted.

"The Führer?"

"Yes."

Schey turned away. He was puzzled. "Why me, sir? Why don't you speak with the Führer yourself? He would have to listen to you."

"It is you, Colonel Schey, who must speak with the Führer on our behalf."

"But why me?"

"Come, do not be so modest."

Still Schey did not see.

"You are a hero of the Reich, Herr Colonel. You have the Führer's ear. You have his confidence. You have his favor."

Schey backed away a couple of steps. The scientist came after him.

"You must do this for us, Colonel Schey. For Germany. We are depending upon it."

Several of the other scientists had stopped their work and were watching Schey.

He was a hero of the Reich, *verdammt*! He had the Iron Cross to prove it. His fingers touched the medal close around his neck. And this is what it had come to. They wanted him to be a favor broker. Marlene was using him for protection. The scientists wanted him to plead their case. And the Führer . . . the Führer looked to him as the ultimate salvation of Germany.

He thought about Oak Ridge and about Los Alamos. He thought about the years he had lost going into deep cover in the United States. And he thought about his more personal losses, Katy and then Eva. But instead of becoming angry, a great sadness came over him. He was a hero of the Reich. Not just for his work in Oak Ridge and Los Alamos, but for what he could do here as well.

Schey nodded. "I will speak with the Führer."

"This evening, perhaps?" the scientist asked hopefully.

"Yes," Schey said. He took one last look at the machine they wanted to tear apart and hide, and then with the scientist he went back upstairs where he retrieved his Luger from the one-armed lieutenant and signed out.

Outside on the street he took a deep breath, then turned and walked up the rubble-strewn street to the ruins of the once-proud Reich Chancellery and around back where he was stopped by the SS guards. He showed his pass and was allowed into the rear courtyard and gardens, where he was again stopped and his pass again checked, even though the guards recognized him.

They saluted, then allowed him down into the Führer Bunker.

The stairs angled back fifty feet beneath the Chancellery, and just at the bottom he checked his Luger with the desk sergeant and took off his gloves and overcoat as he went through the door into the main corridor that ran all the way back to the dayroom.

The place smelled of sweat and cooking and slightly of urine. Apparently, one of the toilets had backed up again. They had been having trouble with them lately.

He could hear music playing softly from the dayroom, and when he came in Propaganda Minister Goebbels was deep in discussion with Luftwaffe Chief of Staff General Karl Koller and an SS general he did not recognize.

"Ah, Colonel Schey," Goebbels said, looking around. He was smiling broadly. "Go right in; he is expecting you."

"Is the afternoon staff conference finished, sir?" Schey asked respectfully. Goebbels was a very powerful and very perverse man. Being around him was like dancing near a high-tension wire, someone had once said.

"Of course, of course. Go right in."

"Thank you, sir," Schey said. He left the dayroom, and went to the rear section of the bunker where the offices, conference room, and the Führer's personal quarters were located.

There were a lot of officers waiting in the corridor or hunched over desks in the various offices. Several greeted Schey warmly. Others ignored him.

Around the corner near the conference room, Keitel, Jodl, and Krebs came past him. They did not even notice his presence.

The Führer momentarily was alone at the long conference table. He was looking down at a large map. He had a slight palsy which caused his head to wobble. His left arm hung slack at his side, and his right hand, raised to his lips, shook slightly. He looked terribly exhausted,

Schey stood there at the corner for a moment, until Hitler, sensing his presence, looked up.

For a moment there was no recognition in the Führer's eyes,

and Schey could do nothing but stare. But then Hitler's face broke into a tired grin.

"Ah. The one man in all of Germany whom I can trust completely." He came around the table, beckoning for Schey.

"I can rely on no one, you know," he said. His voice sounded raspy. "They all betray me. And the whole business makes me sick."

Schey did not know what to say. He was sick at heart. The air in the room was almost too thick to breathe.

"If anything happens to me, Germany will be left without a leader. I have no successor. Hess is mad; Goering has lost the sympathy of the people; Himmler would be rejected by the party. No, there is only me."

32

It was snowing furiously when David Deland tromped up Bascom Hill toward the University of Wisconsin's administration building.

Nothing had been quite the same since he had come home. His father was ill, the weather unsettled, and the war seemed to be dragging on forever.

They had all expected the fighting in Europe to be ended by last Christmas. When the first of the year came and went, the predictions were for February, or mid-March at the latest. They were saying mid-April now. Just two and a half weeks away. He didn't know if he believed it. No one did.

He shifted his briefcase to his left hand, pulled open the door, and stepped inside the big building, crossed the main hall, and took the stairs up two at a time to the university president's office.

He supposed he still wasn't used to his civilian status. No longer did he have to continually look over his shoulder, although he did; no longer did he have to be concerned about whom he talked to, though he tended to be somewhat reticent now; no longer did he have to live with the moment-to-moment fear, although he still awoke at nights in a sweat; no longer did he have to be concerned where his next meal came from or who his friends were.

It had taken him several months to come down from the tremendous stress. And still he had a long way to go.

For a few weeks after he had gotten out, he had remained in Bern with Dulles, doing his debriefings. Then they sent him back to the school in Virginia to teach the new recruits and some of the older hands what it was really like in the field.

But by Christmas he had been released from active duty, and then discharged, providing he would return to the University of

Wisconsin at Madison, to work at the Army Mathematics Research Center.

He had agreed wholeheartedly. But it was much different than he remembered it and far lonelier than he imagined it would be. His friends, even his girlfriend from before the war, had no conception of what he had become. Some of them had gone so far as to tell him to shake it off, to forget about it. But he could not, of course.

E.B. Fred's outer office was usually busy at this hour on a Monday morning. Today only his secretary sat behind her desk.

"Good morning, Mrs. Pett," Deland said.

She usually made some joke with him, but this morning she barely looked up as she nodded. She keyed the intercom on her desk. "He is here," she said.

"Send him in," the speaker on the unit rasped, and she nodded toward the door.

"Is something wrong?" Deland asked.

"I don't know, but they're waiting for you in there. Have been since seven this morning."

"They?" Deland mumbled. He crossed the room and entered the president's office just as the rear door that led out into the corridor closed.

William Donovan, chief of the OSS, was seated behind Fred's desk. He had come here just like this when he had recruited Deland. That seemed like it had happened half a century ago.

Deland's heart skipped a beat. "This is a surprise, sir."

"Come in and shut the door, David," Donovan said.

Deland closed the door, then crossed the room and took a chair across from Donovan. The OSS chief had aged considerably even since Deland had seen him last, just before Christmas. He did not look very happy now, either.

"How is your father?"

"He's holding his own. He'll be back to his department in the fall. But you didn't come here to ask about him."

"No," Donovan said. He was a soft-spoken man. He wore a dark suit and vest, his tie loose. Deland couldn't remember seeing him looking so tired. So wan.

"My discharge is final . . ." Deland began, but Donovan held him off.

"Hear me out, and then you can decide whatever you want. Fair enough?"

Deland nodded uncertainly. This entire business was frighten-ingly reminiscent of his recruitment. Donovan was a very persua-sive man.

"We have a problem in Berlin. A very big problem that cannot wait until the end of the war. *Especially* not until the end."

Deland took a deep breath, held it a moment to relieve the tightness in his chest, and then let it out.

"What I am about to tell you must be considered top secret."

"Then don't tell me," Deland said, suddenly angry. "I put in my stint over there. I did my thing. I don't want to know any more."

Donovan looked at him for a very long time, his eyes penetrating, sad, weary. The weight of the world was in them. He nodded. "All right, David. I guess I understand." He started to rise, but Deland shook his head.

"I'll listen, sir, but I'm not guaranteeing a thing."

"That's good enough for me," Donovan said too quickly. He sat down again.

"By rights, I could walk out of here right now."

Donovan nodded. "We have been working for several years on a weapons project in this country. The British are in on it, but no one else."

"Has it anything to do with the Manhattan Project, sir?"

"Your department is working on it?"

"We've done some of the math. Pump designs. Things like that. Westinghouse and Allis-Chalmers have been up here. Their engineers got themselves backed into a corner."

"It's the same project," Donovan said. He ran a hand tiredly through his hair. "For at least three years Germany had a spy here in this country. He was very good. So good, in fact, that he managed to gather an awful lot of information that would really hurt our position if it ever got out."

"He's still here? Running around loose?"

"No," Donovan said. "Some months ago he managed to get back to Germany."

"Good Lord," Deland said. "He brought his information back for Hitler?"

"We're not worried about that."

"You're not?"

"No. The . . . project is so vast, requires so much industrial potential, that there is no danger Nazi Germany would ever manage to duplicate our work. No chance.''

Deland waited. He couldn't imagine what Donovan wanted.

"The Russians are very close now to Berlin, where this Dieter Schey is presently stationed.''

"The Russians?''

"Yes.'' Donovan licked his lips. "It's possible that Schey, knowing the end is coming, will bargain with his information. Bargain with the Russians. We never thought it would come to this.''

"There is no love lost between the Russians and the Germans. Wouldn't this Schey come back to us instead?''

"No,'' Donovan said, emphatically. "While he was here, he married. His wife . . . was killed in a shoot-out with some of our people.''

"I see.''

"Less than a year later, he had taken up with another woman, one the FBI had its eyes on in Washington. There was another shoot-out.''

"She was killed too?''

Donovan nodded. "In each case, Schey did a lot of damage to us. He's killed at least seven people, possibly more. He won't come back to us. If anything, he'll go to the Russians.''

"How soon?''

"He may have gone already. But surely Berlin will fall within two or three weeks. If it's not already too late . . . we have to put someone inside Germany. Someone who knows Berlin. Someone who is intimately familiar with the city the way it has become. Someone who has field experience. Someone to go in there and find Schey.''

"And kill him?''

"Before it's too late,'' Donovan said. "Before he turns himself and his information over to the Russians.''

Deland thought a moment, his insides boiling. "How do we know he'll go to the Russians?''

"We don't, of course,'' Donovan admitted. "In fact, there are some indications he would not. But it is a risk we simply cannot take. He must be eliminated. He must! I came here to ask you to take on the job.''

Deland had been perched on the edge of his chair. He slumped back now, nearly everything going out of him. It was all coming back to him in a rush. It was the oddest of sensations. He remembered Berlin, and Dannsiger, and Marti Zimmer. He remembered Peenemunde and Major Preuser, and Von Braun himself. And he vividly saw in his mind's eye Wolgast and Katrina Mueller. His heart ached. He could sense her skin, smell her lovely, clean odor, feel her caresses as they made love.

In Bern, Dulles and his interrogators had dwelled for an inordinately long time on Katrina and his relationship with her. Back in the States, in Virginia, the same thing had happened. They seemed less interested in Dannsiger and the business with the underground than they did about poor little Katy in Wolgast.

By now she was probably dead. The Gestapo almost certainly had gone after her. She could not have held out all this time. He was going to have to put her out of his mind, but God in heaven, he was tied up in knots.

"I would have to know this morning," Donovan was saying. "You would fly back to Washington with me. Immediately. From there you'd take a transport across to London. You'd be there by tomorrow afternoon. You'd be briefed on the run and parachuted into Berlin by tomorrow night or very early the next morning—still in the dark, of course—at the very latest. You'd be expected to find and take out Schey very quickly. Twenty-four hours would be optimum."

"Berlin is a very big city, sir," Deland said, but he was still thinking about Wolgast, about Katy.

"Schey's presence has been confirmed. He was on the radio. The Führer awarded him the Iron Cross, in gold. He was promoted to SS-Colonel, as a hero of the Reich. He's a symbol over there now. And he's become Hitler's lapdog. He'll almost certainly be somewhere around the Chancellery or the Reichs Bunker. He won't be far."

"What sort of cover would I have, and how about afterwards? What arrangements would be made for me to get out?"

"You would be an SS colonel with a letter of passage signed by Hitler himself. Your mission is to inspect every aspect of the preparations for the defense of Berlin. You could go anywhere, commandeer any vehicle, any soldier, any supply. Your word would be next to that of the Führer's."

That brought Deland out of his thoughts. He sat forward again. "My God, a simple call to the bunker and I would be exposed as an imposter."

"You have to understand, David, that at this moment the situation is very critical in Germany. Especially in Berlin. We're betting that no one will stop to question your orders."

"So I find Schey and I . . . eliminate him," Deland said without thinking about what Donovan had just told him. "Then what? How do I get out of there?"

"Using your Führer-orders, you commandeer a vehicle and make your way north."

"North?"

Donovan nodded. "The Baltic Sea. Pomeranian Bay. A submarine would be standing by to pick you up."

Deland's stomach tightened. "Exactly where? That is a long coastline."

"Just offshore from Heringsdorf. It is a small town . . ."

Deland closed his eyes tightly. "My God, I know Heringsdorf. It is south of Koserow. Not twenty miles from . . ." Deland opened his eyes.

Donovan nodded. But he didn't look too happy. "South of Wolgast."

"You're bargaining with me."

"There is room for two on the submarine."

"Oh . . . shit," Deland said. He got up. His legs were wobbly. "Oh shit," he said again. He went to the door where he stopped, his hand on the knob. He looked back. Donovan had turned around and was staring out the windows across Lake Mendota. Most of the ice had gone out.

"I'm sorry, David," Donovan said.

"I'll get my things. Where shall I meet you?"

"Truax Field. The operations shack on the flight line," Donovan said. He turned back. "Don't be long."

His father had been sleeping when he left and his mother was at the store, so he wrote a short note and left it for his parents with the nurse. He was glad it worked out this way. Driving down East Washington Avenue out toward the airfield, he glanced up as the capitol building disappeared in a whirl of snow behind him.

His months home had been strange. He had not been able to settle into any kind of a routine. He understood that he had

changed, of course, but he had not realized the extent of his
change until Donovan had shown up.

The snow seemed to part, and he glimpsed the capitol building
in the rearview mirror, its dome patterned after the U.S. capitol
dome in Washington. It was lit by floodlights.

He'd never be able to come back here. There was nothing left
for him. Certainly not his friends. They had nothing in common
with him any longer. Not his parents. They had taught him as a
child that he had to make his mark in the world. And certainly he
would not come back to the university. He felt as if he had gone
as far in academe as he cared to.

It only worried him that he might never find a place that would
be right for him. Everything was so damned lonely. Frightening.

The MPs at the gate had been given his name so that after he
signed in he was waved through. He drove out to the flight line,
where he parked behind base ops, left the keys in the ignition,
and went around to the front door.

Donovan was waiting inside for him, along with the crew of
the DC3 waiting on the apron.

"You made it."

"Are we going to take off in this?" Deland asked.

The pilot, a captain, shrugged. "Depends on how badly you
two want to get to Washington."

"Badly," Donovan said dryly.

"Then we'll go right now. It's not supposed to get any better."

Deland tossed his keys to the sergeant behind the desk. "It's
the '38 Chevy out back."

"I'll take care of it for you, sir; don't you worry about it."

"Yeah." Deland winked. "I don't think I will . . . worry, that
is."

Donovan carried only a briefcase with him. They shuffled
through the snow out to the aircraft, then climbed in while the
pilot and his crew made their preflight checks. The gusty wind
rocked the plane. They could see their breath even inside the
main cabin. It didn't seem to bother Donovan.

"Here's some reading for you," he said, handing Deland
several thick file folders when they were settled in their seats.

As soon as they took off, Deland started through the material,
a life history of Dieter Schey, the man he was going to Germany
to kill. At various spots throughout the dossier, whoever had
compiled the files admitted by notes that certain items of informa-

tion were purely guesswork, while others were even less significant—nothing more than speculation, at best.

Schey's father was a baron, which technically made Schey Prussian royalty. He had been educated in the best academies, had had the best of tutors, and had been the most brilliant student ever graduated from the Abwehr's schools, including a place called Park Zorgvliet.

There were several photographs of him, showing a good-looking, well-built man who could have been mistaken anywhere for a well-to-do American or an Englishman.

"Where'd we get this information, sir?" Deland asked. "I thought all their agents were mystery men with clean slates."

"Dulles got it."

"He speaks English, of course."

"His English is perfect . . . almost too perfect," Donovan said.

The plane was bouncing all over the place. They had been in the air for nearly three hours. Deland was stiff from holding himself against the motion, and his eyes were very tired from reading in the harsh, imperfect light.

He looked up and smiled tiredly. "His Oxford tutors. How'd he get around it here?"

"Everyone thought he was from Connecticut. Or Massachusetts."

"He's a good engineer, from what I gather."

"He's bright, David. Very bright, and very dangerous. He knows his own strengths, as well as our weaknesses."

"Our weaknesses, sir?"

"Our sense of fair play. Our sense of sympathy for the underdog. He'll play it to the hilt. He's a devil."

Deland had read all the files. He remembered every word. He had gotten a far different impression from his reading than he had from Donovan's description. He shook his head.

"What is it? What bothers you?" Donovan asked.

"Schey is not . . . he's not a murderer."

Donovan sighed deeply and looked out the window. The DC3 was set up for passenger service. They were the only two aboard except for the crew. They sat across the narrow aisle from each other.

"He's a highly decorated Nazi. He's killed a lot of people."

"I've killed a couple."

Donovan turned back. "It's different, David," he snapped. "Vastly different, and don't you ever think differently. We're talking about freedom now, democracy versus a terrible regime that thinks nothing of murdering innocent women and children. Gassing them to death and then incinerating their bodies in ovens. My God, the difference staggers the imagination."

It was Deland's turn to look away. Schey was a German. But he was not a killer of women and children. In fact, from what he had read, Schey had killed only in self-defense.

"If you're not one-hundred-percent sure about this, we will find someone else."

Deland looked back. "I'll go. I'll do the job," he said. He glanced down at the files. "It says here he has a son. In Knoxville."

"He abandoned the boy."

After we killed his son's mother, Deland thought. But he didn't say it aloud.

33

The day was very gray and chilly. Canaris was feeling weak this morning. It was a Thursday, he thought. It had been four days since the corporal had damaged his nose. He had not been questioned again, but the corporal had kept up his relentless pressure. These days his rations had been cut to a bowl of coffee and only one slice of bread and jam, morning and night, although he still received a small bowl of thin soup at noon.

He hunched into his overcoat as he sniffed the air, then stepped out into the exercise yard.

His SS guards stepped out of the bunker behind him but remained by the door. One of them lit a cigarette and told some joke. Canaris didn't hear it.

The *Kommandantur Arrest* was a long, low stone building. It contained forty cells, and even from the outside the building looked ominous. There were times when he was absolutely certain that he would die here. But there were other times when his natural optimism soared, and he knew he would survive. It was at those times that he would cock an ear to listen for the sounds of distant gunfire signifying that the Americans would soon be crashing through the camp gates.

The exercise yard for the bunker was on the south side of the camp. The execution yard and crematoria were on the north. Last night he had been awake, looking out his open window, when he realized that a soft gray ash was falling from the sky.

For a long time he had watched the falling ash, and then he stuck out his hand to catch some of it. Suddenly he realized what it was. The crematorium was working. The ash was . . .

He had fallen back inside with revulsion and thrown himself on his bunk, his spirits lower than they had been since his arrest.

There was still a slight odor in the air this morning, a disagreeably sweet, burned odor that turned his stomach when he stopped to think about it.

He walked directly away from the building toward the stone fence. He was not allowed to come within five meters of it, but he always went as close as he could, merely to keep his guards on their toes. It had become a game with him, whose meaning he could no longer remember. But he played it anyway, mostly out of habit.

He had looked closely at his face this morning while shaving. The swelling around his broken nose had already started to go down, but a terrible gray pallor had come to his slack skin. He had lost too much weight. His health would suffer permanently if his conditions did not change soon, he decided, the irony of the thought escaping him at the moment.

His thoughts flitted randomly from his face to his rations, then to the falling ash, but always they dwelled around the same theme: the physical discomforts of his imprisonment. No longer was he so concerned about his defense strategy. Stawitzky was not the ignorant buffoon he had let on to be. He did not yet have enough evidence for a conviction; it was the only reason Canaris was still alive. But he was a skillful *Kriminalrat* who knew how to use fear to break a man's will.

Canaris stopped and looked above the fence, across the stark no-man's land up the hill, to the guard towers fifty meters to the east and thirty meters to the west, and beyond, to the inviting forests of the Oberpfälzer Wald.

Freedom, he thought. The term had never sounded so sweet. Yet he understood that no one in Germany today was free. They were all prisoners caught between the Americans to the west and the Russians to the east, held here by Hitler's madness. The end would be horrible. No better than in here.

He also thought about his career, which had spanned so many years and two world wars—from Kaiser Wilhelm to Adolph Hitler. Were they such different entities?

Someone called his name from the bunker, but he pretended he did not hear. He knew damned well what they wanted. He had come too near the fence, and he was close to the limit he was supposed to walk within the exercise yard.

"Herr Admiral," they called again. They usually called him sailor boy, these days. The rat-faced corporal called him *Schweinhund*. And his official prisoner code name was Caesar. (Stawitzky had let that slip out a week ago.) No one called him Herr Admiral any longer.

He turned, finally, out of curiosity as a Wehrmacht officer, a colonel, his boots gleaming, his cap low, hurried across the exercise yard. The SS guards by the door stood at attention now.

"*Meiner* Admiral," the officer said, and suddenly, like a blinding flash of lightning, and nearly as painful, Canaris recognized the man.

"Hans Meitner," he said, his voice hoarse.

"*Gott in Himmel*," Meitner said, taking off his hat.

Canaris reached out to touch his old friend, but Meitner stepped back a half of a pace and glanced nervously over his shoulder.

"I am sorry, *meiner* Admiral, but the camp commandant, SS-Obersturmbannführer Kögl agreed to this meeting only if nothing passed between us and there was no form of physical contact as well."

Canaris managed to smile. "It is good to see you, Hans. It goes well with you?"

"It was very difficult to get here. I am acting as a messenger for the Führer. He wanted me . . . he ordered me to Salzburg. To speak with our field commanders. But the front is no longer there. I cannot get through."

"Is it bad . . . in Berlin?"

Meitner swallowed and nodded. "I found out that you were here . . . I came as soon as I possibly could. My God, you are going to have to leave here."

"Tell me about Berlin? Are you still at Zossen?"

"You must listen to me, *meiner* Admiral, your diaries have been found."

"Yes, I know that. That fool Stawitzky has twenty pages that were in Oster's safe. He thinks he knows it all. But he can't prove a thing."

"No. Listen to me. There is a lack of office space in Berlin because of the constant bombing, so Buhle moved into your old offices at Maybach II."

"Walter Buhle?" Canaris asked.

"Yes. He's head of Army staff at OKW," Meitner said. "They found your safe. It has been opened, and they have found *all* your diaries."

Now Canaris understood what his old friend was trying to tell him, and suddenly he could feel the chill of the grave. It also bothered him that despite Meitner's close association with a condemned man, he had been promoted and apparently still held the favor of the Führer himself.

"General Buhle is a good man," he said.

"Yes, a very loyal German soldier," Meitner said. "He was at Wolfsschanze, standing not too far from the Führer when the bomb exploded. He was severely injured. He has no love for you."

"What has he done with the diaries? Is he spreading filthy gossip?"

Meitner looked at Canaris with a new understanding, and a great sadness. "He has turned them over to SS-Brigadeführer Rattenhuber."

"I don't know him. Who is he, Gestapo?"

"Rattenhuber is head of the security force protecting our Führer. I am sure he has by now turned them over to the RSHA. Either to Kaltenbrunner or Müller."

Canaris turned away to look again over the fence toward the woods. "This is the end then," he mumbled.

"I have come to take you away."

Canaris turned back and managed a smile. "You still do not understand, do you?"

"What, *meiner* Admiral? What are you saying to me? I think I can get you out of here. But right now, this morning. It will be very dangerous, but what are the alternatives?"

What indeed were the alternatives, Canaris wondered. And what or who, exactly, was Hans Meitner? If he was a friend here to help, his was a misguided friendship. By now it was too late for help. If Meitner was a spy, reporting Canaris' every word, then, too, no help was possible.

Canaris looked beyond Meitner toward the bunker. Perhaps he would be shot down trying to escape. That would eliminate the need for a trial.

He brightened. A trial. Even Kaltenbrunner could not order the execution of the former head of the Abwehr without a trial.

"If you want to help me, Hans, you can do one thing."

"Yes, what is it?"

"Get me an attorney. The best around."

"I don't understand," Meitner said, shaking his head.

"If they have found my diaries, then they know that I *thought* about a Germany without Hitler. But only thought about it. They cannot execute a man for that. A good attorney will get me off."

"Herr Admiral, I have come here today to get you away. I have a car, a driver, and two very loyal Wehrmacht soldiers. They were in the Brandenburg Division . . . in the old days. We can get out of here. Perhaps make it to Switzerland. Perhaps we can find an airplane and get to Spain. To Algeciras."

"Algeciras?"

"Yes, if we can find an airplane. But Switzerland will be easier. We can wait out the war there. It will not be much longer."

"You would give it up? You would give up Germany?"

It was Meitner's turn to look away. He gazed over the fence toward the forest. "Germany is finished. After the war there will be time to return and rebuild." He looked back. "You cannot know how it is in the Reichs Bunker, Herr Admiral. Every day it grows worse. He is a madman. He has deluded himself into believing that somehow God will do a miracle for him. He keeps talking about the parting of the Red Sea. And he's hatched plots to assassinate Roosevelt and Churchill."

"Is there no hope?"

"For us to win the war? No, of course not."

"No, Hans, for me?"

The question seemed to have a great impact on Meitner. He swallowed hard again and glanced up toward the guards by the bunker. "The car is directly in front. My people are just inside the *Kommandantur Arrest*. We will walk back together."

"What about my guards?"

Meitner patted his coat pocket. "I have a weapon. Once inside I will pull it out and shoot them. In the confusion I will give you my overcoat; we will step outside, cross the walk, and get into the car. My guards will be right behind us."

Canaris was ashamed that he had suspected his old friend. "You would do that?"

"We will be out of the main gate and gone before the alarm is sounded. They will not come after us."

"No, Hans," Canaris said after only a slight hesitation.

"No?"

Canaris shook his head, then turned and started slowly back toward the bunker.

Meitner came after him. "What is the matter with you, *meiner* Admiral? They will kill you here."

"I think not."

"Parts of your diaries were shown to the Führer. He went into one of his fits. It was terrible."

Canaris looked at his friend. "What did he say?"

"He is convinced that there is a huge plot against him and that you are one of its ringleaders. He is certain that you have all stabbed him—and Germany—in the back. We would be winning the war now if you and your plotters had not interfered."

"We have lost his war for him?" Canaris asked. Somehow the knowledge gave him strength. The Führer was breaking down as fast as Germany. It was as if they were one and the same being.

He had to smile. He was now coming to the conclusion that Hitler had been teaching his people for years. The people were Germany's body, and he was her soul.

"*Mein Gott*, Admiral, please, you must listen to me. You must save yourself."

"If I went with you now, like this. I would be telling the world that I am guilty."

"He said the plotters must be destroyed at once. Those were his exact words."

"You must do as I ask. There will be a trial, and I will need a very good attorney. The very best in Germany. Preferably someone with no baronage or link with any title. I think just for the moment there is a mood in Germany that runs contrary to the aristocracy."

"I cannot believe this," Meitner said incredulously. "There will be no trial."

"Certainly there will be. We are a civilized nation of laws, Hans, no matter what the Führer has brought us to."

"There will be no attorney."

"Not if you refuse my request. But there is more."

They were getting close to the guards by the door. They stopped again.

Meitner did not know what to say.

"I must know what news there is of Dieter Schey."

For a long time Meitner just looked at him. But then he hung his head. "The spy has returned."

It was a thunderbolt. Canaris could hardly believe his ears.

"Hitler awarded him the Iron Cross. In gold. He is like a puppy dog at the Chancellery and in the Reichs Bunker."

It could not be true. It must not be true. "Did he bring anything back?"

"Yes. The Americans are building some sort of a new *Wunderwaffen*."

"Then our scientists . . ."

Meitner shook his head. "The Führer does not understand it. He calls it Jew science. He refuses to believe it could work, so he has blocked it out of his mind."

"All the work . . . all Schey's years?"

"Wasted. And I think the poor young man realizes it. From what I understand, he was married over there. His wife was murdered by the FBI."

"Yet he returned."

"Yes."

Canaris reached out and clutched Meitner's arm. "He must be killed before he can convince the Führer that the miracle has arrived."

Meitner pulled away as the two SS guards stepped out from the doorway and approached uncertainly.

"I am sorry, Colonel," one of them said.

"Yes . . . I understand," Meitner said.

"It is time for me to get back, in any event," Canaris said looking into Meitner's eyes.

Meitner looked from the guards to the bunker door and back again.

"Have a safe trip," Canaris said.

Meitner had a wild expression in his eyes. He started to reach for his coat pocket, but Canaris knew what was about to happen, so he stepped between the guards and Meitner.

"Give my regards to your friend," Canaris said, and he made a small negative motion with his head.

Meitner was confused. His adrenaline was pumping. "Friend?"

"Yes," Canaris said calmly. "The attorney. You know the one."

Meitner started to come down. He was sweating, and his eyes darted back and forth. His hands were shaking. "Yes," he said. "Yes, I will."

"Then, *auf wiedersehen*, Hans," Canaris said, and he walked back up to the bunker, his guards directly behind him.

Inside, Stawitzky was waiting in the corridor. He was grinning. "A lovely performance, sailor boy."

"What?" Canaris said, only half listening. Meitner's two former Brandenburger troopers were waiting just inside the front entrance. He could see them, their backs turned his way. Four SS guards stood with them by the door. Meitner would never have had a chance.

He looked back at Stawitzky.

"First the fence, then the little display of affection with your colonel friend. What did you hope to gain?"

Canaris shook his head. "I have no idea what you are talking about, you contemptible little toad."

Stawitzky's eyes widened. But then he chuckled. "Your spirit has been renewed by the visit. Old friends do have their uses. But we shall soon put that to rights, I suspect."

"I suspect not, *Herr Kriminalrat*. In fact, I will offer you a piece of friendly advice, if you and your rat-faced corporal will only listen to it."

"And what might that be?"

"There will be a trial soon. My trial. I will be acquitted. Afterwards I shall go after my tormentors with a vengeance that even you will not be able to believe."

"I see," Stawitzky said. He shook his head and motioned for the SS guards to take Canaris back to his cell. "A toad?" he said.

Meitner entered the bunker, passed behind Canaris without looking up, and hurried out the front door, his two men with him.

Stawitzky laughed. "And Krüger will love his new title—rat-faced corporal."

Canaris preceded his guards down the corridor back to his cell and inside, where his handcuffs were placed on him and his ankles were again shackled. They were grinning when they left.

It would not be long now, he thought, crouching down on the floor and tapping the wall with a chain link.

Lunding's reply came almost immediately, and Canaris began telling him about his visit and about his new hope.

34

The bombing had started up again at four in the morning. Schey had been up in the backyard, smoking, when he heard the first bursts out around Spandau. They were probably going after Staaken Airfield again, although there wasn't much left out there these days. Hitler wanted to use some of the broad avenues downtown as runways. It would work.

He could see the flashes far off to the west, and then the dull thumps came as the sound caught up.

They'd work their bombs up here, and then downtown. This apartment was a few blocks south of the corridor. Very little damage had been done here. Most of it had been confined toward the west and, of course, in the east, around Tiergarten.

The Führer was talking about his scorched earth policy again. Yesterday he had actually issued several orders. But Goebbels had taken his mind off the subject with his suggestion about downed Allied fliers. Goebbels wanted them shot. Hitler had agreed. But Doenitz had said, point-blank, that the disadvantages to such a program would far outweigh the advantages.

It was crazy in the bunker. Nothing seemed to make any sense.

The Führer had spent more than an hour talking about the use of Indian soldiers. He thought they were a joke.

"They will not even kill a louse, how can we expect them to defend Germany?" The Führer had laughed. He had strutted around the room. "Give them prayer wheels, and they would work their fingers to the bone."

Schey had averted his eyes. Everyone else in the crowded conference room had applauded.

The Führer stopped at the end of the long table and pounded his fist. "What our real problem is at the moment is concrete."

"Sir?" Goebbels had asked.

"German concrete is simply not standing up to Allied bombs. We must be able to do better than that!" Hitler screamed.

The room was deathly still.

"It is like our German people!" he raved. "If the German people are to be defeated in this struggle, it must have been too weak; it failed to prove its mettle before history and thus is destined only to destruction."

The bombs came closer across Spandau, and Schey flipped his cigarette away. He didn't know what to do any longer. Just lately he had been thinking a lot about his son, Robert, Junior. He wished with all his heart that he could look at his face just one more time. But he knew that would never happen. Robert had probably been taken to the hospital in Knoxville. He had been very sick.

After he got better, he would have been placed for adoption, the records sealed.

Another thought clamped around Schey's heart. What if he had not gotten better? What if he had died in the hospital?

He turned away in a sudden sweat, his heart pounding, his stomach churning.

Marlene, in her nightgown, stood in the doorway. Her face was white. She was frightened of the bombing. It was getting closer.

"Dieter?" she called in a small voice.

"It's all right," he said, choking on the words. God in heaven, it was not all right. What had he done?

"Dieter . . . oh God, I'm frightened."

Schey went across the yard to her, and she grabbed his hand.

"Let's go back down," she cried.

The bombs were definitely getting much closer now on their macabre way up toward the Reich Chancellery. Any day now the Führer would order his bunker sealed. He would order his select few down in the hole, and the doors would close. The final defense of Germany would be conducted from a rat warren. They would be witnesses not only to the final destruction of Germany but also to the complete breakdown of their Führer.

A bomb exploded less than a block to the north, the entire earth shaking underfoot.

"Dieter!" Marlene screamed, and she bodily yanked him down the stairs and into her apartment as three more bombs in rapid succession hit less than fifty yards away.

He felt wooden. Empty inside. He did not know if he would have the strength to remain in the bunker while his Führer, the man to whom he had sworn an oath, the man he had loved above all else, even his own life, disintegrated, bringing his country and her innocent people down with him.

They were in the bedroom. Marlene slammed and locked the door, then threw herself in his arms. She was sobbing; tears streamed down her cheeks and her entire body shivered.

"I can't stand it!" she cried, her voice muffled in his shoulder.

Schey put his arms around her thin shoulders and held her close. "It's all right," he said soothingly.

More bombs were falling outside, but farther away now. They would be safe this morning.

"They're bombing this neighborhood now," she babbled. "They're coming here. They'll be invading next. The soldiers will be here. Russians. They don't take prisoners. They rape the women and then slit their throats. Oh God . . ."

"It's all right," Schey said. But, of course, it wasn't all right. What she was saying rang of truth. He had seen the reports coming from the eastern front. In fact, it would be much worse than she feared.

They parted and he dried her tears with his fingertips. The bombs were very far away now. He cocked an ear. "See?" he said. "It's safe now. They are away from here."

She too listened to the distant thunder toward the Tiergarten, and gradually her shivering subsided, and she began to wilt, her strength fading as her adrenaline cleared.

"Dieter?" she said, looking up into his eyes.

He kissed her, and this time when she melted into his arms, he could almost believe that she was Catherine or Eva, and he responded as he did each time he played the little delusion on himself.

The destruction downtown was awesome, worse than Schey had ever seen it after an air raid. Fires seemed to be burning out of control at every corner. Downed buildings made driving next to impossible. The Kurfürstendamm was completely blocked in half a dozen places, and Wilhelm Strasse was totally unapproachable except from the south, although the square around the

Brandenburg Gate was still open. Ünter Den Linden was completely denuded of trees. It made him sick to see it.

His driver had not shown up. The man had either been killed in the raid or had deserted as so many others were doing just now.

Schey had driven up from Charlottenburg, picking his way as best he could through the mess, circling around, and at other times doubling back when the way seemed completely blocked. There were a lot of Wehrmacht soldiers around this morning. As the front shrank from all directions the troops became concentrated in a smaller and smaller area.

Many of the officers had deserted. Schey had heard the reports. Most of them had apparently headed west or southwest, toward American lines, where they were giving themselves up. Very few talked about heading east to the Russians, although he had heard that some of the scientists from up north had done just that.

A couple of months ago such things would have been unthinkable to him. But lately he too had wondered about desertion. He wouldn't go to the Russians, of course. Stalin, from what he understood, was just as bad as Hitler. But he couldn't head to the west, either. He had been a spy. A hero of the Reich. He had killed civilians back in the States. The coastal watcher in Maine. The FBI agent in Washington, D.C. The cop in Texas, and the two agents in New Mexico, as well as those in the train station in New York City. Back in the States he would certainly be hanged as a murderer.

Suddenly he reached up and unclasped the Iron Cross from around his neck and tossed it aside on the seat. He couldn't even look at it.

In school this business seemed so romantic. Dropped on enemy soil. Working with danger constantly around you. Never safe. On your guard always.

But God, the reality of it. The grinding, crushing, day-to-day business of it. And then, even when you found a safe warm hole where you could hide, at least temporarily, you still had yourself to deal with.

The nearer he came to the Reichs Bunker, the more complete the destruction was, and the more soldiers were in evidence.

He was stopped on Prinz-Albrecht Strasse, as he turned onto Wilhelm Strasse, by four SS-guards. A sandbagged machine-gun emplacement had been set up.

"*Guten Morgen, Herr Standartenführer*," one of the guards said respectfully. He saluted. "Your papers, *bitte*."

Schey handed across his papers, including the special Führer Bunker pass he had been issued several days ago.

When the guard spotted the distinctive seal, he came to ramrod attention. He handed the papers back and saluted again.

"*Alles ist in ordnung!*"

"What is happening here, Sergeant?" Schey demanded, pocketing his papers.

"Why . . . the defense of Berlin, sir."

"Here, on this street corner?"

The SS sergeant seemed surprised. "On every street corner, sir."

Schey looked at the man. He was young, probably in his early twenties. His eyes were clear, and although he was nervous, it was obvious he knew that what he was doing was the correct thing. His superiors had ordered him to do it, and if they didn't know, who would?

"*Vielen dank*," Schey said, saluting, and he headed up Wilhelm Strasse, Gestapo Headquarters behind him.

There was another checkpoint in the next block, but he was not stopped, nor was he stopped around the corner from the Kaiserhof Subway Station on Voss Strasse.

The Führer had puffed up in rage when Schey had relayed the scientists' request that their research apparatus be dismantled.

He had railed for nearly ten minutes about how all of Germany was deserting him at this hour. A man did not have to sell secrets to an enemy to be a traitor to Germany. A man could easily be a traitor by merely turning a blind eye to the traitorous acts of others. Or he could be a traitor by not giving his all to the effort.

Hitler had screamed: "I will not give my permission for the scientists, or for any other man, to turn and run. They will remain in their laboratories. They will redouble their efforts. The tools for the destruction of our enemies are at hand! Nothing must impede progress toward their development!"

Schey had remained in the bunker that afternoon. The Führer had sent a messenger across to the subway station, and Schey had put it out of his mind until now.

The gaunt ruins of the Reich Chancellery were just up the block. There was a lot of activity there this morning. At least a half-dozen troop trucks were parked in front, and it looked as if the engineers had come in to do some repairs.

There was rubble everywhere. The streets here were much worse than elsewhere in Berlin, nearly impassable. Smoke hung thick in the air. It looked like defeat. Everyone acted like defeat.

A large group of women loaded wheelbarrows with brick and pieces of concrete from the street and dumped their loads off to the side. But at the rate they were going, Schey figured it would take them months to clear the road.

He parked in front of the subway station and picked his way on foot over what once had been the broad sidewalk, but now was a hillock of broken brick.

The main entry door had been blown half off its hinges. Schey hesitated a moment at the top.

It was unreal. No one considered this to be an emergency. Not actually. This was business as usual. Almost routine. The destroyers came in the night, and in the morning Germany awoke and picked up the mess. They were like punch-drunk fighters, reeling from the blows raining down on their heads but too numb and senseless to simply lie down. If they did, it would stop. That was the pity of it.

He shoved the door off to the side and stepped down into the front entry hall. It was dark. There were no lights burning, and the windows had been mostly covered by debris. Evidently the power had failed again. It was no wonder.

Schey went downstairs to where the one-armed lieutenant should have been stationed at his desk. But there was no one there this morning.

At first Schey thought the building had been deserted. Perhaps the Führer's message had gone unheeded and the scientists had dismantled their equipment and had left in the middle of the night.

He stepped a little closer, when he spotted a pair of boots jutting out from behind the desk.

"*Verdammt*," he swore under his breath. He knew what had happened.

He opened his holster flap and withdrew his Luger. As he stepped around to the side of the desk, he levered a round into the firing chamber and clicked the safety off.

The one-armed lieutenant lay on his back, his head in a puddle of blood. A single shot had been fired into his face at point-blank range, entering just below his right eye and blowing off a large portion of the back of his skull.

He had been dead for hours. His body was locked in rigor mortis.

Someone shouted something from below, and Schey nearly jumped out of his skin, bringing the Luger up as he spun around. There was a crash of metal, and then everything was quiet. Deathly still.

He glanced back at the body. The lieutenant's Luger was still in its holster. He had not suspected he would die. He had not been prepared.

Schey turned again, paused at the head of the stairs to the lower level, and then started down. Only a very small amount of light filtered down from the open doorway on the street level, but it rapidly became evident that light was coming up from the tunnel as well.

At the bottom he flattened himself against the wall and just eased to the corner.

The tunnel was empty, but from the direction of the laboratory he could definitely see lights, and he could hear the faint hum of an electric subway car in idle. Evidently the underground electrical service had not been interrupted.

He stepped away from the stairwell and hurried through the shadows near the tunnel's curving walls to the access walkway that led a few hundred feet to the old car maintenance area. In the distance, down the track, he could see the back of a subway car. There seemed to be a lot of activity down there. But what the hell was it?

Tightening his grip on his Luger, Schey made his way along the walkway, crouched over and keeping close to the wall. At the far end of the walkway, four steps led down to the level of the siding on which the cars could be run into the maintenance hall.

Schey stopped just within the shadows of the tunnel. Most of the cyclotron had already been dismantled, and the parts were being loaded aboard four subway cars connected together on the main track.

File cabinets and large cases apparently containing blueprints were being stacked at the edge of the tracks by the scientists, while other men loaded the things aboard the cars.

There was an air of feverish activity in the great hall. Most of the lights had been turned off, and no one was doing any loud talking. The only noises were the shuffling of feet echoing in the chamber and an occasional knock as a metal case or part was dropped too heavily.

Some of the men loading gear aboard the train were wearing some sort of uniform. In the dim light he could not recognize it. But something chilly played at the back of his spine.

Standing off to one side of the massive concrete base on which the cyclotron's heavy magnets had rested, was a knot of half a dozen men. One of them was in the odd uniform, while the others were civilians. One of them he thought he recognized as the scientist who had done most of his recent debriefing and who had asked Schey to pass on his message to Hitler.

All of them seemed extremely nervous. Even from where Schey hid, he could see that they kept looking around as if they expected someone to be coming at any moment.

But the uniforms . . . what the hell was going on here?

Schey debated going back up to the street and commandeering some of the SS or even the Wehrmacht soldiers and bringing them back down here. But he decided against it. The scientists were damned near finished. They'd be leaving very soon.

The scientist Schey remembered only as Bertrand stepped aside, giving Schey a clear frontal view of the man in the brown uniform. He wore several medals on his chest. A red star adorned his hat.

He was Russian! The others in uniform were Russian! Here, in the heart of Berlin! These were the atomic secrets Schey had brought back from the States. The scientists had sold out to the Russians.

Without thinking further, his brain numb, Schey stepped away from the protection of the walkway tunnel, raised his Luger with both hands, squeezed off a shot, then a second and a third. The Russian officer fell backwards, his arms flailing. Schey's scientist stumbled and went down, and everyone else in the room scattered.

A bullet ricocheted off the concrete wall just above Schey's head, but still he fired at the scientists and the soldiers by the train.

"Traitors!" he shouted.

Something like a very large fist slammed into his chest just below his collar bone, driving him backward against the rail and nearly flipping him over onto the tracks four feet below.

Other shots were fired, chips of concrete flying, bullets whining off down the tunnel.

Schey felt terribly weak and sick to his stomach, but he managed to regain his balance and he turned and hurried down the tunnel.

At the far end, he turned and fired two shots down the walkway, then pulled himself up the stairs.

Marlene. He could only think of Marlene now. He needed help.

35

The sun shone on the sparkling water, while across Algeciras Bay the great rock pile of Gibraltar stood as a mighty stalwart against the Atlantic. Canaris had stopped his car and gotten out so that he could enjoy the view. Somehow, though, he could not seem to find a way to get back into the car. It was maddening. He could see Dona Marielle Alicia at her little house behind the church. He could almost reach out and touch her. He could see the tears in her lovely eyes. Her lips were moist. She was calling to him.

Canaris awoke. He was drenched in sweat. It was early morning. The sun was just coming up, and he felt stiff and old and very used-up.

He sighed deeply and closed his eyes for a moment, in an effort to recapture his dream. But it had already begun to fade, and by the time he sat up and swung his thin legs over the edge of his narrow cot, he had already forgotten exactly what it was he had dreamed about.

He got up and splashed some water on his face, then combed his thinning white hair as best he could without a mirror.

Lunding tapped his recognition signal on the wall next door.

Canaris glanced toward the foot of his cot. The wall there was scratched from his tapping. Krüger knew damned well what was going on here. So far nothing had been done about it, though. Canaris suspected that Stawitzky monitored their conversations. It didn't matter somehow. Not here.

He crouched down at the end of his cot, his chain dragging across the floor, waited for a break in Lunding's code, and then tapped out his own recognition signal: "Good morning. . . C."

Lunding's code seemed erratic this morning. Over the weeks they had come to know each other fairly well, and now Canaris was certain that his friend was excited about something.

"Slow down; I am confused," he laboriously tapped, letter by letter.

"There will be a trial," Lunding signaled. "Here. Very soon."

"For whom?"

"You. Oster. Sack. Others."

Canaris sat back on his heels. His trial. But Meitner had not sent up an attorney yet. He could not go to trial without counsel. They'd have to understand that.

Lunding was tapping something else, but Canaris interrupted.

"How do you know this?"

"Kögl knows. Trustees. Rumors."

"When?"

"Soon."

Someone was in the corridor and suddenly at Canaris' door. He tapped the danger signal then just managed to scramble back to his cot when the door swung open and Krüger and another SS corporal entered.

The one hung back while Krüger unshackled Canaris' ankles and then released his handcuffs.

"Where is my breakfast?" Canaris demanded.

Krüger didn't bother looking up until he was finished; then he got up and pulled Canaris to his feet.

"My breakfast," Canaris said. His voice was very weak, and his stomach was churning with the thought that his already meager rations would be cut further.

"Put on your shoes," Krüger snapped.

"What is happening here . . ." Canaris started when Krüger yanked him around.

"Forget the shoes," he shouted, and he propelled Canaris out into the corridor.

The other corporal came behind them as Krüger led Canaris down the corridor and then into the interrogation room. Stawitzky wasn't there yet. Krüger roughly tied Canaris to the chair in front of the table, and then he and the other man left.

Canaris' heart was beating rapidly, his breath came in ragged, shallow gasps, but he was unable to control it.

The worktable was loaded with knives and pliers, with needles and things that looked like files or rasps. Many of the tools were covered with blood; others, laid out like instruments at an operating room table, were gleaming.

The door opened and Canaris jerked.

"Good morning, sailor boy," Stawitzky said breezily as he came around in front of Canaris and leaned against the worktable.

Canaris looked up at him. He knew that his lips were trembling; he could not control that either.

"What's the matter this morning; has the cat got your usually very sharp tongue?" Stawitzky asked. Casually he reached behind him and plucked a pair of bloodied pliers from the table.

With a great effort Canaris drew himself up, willing himself toward some semblance of self-control. "There will soon be a trial, and then we shall see."

Stawitzky smiled. "Yes, there will be a trial," he said. He leaned forward. "But tell me, Canaris, how did you know this? Who told you? Your colonel friend?"

Canaris actually managed a slight shrug. "You forget that I was once head of the most powerful secret service in the world."

"*Was*, sailor boy, but no longer."

"Where is my breakfast?"

"In good time, my dear fellow, all in good time. Meanwhile, there are a few things I would like to get straight. Just for the record."

Canaris said nothing.

"Does the name Hans Gisevius mean anything to you?"

Canaris' eyes narrowed. This was old ground. It had been covered at Prinz-Albrecht Strasse. What was the man trying to accomplish now?

"Of course I know the name," he said.

"Of course," Stawitzky said. "And you must have known that the traitor maintained contacts with the Polish Government pigs in Switzerland. You did know that as well?"

"No, I did not. This has already been addressed, *Herr Kriminalrat*."

"Yes, I know. I think Allen Dulles was an old friend of yours."

Canaris again held his silence.

"You know, the OSS chief in Bern," Stawitzky said. He leaned forward, tapping the bloody pliers in the palm of his hand. "The connections are crystal-clear. From you to Gisevius. And from that stinking traitor directly to Dulles."

"No," Canaris said.

"You are guilty, you miserable little bastard," Stawitzky

shouted. "Guilty as hell, not only of plotting to assassinate our Führer but of high treason as well."

"That is not true," Canaris shouted, although his voice was very hoarse and weak.

"You try to topple our government from within, while at the same perfidious moment you treat with our enemies," Stawitzky screamed. Spittle flew from his mouth.

"You cannot prove that."

Stawitzky advanced menacingly on Canaris, his face puffed up and red, an artery throbbing on the side of his neck, the whites of his eyes crisscrossed with broken veins. "You will hang here, you miserable little traitor. You have stabbed the Fatherland in the back for the very last time. You and your bunch of sneak thieves: Oster and Sack and Bonhoeffer and Gehre. Oh yes, Gehre, too. You will see!"

"I have done more for Germany than you can imagine."

"I think you have done more to Germany than even I can suspect. But it will all come out, Canaris. You shall see. And then you will surely swing at the end of a rope."

"It is you who will swing," Canaris shouted.

Stawitzky stepped back and laughed. "Oh yes? And for what, might I ask, sailor boy?"

"The Americans are knocking at our back door. And this is a concentration camp. Those are crematoria in back."

Stawitzky's face screwed up into a grimace. "You little sneaking bastard!" he screamed. He wanted to lash out. It was clear to Canaris. But something stayed his hand. There *was* something even Stawitzky was frightened of.

He finally turned and slammed the pliers down on the work-table.

"Krüger!" he shouted at the top of his lungs. "Krüger, get in here!"

The door slammed open a second later, and Stawitzky spun around.

"Yes, sir," the corporal shouted.

"Get this bastard back to his cell. Get him his breakfast."

"*Jawohl, mein Herr*," Krüger snapped.

Stawitzky looked down at Canaris, then shook his head and left the interrogation room.

Krüger hurriedly untied Canaris' hands and legs, yanked him

painfully to his feet, and started him toward the door. The other corporal appeared. He smiled.

"It's all right, Hans. I will take the prisoner from here."

Krüger hesitated a moment, but then shrugged. "Take the little traitor. The sight of him turns my stomach." He shoved Canaris aside, then left.

"I am Corporal Binder, Herr Admiral. I think your treatment will begin to get better now," the man said reasonably. He looked like some young big-city executive, only with a uniform. He took Canaris' arm and led him out of the interrogation room and down the corridor to his cell.

This was some sort of a trick, of course. A clever method to make him slip up and perhaps tell this one something the others couldn't get from him.

One of his suits, freshly cleaned and pressed, was laid out on his cot along with clean undergarments, a clean white shirt, and a tie. His shoes had been cleaned and were aligned neatly at the foot of his cot.

"There is fresh warm water for you. As soon as you have cleaned yourself and gotten dressed, I will bring your meal."

The corporal turned and left the cell, locking the steel door behind him.

Canaris stood in the middle of the tiny room for a long time, staring at the clean clothes. Gradually he realized that his cell had been cleaned as well. There were fresh bedclothes on his cot.

He went to the water bucket. There was a small piece of soap in the warm water. Beside the bucket was a towel and washcloth as well as his shaving things and a small mirror on a stand.

He turned and glanced toward the door. Were they watching him? Were Stawitzky and Krüger having their little laugh now? What were they trying to do to him?

Of course, if he was going to be tried soon, they'd want to keep up the sham that he had been treated well here, especially if they were uncertain as to how the trial might come out. If he actually was acquitted and was set free, with apologies, there would be hell to pay. He'd make damned sure of it.

He peeled off his shirt and began to wash, the soap and water sensuous on his emaciated frame.

Lunding tapped.

Canaris glanced toward the wall. It would wait, he told himself as he continued with his bath. Lunding would understand.

His hands shook, so he did a poor job of shaving, nicking himself twice in the process, but he did feel much better. Much fresher. He got dressed in his clean clothing and then tapped for Lunding.

"Interrogation easy. Breakfast coming. No leg irons or handcuffs. Talk later."

"Be careful," Lunding signaled.

Canaris climbed up on his bunk and sat there, his knees together, waiting for his promised meal. His stomach was so empty it was hard to sit still. He almost always felt nauseous these days from the lack of food. But this morning he felt worse than he ever had.

It was well after ten before Corporal Binder returned with a small stool which he set down in front of Canaris. He went back out into the corridor and returned, bearing a large tray laden with a bottle of wine, a large iron pot filled with a thick, rich stew, and a small loaf of heavy dark bread.

Canaris' mouth filled with saliva as he smelled the wonderful odors.

"I am sorry there is no butter in the camp at the moment. Even the commandant has none for his table," Binder said.

Canaris tore his eyes away from the food and looked up. He was shaking. Binder smiled.

"Take your time, Herr Admiral. The *Kriminalrat* wishes to speak with you later this afternoon. But until then, you will be left alone. When you are finished, you may signal, if you wish, and go out to the exercise yard."

"Why . . . why . . ."

Binder smiled again. "I only follow my orders, Herr Admiral. But the stew is very good. I promise you. I had some myself." He turned and left the cell.

Canaris looked at the door. Were they watching him now? Watching to see if he would attack his food like an animal?

He turned back to his tray, poured a glass of the red wine, which was surprisingly good, and then tore off a small piece of bread, dipped it in the stew, and slowly ate it, the wine hammering his stomach, nearly making him vomit.

He looked up at the door again and smiled. He would not give the bastards the satisfaction of watching him get sick.

Slowly he ate the stew and most of the bread, and he drank more than half the bottle of wine. His stomach finally settled down somewhat, and although the food and drink were far too rich for him in his present condition, he managed to hold the meal down.

For a long time after he was finished, he sat back, his mind, as well as his body, numb. But then he had the urge to be outside, and he got up and rattled his door.

Binder came almost immediately,

"May I go out for a few minutes?" Canaris asked.

"Of course, Herr Admiral," the corporal said.

Canaris got his overcoat, then went with Binder down the corridor and outside, two SS guards coming out with him.

He stood just outside the doorway for a moment or two. One of the guards lit a cigarette; he offered it to Canaris, who started to refuse, but then shrugged and took it.

"Thank you," he said.

"*Jawohl, Herr Admiral*," the guard said respectfully.

Canaris looked at him in amazement. It had to be the trial. If he were to be acquitted, Stawitzky would have this good treatment to fall back on.

He turned and slowly headed across the exercise yard. The morning was gray and overcast. There was still something of the winter chill in the air. Canaris shivered.

The cigarette made him light-headed. It was the first he had had in months.

He stopped well outside the five-meter zone away from the fence and stared out at the forest. A mist curled through the trees. The scene, if he ignored the fence and the guard towers, seemed so peaceful, as if the war had never occurred.

A great yearning for peace welled up within his breast, and the pain it caused was almost physical when he thought about his missed opportunities.

But even now, he had to admit to himself, if he were free, he would not run to Algeciras. He would remain here to help rebuild his country for the second time in less than thirty years.

He had his memories, though. Of Spain, before the war, when he was a young man looking for submarine bases. Dona Marielle Alicia was the daughter of the wealthiest man in Algeciras. Don Rico was a friend of Germany, and he had taken Señor Guillermo into his home.

Whenever he came to Spain, and that was often in those days, he would manage to stay at least a few days with Don Rico.

He remembered those times so vividly now. He could even see the colors: the marvelous blue-green of the ocean, the striking red of the roses, and Dona Marielle in her yellow gown on the evening that he realized he loved her—and that he would always love her.

They had danced, but they had barely talked that night. Every time he touched her, she shivered, her tiny milk-white shoulders rising up, her large, dark, liquid eyes looking into his, her bosom heaving.

Much later they had had their long talks. It was impossible for them ever to consider marriage. Daughters of wealthy Spanish aristocrats did not marry German spymasters. It simply was unheard of.

But for that evening their disappointments were still in the future. That evening they both knew what they wished to have, in absolute defiance of every code of ethics that existed in Spain or Germany.

Canaris slept in the east wing of the huge villa overlooking the sea. The Rico family slept in the west wing.

She came to him in the middle of the night, across the courtyard, through the gardens, and up from the path that led to the sea.

They stood in front of the doors open to the gentle sea breeze as they undressed and then gazed wonderingly at each other's body.

Even now, standing within the exercise yard of Flossenbürg concentration camp on a chill spring morning, he could feel the gentle caresses of the summer's breeze, feel the incredible softness of her skin, remember her lovely breasts crushed against his chest, and most of all he could sharply recall the unbelievable feeling of wholeness and pleasure while they made love.

"Herr Admiral," someone called from the bunker. "Admiral Canaris."

He turned as Corporal Binder came across the exercise yard.

"It is time to come in, sir. You have been out here for nearly three hours now. It is lunchtime."

36

Dieter Schey came slowly awake, a sickness deep inside of him welling to the surface and threatening to make him vomit. He felt frighteningly weak, and even the effort of sitting up in the bed was almost too much for him.

He figured it was late afternoon. The bedroom door was open, and he could see the last rays of the sun through the living room windows in Marlene's basement apartment.

He sat on the edge of the bed, and hung his head, and closed his eyes. It had been . . . how many days, since he had been shot? He could not remember clearly. But it had been at least two nightmarish days of pain, of strange, feverish dreams, of reliving the shooting over and over again.

Like a silly schoolboy he had remained a perfect target at the tunnel mouth. But something had made him lose all of his training in a flash. The Russians were there in the tunnel, were being given the American atomic secrets by the Reich's own scientists. By good Germans. Everything he had gone through— the years of deep cover in the United States, the killings, the murders of Katy and Eva—all of it had culminated in one instant of mindless revenge when all thoughs of self-preservation went out the window.

Fortunately, he had not been stopped on the way out of the area, and somehow he had made it here, to Charlottenburg and Marlene.

He lifted his head and opened his eyes. Marlene, dressed to go out, stood in the bedroom doorway.

"What are you doing, Dieter?" she asked. Her voice sounded hollow.

Suddenly she loomed over him and laid him back in the bed.

"Where are you going?" he asked. His voice was very weak.

It did not sound like him to his own ears. He reached up to touch his face. There was a stubble on his chin.

"Listen to me, Dieter; you are too weak to try to get up," she said. She sat with him on the bed and looked into his eyes. She was frightened. He could read it there.

"How long . . ." he croaked.

"Four days."

He could not believe it. Impossible.

"It's Sunday, Dieter," she said. Her eyes were filling with tears. "They're looking for you. They think you've deserted."

"The SS has been here?"

"Not yet, darling," she said, brushing a strand of hair away from his forehead. "They don't know about this place. Remember?"

But he hadn't deserted, goddamnit. He had killed at least one of the traitors. They'd have to understand.

He thought he had given voice to that, but he had not because Marlene pulled the covers back over him. "Don't try to talk," she said. She reached down and kissed him lightly on the lips. "Sleep," she said. "I'm going to try to get us something to eat. I'll be back soon."

"Marlene?" he asked.

"It's all right; the SS won't find you, my darling," she said. Tears rolled down her cheeks.

Was he going to die, he wondered? Was that why she was crying? He felt so terribly weak. And then there was that something else at the back of his mind. Something he had resolved on the way out here from the subway station laboratory. She didn't know about it, and he had to keep it from her. She would worry too much.

When Marlene left the apartment, tears were pouring from her eyes. She went out the front way, careful not to bang the iron gate at the top. It was dusk. It would be dark very soon.

She stood on the sidewalk, looking up and down the street. Very few bombs had hit this street, so she could almost pretend that there was no war, that the city around her was not mostly destroyed. She could pretend that her man was back in their apartment, sleeping after a hard day's work. She could pretend that she was simply on her way to the market to pick up some

fresh meat, perhaps some potatoes, a little lettuce, a few freshly
baked rolls . . .

Why had it turned out this way? How in God's name had
she been reduced to this?

Stiffling a sob, she headed up toward Königs Allee, the heels
of her last decent pair of shoes clattering on the pavement, her
heart hammering in her chest.

She had only two choices. Certainly, remaining in the apartment with Dieter until the end for them came was not a viable
option. It left her only the Resistance or the SS. She had had no
problem with her choice.

The big man whom she knew only as Bernard suddenly appeared from the doorway of a partially bombed-out ruin of a
building.

Her heart leaped into her throat. Her hand went to her mouth.
"Oh," she said in a small voice.

"You have found him for us, Fräulein?" the man said. He had
a pleasant voice. But it was obvious he was weary.

She had done a lot of work for the Resistance over the past
months. She had associated herself with any SS or Wehrmacht
officer she could get close to, reporting back to Bernard whenever she had learned something. It was why she had sought out
and attached herself to Schey. Until now, though, she had not
had the courage to tell the Resistance about him. Somehow,
despite herself, she had fallen in love with him.

"Yes," she said timidly. She kept walking. The man had
taken her arm. It looked as if they were husband and wife, out
for a stroll during the lull in the bombing. It was not an uncom-
mon sight.

"Yes, where is he?"

God help her . . . "In my apartment," she said. "He is
wounded."

The man stopped her, a play of emotions across his face. "Do
not go back to your apartment, Fräulein. Find someplace else to
live. There are plenty of apartments empty in Berlin now. The
war will be over in a matter of days, in any event."

"What are you going to do? . . ."

The man pulled out a package from his coat pocket and handed
it to her. They were captured American C rations. A lot of SS
officers would have paid in gold for the food.

"The SS are looking for him," she blurted, taking the food. She felt so damned guilty.

"What for?"

"They think he has deserted."

The man smiled. "Just go away now, Fräulein. If we need you, we will find you." He turned and walked off in the opposite direction.

Marlene watched him go, and then she held the C ration package tightly against her breasts, and her mouth began to water. God help her, she was so hungry.

The Westland Lysander's big Bristol Mercury engine made all normal talk impossible. Deland, dressed in olive drab coveralls over his SS colonel's uniform, sat back in his seat, his eyes closed, although he was far from sleep. He wore a headset which connected him to the pilot. There was no one else with them.

It had been a fairly routine flight over the channel, then across Holland and into Germany. There weren't many Luftwaffe planes up in the air any longer. There had been reports of a new-type, very fast German aircraft called a jet. But there weren't many of them, and in the two days he'd spent in England, waiting for the weather to clear, Deland had heard that Allied bombers had taken care of the factories that made the special fuel the new jets required.

He had gone over the operation plans a hundred times in a briefing room at Tempsford in Bedfordshire, outside of London. He was to be dropped in a field outside the village of Nauen, about twenty miles west of Berlin. It would be up to him to make his way into the tiny town where he would be met by one of the leaders of the Resistance who would provide him with the initial intelligence and his transportation. Schey had been spotted somewhere in Charlottenburg. It was going to make the job much easier. Charlottenburg was wide open, and it was to the west.

Deland never stopped to ask why, if Schey had been spotted in the Berlin suburb, the one who had spotted him didn't go in and do the job. He was afraid of the answer he would get.

"Hey, Joe," the pilot's voice blared in the headset. "You about set back there, mate?" They were called the Moon Squadron out of Tempsford, and the agents they had been dropping into France and Germany and Denmark from the very beginning were all called Joe.

Deland sat up with a start. The pilot was grinning over his shoulder at him. Deland smiled and gave him the thumbs-up sign.

"Okey-dokey then; we're just a couple of minutes to the drop zone. You can open the gate about now."

Deland pulled the headset off and laid it aside, then undid his seat belt and pulled himself across to the port-aft perspex window and undid the latch. The cold, howling gale filled the cabin, and Deland reared back, flopping into his seat. He reached down and fumbled with the straps holding his parachute. When he had them secured, he picked up the headset.

The pilot was looking at him. His voice came over the earphones. "On the count of three, you go. One is blinking red. Two is amber. And three is green."

Deland nodded.

"Sixty seconds to target; take your position. And . . . good luck."

Deland grinned. He laid the headset down and awkwardly pulled himself back to the opening in the side of the cabin. He clipped his rip cord snap shackle to the overhead ring, pulled his collar up, then took a deep breath, held it a moment, and let it out slowly. The red light was blinking.

"One," he shouted.

There was nothing outside but a cold, windy blackness. A void.

The red light went out and the amber began blinking.

"Two," he shouted.

He gripped the side of the opening, braced his feet for the proper push off, and the amber switched to green.

"Three," he shouted madly, and Deland pushed his way smoothly out the door, the slipstream pulling his body, the Lysander's horizontal stabilizers and elevators flashing overhead, then a tremendous jerk as his arms seemed to be pulled out of their sockets, his back nearly dislocated.

The roaring noise was gone, the wind diminished to a gentle breeze, and the heart-clutching fall had been reduced to an almost pleasant sway.

To the east he could see a number of fires. There had been a bombing run over Berlin earlier tonight.

Below was a vague, quilted pattern of blacks, very dark grays, and only slightly lighter grays. He could see a road, but no town.

There were patrols around Berlin. He had been warned that because of the increased bombing, he would be shown little or no mercy should he fall into enemy hands. Especially dressed the way he was, with the forged Führer-letter.

But that was a moot point now. He could not turn back and simply go home. His escape lay far to the north. To the submarine. To Katrina in Wolgast. If she was still there. If the Gestapo had not arrested her and killed her.

The thought of Katrina in a Gestapo cell being tortured was almost more than he could bear. He had managed, for the most part, to put the thought out of his mind all these months, but now it reared its ugly head again.

First he had to land without hurting himself. Then he had to make it to the Nauen road without detection. Then he had to make his contact. The staff car would be hidden in a barn, just before the town, on the main road into Berlin. There was a certain twisted tree marking the dirt track. His contact would be there with his instructions. Then he had to find and kill Schey. And somehow make his way north, across enemy lines, between Russian troops to to the east and Allied troops to the west.

The side of a grassy hill was suddenly coming up at him very fast. He got the impression of a broad clump of trees to the west and a road off to the north, but then he hit, willing himself to go loose, willing himself not to stiffen against the fall, willing himself to roll with the impact as he had been taught in one very brief afternoon of training.

He banged his left elbow on a rock, his fingers going numb, and then he was tumbling end over end, the parachute dragging him down the hill, until he managed to dig in his heels, grab the straps, collapse the chute running to them, and pull the fabric in close to his chest in a huge bundle.

There were no sounds. No sirens. No dogs barking. No troops coming.

Deland lay on the heap of the parachute, his heart hammering, the fingers of his left hand tingling.

He jumped up, released the parachute straps from around his chest and between his legs, and then bundled the entire thing up and raced off toward the protection of the trees below in a shallow valley.

It was chilly here, but he was sweating by the time he made it into the woods and crouched down. He watched the crest of the hill intently for the sign of any pursuit. The road and the town were just a couple of miles on the other side. If there were troops stationed there, they could easily have spotted him coming down.

After a few minutes, however, he pulled off his coveralls, having a hard time getting them over his uniform boots. Then he opened his pack and unfolded his entrenching tool.

Within five minutes he had managed to scrape a hole deep enough to dump the parachute, his coveralls, the shovel, and the pack, after he had removed his black leather gloves and his SS-uniform hat.

He pushed the dirt, and then the leaves and twigs, over the hole, brushing the ground to make it seem as if it hadn't been disturbed. Then he put on his hat, pulled on his gloves, and started around to the east of the hill, in the general direction of the highway.

It was a moonless night and yet he still felt very exposed out here. He would be hard-pressed to explain what he was doing wandering around the countryside, Führer-orders or not.

After twenty-five minutes he had made it around the base of the hill, and below him, across a small creek, was the highway. He could see the fires in Berlin as several soft red glows on the horizon to the east. Of the town of Nauen he could see nothing. The barn was back toward the west.

He worked his way down into the narrow draw, then about fifty yards downstream, he found a place where a half-dozen big rocks had partially blocked the gentle flow, providing an easy path across.

On the other side he started up the cut, when he heard the sound of several trucks coming up the highway from the east.

He was just below the level of the roadway, and he threw himself down, flattening himself against the ground. Three troop trucks went by, their engines clattering, thick black smoke coming from their exhausts. The rear cargo flaps were open, and Deland could see the troops inside. They were dressed in gray Wehrmacht uniforms, but he got the distinct impression that they were merely children. Young boys of no more than ten or twelve.

He had heard about it. But he had not believed children were being conscripted until now.

Up on the highway there was no sign of traffic, although from here the fires in Berlin were distinct on the horizon. He even imagined that he could smell the smoke and the plaster dust.

He straightened up his uniform and started toward the west, his back straight, the heels of his boots digging into the asphalt, his stride long, purposeful.

The road curved gradually around the base of the hill, then dipped down on the other side, curving sharply out of sight to the north.

Nauen would be a mile farther beyond the curve, the twisted tree and the barn just at the curve if the maps he had studied were correct.

If he had felt exposed out on the field, he felt absolutely naked here. If a patrol came by, he decided, he would tell them that he had had an accident. He would use his letter to commandeer a vehicle, and from that point he'd have to play it by ear. Somehow he would make it into Berlin. Of course, without his contact his mission would have to be scrubbed. Charlottenburg was a large area. He'd never find Schey without help.

Within another few minutes Deland had made it around the curve, and about a hundred yards farther was the twisted tree, a narrow dirt track running down toward the base of a hill.

Deland hurried across the road and then down the path where he saw an old, dilapidated barn with a broken stone foundation and gaping holes in the roof.

He stopped twenty yards away, unsnapped the flap of his holster, and drew out the Luger. He levered a round into the chamber and then started forward again.

As he walked, he began to whistle the tune to "Little Brown Jug." It was their recognition signal. The Resistance was there in the barn. He did not want to be shot as an SS colonel.

Ten feet from the barn someone stepped out of the shadows to the side.

Delan stopped, raising his Luger.

"I didn't know it was going to be you," Dannsiger said.

Deland stepped closer, and suddenly he realized who it was. His hand shook as he lowered the Luger. "My God. I thought you were dead."

37

There had been a current of excitement all during Saturday, and now today as well. Binder refused to be drawn out by Canaris, but Stawitzky had stopped by for a short chat about the old days in the Abwehr. Before 1939. He was almost friendly. Canaris spotted Krüger out in the corridor. He was grinning, his lips drawn back over his teeth like a rat's.

Lunding had been silent for most of the day, although he had signaled that there seemed to be a great deal of activity in the camp the last time he had been allowed out.

At noon, Canaris had asked Binder if he would be allowed his exercise period, but the corporal just shook his head, left the tray of food, and got out.

The meals came three times a day, each full and well-balanced with either meat or chicken, plenty of vegetables, and always the heavy dark bread which reminded Canaris of Bavaria.

Mostly he had wine to drink with his meals, although for Saturday's dinner he had been given two large steins of thick, rich beer, which he had thoroughly enjoyed.

Something was about to happen. There was no doubt in Canaris' mind. But what?

For a time, gazing out his window that looked across the exercise yard and beyond the fences to the woods, he speculated that the Americans had finally advanced within striking distance and soon would be here. It would explain the activity, the fine rations, and the good treatment.

Yet, somehow, he knew that wasn't the case, and when Binder brought his dinner tray shortly before six, the corporal seemed especially nervous and ill at ease.

"What is it, Corporal?" Canaris asked.

Binder went back out into the corridor without a word. Canaris thought he was leaving, but he came back a moment later with a

329

clean, freshly pressed white shirt. He looked very guilty and just
a little frightened.

"Why are you giving me this shirt now?" Canaris asked,
rising. He was truly alarmed.

Binder said nothing. He just held the shirt out. Canaris took it.

"Can't you speak to me? Can't you tell me what is happening?"

Binder glanced over his shoulder. He was really frightened.
"You are to clean up after you eat your meal. Shave. Put on your
clean shirt. And wear a tie."

"What is it?"

"Colonel Oster is already in trial. He has confessed."

It was as if a gigantic hand had clamped itself around his heart.
Canaris staggered, and sat heavily on his cot.

"Hans? The trial?"

"There are others, Herr Admiral. Other prisoners have been
brought here. I don't know who they are, but . . ."

Canaris looked up. "Do you know the name Meitner? Hans
Meitner? He was the colonel who came to visit me."

"No, sir. I do not know him," Binder said. He stepped back
as if to go. "Please, Herr Admiral, have your dinner and change
your shirt. Your trial is . . . next." He turned and left the cell.

Dinner was a small baked chicken with *Spaezle* and some raw
cabbage soaked in vinegar. There were two steins of beer.

His trial! Meitner had evidently failed. There would be no
defense counsel. The RSHA had finally gotten its way. They had
his diaries. There was no hope!

He pushed his tray aside and got down on the floor at the foot
of his cot. He tapped for Lunding, but there was no answer, and
after five minutes he gave up. His friend was either out of his cell
or asleep. He would try later.

He dragged himself back to his cot, picked at his food for a
moment, but then began to eat in earnest. He had spent too many
months half starving to let any opportunity to eat pass. Besides,
he told himself, if there was to be a trial tonight, he would need
his strength. All of his strength. They might convict him, but
they were going to have a fight on their hands.

Canaris had finished eating, had cleaned up and was dressed
and waiting for them when they came a few minutes before eight.
Binder, Krüger, and two other SS guards all crowded into his

tiny cell. All of them were respectful. Even Krüger tried to be as considerate as possible while he placed fetters on Canaris' ankles and handcuffs on his wrists.

No one said a word as they led him out of his cell and down the corridor past the guardroom, his chains clattering on the floor.

His heart was pounding very hard, and it was difficult for him to catch his breath.

They turned to the right outside the front door and went down the walk alongside the main driveway. The night was cool. But it felt good to be outside. Canaris had been this way only once before, when he had first been brought here from Berlin.

They crossed the driveway and entered what appeared to be one of the administration buildings. Otto Thorbeck, whom Canaris recognized as the SS judge based down in Nuremberg, was waiting in the entryway.

He preceded them as Canaris was led down a short corridor and into a large room that had been set up as a courtroom.

Seated at the bench were the camp commandant Kögl, Stawitzky, and Colonel Walter Huppenkothen, his old adversary from the Prinz-Albrecht Strasse interrogations.

There were two recording secretaries seated to one side, along with Thorbeck who had positioned himself at the open door to a side room. Canaris just caught a glimpse of a long table filled with files and other papers. Evidence, he figured.

He was directed to a chair facing the bench, then Binder, Krüger, and the other two guards withdrew to the back of the room.

Huppenkothen raised a gavel and slammed it sharply on the table. He seemed angry, and although he was looking up, his eyes refused to meet Canaris'. The others were the same. They were all frightened. This was to be a sham.

"The Schutzstaffel Summary Court, District Headquarters, is hereby convened in the matter of Admiral Wilhelm Franz Canaris, charged in the first count: That since 1938 the accused has been a vital and active link in plans for a coup d'état against the lawful National Socialist Government of our Führer Adolph Hitler; in the second count: That the accused did conceal within the Amt Ausland/Abwehr, while he was head of that body, the said conspiracy and conspirators; in the third count: That the accused, during the winter of 1939–40, did attempt by verbal and other means to incite various German military commanders into rebellion; and in the fourth count: That the accused was privy to secret illegal negotiations on Germany's behalf between one Josef Müller and the Catholic church, to wit, the Vatican.''

Huppenkothen had been reading from the indictment. He looked up. ''You are charged with *Landesverrat*, to wit, treasonable activity against the state, as well as *Hochsverrat*, high treason. How do you plead?''

So that was all of it, Canaris thought, his mind racing. They had not charged him with the July 20th assassination attempt on the Führer, nor had they said a thing about his diaries. Was there hope after all?

''Before I plead, *Herr Standartenführer*, I wish to raise a number of points of law,'' he said. His voice was surprisingly strong, although he could not trust himself to stand yet.

Huppenkothen sighed deeply, but nodded.

''First, I have no defense counsel, contrary to law. Colonel Hans Meitner was my appointed . . .''

''Colonel Meitner is dead. He was killed in action two days ago,'' Huppenkothen snapped.

It was as if all the air had suddenly left the room.

Stawitzky leaned forward. ''You have had ample time to provide yourself with counsel.''

Canaris tried to order his thoughts. ''I request a delay in these proceedings, to provide me time to . . .''

''Denied,'' Huppenkothen said.

''On what grounds?''

''The exigencies of war. Proceed.''

Canaris took a deep breath. ''I am a member of the Armed Forces. An SS Summary court has no jurisdiction in this matter.''

''Superseded on the orders of the Führer.''

''Then venue belongs in Berlin, not here.''

''Superseded!''

Canaris sat back and shook his head. ''This is a sham. If you want my help to proceed with it, you will be disappointed.''

Stawitzky was smiling. The camp commandant, Kögl, was bored. Huppenkothen was angry and impatient.

''How do you plead?''

''Not guilty to all charges,'' Canaris said. He looked off toward the windows. Arc lights had come on across the compound. There seemed to be some activity out there, but it was impossible from here to tell exactly what was going on. He kept thinking about poor Hans, whose only crime had been to befriend an accused man.

Otto Thorbeck stepped into the side room and brought out several fat file folders which he placed before Huppenkothen and his two newly appointed associate judges. They were Oster's files. Canaris was reasonably certain of it. It was the same material that had been used against him from the very beginning. Not very convincing. Why hadn't they brought his diaries? Perhaps they were saving them for the very end?

Everything, all the questions, the results of all the interrogations from the Frontier Police College, then Prinz-Albrecht Strasse and finally here, came out now, as Huppenkothen spoke.

The words flowed around Canaris—meaningless, in one sense, because he was so intimately familiar with the material, and yet made more ominous than ever before because of the nature of this proceeding.

He glanced from Stawitzky on one side to Huppenkothen in the middle and Kögl at the opposite side of the bench. Then he looked at Thorbeck. They all understood what was happening here. They all understood the sham. They were simply going through the motions so that it would all be down in black and white on paper.

Was Wilhelm Canaris murdered? Of course not! There was a proper trial! Rules of evidence were meticulously observed. The question of jurisdiction and venue? . . . Everything was breaking down because of the war. We did what we could in the name of justice. But traitorous acts must be dealt with. Swiftly. Harshly.

The courtroom was suddenly silent. Canaris blinked. They were waiting for him to speak. He would speak indeed. As he had for all of these months.

"As you well understand, gentlemen, at the time I was supposedly committing these acts of treason, I was head of Amt Ausland/Abwehr. In that position, may I remind you, it was my job—my duty—to involve myself in every aspect of intelligence-gathering. Within, as well as without, Germany."

"You knew about the coup d'état plans?" Huppenkothen asked indifferently.

"Of course, I knew about the plans all along. I followed them with great interest."

"Why didn't you say something?"

"Because the plans never materialized. It was merely talk. If and when it had become dangerous to the Reich, I would have acted."

"They said you were a part of the planning itself."

"They?" Canaris asked imperiously. "Who are they?"

"Colonel Oster, for one," Stawitzky interjected.

Canaris shook his head. "Naturally he would think such a thing. I was going along with them to better ascertain their true intentions."

"I see," Huppenkothen said. "But let's come back to that in a moment or so. I would like to explore now, the winter of 1939–40. There were certain discussions you had with a number of our military commanders."

There was no direct evidence for anything they had charged him with, unless they brought out his diaries. He kept expecting Huppenkothen to motion to Thorbeck, who would then slip into the side room and come out with the three books. At that point it would be over for sure. Just the threat of that happening began to wear Canaris down.

For months, until just recently, he had gone without a decent diet. For months he had been forced to lead an almost underground, and certainly an unnatural, life. His strength began to fail him now, when he needed it the most.

Sometimes his interrogators laughed at him; at other times they shouted, but it was meaningless sound. He had no real sense of the passage of time, although he suspected that the trial was going very fast. Too fast.

Suddenly Stawitzky stood over him. "You miserable, stinking little traitor. You wanted to kill our Führer. You wanted to deliver our armed forces to the enemy on a silver platter."

"No . . ." Canaris started to say, when Stawitzky reared back and smashed his fist into Canaris' already damaged nose.

The pain was unbelievable, although he did not black out. The room spun around and around, and his stomach churned. There was a movement, and they were shouting something, but it was all so indistinct, so unreal, that he could not focus on any of it. He could only try to hold on to his own sanity, his consciousness, for as long as possible.

Hans Oster was suddenly there in the courtroom. He stood across the room from Canaris, who was slowly beginning to see and hear what was happening.

"You were with us, Willi," Oster was saying, as if from a very great distance.

"No," Canaris mumbled. It was hard to talk. His face seemed swollen and very numb.

Oster was mad. "Oh yes, you were. In every phase of our activities. He was there."

"No," Canaris cried again. "It was all for show. Don't you understand?"

"No," Oster shouted. "That is not true. I can only say what I know—I'm not a rogue."

Thorbeck came around to the side. He looked a long time at Canaris. "Colonel Oster was your chief of staff. Are you telling the court, Herr Admiral, that he is falsely incriminating you? Is that what you are telling us?"

Canaris looked from Thorbeck to Huppenkothen and the others on the bench, and then to Oster . . . poor Hans. He shook his head. There was no fight left in him. "No," he mumbled.

"Speak up," Thorbeck boomed.

"No," Canaris said, looking up.

It was after ten when they passed the guardroom in the bunker and walked slowly down to the cells. Canaris, through pain-dimmed eyes, had glanced at the clock.

The verdict had been guilty, of course. The sentence, death. It had all been predetermined.

Meitner had warned him that the Führer had gone into a rage when he had learned of the diaries. He had ordered all of the conspirators destroyed. And now, despite the illegality of the trial, despite the fact he wasn't really guilty of any crime against the Reich, and despite the fact the war would be over any day now, the end was at hand.

Corporal Binder was especially careful with Canaris as they entered the cell, but Krüger was swaggering now, and he shoved Canaris toward the cot, making him stumble.

"You little traitor," he spat.

Binder turned on him. "You *Schweinhund*, keep your hands off your betters!"

Krüger stepped back, surprised. But then a slow grin spread across his face. "All right, Binder. You may have your way. But I will not forget this."

"See that you don't," Binder said. He turned and helped Canaris to his cot. "How do you feel, Herr Admiral? Can I get you something?"

Canaris looked up. He shook his head. It was very hard to keep focused. It was as if he were in a dream. Time kept slipping away from him.

"I'll check on you a little later, if I can," Binder said. He turned and left the cell.

Canaris lay back and closed his eyes. The room wanted to spin at first, but then it settled and he dozed off.

He kept seeing Huppenkothen and the others in court. Then Meitner's image swam into view, but his old friend was crying. He saw Baron Kaulbars and Uncle Mau and the others back in Berlin. His dogs, Kasper and Sabine, were there, as were Motte and the other Arabians.

Later—he did not know how much later—he could hear Lunding tapping on the wall from the next cell. For a long time Canaris lay where he was, half listening to Lunding's code but not understanding it. He was too tired. The man had been a great comfort these weeks. Now, however, he wanted simply to sleep.

But the signaling continued, and finally he dragged himself up and then sank to the floor at the foot of his cot, his head resting carefully against the wall. He waited for a break. When it came, he began his message.

"Nose broken last interrogation. My time is up."

Lunding tapped something in response, but Canaris could not make it out.

"Was not traitor. Did my duty as German."

Again Lunding signaled something. Canaris could read the urgency in the message, but he could make no sense of it. He was so sleepy.

"If you survive, remember me to my wife," he tapped, and then he turned away. He looked at his cot. It seemed an impossibly long distance up. He could not stay here on the floor.

Somehow he managed to drag himself back up. He pulled off his coat and tie, then took off his shoes and socks, and lay down on his back. He closed his eyes and was asleep almost instantly.

He dreamed again. But this time his images were unclear and very far away. He felt yearnings, but no desires for anything concrete on which he could focus. It was frustrating, but even in his dreams he could sense the passage of time, and he was not surprised or shocked when a commotion out in the corridor awoke him.

It was still early morning. The sun had not come up yet, although the yard outside his window, lit by arc lights, was almost like day.

He could hear guard dogs barking, and a number of voices seemed to be arguing. There were many people outside his door.

His cell door came open. "Out you come," someone shouted.

Canaris did not recognize the voice, but he sat up and managed to get to his feet when Krüger and several other SS guards crowded in. They roughly unhooked the shackles from Canaris' ankles and the handcuffs from his wrists.

He was led out of the cell, then down the corridor, and around the corner from the guardroom.

Karl Sack was there, along with Bonhoeffer and Gehre. They were nude. Their emaciated bodies were blue-tinged in the harsh overhead lights. No one said anything. They all averted their eyes.

"Get undressed," one of the guards told Canaris. "You, too," he said to someone behind.

Canaris turned as Hans Oster came down the corridor. His old chief of staff acted as if he were drunk or on some sort of drugs. He did not seem to recognize anyone.

They got undressed, and Canaris shivered. It was very cold.

His arms were tied painfully behind his back, and then he was led to the rear door, the others directly behind him. His guards seemed to be in a big hurry. Everyone was nervous.

At the door, though, they hesitated a moment. There were a lot of SS guards and officers crowded into the tiny space now. Huppenkothen was just within the doorway, as were Kögl and Stawitzky. Thorbeck stood to one side, and there were others whom Canaris did not recognize.

He looked around for Corporal Binder, but the man was no where to be seen.

"All right, Caesar first," someone from behind said, using Canaris' prison code name.

The door opened and he was pulled outside. The early morning air was intensely cold. The entire yard was lit up by strong lights. The stones were very hard on his feet, and it was windy.

At first Canaris could not see where he was being led because the lights were blinding him, but then they stopped in front of a low stepladder over which dangled a noose. The rope was attached to a large hook in an overhang at the edge of the building.

''Up you go,'' his two SS guards said, half guiding, half lifting Canaris up the two steps.

There was no ceremony. No reading of the sentence. Nothing.

Canaris managed to glance back toward the door as the noose was put around his neck and tightened. He could see Huppenkothen and Stawitzky there. Neither one of them was smiling now.

He just looked back when he felt the steps jerked out from under him, and the noose pulled up so terribly . . . Dear God . . . he was dying here! . . .

38

And still it was the same night. Marlene had not returned yet, and Schey was very worried about her. The Allies had come through an hour ago, but most of their loads had been dumped on Tiergarten, Mitte, and Wedding, not here.

He had dragged himself out of bed, wakened by the noise of the bombing, and he had gone up the back way to stand in the courtyard as he smoked his last cigarette.

The smoke made him light-headed, and for a while, as he watched the flashes toward the northeast and listened to the dull thumps and rumbles, he had to reach out and hold on to the corner of the doorway so that he would not fall down.

He was very weak. He could not remember when he had eaten last, although vaguely, at the back of his mind, he thought Marlene may have fed him something. Days ago, was it?

After the bombing he had gone back into the apartment and rummaged around for food. He only found a bit of coffee and a tiny packet of raw sugar that Marlene had been saving. With difficulty he brewed the coffee on the gasoline stove, and when it was done, he poured all of the sugar into one mug and brought it over to the small table in the sitting room.

He sipped the coffee, burning his lips, the ultrasweet taste turning his stomach. But he continued, alternately blowing on the hot brew and then sipping. The sugar, he knew, would give him energy. He was going to need it.

For a long time he sat in the darkness, sipping his coffee and listening for any kind of a sound. The family that had lived upstairs had moved away weeks ago, and now there was no one left in this building, though other buildings on this street were occupied.

The Russians were coming and everyone was frightened of what would happen if they were caught here in the city. A lot of them had gone out into the countryside. Of course, the army was stopping them now, but at first a lot of them had gotten free. If the Führer could remain here in Berlin, then his people certainly should not be allowed to desert.

Besides, the people in the country didn't want Berliners in any event. There had been reports of Germans attacking and killing Germans!

For a time, as Schey sat there in his stocking feet, his chest bare, he thought about the United States and tried to compare his life there with this now. But after a while he realized that he was not being fair. His life in Bavaria, however, and later, in Rudesheim on the Rhine and here in Berlin, before he was posted overseas, had had a quality to it, had had a gentleness, a softness, and even a sophistication that was certainly beyond anything he'd encountered in Oak Ridge or in New Mexico.

The U.S. was very big, very rawboned, very back-country, while Germany had the charm the Americans used to call "Old World."

There was no comparison in that respect. None at all, in his mind. And besides the hurt in his chest from his wound, there was an even deeper ache in his gut for the time past.

His Iron Cross, the metal softly gleaming, was hung by its ribbon over the lamp shade on the table. He reached out and touched it. The medal turned, catching a stray reflection.

He'd expected a parade ground ceremony, of course. His peers were supposed to be there. There'd be pomp and speeches; there'd be a band; his father would be in the stands, and *der Führer* would come out with his entourage. He'd say a word or two, and then place the medal around Schey's neck.

He had not expected the sniggers. He'd not expected the sideways glances, the raised eyebrows. He'd not expected the urgent messages interrupting the ceremony, the bombing raid that afternoon, nor the fact that the assembly had taken place fifty feet underground.

He turned his eyes away from the medal. Nor had he expected to be put on the radio, exhorting his fellow soldiers and countrymen never to lay down their arms, to fight until the very end for the honor and the glory that was Adolph Hitler.

God in heaven, had he been so wrong? Had his entire country been so terribly wrong all this time?

Scorched earth. *Der Führer* had given the order for everything to be destroyed. Bridges. Factories. Farm fields. Everything. When the enemy came across the frontier, they'd find nothing but scorched earth.

Schey finished his coffee, then dragged himself away from the table and back into the bedroom; there he sat heavily on the bed and reached for his Luger where it hung in its holster. He pulled it out, checked to make sure the clip was full, and then closed his eyes against the tears.

Der Führer . . . his Führer . . . was mad. If he were allowed to continue, all of Germany would be destroyed. Every person, every man, woman, and child, every last blade of grass would die.

He had to be stopped!

Schey reached for his boots.

The other three men in the barn kept looking at Deland as if he were some sort of a monster.

"It's the SS uniform," Dannsiger explained, looking up from the map spread out on the flat hood of the *Kriegswagen*. It was a Volkswagen. A people's car. Dr. Ferdinand Porsche had designed it at the Führer's behest. This was the military model, Germany's answer to the American jeep.

"Are they coming into the city with us?"

"None of us are coming into the city with you, Edmund . . ." Dannsiger said, but he bit it off, suddenly realizing that he did not know Deland's real name. "What does your pay book call you now?"

"It's better you do not know," Deland said. "I am Edmund."

Dannsiger nodded. "Marti wondered about you."

"Did she escape?"

"No," Dannsiger said. He looked at the map. "I will have to show you here where his apartment is located. And then I am leaving."

"Where are you going?"

"West. We are going to try to get to Hannover. Or somewhere near there."

"Because of the Russians?"

Dannsiger nodded, grim-lipped. "It will not be long. And it will not be very pretty."

"Has there been any report of Russians already in Berlin?" Deland asked.

Dannsiger was startled. "Advance units?" he asked. But he answered his own question. "No, I do not think so. They would have to be either very brave or very stupid, or both. Berlin is a very difficult city just now."

Deland nodded. He looked at the street map. "You said something about him being wounded."

"His girlfriend said he had been shot. She had no details, but she said he is very weak. The bullet is still in his chest. He apparently isn't able to leave the apartment . . . just here." Dannsiger pointed a pencil to a street just off Reichenhaller Strasse. "It is number 37, in the basement. There is a front entry as well as a back."

Deland leaned closer toward the map and studied it for a long moment or two. There was no alley behind. "How about the buildings around it? What kind of shape are they in?"

"There have been a few hits in the area, but very few. The block is in fairly good condition. There is a series of courtyards in the back, however. They can be reached through the tailor's shop on the corner."

"There is no one in that building?"

Dannsiger looked up and shook his head. "No. They have been gone for a very long time."

"Were they Jews?"

Dannsiger nodded.

Deland looked at the map again, then straightened up. "How about gasoline?"

"The tank is full. There is another twenty liters in a can in the back. It is more than enough to get you into the city and then back out again to your rendezvous . . ." He held up his hand before Deland could speak. "No, I do not wish to know about your escape plans either."

Deland looked at his watch. It was after midnight. "Is this place safe?"

"For now, yes. But not for overnight. It will be checked," Dannsiger said.

"Why didn't you do it?" Deland blurted.

The others turned away suddenly and shoved the barn door the rest of the way open. There were two motorcycles in the shadows.

They pushed them outside. They evidently planned to ride two to a machine.

Dannsiger looked at him for a long time. "Good luck," he said, and he started to turn away. But Deland went after him.

"Goddamnit, I asked you a question. What's the matter? Why didn't you just go in and kill him when you had the chance? It would have been so much easier than dragging me all the way back here. What's the matter . . . is he some kind of a superman?"

Dannsiger turned on him. One of the others had his gun out.

"Dieter Schey is a hero! A German, just like me!"

"A Nazi."

"A decorated man! He has the Iron Cross! He has given his soul for Germany! Can't you see that, you bastard? You heartless bastard!"

Dannsiger turned again and hurried out of the barn. This time Deland did not try to stop him. He felt like such an insensitive fool. Although it was the answer he had expected, it was the one he had feared most.

Fifteen minutes later he heard the sounds of the two motorcycles starting up, but it came from a long way off. Possibly on the other side of the village.

He looked at the map again, then folded it up, switched off the battery-operated lamp, and tossed them in the car. At the barn door he looked outside, but there was nothing to see. He was on his own now, in more ways than one.

Deland entered Berlin proper on the Hamburg Highway past Spandau, barely slowing down for the first two sandbagged checkpoints, but then he came to the barrier across the road, and he pulled up.

There were a lot of soldiers here, most of them Wehrmacht, but the commanding officer and at least two others were dressed in the black SS uniform with twin lightning bolts at the collar. It was the first Deland had heard of an Army unit mixed with SS.

Two Wehrmacht soldiers approached, and when they realized it was an SS colonel behind the wheel, they came to attention. An SS captain came from around the barricade, a Schmeisser machine pistol at his chest.

He came to attention and saluted. "Your papers, *bitte*, *mein Herr*," he said respectfully, but firmly.

Deland eyed the man, then slowly opened his door, got out, and deliberately took off his gloves. He glanced up toward the barricade, then back at the SS officer and the two Wehrmacht soldiers.

"*Wie heissen Sie, Hauptmann?*" Deland snapped.

The captain sucked in his gut. "*Wolner, Herr Standartenführer. Hans Wolner.*"

"*Ja*, well, Wolner, look back up there to the north and tell me, what do you see?"

The captain looked nervously over his shoulder. "Why, forest, sir. Trees."

"And what is in the forest, *Hauptmann* Wolner?"

"I . . . I do not know, sir."

"No, I suspected as much. An entire Soviet division could be hiding there, you idiot!" Deland screamed. "See that the forest is swept and posted! Or I will see that you are shot as an incompetent who is unfit to wear the uniform!"

"Sir!"

Deland allowed himself to calm down; then he took out his Führer-letter and handed it to the captain. "I assume you can read?"

"*Jawohl, Herr Standartenführer* . . ." the captain started to say. But he had begun to read the letter, and he suddenly realized what it was. He paled. He looked up. His lower lip quavered, and his hand shook as he handed the letter back. He was speechless.

"*Gott in Himmel*," Deland said, half to himself. "And this is the defense of the Fatherland?" He shook his head, pocketed the letter, and before he got back in the car, he glanced at one of the Wehrmacht soldiers. "Your button is undone," he said resignedly. The soldier nearly fainted.

By the time he had the engine started, the center row of the thick steel spikes had been rolled back, and he drove through. Sweat was pouring down his side beneath his tunic, and his legs were so weak that his foot shook on the clutch when he changed gears.

Deland knew Charlottenburg fairly well, so it was easy for him to find the proper street. He drove past the building, then around the corner and continued another block, before he parked his car.

He walked back the way he had come. Nothing moved in the city. The fires he had seen outside of Nauen were still burning. They made the entire horizon to the east and northeast red and pink. The bombing raid had definitely hit Tiergarten, and probably Wedding. Perhaps Mitte as well.

At number 37 he carefully opened the gate so as not to make any noise and went down the stairs to the basement apartment. He unsnapped the flap of his holster, withdrew the Luger, and made sure a round was in the firing chamber and the safety was off. He held the weapon out of sight at his side as he reached out with his left hand and knocked at the door.

"Colonel Schey," he called. "Are you there?"

Deland thought he heard someone moving around inside. But then there was silence.

"Colonel Schey," Deland called again. He knocked. "I am Colonel Hessman. I have come to talk to you. On *der Führer's* behalf. He has sent me. I have a letter."

There was continued silence.

Deland reached out and tried the knob. The door was not locked. He shoved it open, but then stepped aside.

He could smell coffee.

"Colonel Schey?" he called. There was no answer, and Deland rolled left into the apartment, stepping quickly back to the right and crouching low, the Luger out in front of him. "Schey?" he called softly.

"I am not a deserter," Schey said. He was in the back. Deland crouched a little lower.

"No one says you are a deserter." The apartment was mostly in darkness. Only a small amount of light coming from outside provided any illumination.

"I was wounded. By Russians. Here, in the city."

Russians? Christ, was he already too late? "What Russians? Where?"

"In the laboratory at the Kaiserhof," Schey said softly. "The scientists were giving everything to the Russians. I managed to shoot two of them." Schey appeared at the bedroom door.

Deland almost brought the Luger up and shot him then and there, but something stayed his hand. The Russians. Schey had shot the Russians. Christ, had Donovan been that far off? "Is that how you were wounded?"

Schey nodded. "There was shooting." He looked beyond Deland to the doorway, as if he were expecting someone. The girlfriend Dannsiger had mentioned?

"Was it the American atomic bomb secrets?"

Schey nodded again. His shoulder was bandaged. But a lot of blood had leaked out. "Yes," he said. "I slowed them down." He was dressed in his uniform, his tunic unbuttoned. He held his Luger in one hand and his Iron Cross in the other.

"The secrets you brought back from America?"

"Yes. What a joke."

Deland's insides were tied up in knots. He brought the Luger up. "Drop your weapon, Colonel Schey," he said in English.

"You stupid bastard, I'm telling you . . . ." Schey began, but then he rocked back on his heels, thunderstruck. "English," he said. "My God, you're American."

"Drop your weapon, damnit!"

Schey just looked at him. "Why?" he asked, in English. "You did not come all this way in that uniform to kidnap me and take me back for trial."

Deland couldn't say a thing. His hand was rock-steady, but his knees were terribly weak.

"You've come to kill me . . . because of what I did? But no, it wouldn't be that. It would be the Manhattan Project secrets." Schey smiled. "Well, it's too late. I've given everything I know to my scientists. And they in turn have sold out to the Russians."

Deland didn't know if he could just pull the trigger and kill this man.

Schey raised his Iron Cross so that it caught a bit of light. He looked at it wonderingly. Then he looked at Schey.

"Back in the States, at the hospital in Knoxville, Tennessee, is my son. Robert Mordley, Junior. I had to leave him when his . . . ."

"Mother was killed?" Deland finished it.

"You know?"

Deland nodded.

"I was going to return to the Führer-bunker tonight to assassinate . . . my Führer," Schey said. "I was getting dressed to go." He lowered his head. "But I could not have done it, you know."

"He has brought all this down on your people. He has killed millions of Jews . . . or I suppose that doesn't matter to you."

"It matters very much," Schey said with much feeling. He tossed the Iron Cross to the floor at Deland's feet. "See that my son gets this, will you . . . ." he started, while at the same moment he brought the Luger up.

"No!" Deland shouted, and he fired a single shot, catching

Schey in the chest, just to the left of his breastbone, driving him back into the bedroom, his shoulder bouncing off the door frame.

Deland leaped forward, his mind numb. Schey lay sprawled at the foot of the bed, his eyes open, his head at an odd angle, his chin on his chest. He still held the Luger limply in his hand. He was dead.

He had known that Deland could not simply pull the trigger on a helpless man. He had precipitated the action.

Deland holstered his Luger, took Schey's, and slid the action back. There was a loaded clip in the butt, but no shell in the firing chamber. The gun had not been ready to fire.

Schey had been a remarkable man. From what Deland had read of his exploits, he had not thought it possible for one man to have done so much. But now, for no definable reason, looking down at him, Deland was certain reports contained only the half of it.

He dropped Schey's Luger, then got to his feet and went back out to the front door. With the car, his uniform, and the Führer-letter, he did not think he'd have much trouble getting up to Wolgast. If Katrina was still there, he knew she would come with him. There had never been any doubt in his mind. He had promised her that he would be back. And they loved each other.

Outside, he suddenly remembered something, and he went back in. Schey's Iron Cross lay on the floor where he had tossed it. Deland picked it up, put it in his pocket, and left.

Oh, the older man knew that a lot of heroes turned out happy in the end. But he also knew that they all wondered, at least once in their life, what had been of most importance: their contribution or all the crowing about it afterwards?

—Fuckin' shit, don't leave me hanging like this, man, the younger man said.

Just about everyone had left the club by now. It was very late. The bartender came over and nodded toward the door. It was time to leave.

Surprisingly, the younger man rose without a fuss. —Come on, he slurred.

The older man finished his beer and got to his feet. Together they staggered out of the bar. It was very cold. The wind blew the snow down State Street in long swirls. He couldn't see Bascom Hill from here, but the capitol dome was lit brightly. It looked cold and forbidding.

—So, what happened? Did Deland get out of Berlin okay? I mean, the fuckin' krauts were getting jumpy. How many times could he run into a stupid captain with his head up his ass?

—He got out all right, the older man said.

—Yeah, but how?

They crossed State Street and headed up toward the older man's apartment on Langdon Street. The younger man seemed mindless of the cold or of where they were going. He wanted to hear more. The older man suspected he had wanted a love story out of it. From the ashes of war comes true love. Well, it had happened that way. At least in part.

—He drove back to the same SS captain on the Hamburg Highway near Spandau and got back out.

—Oh man, the poor son-of-a-bitch must have been shittin' bricks.

348

—*He went through Nauen, then swung northeast back toward Peenemunde. He wasn't stopped once. Not even when he got to Wolgast.*

The younger man's face was more animated then it had been all night —*She was there? His Katrina Mueller?*

—*She was there. Waiting for him.*

—*But what about the Gestapo?*

—*They believed her. She had an unblemished record. She had lost a brother on the Russian front. They just believed her.*

—*Man, oh . . . man, the younger man said, thinking about it.* —*But then what? They made it to the submarine?*

—*Her father arranged a boat for them.*

—*They came back to the States?*

The older man nodded. They had reached his apartment in a rundown area of student housing. He had been here for a couple of years now. Trying to find himself, he supposed. Without much luck. Trying to live up to . . . what?

—*Come on, he said, and he helped the younger man up the steps.*

—*No, wait a minute now.*

—*It's all right. I want to show you something.*

—*I want to know about Deland and Katrina. They came back to the States. Did they get married?*

—*They got married, the older man said. They were in the corridor, and they continued up to the second floor and into the older man's apartment. He turned on the lights.*

—*Jesus, the younger man said in awe.*

There were a lot of photographs and maps pinned on the walls. There were books and articles clipped from magazines lying everywhere. All of it the product of years of research by the older man.

For a long time both men were silent, each with his own thoughts, his own impressions of the moment.

Finally the older man went to the desk, picked up two small, polished wooden boxes and brought them back to the younger man.

He opened the first. It contained a Nazi Iron Cross. In gold.

The younger man's eyes went wide.

—*Colonel Dieter Schey's award, the older man said.*

The younger man's eyes went to the other box. The older man opened it.

—Major Robert David Deland's Congressional Medal of Honor.

—For service behind enemy lines.

The older man could feel tears filling his eyes. His stomach ached, and his throat constricted. *—For going back and killing . . .*

—Your father. You're Robert Mordley, Junior.

The older man couldn't trust himself to speak. He nodded.

—But then, how the fuck did you get Deland's medal . . . the younger man began, but then another stunning revelation hit him. —Fucking far out, man, he said in awe.

The older man turned away. He had made the other man understand, hadn't he? At last?

—You're adopted. Your name now is Deland. Deland and Katrina were married, and they adopted you.

Deland nodded.

The younger man stepped farther into the room so that he could better see the maps and photos and other products of Deland's research.

—And you were just told?

—A couple of years ago, Deland said.

The younger man was shaking his head. *—You poor bastard. Two fathers, both heroes, and one kills the other. And you think you understand now, about heroes? You think you've got it pegged?*

Strangely, the younger man no longer seemed as stoned as before. He looked again at the two medals Deland held in his hands.

—Shit, you don't understand a fuckin' thing, my man. I suspect that if you go home to your father, he might be able to explain it to you, if you'll listen. He gave you the medals. He must have already tried to make you understand.

The younger man waved his arm around at the things in the room.

—You sure as fuck won't understand it from this shit.

—Better than you will ever understand.

The younger man laughed derisively. *—You think it's some kind of romantic bullshit? Tragic, and all that crap? He opened his coat and reached up under his sweater.*

Deland watched him, and he knew now why the younger man seemed so familiar to him. He understood now what it was about the younger man that was so recognizable to him. He had studied heroes for so long he should have recognized it right off the bat.

—Pleiku, the younger man said, tossing his Medal of Honor across to Deland.

They were heroes all . . . men true to their ideals, right or wrong; men true to their countries and to their medals.
What waste, their lives in war!